SOUNDS OF A DISTANT TRAIN

DAN GOODIER

Sounds of a Distant Train

Print ISBN: 979-8-35093-134-1
eBook ISBN: 979-8-35093-135-8

Printed in the United States of America

Sounds of a Distant Train

CONTENTS

To Susie,

Every line I will ever write about love, kindness, strength, or hope is inspired by you. Thank you for all of it, and for everything else we share.

As for those beautiful, sapphire blue eyes of yours…
that's a story for another day.

PROLOGUE

As I look back, I think the greatest influence in my life was growing up in a small town. Though stereotypes can suggest simplicity and calm, real-life experience has time and again revealed there is far more to understand than could possibly be measured by one's first impressions. That is certainly the case with my upbringing. I am Emmet North.

The bungalows, church steeples, and painted storefronts only offer hints about the remarkable lives of the people who dwell within. Consequently, the familiar Currier and Ives images often belie the complexity of the interactions they share. Love, conflict, exhilaration, hope, disappointment, and grief all occur in a small town just as in the larger cities of the surrounding world.

The differences lie in how closely entwined the lives of friends and neighbors become within the small-town culture. If something happens, it likely involves someone near to you, even someone you care deeply about. Or maybe it happens to you.

In the world of my youth, this familiarity and intimacy amplified the feelings shared among friends and enemies alike. Even our natural environment often played a significant part.

No matter who you are or where you call home, some aspects of every life are bound to be difficult or even extreme. However, when something bad happens, it is the way we react and hopefully persevere that ultimately matters. I would contend this applies to people, a town, or even a country as resilient as ours. It is what lasts beyond the worrisome times and stays relevant over the course of our lives. Perseverance is the essence of survival and, ultimately, of redemption.

As is often true, human caring and understanding can spring up like a fountain and thus turn defeat into victory, confusion into clarity, or calamity into atonement.

Occasionally, average people can be the source of profound creativity under the most unusual of circumstances or in the unlikeliest places. I think it is correct to say my hometown was one such place.

I have drawn an imaginary circle around the events of a two-year period encompassing 1967 and 1968, a time filled with remarkable changes for my family, my hometown, and, coincidentally, the history of our nation.

Though the memories remain clear and strong, the circle is not without flaws. This chronicle of thoughts and stories is an opus whose imperfect alchemy consists of common elements that, when mixed in certain random measures, produce notably uncommon outcomes. Such is the nature of life.

Most of what I share represents people, places, and goings-on of which I have explicit, firsthand knowledge. Some of this comes from tales passed along to me from my parents, my closest friends, or other trusted sources. In a few cases, I have included certain acts, events, or discussions of which I have no direct personal knowledge. Those are based on what I can best describe as simply the way I believe they happened. I leave it to you to decide whether to accept or question their relative validity.

I offer these stories from the end of my childhood. The accounts are correct according to my best recollections, even the parts I wish were not.

Today, I stand beside Lake Pepin in a place where I can clearly see the shoreline, and still gaze out across the ever-changing waters and beyond the limits of my aging vision. I am instantly pulled to a time long ago when my friends and I inhabited this place and experienced all the richness it provided. The afternoon sunlight sparkles on the surface like a billion diamonds. The sounds of the lake are exactly as they were then. I can almost hear the laughter of young voices, now long exchanged for their more brittle adult versions.

The waves tell the story. In the early years, they were part of a playground for my childish imagination. They cast themselves at my feet as I ran in and out of their reach. On blustery days they became snow-capped mountains, and on calmer ones, a place for mothers and their babies to splash and play. Then, everything was a new adventure to be experienced, every wave a promise of what was to come. It is impossible to know how many of those promises became reality and how many just washed upon the beach, only to recede and be replaced by another.

Now, it seems the waves stand for an endless succession of memories. They remind me of who we were then and of the power of friendship as we knew it. I try to recall and examine the entirety of these memories, most of which exemplify some of the best times of my life. But not all.

Down the lake, a train blows its horn, and my eyes quickly turn toward the sound. For a few seconds the waves go silent and the world around me stands still. A sudden feeling rises in my stomach: instinctual fight-or-flight radar. It's like what I occasionally experience because of my fear of heights, yet this is far worse. My jaw aches, and I realize I am clenching my teeth.

Despite the visceral response, I am compelled, almost against my wishes, to once again consider the extreme and unpleasant context of the remarkable circumstances that caused it. Even the most difficult memories are kept for some reason. Everything in life is important in its own unique way.

As this moment of surprise subsides and the calming sound of the waves returns, I resume my contemplation of a time when the world as I knew it seemed to be coming apart but then struggled resolutely to recover

. . . to change. Now in the fourth season of my life, I am more able to clearly see how profound these events from my youth turned out to be and how important it is to share them, if for no other reason than to document a small part of the history of my hometown.

CHAPTER 1

ALONG THE MISSISSIPPI

Bay City, Wisconsin, offered a wondrous playground for kids to grow up in. My friends and I spent our young lives exploring the shores of Lake Pepin and the Mississippi River, which formed the border with Minnesota. As the Great River winds its way to the Gulf of Mexico, the Mississippi undoubtedly has served a similar purpose for millions of kids.

We enthusiastically immersed ourselves in the beauty nature provided, and yet, we often were unaware of the inherent dangers in our immediate surroundings. When we were together, we felt safe, even when our play led us to take certain chances. Steep and craggy bluffs represented rock-climbing opportunities that simply could not be ignored. And as every kid eventually discovers, any body of water large enough to skip a rock on its surface is fair game for testing the boundaries of youthful creativity. Our nonchalance toward risk was part of the excitement, part of life's adventure.

In addition to the recreation it offers, the Mississippi is a thriving and muscular inland waterway for commerce. A busy industrial system is created by the grain, coal, lumber, and just about anything else that can be loaded onto the giant barges and floated up or downstream.

The intense and difficult river work begins in our northern location as soon as the ice melts enough to break up in spring. It usually lasts into early December, when nature once again proves how even the best efforts of humans and machines are no match for a Wisconsin winter.

Less visible, and much less understood, is the illegal trade that is a small, yet significant part of the Mississippi's complex character. Smuggling of stolen goods, drugs, guns, and even people all too often went unnoticed and without consequence.

I would wish to stress that the great majority of the barge and shore workers are honest, hard-working men and women who provide important services up and down the commercial backbone of our country. However, there will always be a few who recognize and exploit the criminal opportunities presented by the lightly patrolled vastness of the Mississippi waterway and its seemingly endless network of backwater channels. To that extent, the Mississippi casts a long shadow, one that stands in stark contrast to the joyful innocence of children playing along the shores of Lake Pepin.

Drug use was becoming commonplace in the late 1960s, even in small communities like Bay City. Though it was difficult to know where they came from and exactly how they reached us, common sense would suggest the Mississippi may have had something to do with it in our area.

My parents were several years older than most of my friends'. Consequently, our lifestyle was a bit out of sync with the times. Or maybe the clocks just ran a little slower in our house or in our town.

In my youngest years, I guess I didn't fully realize we were poor. But by the time I reached my teens I'd come to recognize the slightly different standards by which most of my friends lived. I didn't feel bad about it, really. It was all I knew. Rural and urban regions alike were home to growing numbers of poor people just trying to survive. It was who we were, and the challenges we faced certainly were shared by many.

Eventually, I grew to realize *poverty* is a relative term. Some of the wealthiest people in the world are also some of the loneliest or most morally bankrupt. Conversely, some of the poorest lives are made utterly rich by the people who surround them. In this sense, I was one of the fortunate ones. I had some good and close friends who didn't seem to care about such matters. Heck, we just wanted to have fun.

Of course, the friendships you share as a kid seem like they will be with you forever. Though most will prove to be temporary, the experiences we share in childhood teach us lessons that resonate for a lifetime. The people, places, and moments of our young lives create some of the most priceless memories of all, strung together like precious beads on a fine line in time—stretching out to connect the past with the present. For me, many of these memories are as vivid today as when the events that inspired them first occurred.

At that time, the nation was still reeling from President Kennedy's assassination. We hadn't yet realized we would never get over it. We remained hopeful. Our country had bought into the fairy tale of John F. Kennedy's Camelot. When he was killed in 1963, so was the inspiration for his fragile dream. In Catholic homes, JFK's picture was often displayed near that of the pope.

Lyndon Johnson inherited the presidency under the most unimaginable of circumstances. He bargained and bullied his way to achieving his own national vision to divert the country's attention and potentially create some cause for optimism. President Johnson called his image of America "the Great Society." For a lot of us, it sounded pretty good, and I guess we wanted to be part of something we could be proud of, kind of like rooting for a winning team. For the most part, it seemed the greatness was not reserved for towns like ours.

As we grew older, a lot of what was happening in the world around us became increasingly harder to overlook. But despite all the complexities and unknowns, being a kid was a significant equalizer. Our collective creativity simply did not allow for very many walls or boundaries. If we could imagine it, we could usually act it out. If you could run fast or catch a ball or belch the alphabet, you would be okay, accepted by the other guys. I guess you could say we measured our worth by different criteria than most adults did.

What we knew of life beyond our town came to us mostly from our televisions and secondly from the newspapers. The evening news revealed stories about racial bias and all-too-familiar reports of open conflict. News anchor Walter Cronkite's trusted voice explained how volatile interracial confrontations were increasingly becoming an issue, but especially in the larger cities.

Bay City had not yet become integrated. However, even though we didn't always relate on a personal experience level, we could generally grasp the magnitude of the issues, even at our age. But like a lot of other worldly things, much of it just seemed beyond what my youthful mind could completely comprehend.

On the other hand, my older brother Jack often paid close attention to the news to absorb the meaning of such information, even more than most adults. Jack just needed to understand why things were the way they were in the world around us. It was one of many things that set him apart from the rest of us.

Equally confusing were the terrifying real-time live scenes of war, which were for the first time available in the living rooms of virtually every home. They were graphic, omnipresent, and they reminded us how the Vietnam conflict had divided our country in ways we never had seen before.

As we grew into our early teens, military service became a subject of great concern for our parents, who dreaded the possibilities regardless of their political affiliations. Our parents understood that no matter who you vote for, war doesn't play favorites.

For my friends and me, party politics was an unknown language, except we probably all would have said we hated Nazis, had anyone asked.

I am often struck by similarities between the times we live in now and those of the period I am writing about. In some ways, things appear relatively unchanged since those days. As it was then, I guess a lot depends on your point of view.

I know this for certain: a person's personal journey is inevitably a steep and winding path. It is most certainly a unique experience for each of us. The people we meet along the way represent our lives' intersections, the forks in the road. Without exception, each one shapes our future and changes us somehow.

That said, we couldn't possibly have predicted the changes coming to my family and to our town, or the amazing occurrences that caused them. Nor could we have predicted how the crushing importance of those events would cause such a massive slipstream effect in our lives, just as the period between 1967 and 1968 shaped the history of our country and of the world for all time.

Perhaps the clocks sped up during that time, or maybe our small-town existence caught up with the rest of the world for a while. We didn't always want it this way, but it happened anyway, and we became swept up in it without our permission—and without any warning.

CHAPTER 2

Spring 1967

It was a time when school children practiced tornado drills, fire drills, and nuclear attack drills. When the signal was sounded, we marched in military fashion to the places our schools had deemed safe from high winds or outside to escape the imaginary fire. Strangely, when we performed the civil defense drills—the ones preparing for nuclear attack—we merely slid from our varnished maple seats and huddled under the desks as instructed.

Our teachers surely realized this did nothing for our actual safety from an atomic bomb blast or the deadly unseen fallout we feared most. But like their students, they dutifully acted out their parts because it was expected of them.

We had all been through many bad summer storms and the accompanying damage caused by the unforgiving force of wind or a random lightning strike. Unfortunately, some also had real-life experiences to remind us why we diligently performed the fire drills.

But nobody really understood what a nuclear attack would be like. Radiation was the unknown and unseen enemy. Many of us had seen flickering images of the Hiroshima and Nagasaki mushroom clouds on television or on a newsreel in a movie theater, but thankfully this was as close as any of us had come to this extremely complex and frightening reality. Still, even in our little town, a few houses were equipped with fallout shelters in the basements.

My father's name was Marion, but he went almost exclusively by Brick. Dad was an imposing, barrel-chested man whose biceps and forearms were built over a lifetime of hard work. His nickname came from his years as a bricklayer. Though he hadn't done any major contracting for several years, he still picked up enough work to stay busy with smaller projects or whatever odd jobs were available. In a small town like Bay City, people tended to take on whatever job would pay, with little regard to whether they had ever done it before.

His black hair and paintbrush mustache were beginning to show streaks of gray, and deeply etched lines framed the corners of his eyes. Not all of them were caused by smiling.

My mother was Rachel, a full-blooded Swede who wore her light brown hair in long braids wound in a tight circle around the back of her head. A kind and hard-working mother and wife, she was the center of our family's universe.

They were in their late thirties when they married. By the standard of the day, they were already old.

My brother Jack is two years older than me. When he was a toddler, he contracted a bad case of asthma, which seemed to stick with him for several years. Now in his teens, he was still too slim to look completely healthy.

Jack was the intellectual superior of virtually all his peers and many grown-ups. It made him something of a curiosity when he was a little boy. He even auditioned for an early TV game show called *Giant Step* starring a budding actor named Burt Parks. Precocious children answered difficult questions designed to show off their intelligence and how cute they were.

When we were still living in Red Wing, Minnesota, a couple of well-dressed execs from WCCO-TV in Minneapolis came to our humble house to interview him. It turned out Jack was much too smart to be very cute, even at an early age. He didn't make the cut.

Eventually, his intelligence began to set him apart from the other kids. Especially in social situations, it was increasingly more of an obstacle than a gift. Early in life, being different is often a source of ridicule, regardless of what that difference is. His world became defined primarily by his precious books, which he read voraciously. In turn, they fueled his insatiable search for knowledge. And so it went. The more he learned, the less like his peers he became. Unfortunately, that applied to me, as well.

I understood Jack as much as he would allow. We shared a bedroom in our tiny home, and a thousand experiences only brothers could share, even if we were somewhat mismatched. While Jack was painfully introverted, I was generally outgoing and got along with most kids and adults alike, competing or cooperating as the situation demanded.

I occasionally found myself defending him from the meanness of other kids. I wasn't afraid to step into a confrontation on his behalf, even if it meant taking on an older boy. I'd been told how smart Jack was so many times that I just accepted I was never going to live up to that standard. So, I learned how to fight instead.

This role reversal generally worked against both of us, causing Jack the humiliation of my childish defense in addition to whatever started the ruckus to begin with. It also caused me to receive at least one nasty black eye. As brothers, Jack and I struggled to find common interests. Still, in some ways I suppose I idolized him. Perhaps I still do. Yet I think he resented me because I had friends while he had books.

\+ + +

Bay City is located at the head of Lake Pepin on a wide, flat, twenty-one-mile stretch of the Mississippi River. For thousands of years the area was home to Indigenous people whose rich culture was derived from hunting and fishing along the lake and the surrounding bluffs.

Lake Pepin was "discovered" in 1680 by European explorer Father Louis Hennepin. At that time, he called it Lac de Pleurs, or Lake of Tears, because he had observed some Dakota Sioux people crying over the death of their chief's son. The name Lake Pepin first appeared on a map drawn in 1703.

In 1851 Congress created the Indian Appropriations Act, which began a process designed to force Native people to move onto reservations to free up land for new settlers. One such community was established on Prairie Island near the place where Red Wing, Minnesota, would be settled. The village of Bay City was originally known as Saratoga but was renamed in 1886.

The lake increased to its current size in 1938 when the Army Corps of Engineers built a series of locks and dams to control flooding. Ironically, Lock and Dam Number 3 near Red Wing *caused* significant permanent flooding of acreage within the Prairie Island Indian Reservation, and thus reduced the usable land from 534 acres down to approximately 300. Several Native burial mounds were lost to the waters.

Except for this utterly unconscionable outcome, the mitigation strategy worked well until the spring of 1967 when the Mississippi swelled beyond anyone's imagination. Like many others, our house was flooded with a couple feet of dark and unforgiving water. As it overtook the safe boundaries of our world, a series of events began that would alter the course of our lives for many years to come and define our family in ways we only partially understood at the time.

This was the year a lot of things seemed to start coming into focus for me. It was a time of questions and experimentation. It would also prove to be a time of new feelings, responsibilities, and commitments. In other words, I was a teenager.

Unlike a flash flood after a summer rainstorm, the flood of 1967 was caused by a rapid spring thaw after an extremely snowy winter. The weather became unusually warm in early March, causing the hills and gullies to run wild with the torrential flow that eventually reached Lake Pepin. We watched the flood waters rise slowly and relentlessly for several days before Dad and Mom finally decided we had to move out.

I remember standing together on the street in front of our house with all our belongings on a neighbor's trailer and a borrowed pickup truck. The pavement was just a couple of feet above the water level in our fully engulfed front yard.

My folks held each other closely and silently grieved as the first water lapped at the threshold and then painfully spilled over onto the living room floor. Jack and I didn't really know how to act. It was all so serious and yet we had nothing to compare it to. The hundred-year flood was something nobody thought would ever happen, but it did. We stood off to the side and behind them. I purposely leaned into him, causing him to lose his balance. He punched me on the shoulder. We didn't say a thing.

We had lived in our current home since moving from Red Wing in 1959 when Highway 61 was blasted through the solid limestone hillside along Barn Bluff. Several neighborhoods, including ours on Green Street, would eventually be swallowed up by the highway construction. The state had condemned all the properties they needed to build on, and Dad and Mom were paid what ours was deemed to be worth. Back taxes were owed, so there wasn't much left after the debts were settled. By the time we left Red Wing, we didn't have a lot of choices.

Ours was one of the last dozen or so houses standing before the wrecking ball finished its thankless work. The few other remaining ones would be moved to available vacant lots around the city. At first, Dad had refused to move us out because I had been sick with pertussis, or whooping cough. Eventually his resistance was met with an ultimatum, and we left the only home Jack and I had known until then.

In the time leading up to our departure, Dad had managed to assemble a crew and move a small, detached garage over the Eisenhower bridge and across the remaining eight-mile stretch to Bay City. He had snatched the garage just ahead of the demolition crews. No permission was asked or granted. He just helped himself to it, and nobody cared. The garage building would form the structure of our new home.

He also had squirreled away many other building components like windows, doors, kitchen cabinets, and even a big, enameled fuel oil heater, all scavenged from neighboring homes. By then, Green Street looked like a war zone. Our house may have been the last one still inhabited.

A few months before we moved, Dad bought a 1949 Pontiac Silver Streak from a guy who had lost both of his legs to diabetes. It was not very dependable. Often a repair had to wait until an odd job came along to pay for it. Consequently, we usually walked when we needed to get around town, using the Pontiac only when necessary or for special occasions.

My uncle Harry was our go-to driver if we had to go farther than the Pontiac would predictably be able to handle. He was Mom's older brother, and as nearly as I could tell, he seemed genuinely happy to help as needed. Harry had lived in Bay City for several years, and he helped identify an affordable lot for my folks to buy.

Our new house was not finished when we first moved in. It had only three rooms: a kitchen, a living room, and a large bedroom with two double beds. Jack and I shared one and our parents the other. It was all the original garage structure could accommodate.

Though water would easily percolate through the sandy soil, the house was built on a flood plain. A conventional septic system was out of the question. For the time being it was a moot point. Since there wasn't enough money left to pay for a holding tank, an outhouse was the only viable choice as our toilet. It was a big downgrade from the old Green Street house.

Though we did have a well and a fresh water source in our kitchen, the wastewater was diverted away from the house into a sandy pit where the holding tank was supposed to be. This awful arrangement became known as "the slop hole." It was as delightful a place as its nickname suggested. Smelly, wet, and a little dangerous, it somehow kept the gray drainage water below the frost line.

A large, round wooden lid was set over it and a slatted snow fence put up around it to ensure only the most minimal level of safety. Gaps in the soil around the top provided glimpses of the underlying mess. The slop hole was to be avoided, if possible . . . a place of lost baseballs, dead frogs, and perpetual clouds of insects.

A few months later, Dad added the second bedroom and a small unfinished room designated to be a future bathroom. Jack and I were ecstatic with the new sleeping arrangement. I imagine Mom and Dad were even more so. Just the potential of an indoor bathroom was an encouraging sign. For the time being, though, we continued using the outhouse.

Our new room allowed for two single beds with a nightstand between, and a large dresser that we shared. Besides storing our clothes, we still managed to find room for agates, snail shells, and other treasures gathered from the fields and along the lakeshore.

One of the first things Jack and I did was set up our stereo. A red and white Sears "Airline" record player was placed in a prominent location atop the dresser and in front of the mirror. Music was one of our greatest avenues of escape, so it got a lot of use.

Within the confines of our shared existence, Jack's musical taste dominated. The simple-minded fluff of the daily AM radio play lists was replaced in our room by edgier and more complex themes. He introduced me to the Rolling Stones and the Beatles, and to Jimi Hendrix and the Doors. I responded with the puppy-like dedication of a younger brother and a burning desire to be cool. This was extremely important at our age, and I respected Jack for his eccentric coolness even though I never really wanted to be quite like him.

During the period our house was flooded out, our parents rented one of the only available vacant buildings in town. We moved into the abandoned barbershop on Main Street, next to Taylor's Hardware Store and across the street from Hunt's Tavern, where Uncle Harry worked and lived in an upstairs apartment.

Mom and Dad hung curtains in the front window with the chipped barber pole sign painted on the inside of the glass. We slept upstairs in an unfinished attic with exposed sidewall studs and rafters. The first floor acted as a combination eat-in kitchen and living room. Mom's gas range was installed next to the old barber chair. The shabby upstairs bathroom was the first indoor plumbing I had known since the house on Green Street. It was one of the only things I liked about the place. That and the slight odor of talcum powder, which I found oddly pleasant.

Other families inhabited the long-closed bank building, Tremseys' Resort cabins, and the upper levels of several other buildings not originally intended to be used as apartments. Overall, it made for an interesting living situation for the kids. At first, it was like camping out.

A helpful guy from the Savings and Loan held a meeting at the old village hall to explain how families could get low-cost loans to make the necessary repairs on their houses after the flood. Shortly after the agreements were signed, truckloads of building materials began showing up and getting unloaded and neatly piled in front of the houses along our street and down on Lakeshore Drive.

It would take several months to rebuild all the houses to a livable state. Groups of neighbors worked first on one house and then on another, without any expectation of pay. If anyone made a fuss over it, shoulders shrugged, eyes were averted toward the floor, and someone would say it was "just the right thing to do."

For a while, Bay City's historical population of 327 dwindled a bit because of the flood. During the summer of 1967, several families would move away to surrounding communities, taking their sons and daughters to higher ground in Ellsworth, Hager City, or Diamond Bluff. The population signs never changed. I guess 327 was maybe more of a goal after that.

It rained hard the first night we slept in our new room. The sound on the roof seemed extra loud because of the lack of insulation. It helped me to go to sleep. The steady noise must have kept Jack awake.

I woke up after the first night to find something Jack had drawn on a brown paper grocery bag while I was sleeping. He did this from time to time. I always tried to sneak a peek, and he might have even left them lying around so I could discover them. This one was a pencil drawing of what appeared to me to be an angel falling from the sky. The details were strikingly realistic. The angel's sinewy body was drawn in an awkward, doll-like position, with his damaged wings pointing skyward as he fell.

Mostly, I had come to accept my own ineptitude as compared to his blossoming genius. Jack was Jack. I tried to put it back exactly where I found it, so he wouldn't realize I had seen it.

However, curiosity finally got the best of me. When I asked him about it, Jack said, "It's not an angel, it's Icarus. He escaped from an oppressed land on wings made of wax and feathers, but he flew too close to the sun and his wings melted. He fell to his death into the sea."

Jack paused and waited for a moment before asking, "Well? What do you think?"

"I don't know, Jack. It's pretty strange stuff. Maybe I should ask you what *you* were thinking. I mean, instead of sleeping like regular people."

"Yeah, sleeping is kind of overrated. Well, maybe Icarus symbolizes freedom. I haven't quite figured it out yet. Maybe it has something to do with how we all want to be free but sometimes we can't handle the responsibility that comes with it."

"He's got a weird look on his face. Is he supposed to be screaming or something?"

"Ha! I'd better work on that a little more. He's *laughing*. Icarus laughed as he fell. Why he did that is a point of discussion. One theory suggests he felt the joy of flying even if it was so short-lived. I think a little freedom is better than none. You know? Of course, freedom means different things to different people."

"Yeah, sure. Jack. You do realize you're a little crazy, right?"

"I live to entertain you, M."

CHAPTER 3

A Different Kind of Flood

I recall, on a sunny Friday morning in June, standing in the open doorway and playing the Byrds' version of Dylan's "Mr. Tambourine Man" on the Airline at a somewhat too-high volume. Summer vacation from school had recently begun. It was rare for me to be alone in the barbershop. Mom had a doctor's appointment in Red Wing, and Dad and Jack had gone with her.

Bob Dylan's lyrics seemed profound and mystical. I played the song over and over, trying to grasp its meaning. Through Jack, I was introduced to a more sophisticated viewpoint than those I generally shared with my friends. He could probably interpret it for me, but I was hoping I wouldn't have to ask.

Kids and dogs moved about on the sidewalks outside. Cars and bikes shared the streets without mishap. Flies buzzed and landed on the warm pavement. Dust particles floated in the sunlight. The world of my childhood was about to change forever.

Earlier that morning Uncle Harry had driven the family to Red Wing. The Impala was his pride and joy. It was a two-tone red and white convertible with overdrive. Having returned them home again, he angle-parked in front of the barbershop just as the Byrds were finishing the second verse. I hurried to turn down the volume as Mom, Dad, Harry, and Jack silently filed in. I could tell something was wrong as soon as I saw them.

Harry seemed uncomfortable and mumbled an excuse for leaving right away. Dad stared at the floor with red-rimmed eyes, and Jack appeared angry about something. I looked to Mom for the answer.

She smiled and said, "Honey-boy, we need to talk."

Then she calmly and quietly told me she had cancer, and she needed to go away for treatment at the University Hospital in Madison. She said Jack and I would have to help Dad out, and we shouldn't worry because he would take care of us until she got back. I asked her if it was serious.

Mom smiled again and nodded, saying only, "Yes." Tears were beginning to appear in the corners of her eyes.

I cannot remember being more frightened than I was at that moment. As it was with the great flood our town had endured, our home was once again engulfed by the shock, sorrow, and fear of an unknown threat we had not considered before. There was no escaping it. We were forced to deal with it, and it wasn't going to ease up anytime soon.

Over the next few days, we talked a lot about cancer. The doctor had said the best treatment option for Mom's condition was a combination of surgery and radiation. It was a relatively new approach and was still being evaluated, but the early results were promising. It seemed confusing that we had been programmed to fear radiation from a hydrogen bomb, but now we were told radiation treatments were my mother's best chance for survival. Though I tried to be positive, I couldn't help being afraid.

Mom had cancer of the uterus, and the treatment would likely be almost as debilitating as the symptoms of the disease itself. She explained what we should expect. There would be weight loss and some pain. She may even lose a lot of her hair. We already understood enough to know this was very serious and even life threatening.

Madison was three hours away, but because of the driving issue it might as well have been on the moon. We weren't sure how long she would be gone, but probably a few months.

When the time came, she left in a tan Rambler Ambassador sedan driven by a cheerful volunteer from the American Cancer Society. We hugged and cried, not knowing for sure whether she would *ever* return at all. All too quickly, Mom was gone from our sight.

Dad took it badly. He sat nearly sleepless in the barber chair for two days, only getting up a few times and moving around slowly, as if in a trance. She had made tuna casserole and baked some fresh bread, taking care of us up to the very last minute. He hardly ate anything. At mealtime Jack and I warmed it up in a pan on top of the stove, mostly trying to keep quiet and respect Dad's sadness. The three of us were just waiting and hoping for some of the initial shock to pass. Meanwhile, it was Mom who would be going through the hardest part, alone and far away from her home and family.

In the early morning after the second day, Dad woke Jack and me up. "Are you hungry? Let's get some pie."

It sounded good to me. Jack said we should go without him, and he rolled over and went back to sleep. I got dressed, and we set off for Stella's Café. It was still dark, and the cool air felt good. I could almost match the length of Dad's stride with my own.

On any given morning, the counter at Stella's was lined with most of the local dignitaries. This morning's crowd included Mick and Hap Swenson, two grizzled and weather-worn brothers who owned the last big commercial fishing operation on Lake Pepin. As was frequently true, they were having a substantial breakfast before heading off to work on their fishing rig.

Wayne Button was still dressed in the wool sport coat and plaid shirt he had gone drinking in the night before. Wayne worked on the Swenson brothers' seine boats harvesting carp, catfish, and other rough fish for the markets in Chicago and New York. His breath still smelled of last night's stale booze, but it didn't stop him from flirting with Stella. Wayne's bowed legs were vestiges of his early days as a rodeo rider in Montana. His crooked nose had been broken more times than he could remember. Most times by horses, and once or twice by another cowboy.

The café was owned and operated by Stella Person. Stella was a short and energetic woman with a gift for multitasking the many duties of cooking and serving meals while keeping conversations with just about everybody in the room. Her pink uniform strained in several areas, but especially where her chest threatened to escape over the top of the zippered front. Wayne was clearly interested.

Jerry Wold was consuming a high dose of caffeine before facing the challenges of his job pumping out septic tanks. He owned his own pump truck, and like a lot of independent businesspeople, he made a decent wage for performing a hard job. Jerry liked to say, "Poop is my business, and business is good."

Dale Thorsdall looked typically suave with his slicked-back hair, gold chain bracelet, Bermuda shorts, and loafers with no socks. He was reading the morning paper and inhaling a cigarette between sips of coffee. Dad and I sat down next to him.

Dale sold insurance. He was divorced and lived by himself in a nice house down on Lakeshore Drive. Currently, he was staying in his big Winnebago camper while his home was being repaired. Dale was also the mayor of Bay City, a job that paid $100 per month.

Dale said, "Hi, Brick. How is she?"

"Good morning, Dale. I guess we'll have to wait and see."

I listened for any other information, but it didn't come. Several of the regulars and Stella all expressed their concern.

"These things happen."

"It's not up to us; it's God's plan."

"It's a shame, but what are you gonna do?"

I grew more and more frustrated with each trite comment. *Mom* was the one who was going to go through this nightmarish process. *She* was the one who would lose weight and lose her hair and throw up every day. Why were they giving Dad all their sympathy? I felt invisible.

Finally, I lost control and shouted, "She's not dead! She's just sick!"

Then I broke down and began sobbing uncontrollably out of shame, fear, and relief. I was at once embarrassed and intensely aware of being far too old to be crying like a baby in public, but I was lost in the overpowering emotions a boy feels for his mother.

Stella came around the counter and put her arms around me, pulling me into the cushion of her chest. I hugged her and cried without holding back. After I stopped, she brought out two pieces of the best apple pie in the world and put two scoops of ice cream on each piece. When we left, she didn't charge Dad for the pie. It was barely daybreak.

"What do you say, M? Let's go up to the house."

"Okay, sure. I'm sorry about bawling like a big calf back there."

"It's all right, son. How the heck are we supposed to act anyway?"

We walked across Highway 35, through the ditch, and over the railroad tracks. Turning west, we cut through Brown's Seed Corn property and behind the old Bay City Grade School. The big square brick building was empty now. Its cornerstone was marked 1905. For decades, each classroom housed two grades, which wasn't too bad considering a few one-room schools were still operating. All were bursting at the seams with kids in those days.

I attended Bay City Elementary School from first through fifth grade. My class was the last to graduate after our school was absorbed into a consolidation plan. One immediate result was the Bay City kids and those from other surrounding towns would be riding a bus to the new Prairie View School west of town near Hager City.

Prairie View was a major improvement over the fractured classroom experience of Bay City. I spent one year at Prairie View before beginning the longer daily bus ride to the junior high school in Ellsworth, Wisconsin.

Ellsworth Junior High was a blend of kids from the surrounding towns and farms. There were country kids, city kids, and kids like me from small towns scattered across the counties served by the Ellsworth school system. But as far as ethnic diversity, there were few non-white kids in the entire Ellsworth district and none who lived in Bay City. Most of us were of mixed Scandinavian or Irish heritage.

This fact was not completely lost to us. Like other aspects of our earliest cultural awareness, we were being taught to think about the ways in which people of differing ethnic backgrounds communicate. Many of the examples we heard about in class suggested people of different colors or cultures could live together in harmony. This was in stark contrast with what we saw on television during the evening news.

And yet, Jack seemed to be a good filter of the sensational news stories, and his opinions usually made sense to me. Mom called him an old soul.

"Every heart beats the same red blood. People are people. The rest is what we choose to make of it."

"Geez Jack, where does this stuff come from? So, are you, like, from some ancient, all-knowing alien race or something?"

He smiled and said, "It's from a country-and-western song, I think."

"You're kidding, right?"

"No, really. Don't tell anybody. It's my main source for wise or profound statements."

"Ah, geez."

The sidewalks stopped at the end of the old schoolhouse block, and we continued walking on the street leading to our house. We walked past Swenson's Fish Market and Patterson's house, where David Patterson lived with his dad and his uncle Art. David was somewhat mentally challenged, and his distinct speech impediment often became the focus of other children's cruelty. David's uncle looked after him when his dad was at work.

In our younger years when we went to our friends' houses to see if they could come out and play, we didn't knock on the door, and most of the houses didn't have a doorbell. Instead, we stood outside the house and loudly shouted, "Here for . . ." and called out the kid's name. We often stood there shouting out our proclamation several times before the friend appeared or a parent showed up to say they were not available to play.

However, David's speech pattern shaped his words a little differently from the other kids. He would stand in my front yard and holler, "*Hee foh Ay-mot!*" at the top of his lungs. Though I found it a little embarrassing, I never told him so. I just hurried up when I heard him calling.

He was the only neighbor kid who would play with me when we first moved to Bay City. At the time, he was still a grade ahead of me. In a year or so we outgrew the friendship. I am certain it was frustrating for David to be older and more physically powerful than his playmates, and yet unable to keep his younger friends very long.

However, in the period while David and I were playing together every day, we managed to share at least one major adventure. David was something of a pyromaniac, which appealed to me a great deal as a young boy. Together we burned down imaginary forts and the headquarters of the entire Nazi army, not to mention a few replica houses of some of the neighboring boys we didn't like very much. After a few smaller fires, we were ready for bigger things.

The Patterson's martin house—a type of apartment-style birdhouse—was quite large and, as we learned, could hold an unbelievable number of matches. It took a long time and a lot of petty match thefts to fill it up. It had to be just right. As David said, "We plan 'na shit outa shit."

We were careful not to get caught. We didn't consider it as stealing—more like a spy mission. Over the course of a couple months, we completely stuffed the Martin house with matchbooks and stick matches taken from our homes and from the gas station downtown.

Eventually, we were ready. On a sun-parched day in July, we stuck a piece of rolled up newspaper into the front door of the birdhouse, lit the makeshift fuse, and torched it in a blazing whoosh of explosive fireball glory. The big, flaming reddish-orange ball rolled upward through its own smoke and quickly began scattering smoldering ash and chunks of burning birdhouse across David's backyard and along the railroad tracks bordering the back of the Patterson property.

We were incredibly impressed with our work. However, our elation was unfortunately short-lived. Somebody called the volunteer fire department, and David and I got into a bunch of trouble for it. The upside was that getting in trouble has a sort of bonding effect when you are a kid. To tell the truth, I doubt either of us had any real remorse for the whole thing. But for a short time, even the older guys thought we were cool.

Next door to the Patterson house lived Sam Most. His tiny house was right across the street from ours. He was around ninety years old and lived alone in squalid conditions. Sam was a white-haired, mildly senile old fellow whose mustache was permanently stained yellowish-brown from chewing and spitting tobacco. He was fortunate to live on the high side of the street. If the flood water had gotten deep enough to reach his house, he probably would have just stayed there and drowned out of sheer stubbornness.

When I was a little boy, Sam told me he would help me learn how to ride my first bike without training wheels. I dutifully brought it across the street and up the small hill onto his front yard, where he removed the training wheels with a pair of pliers and several choice expletives. Then I crawled up onto the seat with Sam holding the big new bike steady.

He asked, "Are you ready?"

"Yup."

"Set?"

"Yup."

He never said "go." I don't know what I thought was supposed to happen, but I wasn't expecting Sam to just give me and the bike a good shove. I flopped backward as I took off down his hill and across the street, gaining speed as the bike launched down into our front yard. All the while, Sam was yelling, "Ride, dammit! *Ride,* boy!"

I crashed near our apple tree with Sam cackling like the crazy old coot he was. My testicles got mightily crunched on top of the bike frame when I tipped over. I never trusted him again. Testicular pain does that.

This morning he was sitting in his lawn chair at the front edge of his yard. As we approached, I noticed his false teeth were lying on the ground next to the chair. He was casting a fishing line across the pavement and into our yard, slowly reeling it back in. It was a surreal scene, to say the least.

Dad asked, "Sam, what the heck are you doing?"

"Fishing," he said, and spat.

Dad and I looked at each other. Finally, he said, "Fish in your own yard, Sam. I might want to try that spot later."

The old man just smiled his toothless smile and kept on fishing and spitting.

I'd been in our house often since the floodwaters subsided, mostly to help with sweeping up after the workers. Dad and some of his buddies had cut off the lower half of the sheetrock walls and removed the wet insulation. The rest of the house had to dry out for several weeks before the actual repairs were started.

By now most of the rough work was done, and the trim carpentry had begun. Today, there was a wallpaper sample book on the counter.

Dad asked, "What do you know about wallpaper? I've had this book for a few days."

I smiled, raised an eyebrow, and said, "You're in luck. I have an uncanny knack for this sort of thing."

"Good," he said. "We need to get this done before your mother gets home."

For a second our eyes met. Then we both looked away and he opened the sample book. We carefully examined every pattern and finally settled on a white background with miniature roses on it and a wide rose pattern border. We were very proud of our choice, though I realize now it was probably quite dated even then.

Jack was up and reading in the barber chair when we got home. He nonchalantly mentioned Mom had called. We asked him a bunch of rapid-fire questions about what she had said. He grudgingly answered our questions before returning to his H. P. Lovecraft horror novel.

Then we called Mom and asked her the same questions all over again. It helped a lot to hear her voice. She seemed strong and resolute. She said she was going to beat this darned disease, and we believed her. She told us we needed to do our part and not lose faith. We promised we would not. Before she finally hung up, she told us how much she loved us, and we told her we felt the same. Among all the other uncertainties, it was never in doubt.

The absurdity of living in a barbershop was hard enough but learning how to function as a family without our true leader sometimes seemed like madness. We were equals in a sense, for the three of us had depended on her far too much for our daily support systems. She was the glue. Without her, our roles and relationships with each other were noticeably changed. Something extremely important was missing, and it would be this way until she returned.

Dad had a kind of seniority, and we respected him. He was, of course, still our dad. But he was as worried as we were, and we all had a lot to learn. In some ways we were more like roommates than a father and sons.

As I lay in bed, I thought about the wallpaper and hoped it would be good enough, though I knew it never could be. Still, I wanted her to like it because I had picked it out.

Monday morning, we placed our order at Taylor's Hardware. Dad and I proudly showed off our choice, and the clerk endorsed it, as if the cheery rose pattern could solve everything. Three hours and a world away, Mom began her radiation treatments.

CHAPTER 4

THE DRIVE

A few weeks went by, and a pattern of sorts began to develop. We called Mom every other day. It soon became clear she had good days and bad ones. In between the calls we tried our best to go about our usual lives.

One morning in the café, Dale Thorsdall approached Dad with a proposition.

"Brick, c'mon over. I've got something I need to talk to you about."

"Hi, Dale. What's up?"

"Well, the Village Board met last night, and we need to hire a new village custodian. What do you say? Are you interested?"

"Are you offering me a job? Uh, sure. Absolutely."

"Great. Oh, by the way, you'll also be the town constable. Sound good?"

"Well, not *as* good. Do I have to carry a pistol?"

"Oh, *hell* no. I'm not authorized to issue you a weapon. But I guess if you think you need one, you should probably buy yourself a gun and then be damned sure not to let me know about it."

"I'd prefer not to do that. What exactly does this job pay?"

"Accept it first, and I'll tell you."

"Okay, I accept. Now, what am I making?"

"Seven bucks an hour as custodian, no overtime, and fifty bucks a month to be the constable."

He reached into his front pocket and produced a shiny, nickel-plated badge.

"And you also get this. But you can only wear it after your custodial workday is done or when you are patrolling our town. Or, I suppose, any other times when you think it might be right."

"Hmm. Thanks, Dale. It's a good offer. We need the money. A steady paycheck will sure be a good thing. I really appreciate it."

"You're welcome, Brick. Bay City needs you. Hell . . . *I* need you. There is a lot to do, and I know you'll do a great job."

"When do I start?"

Dale smiled a broad smile, and the two men looked each other in the eyes.

"Yup, I get it." said Dad. "Do I have time for a cup of coffee first?"

"You bet. It's on me this morning. The Village Board wishes to congratulate you on your new position. By the way, when it comes to all the 'power and glory,' you are officially second in line in behind me, your venerable mayor."

"Well, you know what they say: when you're not the lead dog on the sled, the view never changes."

"Oh brother. So much for gratitude."

"No, really Dale, thanks a lot. I guess I should ask you what exactly you want me to do. And I probably should also let you know my car doesn't run very well most of the time."

"Oh hell, Brick, I want you to do whatever needs to be done. It's *our* town now, and I intend for you to keep everything looking sharp and running right so nobody ever calls me to complain. That's the most important part. You can use the village tractor to get around. It's parked in the fire hall, and the trailer is down behind the old jail."

"Uh, I don't really have to ever put anybody in the jail, do I?"

"Don't be ridiculous, Brick. The jail is where we keep the gas cans. Mostly, the Pierce County cops handle any actual arrests. You get all the easy stuff. Hey, have you ever known *anyone* to end up in that ol' birdcage? Maybe you'd better check for skeletons before you go in there. If we ever did lock anybody up, I'd bet good money we forgot all about 'em."

Word of Dad's new job spread quickly, and soon it seemed the whole town felt good about helping our family out. Dad worked hard during the day cleaning the streets, mowing the park lawns and the two church lawns, and generally keeping the town in decent repair. Neighbors waved and wished him well. Occasionally, he was offered a fresh, warm cookie. He rode around on a big blue tractor with a yellow sign stenciled on the hood that read "Village of Bay City."

On Friday nights, he worked security for the dances at Horton's Ballroom. In between the new job hours and on weekends, he worked on the house repairs.

Jack read nearly nonstop. Though he seemed to grow even smarter and more introspective, he couldn't seem to admit how much he missed Mom. He built his emotional walls so well even I began to back off and give him the solitude he demanded and yet, so despised.

This was about the time I met Darla. She and her parents had moved to town just before the Fourth of July from Redondo Beach, California. She was tall and tan and had big brown eyes. Compared to other girls my own age, I guess you could say she was an early bloomer. She just seemed so—Californian.

The first time I saw her she came riding up to the barbershop, parked her bike, and looked in the window of the door with her hands cupped on either side of her face. She was bent forward, and I could plainly see down the front of her shirt. When I realized I had allowed my gaze to wander, I quickly shifted my eyes upward only to meet hers. She smiled.

I felt my heart beating in my chest as I hurriedly moved to the door and opened it a bit too suddenly. Darla looked startled, but she quickly regained her composure.

"Who are you?" she said.

"Who am *I*? I'm Emmet North, but mostly everybody calls me M. I live here. Who are *you*?" I replied. Even as I said it, I felt foolish.

"So . . . you live in a barbershop?"

"It's only temporary. You know, the flood and all."

She sized me up. "I'll call you Emmet, because I am clearly not *everybody*. What color are your eyes? Hazel?"

"Well, green, I guess. And yours are . . ."

"Beautiful? I know." She fluttered her lashes for effect.

"I was going to say brown."

"Very funny. You're a real comedian. Want to take a drive?" she asked.

"But I wasn't—well—uh, sure. A drive sounds good."

Her name was Darla Day, and she was fourteen, a year older than me. I got my bike from behind the shop, and we started off toward the other end of town. As we rode, she told me about how her father had been transferred to a new job with 3M in St. Paul, and how great Redondo Beach was, and how crummy Bay City was.

Her father was Martin, or Marty, and her mother was Doreen, but she preferred Deedee. I pointed out our real house before we turned left toward the lake and continued toward hers. By the time we reached her place, I was unquestionably smitten.

Darla lived in a double-wide mobile home a few blocks from our place. A month ago, the land had been empty. Now, this shiny portable house had been planted between two vacant lots that were essentially dry plots of sand burrs and dandelions.

In contrast, Darla's yard had lush, green, freshly laid sod and a big round aboveground swimming pool with painted corrugated aluminum sides. It seemed glamorously different than its surroundings . . . like an oasis. The trailer was pastel pink with white trim, and it had flower boxes with fake pink geraniums in them. The pool liner was dark blue and had stenciled sea horses in a ring around the top.

Standing in front of her house, Darla seemed even more sophisticated than when I'd first seen her. A gray Ford station wagon was parked out front. She went into the trailer and returned almost immediately, bouncing down the steps dangling a set of car keys in her left hand.

"My parents took the Riviera," she chirped. "Hop in."

"What? Are you kidding?"

"I asked you if you wanted to take a drive. What did you think I meant, on a bike?"

"Well, yeah. I guess so."

"Are you in or out?" The tone in her voice was both a challenge and an invitation. I was in the front seat before I knew what I was doing.

"Uh, have you done this before?"

"Sure, lots of times."

She started the engine and revved it up higher and tighter than any half worn-out station wagon engine ever was revved before. She smiled a sultry fourteen-year-old smile and dropped the transmission into drive. We pulled out of her parents' yard and turned left, heading toward the Legion Club's baseball field, which was still waterlogged from the flood. The car lurched a few times, but overall, Darla seemed to be a competent driver, at least to me.

In addition to bordering on the back of my family's lot, the road to the ball field eventually led to Johnsons' Woods. Darla drove down the muddy dirt road and parked behind the bleachers, grinding the gears mercilessly as she shifted into park before the vehicle had fully stopped.

"Oops. So, what's your story, Emmet North?"

"What do you mean?"

"You know, what do you like to do? What *is* there to do in this town?"

"I don't know; mostly I hang around with my friends. Sometimes we play football. Sometimes we swim or fish."

"Fishing?! Yuck! Don't you ever do anything *fun*?"

"Like what?"

"Like go to a drive-in or stay up all night and drink Ripple on the beach. You know, *fun*!"

"Well, sure. I guess so." I didn't know what Ripple was.

"I saw you looking at me back there at your house."

"You did? Oh geez."

"You were pretty obvious." She giggled.

"Sorry."

"It's okay. I didn't mind." After a pause she asked, "I heard your mom has cancer. Is it true?"

"Yes."

"Will she be okay?"

"Yes! Definitely." I was more emphatic than confident.

"Great. I'm glad to hear it. How long has she been gone?"

"Around a month, I guess. It seems longer."

"When will she be back?"

"I don't know. Soon I hope."

For the first time since I'd laid eyes on her, Darla was quiet. She looked me up and down as if studying me. She was thinking about something. I just didn't know what it was. I was a little uncomfortable. Eventually Darla took the initiative.

"Do you want to drive this heap?" she said.

"Uh, okay."

We traded places without opening the car doors. When I slid across the bench seat and under her, I immediately became aware of the way her hair smelled sweet like flowers, or maybe Prell shampoo.

I turned the key and revved the engine. In a lame attempt to impress, I turned up the volume on the radio. Van Morrison was singing "Brown Eyed Girl." I shifted into reverse, and instantly the motor died. Smiling sheepishly, I tried it again. This time I managed to back out and shift into drive.

We took off down the muddy ballpark road leading back in the general direction of my normal life. When we reached the blacktop road, I turned hard on the steering wheel, but we were going too fast. The driver's side tires caught the soft shoulder, and we started drifting into the ditch.

"*Hit the brakes!*" Darla shouted.

My foot froze. Instead, I shoved the gas pedal to the floor, and we careened down the ditch, bumping and swaying uncontrollably. By the time I figured out how to stop the wagon, dirt and grass were sticking out of every crack and crevice of the undercarriage like a hula skirt. The radio still blared even after the engine died.

I turned off the key, and we sat there breathing hard and not talking. Then Darla got a strange look on her face. She slid over next to me and ran the palm of her left hand across my short dark hair from front to back. Without hesitation, she gave me my first *real* kiss.

I could feel my cheeks getting flushed. I should have realized this was about to get complicated. But like every other darned fool who has just kissed a pretty girl for the first time, I was already hooked. All I could do was insipidly smile and drive her home.

"Don't be too proud, Mr. North. You could use some practice. And I'm not just referring to your driving skills."

We left the car where we found it, dirt and grass and all. Darla said she would take the blame for it. It wouldn't be the first time. I rode my bike back to the barbershop, a changed man.

I was suddenly dangerous and daring, a rebel drag racer with a hot movie-star girlfriend on my arm. I imagined myself smoking a Chesterfield and screaming down the street in an XKE Jaguar like James Dean. There was no stopping me. I rode fast and hard. I dodged around imaginary boulders and palm trees like the ones in Redondo Beach. When I got to the shop, I pushed the pedal backward, engaging the brakes and laying down a rubber streak two feet long on the sidewalk. Then I swaggered into the shop.

Jack looked up and said, "Welcome home, Beaver."

"Bite me, Wally."

A trace of a smile passed between us. I wondered if Jack had ever been kissed. I thought not. I wanted to talk to him about the whole adventure, but I didn't think he could keep it a secret. I didn't want Dad to know what a wild man his son had suddenly become. I thought it best to just keep quiet about it. I softly whistled "Brown Eyed Girl" as I headed upstairs.

"What's with you, Junior?"

"Nothin', Jack. Nothin' at all."

The weekend was coming on, and I was the newly self-appointed Prince of Bay City.

After a while Dad came home and announced that we were going out for supper at Horton's Ballroom. Jack and I were up for any meal we hadn't cooked ourselves. A great fish fry was held every Friday night in the basement of the hall. It was an all-you-can-eat-for-a-buck-and-a-quarter affair.

Dad said we could stay for the dance if we promised to stay sober and not hit on any ladies in the bar. I figured Jack was up to the task, but I wasn't sure I could be trusted.

"Okay, we promise," I lied.

People came from miles around for the fish fry. Boris Rose and his wife Shirley cooked. Boris and Shirley worked part time at Swenson's fish market, but their true calling was frying fish in mass quantities. Boris was well over sixty, and Shirley was in her thirties.

Shirley's long black hair hung nearly to her waist and was pulled back into a ponytail. Impossible not to notice, she had a pronounced overbite which unfortunately made her look less intelligent than she really was.

Boris was a Norwegian who had come from Canada a long time ago but still carried a strange Norwegian/French-Canadian accent few people recognized. He chain-smoked non-filtered cigarettes and wasn't very careful about where the ashes fell. The boiling grease in the deep fryer hid a multitude of sins.

The fish was beer-battered, hand-dipped, and delicious. There were hash browned potatoes, baked beans, coleslaw, orange Jell-O, and heavily buttered buns. Jack and I tried to figure out who among the people in line had brought plastic bags to smuggle some fish home in their purses or bib overalls. Desperate times called for desperate measures.

Dad wore his nickel-plated constable star on a blue shirt he had carefully ironed before leaving the shop. He looked strong and proud.

After we had eaten our fill, it was time to go upstairs so Dad could patrol the dance hall. For once, Jack didn't have a book with him. We found a small table in the back of the hall. Dad got us two O-So Grapes and gave each of us 50 cents.

"Don't spend it all in one place," he said. "And remember to stay out of trouble. I would hate to have the two of you end up being the first guys I have to arrest."

The music started at eight o'clock. Dad started the slow circling walk around the perimeter of the dance hall that he would repeat many times before midnight when the dance ended. Several of the dancers greeted Dad.

"Hi, Brick."

"What do you say, Brick?"

One of the farmer's wives said, "Save me a dance, will you, Brick?"

He just smiled and kept walking slowly. The band was the Ramblers, a polka band from Ellsworth composed of three teachers moonlighting to supplement their income and drink a few free beers. The instrumentation consisted of an accordion, a tuba, and drums.

They were well-trained musicians, but their song choices were extremely questionable to my young ears. They played the usual choices of mainstream polka favorites like "Beer Barrel Polka" and "She's Too Fat for Me," along with some modified country arrangements like "The Tennessee Waltz" and "I Walk the Line." Any of the non-polkas had been "polka-tized" nearly beyond recognition. This would have been tough enough to take, but for reasons known only to the band, they also included arrangements of current hits by Neil Diamond, Jay and the Americans, Tom Jones, and the Beach Boys.

When the lead singer broke into "I wish they all could be California girls," the combination of a polka beat and surf music caused Jack to blurt out, "Is this hell?"

I swear if I had heard "Mr. Tambourine Man," my head would have exploded. But the crowd loved it and rapidly reached a fevered frenzy born of cheap beer and a need to blow off some steam from the work week they had just completed.

Before long, Jack had heard enough. He gave Dad the index finger wave and punched me on the shoulder before heading out the door and back across the railroad tracks to the barbershop. As he walked away, the Ramblers kicked into an off-kilter rendition of a Herman's Hermits tune. I was pretty sure Jack was right. It seemed like the end of the world might be coming soon, at least musically speaking.

I sat there drinking my O-So Grape and waiting for another sign from above. It never came. Dad finished a little after midnight and received a $10 cash tip from the bartender.

"What do you say? Let's go home."

"Sure."

The Ramblers were talking to some glassy-eyed ladies at the bar. I nodded to the tuba player as we walked by and out the door. He nodded back. It was clear we were both men of the world.

Dad and I walked side by side in the cool late-night air. I matched my stride with his, proving beyond doubt I was a grown man now.

We could hear the train's horn far down the lake at Stockholm. It would blow again at Maiden Rock and then again just before it made its way to Bay City around twelve thirty. I noticed it was a freight train. At this time of night, the actual freight loads were quite scant, but a seemingly endless parade of empty boxcars needed to reach the Twin Cities before morning. We hurried to get across the tracks before it reached town so we wouldn't have to get stuck on the wrong side and wait for the train to roar pass.

The horn had a deeper and throatier sound compared to its passenger train counterpart, the Twin Cities Zephyr, which was the pride of the Burlington line. She roared through town every Monday through Saturday on the early morning run to Chicago and again in late afternoon on the return run to St. Paul. The Zephyr's horn was brilliant and almost musical in its tone. Tonight, the mournful sound of the freight train seemed weary and only served to remind us it was time to sleep.

CHAPTER 5

THE BEACH

My three best buddies showed up Saturday morning with a plan. Tom Freeman, Rex Hillstad, and Denny Berg had cooked up a great caper. We would sleep out on the beach, and Denny's older brother, Nate, would buy us a pack of cigarettes and a *Playboy* magazine. Nate was not doing this out of the kindness of his heart but because Denny had caught him helping himself to their father's Old Crow whiskey, which he valued above all else. In return for his silence, Nate agreed to do his brother this favor.

Personally, I couldn't inhale a cigarette without coughing madly. Still, the idea sounded pretty good to me. We agreed to meet up around six thirty under the west-end viaduct, where Nate would have made his drop earlier. A pack of Marlboros and Miss July would be stashed in the girders of the viaduct bridge. It appeared to be a very well-conceived plan.

Denny used to live in Florida. He had been badly hurt in a car accident when he was just a toddler. His mom died in the wreck. After the accident, his dad moved Den and his degenerate brother north to Bay City.

Denny's injuries made him walk kind of hunched over like an old man. He was a natural comedian. His quick wit made him popular despite his somewhat unique-looking, little-old-man stature. His black hair was pasted across his forehead in a careless swipe. Occasionally he flipped his head sideways to get it out of his eyes.

Rex was red-haired and freckle faced. He was stocky and strong. His folks were divorced, and he lived with his mother on the other end of town. Due to a strange incident, Rex had attained folk-hero status among his friends and even the adults in our town. A few summers earlier he was floating in an inner tube, just relaxing and soaking up rays, when a large snapping turtle lopped off two of his toes. As it turns out, snapping turtles have little discretion when it comes to their dining habits. The foot looked about as nasty as you would imagine, so he immediately became famous. Rex was always happy to slip off his shoe and sock to show off the damage. All mangled and grotesque, I thought it was about the coolest thing I'd ever seen.

Tom was a blond, curly headed string bean who looked a little book-worm-y, but he was deceptively athletic. He was smart and I guess good looking, in a sort of geeky way. He had been my best friend since grade school and right after I stopped playing exclusively with David Patterson. On about every level, we just clicked.

His nickname was Jelly. Unlike the drama Rex experienced, Tom's nickname was coined by his doting mom, in response to his love of grape jelly when he was just a baby. Her version was "My little jelly-boy." I am sure Tom regrets ever sharing that with us. We shortened the title down to Jelly, only because Tom seemed to be marginally okay with it.

Together, we called ourselves the Baytown Mafia. With our plan in place, we had all afternoon for other things. Now we just needed to figure out how to spend the rest of our day.

"What do you want to do?"

"I don't know. What do *you* want to do?"

"Let's go swimming."

Jelly bobbed his head and said, "*Right on!*"

We laughed. He was trying so hard to be cool.

"Bite me, you a-holes," he whined.

"*Right on!*" I added.

Denny added, "Right on, *man!*"

Then Rex: "You mean right on, *my brother*!" That just about covered it.

We went home to get our suits. We had our choice of the main beach on Lake Pepin or any of a handful of nearby ponds fed by artesian wells. Artesian water is cleaner, but much cooler. The day was warming up fast, so we headed for Northwestern Pond. Northwestern was a formidable little pool with artesian wells pumping into each end and an overflow spillway to the slough leading out into the harbor.

Occasionally, in late winter, one or more bald eagles could be seen standing on the edge of the ice encircling the open water caused by the flowing streams from the wells. If you were lucky enough to come upon one of these large and noble birds as they were fishing, it was a sight to be remembered. I thought they resembled monks with white hooded robes as they hunched over, peering into the clear water and patiently waiting for a shad or sunfish to stray too close to the surface.

Years earlier, when commercial fishing was still big business on the lake, Northwestern was used as a holding pond for timing the market to get top dollar. The carp are primarily used to make gefilte fish, a popular traditional dish generally served as an appetizer in many Jewish households.

By the 1960s, Swenson's fishing crew was selling their catch as fast as it was harvested. Money was tight, and the markets didn't fluctuate more than a few cents a pound.

When we were still little kids, I ruined a new pair of penny loafers trying to float a raft across Northwestern with Tom after Sunday school. The contraption had been cobbled together by some older guys. It was made of old lumber and some empty steel barrels for flotation. Unsurprisingly, the barrels weren't very dependable. The water was up to our knees before we made it across the pond and into the shallows. We had to wade the rest of the way to shore.

Neither of us could swim yet, and we had no business trying the stunt. It was one of just a few times I ever saw Mom lose her temper. She was very upset about the shoes, but when she realized we could have drowned she spanked me harder and longer than my crime deserved.

She sobbed uncontrollably all the while she was whaling on me. I thought she had gone crazy. Afterward, I just stood there too scared even to cry as she knelt and hugged me, telling me she loved me over and over.

I stroked her hair and said, "It's all right, Momma, it's all right." I guess I was about seven or eight.

When we got to the pond, we realized we were not the first swimmers to seek this private sanctuary from the heat. Two girls were sunning themselves on the sand. I instantly realized one of them was Darla. I didn't recognize the other girl. They both wore white bikinis, which made their tans look darker. As I would soon learn, their skin was coated with a mixture of baby oil and iodine. Their bodies glistened in the hot sun, and we stared dumbfounded. Jelly whispered, "Wow. They're beautiful."

The three of us whispered in unison, "*Right on!*" Then we all broke down laughing. Darla and the other girl sat up.

"Hi there, Emmet. Who are the dirtballs? Step over here and let us get a good look at the local talent."

"What did she call us? Dirtballs?" Rex clearly considered the term a compliment.

"Never mind," I said. "C'mon."

We trudged over the sandy ridge and walked up to the girls. Darla started the introductions. "Carmen, this is Emmet North."

"The stunt driver?"

"The same."

"Very funny," I said. "I'm a little rusty."

Carmen asked, "Who are these guys? Let me guess . . . I know, the Three Stooges! Darla, I kinda like little Curly there." She pointed at Tom.

"Let's kidnap him and hold him for ransom."

Darla pretended to play along, "Too risky. He might be missed by the other members of the chess team. This other one is more my style," she said, pointing a curved index finger at me.

"He's a little swarthy and obviously not too bright, but I think he could be useful in the right situation."

I blushed and introduced the Mafia.

"Darla, Carmen, this is Rex, Denny, and Tom, but most people call him Jelly."

Tom had been thinking. "What's with the 'stunt driver' routine?"

"Never mind, I'll tell you later."

When Carmen stood up Denny inhaled so fast, he choked a little and had to cough. She was Darla's older cousin from Minneapolis, and she was staying overnight at Darla's house. Carmen was sixteen, and by all appearances she was all grown up. There were peaks, valleys, and curves everywhere.

The three boys stared. Tom made a gurgle-y sound as he loudly swallowed the saliva which had suddenly appeared in his mouth. This time, I made sure to maintain eye contact with Darla.

Carmen finally said, "Let's get wet, you hoodlums."

We ran to the water and dove in. Denny started splashing water in Rex's face. Darla and I stood there a few feet apart, face to face and smiling, neck deep in the cool water.

Carmen started swimming for the far shore. She had a surprisingly strong and choppy stroke. She was a third of the way across the pond when Jelly took off after her. The race was on. He swam like a man possessed and slowly began to gain on her. Tom looked like Johnny Weissmuller in the old Tarzan movies, where they sped up the camera and made the great Olympic swimmer look even more superhuman.

Carmen's feet touched the other shore before Jelly caught up to her. She turned around and passed him as he waded the last ten feet. When he hit the sand, he spun on his heels and reentered the water like a knife. Carmen didn't stand a chance. He passed her in the middle of the pond as she began to tire and made it back to our side while she was still about ten yards away. By now, we were cheering.

As she arrived on the beach Carmen was breathing hard, but she managed to smile and say, "It was rigged."

Jelly said, "You wish." He panted as he bent forward at the waist with his hands propped on his knees. Then he looked up at Carmen and smiled. "It's the awesome influence of clean air and small-town living."

We swam around for a while and eventually had to get out of the cool water in favor of returning to the hot sand. I lay down on my back and closed my eyes. Darla was lying next to me. The tips of her fingers were touching mine. Carmen and my three best friends were scattered across the beach in various angular poses.

I could see Carmen occasionally looking at Rex's foot. Finally, she gave in to temptation and asked, "Hey, Rex—can I ask what happened to your foot? I mean, you don't have to tell me if you'd rather not talk about it."

Tom chortled, "Rather *not* talk about it? Try to stop him."

"No, it's okay. I don't mind. A big old snapping turtle bit off my toes. I watched one of 'em sink down in the water, but I think he ate the other one. It happened right here in this pond."

"*Eee-yooo!*" Carmen and Darla reacted in unison. We laughed and as always, Rex basked in the attention. The world was close to being perfect. Then I had to go and mess with perfection.

"We're camping out on the beach tonight. Want to join us?" Immediately Denny, Rex, and Jelly sat straight up.

Darla's eyes were closed. "Sorry, we can't. I'm grounded and I can't leave the house after dark. Try to guess what for."

I had dodged the bullet, but I just couldn't leave well enough alone. "C'mon, maybe you could sneak out. There's a full moon. It would be easy to find us."

By now the Mafia were trying every nonverbal signal they knew to get my attention. Tom pursed his lips, opened his eyes wide and tilted his head to one side. Denny gave the universal "stop or I will kill you" sign by drawing his index finger across his throat.

Darla was weighing the possibilities. "Well, maybe we could, but it would have to be pretty late, after my folks go to sleep."

Carmen sat up and said, "We'll bring the beer."

Now I sat up. I looked at Rex. He was frowning darkly. He held up his right fist with the back of his hand pointed at me. His middle finger slowly uncurled. I silently mouthed the word "*What?*" The girls were already plotting their moonlit escape from the pink trailer.

It was around 4:30 when we split up and headed home. Rex, Tom, and Denny clearly were not happy about my spontaneous invitation. After I told them about the station wagon incident, they sort of changed their minds. I made them swear secrecy, something I never really expected of them. The act of swearing something was far more important than the actual secrecy anyway.

Jelly's assessment was, "They'll never show." I remained hopeful.

Our parents were used to us camping on the beach. It had been done for generations, and in those days, it was considered safe. I didn't have a sleeping bag, but Dad gave me a pillow and an old quilt I had used before. The stage was set.

As it turned out, Rex's mom wouldn't let him camp out because he had to usher at church Sunday morning. Rex belonged to the Lutheran church at the other end of town from our house. The Methodist church was on our side of town. In Bay City, this was a main consideration for deciding why Lutherans were Lutherans and Methodists were Methodists. The Catholics had to go to Red Wing or Ellsworth for Mass. The Baptists usually just suffered silently and attended one of the more available choices. At any rate, Rex was out of the camping adventure.

At six thirty, the remaining three of us assembled under the viaduct bridge. Denny scrambled up the embankment and zeroed in on Nate's hiding place. Regardless of our high expectations, there was no pack of Marlboros and no *Playboy*. Instead, Nate had left a box of Swisher Sweets Willow Tips. These were smallish cigars with plastic mouthpiece holders attached. To make matters worse, they were flavored with a mysterious blueberry taste. The label said, "For a Fresh and Fruity Smoke."

Nate had left a scrawled note to us saying, "Smoke this you pansies."

Denny apologized for having such an idiot for a brother. Jelly didn't think the Willow Tips were so bad.

"It could be worse. I've smoked 'em before."

"Are you kidding? What possible reason could you have for smoking one of these?" The only thing that kept me from laughing out loud was how mad I was at Nate.

"All right," Jelly said, "I didn't really. I was just trying to make you feel better." Something about the look on his face made me think maybe he really had smoked one of the goofy things, but I let it go. We headed back toward the lake.

Lakeshore Drive ran down the hill from Main Street and curved to the west, running parallel to the lake for ten or twelve blocks before ending at Fishermen's Point, known to the locals as simply "the Point." Cars couldn't drive all the way out to the end of the rock-and-sand peninsula. The Point was our most favored destination for camping.

There were some huge old cottonwood trees with water lines ringing their trunks from a hundred years of lesser floods than this spring's. The watermark from this year's flood was the highest of all, a good five feet from the ground. The Boy Scouts and 4-H had cleaned up the lakeshore after the flood. There were still several large piles of driftwood and branches left for the campers to use as firewood.

We pitched our camp where we had many times before, placing our sleeping bags and blankets on a patch of sand close to the foot of the biggest cottonwood. This majestic tree was known as the Kingfish.

The Kingfish had seemingly always been there at the head of the lake, like a sentinel guarding our town and keeping it safe from too much modern influence. It was a massive tree, ancient by any standards. Tall and straight, it looked strong enough to stand there forever.

The giant tree was a rune of sorts. So many kids had carved their initials into the bark as to cause the appearance of graffiti stretching from the ground up beyond the point of them being easy to decipher. A hodge-podge mixture of new and old markings ran together in a language all their own. Yet many of the hearts and names or initials were easily readable and familiar to us.

The Kingfish was a kind of marker of recorded history and a symbol of the many generations who had grown up in our town. It had stood there for over a century bearing witness to lives come and gone and as a testament to young love, and occasionally young lust.

The names far outnumbered my generation alone. They included those of our parents, our grandparents, their cronies and sweethearts. Several of the same names could now be seen on the headstones at the cemetery up on the hill and near the edge of town. Though many of the other trees were also marked, none was as prestigious as the great Kingfish.

Leaving your mark on that old tree meant a little more—something a bit more permanent.

By the time we arrived, it was almost eight o'clock. The sun would be down in an hour or so. We set about gathering the best driftwood we could find to feed our campfire through the night.

By eight thirty we had a good blaze going in the dwindling daylight. Our quilts and sleeping bags were placed around the fire in a Y formation, far enough back to keep the majority of sparks from landing on them.

The sun slid the rest of its way down the sky, and the sounds of night-time gradually began. Crickets and frogs were all around, and back across the slough in the swamp we occasionally heard the slap of a beaver's tail. An explosive report from a beaver's tail could scare the bejesus out of you if you didn't know what it was. We settled in and got comfortable, just soaking in the soundtrack of the gathering night.

And always, there was the rhythmic washing of the waves on the shore. The meter and pattern rose and fell with the size-cycle of the waves. By morning they would be smaller and the splashes less pronounced. Tonight, the sound was plainly audible. We sat staring at the fire and listening to the sweet song of our surroundings. Jelly broke the silence with, "They'll never show."

The Mississippi's main channel runs along the far side of the lake and causes a steady and permanent current to pull away from the shore. When the wind blows in the same direction, it can become downright treacherous. Many small kids have lost their toy boats to the deceptive current. A weak swimmer can be pulled into deep water before they know what is happening. That night, the river and the lake were mostly without traffic of any kind. As the darkness grew deeper, some tiny points of light appeared along the shore and across the lake. The serenity of this familiar scene could calm even the most restless soul.

By eleven o'clock the moon was shining full and round, and bright enough to let us see when we moved around. Denny was the first to spot the yellowish point of a flashlight beam bouncing along, coming down the path along the slough. This was the less-traveled way to get down to the lakeshore. At one point you had to walk on a narrow timber spanning the six-foot gap where the overflow from Northwestern Pond emptied out. It was not a good route to travel at night. Darla and Carmen had arrived.

"Howdy, pilgrims. How 'bout rustlin' us up some grub? We're hawng-gry." Darla's imitation of John Wayne was only marginally recognizable.

Carmen looked around and asked, "Where's the other one? Did the turtles eat him?"

"Rex couldn't come. He had a religious experience." Denny held his hands up over his head and wiggled his fingers.

Darla came over and sat down next to me. "Nice night."

I smiled. "It is now."

Carmen plopped down between the two boys. Jelly squirmed a bit and made room for her. I was relieved to see that they hadn't brought any beer. I thought maybe Carmen had been serious. At any rate, I felt like my life was exciting enough lately. Jelly had brought some Hershey bars, and Denny had a Styrofoam minnow bucket with some iced Mountain Dews.

"What's in the cooler?" Carmen was hopeful.

"Yahoo. It's Mountain Dew." Denny droned the soda's advertising slogan with an exaggerated flat affect. The girls chuckled and helped themselves to a can. We sat together and watched the fire for quite a while. We didn't feel the need to talk very much. Occasionally, somebody made a wisecrack or put a chunk of wood on the fire when the flames got too low.

Carmen finally said, "Boys, this party could use a little livening up. Let's go swimming."

Jelly said what we all must have been thinking. "Oh man, I didn't bring my suit."

Carmen casually replied, "Sounds like a problem." She asked in a matter-of-fact tone, "What's it going to be, kids? Swimming by moonlight or a nice little 'Kumbaya' singalong?"

As she stood up, Carmen pulled her shirt off in one fluid motion, revealing a flowered print bikini she was wearing under her street clothes.

Darla looked at me and shrugged her shoulders. "Are you up for it?" As she wiggled out of her clothes, I realized that Darla had planned ahead and brought her swimming suit along, too.

My voice cracked but I managed to mumble, "Sure. Yup. You bet. Why not?"

Tom stared wide-eyed, gulped, and said, "I'm flexible."

Denny said, "I hate that song." He stood up fumbling for his belt.

We moved away from the fire, opting for the meager privacy offered by the dim moonlight. Carmen and Denny made quite a pair. Carmen was arguably a fine example of what God had in mind when Eve first strolled in the Garden of Eden. Denny, on the other hand, looked like a skinny troll as he hopped on one foot and pulled off his blue jeans. In a minute we were wading out into the blackness of the lake, the girls in their fashionable swimwear and the guys in our tighty whiteys.

The water was warmer than the night air, and it felt good. The moonlight reflected white on our bodies. We laughed and shushed each other for laughing, as if someone would hear. Unlike the sand of Northwestern Pond, the lake's bottom gave way quickly to fine, soft mud. Originally it was topsoil, washed from a thousand surrounding hillsides and valleys since the dawn of time. Nothing else in the world feels like Mississippi mud squeezing between your toes.

We went out quite far before the water was up to our shoulders. Without thinking we formed a circle facing inward, our elbows occasionally touching and our toes wiggling in the mud.

Over in the main channel of the river, a paddle wheeler from the Red Wing harbor had pulled up and parked in the shallows. *Harvest Moon* was her name. The Saturday night excursion trip provided tourists with a prime rib dinner and dance cruise complete with a complimentary glass of champagne. A tuxedoed orchestra played big band music and other favorites from our parents' generation. We could hear the faint sound of the music and of ladies laughing with their high voices. The band was playing "Pretty Red Wing." It was nearly midnight. Darla spoke in a soft voice. I wasn't sure if she was talking to me or to all of us.

"Look up. Aren't the stars beautiful tonight? If you could have one wish, what would it be?"

We thought about it for a while. Jelly said, "Maybe I'd wish I could travel and see the world. Except Vietnam. That can wait."

Denny said, "I'd wish I had some decent trunks on before I walk back out of this water." We chuckled.

Carmen spoke softly, almost like a confession. She said she wished she could be an actor. I think it surprised us a little, but it seemed pretty cool.

Darla looked at me and quietly said she wished my mom would get home soon. The others said they did too. I was a bit uncomfortable with their genuine concern. I was used to being their informal leader and I guess I had a hard time being the focus of their sincerity. I had a fleeting thought about Denny's mom.

In my best fake Miss America voice I recited, "I would wish for world peace."

Nobody laughed. A few seconds of silence passed before I said, "Okay. I wish my mom would come home soon, too. I really miss her. But right now, I guess I just want to enjoy our time together. I feel bad about my mom almost all the time. Being with you guys is about the only time I don't."

It was late when we finally waded out of the lake. The others went ahead, and I held Darla back on purpose. We kissed for the second time, and this time I knew enough to kiss her back. We held hands as we walked to the shore. By the warm coal bed of the campfire, Darla and I shared my quilt. Carmen sat between Denny and Tom.

So, we relaxed there by the dwindling fire with no real regard for our lack of proper swimming garb. It just seemed like a form of shared honesty. We were a group of friends, our own tribe. I suppose I'd never experienced this kind of intimacy. We were young and in control of the moment, something we didn't feel very often. We didn't need anything more. We talked and laughed for several hours through the rest of the night.

Finally, the earliest light of morning was beginning to show over the eastern shoreline. Darla and Carmen had dressed and were hugging us and saying what a great time they'd had. Darla kissed me again for the third time, but this one was a short peck on the cheek. She squeezed my hand hard when she did it. Somehow, it was the sweetest of the three.

The girls headed back down the path and along the slough. They crossed the Northwestern overflow and by the light of their flashlight, managed to get safely back to the pink trailer and into bed without being discovered.

I can easily say without any hesitation this was one of the best nights of my life. Denny pulled out the Willow Tips.

"Boys, I'd say it's just about time for a cee-gar."

We were feeling pretty smug. Tom stared out into space as he puffed on his Willow Tip.

"Mr. North, Mr. Berg, it's truly a rare a wonderful thing."

"What is?" Denny couldn't see what Tom was imagining.

"Life, gentlemen . . . the Big Enchilada . . . the pearl in the oyster."

"Yeah, especially the 'swimming in our underwear' part."

"I believe you are correct, Mr. Berg. I think that is an important ingredient."

Tom was enjoying his manly and intellectual dissertation. He was Hemingway, staring at the early tropical sunrise through the glass of an imaginary empty rum bottle.

We sat there as the sun came up, puffing our blueberry cigars, still in our underwear and rolled up in our blankets. The waves were calmly lapping the shore, and the coals of the fire were almost burned down to ashes.

It was Sunday morning and still a couple hours until Rex would be getting up for church. We got dressed and packed up our stuff. Before we left the Point, we put our arms around each other's shoulders in a three-man huddle, and though we would not have admitted it, we hugged each other. Some things in our world were bound to be changing, and this precious time couldn't possibly last too long. Still, we had no way of knowing just how soon those changes would come or how intense they would be.

CHAPTER 6

Our Pilgrimage

I was back at the barbershop around six thirty in the morning. Dad was already up and drinking coffee. I must have looked a little rough.

"Early riser, eh?" The corners of his eyes crinkled when he smiled. His mustache almost succeeded in disguising it.

"Didn't sleep much."

"Guilty conscience?"

"Full moon." I smiled.

Dad appeared to be amused and at the same time he didn't want to show too much approval for me staying up all night.

"What's that smell?"

"It's just, uh, the campfire." My gaze wandered around the room.

"It smells kind of funny. What kind of wood were you burning?"

"I think it was . . . blueberry wood."

A look of partial understanding came over his face. "Yeah . . . blueberry." I knew he suspected something.

I said, "It's a fresh and fruity kind of smoke." I could see he wasn't amused. Fortunately, Dad let me off the hook by changing the subject.

"I took Monday and Tuesday off. We're going to see your mother."

"*WELL, ALL RIGHT!*" I shouted.

"Shh! Your brother is sleeping!"

Dad was trying his best to be stern. I started laughing uncontrollably and blew a little snot out my nostrils. I covered my mouth until I had to let out my breath. Then I coarsely whispered, "Well, all right!"

Dad started laughing, too. Upstairs, Jack stirred awake. A sleepy and confused voice asked "Uh, what time is it?"

I used a haunting voice and called softy, "It's only a dream. Go back to *sleeeep*." Jack groaned and rolled over.

Over on the table was an artist's sketchbook. Jack had been drawing a lot lately. Ever since we were little kids, he had sketched cartoons, and he was very good at it. The Icarus drawing was a current example of his true potential.

"What's this, Dad?"

"I got it for Jack. He wants to draw, so . . ."

"Can I look at it?"

I opened it up before he had a chance to answer. What I saw was unexpected. On the first page was a portrait of a woman in its early stages. She had long flowing hair that swept forward over her shoulders. The shape of her face was drawn, and the outlines of her mouth and nose were there. But what grabbed me and pulled me in was the photographic clarity and precision of the eyes. They were deep and shining pools—a little sad, but understanding, and infinitely wise. It was our mother.

Jack had perfectly captured the look we both had seen so many times before. But this was not Mom at her current age. The woman in the picture was likely in her late teens or early twenties. The likeness was remarkable.

Of course, neither Jack nor I had known her then. Somehow, he had managed to create this image from within his mind's eye. Dad came over and looked at it.

"My God, how does he do it?"

We admired it for a few more seconds, and then I closed the cover. I felt as though I'd looked into Jack's most private and personal thoughts. The same emotions I struggled to deal with by talking with my friends or by crying, Jack didn't seem to show at all. I realized I had been very wrong. He was confronting Mom's illness in his own way. The portrait was powerful stuff.

The rest of Sunday passed by, punctuated only by a phone call from Darla. She and Carmen had made it home safely and without being caught. I told her we were going to Madison for a couple days to see Mom. I said I was going to tell Mom all about her.

"Really, what will you tell her?"

"Oh, I don't know, maybe what a great driver you are."

"Shut up! What will you really say?"

I had to think about it. "I guess maybe I'll tell her you're my best new friend. What about that?"

"Emmet, you are so sweet."

". . . *and* what a great driver you are!"

"Okay, smart guy, simmer down. It's important what your mom thinks of me. Give her a big hug for me. I'll see you in a couple days."

Monday morning Harry rolled up in the Impala at seven thirty on the dot. My uncle lived in a tiny apartment above Hunt's Tavern where he acted like sort of an all-purpose caretaker for the place.

The bar catered to anglers and hunters. Harry mixed drinks, swept up, and swamped out the bathrooms at closing time. He sold minnows from the tank in the garage and fixed the coolers when the compressors overheated. If somebody wanted a burger or a grilled cheese sandwich, he fired up the grill. Harry referred to himself as "chief cook and bottle washer."

Molly Hunt was the owner and a widow for many years. She was kind of sweet on Harry, and it made it possible for him to drop what he was doing just about any time Dad needed a lift somewhere or if the fish were biting. So, because the Pontiac was not a good bet, Harry again acted as chauffeur.

We piled in and hit the road. The Impala was a real cruiser. It was equipped with a 348-cubic-inch powerhouse of a motor with a factory four-barrel carburetor and dual exhaust. It had an automatic Turboglide transmission with a super low first gear. When Harry was feeling a little frisky, he would hit the gas and lay down a short patch of rubber.

It also had a strange Kleenex box holder on a pivoting hinge that allowed it to be out if you needed a tissue and in for efficient storage. The Kleenex box slid in from an opening on the back. This odd accessory had a Chevy insignia on the front. More than one person mistook it for an eight-track tape player.

I kidded him by saying, "Uncle Harry, put in a tape, will you?"

He caught the joke and played along. "Okay, M." He pretended to push a tape into the Kleenex holder and turned on the radio, making a sort of tick-tock sound with his tongue.

On the radio, Smokey Robinson was singing "Tracks of My Tears." His incomparably high voice was impossible to sing along with. Collectively our falsettos were atrocious. Fortunately, we soon quit trying to sing along and just sat back and listened to a legend.

Jack said, "Smokey's the best." We nodded in agreement.

For three hours we rode across the Wisconsin countryside, past Eau Claire and Black River Falls, past Tomah and the Wisconsin Dells. We made small talk and listened to the local radio stations until the signals faded, and then Harry would find the next one.

We ate a big breakfast at a truck stop outside of Sun Prairie. The waitress who took our order explained the brunch menu replaced the regular breakfast menu beginning at ten o'clock. Harry asked her what the difference was in the brunch menu.

"No difference. We just charge fifty cents more." She wasn't kidding.

Finally, we reached the city limits of Madison around eleven thirty. We were a little restless and stiff from riding so long. As we drove up East Washington Street toward the State Capitol building, I was awed by the beauty of the white rotunda shining in the morning sun. Dad said, "It's really something, isn't it?" We agreed.

Harry slowly motored around Capitol Square, just taking in the scene of lawyers and legislators and normal people hurriedly walking to their destinations nearby. University Avenue radiated south from Capitol Square. As soon as we turned onto it, our focus changed, and our anticipation intensified. Mom was just a half mile away.

"Dad, why did she have to come all the way to Madison? Couldn't they do her treatment in Red Wing or even in Minneapolis?" As with almost everything else, Jack was thinking about Mom's situation from a more complex perspective.

"Well, son, they probably couldn't do the treatments in Red Wing. But a few hospitals in the Twin Cities maybe could have handled 'em. It's just that University Hospital is a research and teaching facility. Mom's treatments cost a lot of money—so much we never would have been able to pay for them. In this hospital she gets it done for free. The Cancer Society set it up. The young doctors and medical students learn about the disease and how to treat it, and in exchange, her care doesn't cost anything. If we lived across the border in Minnesota, she could have gone to the U of M hospital."

"So, she's a—"

"She's a *volunteer* for a case study in a very important system. Someday your mother will be part of a group of patients responsible for helping to cure this damned disease. She's a sort of pioneer, son."

Dad had interrupted Jack just before he could use the term "guinea pig." I know Jack was grateful for it.

University of Wisconsin Hospital was an expansive series of multistory buildings. We stopped at the main entrance and asked directions. Mom was staying in the dormitory on the rear of the property. Harry wheeled around the block, where we found the modest two-story house with a slate roof.

Dad opened his car door before Harry could shift into park. We nearly ran up the steps and onto the porch. Dad rang the doorbell, and a lady came to greet us. She was very friendly and led us down the hall to Mom's room. Dad knocked softly and opened the door a crack.

"Rachel? We're here."

The next few seconds provided a blur of activity. Mom rushed over and threw open the door, hugging Dad and Jack and I all together and then one at a time. She thanked Harry profusely and invited us in.

"I can't believe you made it. Oh, I'm so glad to see you all. It's been so long. Let me look at you."

Dad managed to choke out, "I love you, Rae."

The three of us had probably all lost a little weight. Mom noticed it and made a point of telling us she would "fatten us back up" as soon as she got home. When she was done loving us up, she stood back, and for the first time we were able to get a good look at her.

She had lost a great deal of weight, too, almost thirty pounds. It was most noticeable in her face. Her cheeks and eyes were a little sunken in. Still, she did not look terribly ill.

Harry said, "You're too skinny, Rachel. You look like you did in high school."

She wore a colorful dress that must have been new because it fit her well. She was also wearing makeup, something she never did unless she was going somewhere special. She had deep rose-colored lipstick and blush on her cheeks. And finally, she was wearing a lightweight white stocking cap on her head. We knew what it meant.

She said, "Sit down. Sit down. We need to catch up. I want to know everything."

The room was small but cheerfully decorated. The walls were light blue, and there were linen draperies. It was surprisingly homelike. Our pictures were lined up on the nightstand.

We talked nonstop. She told us the treatments were difficult to tolerate, and she seldom felt like eating. She explained how several women who had recovered from cancer volunteered at the dormitory and supported the ladies who were undergoing treatment. They encouraged wearing makeup and dressing nicely every day, even if you felt like staying in your pajamas. This was to help support self-esteem and fight off depression. Mom said it helped. The new dress came from clothing donated by local dress shops. She said it was better than anything she could ever afford to buy.

She had been learning how to crochet from one of her dorm neighbors. She gave us each a potholder she had made. They were all cream-colored and had a pattern resembling pineapples. She was very amused as she clapped her hands together and laughed at the puzzled looks on our faces.

"It's all I know how to make. You'd better like them."

I told her about Darla. Well, not everything, but about how great she was and how I was supposed to give Mom a big hug from her. Dad talked about his work and about the local gossip, including the unlikely pairing of Wayne Button and Stella Person. Jack said he had a surprise for Mom when she got home. Dad and I knew what he meant.

Harry sat back and smiled and mostly took it all in. He excused himself from time to time to go outside for a smoke. The lady who had shown us in frowned darkly at him every time he did it.

Eventually we got around to talking about her hair. It had been her pride and joy since she was a young girl.

She asked, "How do you like my hat?" She preened and struck a glamorous pose. Then she told us about the day she began losing her hair. First it came out in small pieces on her brush and soon in clumps. Like many of the other ladies, she decided to cut it very short to support a sense of control over the unbearable and inescapable outcome.

"It's much easier to take care of now." She smiled, but tears were beginning to show up in the corners of her eyes.

Then she straightened up and stepped back. Reaching up, she slid the cap down the left side of her head and looked straight at us in a sad and expectant sort of way. It was very different to see Mom looking like this. We were used to the long braids wound tightly around her head. Though it was a surprise, we didn't let on.

Dad said, "Hair or no hair, Rae, you're still the most beautiful woman I've ever seen." She caught her breath in a little sob and kissed him on the lips. Afterward she left the cap off and we grew used to the new look in a little while.

It was just so good to see her, and she was much more energetic than any of us imagined she would be. I had pictured her flat on her back in a hospital bed with tubes everywhere. This was exponentially easier to understand.

The next morning, she would go next door in the cancer center for another radiation treatment. She said it would be okay with her if we didn't stay for that. It was her way of asking us not to.

Mom made chicken sandwiches for supper from the little refrigerator in her room. We were hungry, and it tasted good because everything she made tasted good. Being able to have a meal together with her made us feel stronger. I guess there are different ways to be hungry. Sometimes it comes in the form of loneliness. She made us feel emotionally more satisfied, more complete.

We finally left around eight p.m. and checked in to a hotel called the Lagoon. There were two double beds. Dad and Harry bunked together in one, and Jack and I were in the other. By the time we settled down for the night, we had shared many positive and reassuring comments about our mother.

The lights were still on, and I was reading an article from a *Life* magazine intentionally left on an end table by a chair in the corner of the room. The magazine was several months old.

A large picture portrayed an attractive young black woman standing next to a group of somewhat older and slouching white guys. Aretha Franklin was smoking a cigarette. As was often the case with the photographs of *Life*, the shot was not intentionally posed nor even planned. The *Life* photographers just took pictures of the way things happened to be in the moment. Many were masterpieces.

The young vocalist looked naturally glamorous, but the guys in the picture looked like they could have been a group of blue-collar working stiffs from Bay City or anyplace, really.

The caption under the picture read "R-E-S-P-E-C-T Sock it to me!"

The article read: "Since it first burst on the music scene in early 1967, Aretha Franklin's 'Respect' has gotten a lot of it. The funk is undeniable, and the greasy sound of the Muscle Shoals Rhythm Section causes a fair amount of discussion when listeners begin to realize the band affectionately known as 'The Swampers' are a bunch of white session musicians whose groove is a perfect match for the Queen of Soul's vocal style. The song itself has become a sort of anthem for women and for the American black population who at first requested, and then demanded the respect they deserve. Aretha Franklin has delivered a powerful voice along with the passion behind the message."

"Hey, Jack."

"Yes?"

"What do you know about Aretha Franklin?"

"Only a little. She's pretty cool, and she sure has a great voice."

"What about the Muscle Shoals Rhythm Section?"

"Uh, not a lot. I think they're playing on a lot of records these days, though."

"This magazine says they're white musicians, but their sound is popular with black singers."

"Yeah, I guess so. Why do you ask?"

"Well, with all the fighting going on all over, how is it this music is even happening? I mean, I'm glad it is, 'cause it's great stuff. But it seems like it might be, you know, kind of put down by—well, maybe by a lot of people."

"Yeah, I get it, but I think musicians are mostly color-blind when it comes to the 'black music/white music' thing. It's the music that matters and not so much the musicians. It's always been this way, and I think it probably always will be."

"I guess so but try telling that to the Beatles."

"Ha! Good point. I think those cocky English guys are going to be a flash in the pan. They're just not authentic enough. Now, Bob Dylan—there's a guy who'll be around a long time. His stuff is the real deal."

"Yeah, I guess. Dylan's good but his voice stinks. I can't understand him."

"You prove my point, Little Brother. The *music* is what matters, not the musician."

Somehow Jack always seemed to have a way of being right even when he was wrong. I liked the Beatles.

Dad and Harry had turned on the TV to the *Red Skelton Comedy Hour* program. The announcer's booming voice proclaimed, "Ladies and gentlemen—Red Skelton!"

The aging comedian strolled onto the stage looking bountifully cheery as he began his monologue.

"Good evening, folks. Say, have you heard the news? A Martian landed his flying saucer in Times Square today and he pulled up to a parking meter. A crowd gathered as he crawled out of his spaceship. He had one great big eye and four arms and a horn sticking out of his forehead! He looked at the parking meter with a confused look on his creepy Martian face." The audience laughed as if on command. "Finally, he turned to the crowd, held out a piece of paper with some strange-looking writing on it, and asked, 'Does anybody have change for a Hern?'"

Again, the TV audience exploded with laughter. So did Jack. His was a deep belly laugh, something we didn't often hear from him. Dad and Harry looked blankly at each other.

Harry said, "I don't get it."

I said, "Neither do I. Jack, there's no such thing as a Hern, is there?"

As Jack regained his composure he explained, "No, that's why it's so hilarious."

"Okay. I guess. I just don't really think it's very funny."

Dad got up and turned off the TV. "All right, fellas, I think it's about time we get some shuteye. Hey, Harry, do *you* have change for a Hern?"

"Still not funny, Brick."

Finally, our relief gave way to utter fatigue. We were physically and emotionally exhausted. I think we broke the world record for snoring that night, but nobody cared. We slept like babies.

The next morning, we stopped back at the dormitory and spent some more time with Mom before she had to go for her treatment. It was sad to say goodbye, but not nearly as hard as when she'd left home. The last thing she said before we got in the Impala was, "Don't worry, God will take care of me—of all of us." She was half finished with the radiation.

We were pretty upbeat on the way home, and the drive seemed shorter than the way there. When we got back to Bay City, Dad tried to give Uncle Harry some money for driving, but he wouldn't have it.

"Brick, I was glad there was something I could do. You and Rachel have been good to me. And after all, she *is* my sister. You know I want to help."

It was true. Harry ate a lot of Sunday chicken dinners at our house. Dad thanked him, and so did Jack and I. Harry said it was worth more just to have the privilege anyway.

After dark, as Jack and I lay in our beds in the barbershop attic, we talked for a long time about our impressions of the Madison experience and of our mother's state of health. We both noticed she was really thin, but we agreed she seemed fairly strong and her will was unquestionable. Jack described in detail how the human body reacted to controlled doses of radiation. It was more than I wanted to know.

We chided each other about the potholders, and it felt good to laugh. I finally confessed I had looked at the portrait. The only thing he said was, "And?"

I said I wondered how he could have imagined Mom as a girl. He told me that wasn't the hard part. He said he had started over four times before he was finally satisfied with the eyes.

"Well, it's perfect, Jack. Even better than Ichabod the Crazy Angel."

It was getting late, and we were both tired. Jack smiled that sort of all-knowing crooked smile of his. "We'd better get some sleep. Goodnight, M. Oh—M, it's Icarus."

"Whatever. Goodnight, Jack. I love you."

"I, ah—I love you too, pal." He seemed uncomfortable saying it.

Summer was slowly winding down. In a little over a month, we would be back in school. We had seen a lot of changes since the spring flood brought us to the barbershop, but clearly the dangerous unseen enemy threatening our mother's health was the most significant. Maybe, just maybe, she was getting a little better.

During the night I had a strange dream about Mom. I was standing in the doorway of our house and watching her as she sat out in our yard. She was barefoot and wearing the same colorful dress from Madison. Her lips were moving, and I realized she was praying. Though I was listening intently, I couldn't hear her voice. She was smiling and looking straight at me as she prayed.

Above her, I began to see her words—not *hear* them in a traditional sense, but sort of *see* them appearing in the air above her head like the floating down of a dandelion. Somehow her words had conjured a visible image, and yet I couldn't hear the actual sound of her prayer. Nor could I make sense of the words as they swirled, floated, and eventually drifted away.

I didn't fully capture what my presence in the dream meant, but I clearly understood that Mom's unwavering faith was causing it, like music from the vibration of an instrument's string in the air.

Her deep and sacred love for us somehow kept our family close. This and her spiritual strength. She simply refused to let even her illness or the miles between us tear down the ties we shared. I wished I could be more like her. I wished I had cancer *instead* of her.

CHAPTER 7

McCREEDY

Saturday morning rolled around again, and Rory McCreedy was organizing a football game. Bay City wasn't big enough to field two teams of high-school-aged boys, so the big guys took turns as captains of the teams, and the younger boys were highly encouraged to play. More than that, actually: it was a combination of peer pressure and outright enforcement. Sometimes you played whether it was convenient or not.

Tom came by, and we tossed a football back and forth as we began our hike to the field by the old school. We stopped off at David Patterson's house to let him know about the game, too. I knocked on his back door, but there was no immediate response. I knocked louder. There were sounds of running footsteps inside.

Then we heard David's voice. "Say the words."

"David, it's me and Tom."

"Say the words."

Without much enthusiasm, Tom and I complied with David's wish. "Here for David."

The door flew open, and David shouted, "Boo!"

Tom rolled his eyes. I said, "Hi, David. C'mon with us. McCreedy's got a game on."

As always, David was excited about a football game. "Hey, hey! Was that cool?"

"Was what cool? That you tried to scare us? Yeah, David. It was pretty cool."

"Ay-mot, *you* cool. You too, Tom Jelly. You both cool."

When we got to the school, four of the little girls from the neighborhood were jumping rope on the cracked blacktop basketball court. Two of them swung the rope, and the other two jumped in. In unison the girls chanted the poetry so adeptly created by poor and tough children:

"Three Irishmen, three Irishmen, digging in a ditch

One called the other a dirty son-of-a

Peter Murphy, Peter Murphy sitting on a rock

Along came a bedbug and bit him on the

Cocktail, ginger ale, five cents a glass

If you don't like it, stick it up your

Ask me no questions and I will tell no lies

Johnny got hit when the Irishman spit, right between his eyes!"

The girls laughed at how clever they were. Jelly said, "You shouldn't talk like that. I'll tell your mothers."

"Shut up, Tom *Free*-man!"

"Yeah, shut up, *Jelly*-man!"

"Up your ass with Mobil gas—down your spine with turpentine!"

Tom rolled his eyes. "I give up."

They started jumping and chanting again. This time they aimed it at Rex. Like every redhead I ever knew, he hated all the crap he took because of the color of his hair.

"Red, red, wet the bed, wiped it up with gingerbread. Red, red, wet the bed . . ."

Rex's face got even redder than usual, and he took a step toward them. "I oughta . . ."

Right about then McCreedy showed up. All four of the little girls stopped and said in unison "Hi, Rory," their little sing-song voices showing obvious admiration patterned after their older sisters' feelings about McCreedy.

He was tall and good-looking, with a shock of wavy, light-brown hair. Rory McCreedy was the sort of genetic accident that produces a kind of physical perfection only once in a kajillion births. When he smiled, the dimples in his cheeks had dimples, and they melted even the icy hearts of the four, little rope-jumping girls.

"Girls, I don't like it when you talk naughty. Don't you know any nice rhymes?"

They immediately started jumping and singing, "*Bluebells, cockle shells, eevy-ivy-over. Ashes, ashes, we all fall down.*"

"That's better." McCreedy smiled and we all smiled.

One of the little girls whispered to her friends, "He's *handsome*!"

McCreedy was the kind of guy who caught the eye of a lot of girls, mostly those a lot older than the rope-jumpers. Though he dated, it seemed as though he was never in a steady relationship for too long. During the season, football was his main focus.

Rory McCreedy was the second-string quarterback on the varsity team. As far as raw talent goes, he was a natural—the genuine article. He pitched on the baseball team and played forward on the basketball team. But football was his favorite sport and his true passion. He seemed to know every imaginable statistic about every team, but especially the Green Bay Packers.

However, even though he was a dyed-in-the-wool Packers fan, McCreedy's real idol was Johnny Unitas, the great Baltimore Colts quarterback. He said Unitas should have been a Packer. According to Rory, Unitas had "a rare combination of deadly accuracy and arm strength."

Without any formal discussion about it, McCreedy was in charge. At sixteen, he was already an imposing figure at over six feet tall. He had a lean build and looked completely comfortable with a football in his hand. Besides, he was a great guy who assumed a kind of mentorship role among the kids of our town, teaching and coaching without really thinking much about it. When McCreedy wanted to play ball, we played.

In spite of having a rifle arm which could rocket a football over forty yards in the air, the only knock on McCreedy was his accuracy. Generally, this is what kept him on the bench most of the time. He didn't seem to mind, though. He practiced hard and was a student of the game. He said when it was his time to shine, he would be ready. All I know is he always seemed to shine in our Saturday games.

At around ten a.m. we assembled on the old school playground. Besides the Baytown Mafia boys, the usual players included Kenny Sprague, Pat Swenson and his younger brother Rick, the Coleman brothers, Jim and Woody, and of course David Patterson.

Woody Coleman was the same age as Rory, and his best friend. Woody wore round wire-rimmed glasses whose lenses were so thick they magnified his eyes. He was nearly blind as a bat without them. Rory and Woody were always the captains. They assigned us to their teams to try to balance out the talent and general lack thereof.

Anyone not picked for McCreedy's team was a bit disappointed because he always won, but he made sure every kid got to be on his team at one time or another. Woody's team was relegated to an assumed losing status even before we began. It was understood going into the game, and it was okay with us.

Today Rory's team was Rex, Jim, me, and David. The game was on. It was McCreedy's five against Woody's six, and they didn't stand a chance.

Without exception, McCreedy played every down like it mattered. When he barked "huddle up," his team huddled. He clapped his hands when we broke huddle, and he spat commands to his team when we were on the line.

He also carried on a running play-by-play narration of the game during every play. Occasionally this was so comical it distracted even his own teammates, along with the opposition. Sometimes we just had to laugh at how great this guy was.

"Patterson! Block *everybody* and don't let 'em get to me."

David Patterson enthusiastically approved of the plan. He smiled broadly and shook his head at McCreedy.

"Okay, Ro-ey. *Evvy-body!*"

As he spun around, his demeanor instantly changed from the smiling and appreciative David to someone else. A dark and intense scowl came over his face. He would block and shove until Rory told him to stop. I swear, when McCreedy told him to "block everybody," David would do it even if he broke every bone in his body trying. Next to me and a couple feet away, I could hear his teeth grinding as he got set in his down stance. It was a little scary.

McCreedy said, "Down. Set. Blue 26, Blue 26!" We looked at each other. What did it mean?

"Blue 26!" His voice was more insistent. Nothing happened. It was obvious nobody had a clue what "Blue 26" meant. Rory said, "Time out! Huddle up, you rookies."

In the huddle McCreedy told Rex, "When I say, 'Blue 26,' I want you to split out wide and go deep. Don't worry about going too far downfield, I'll get you the ball." Rex was ready now. They broke huddle.

"Blue 26!" Rex split out wide. Jelly went out to cover him. "Hut, hut!" I hiked the ball. We blocked and shoved each other. David was a twisting, snarling, and blocking maniac.

McCreedy started his play-by-play: "Unitas fades back. He surveys the field. He cuts left. He sets. *And he fires*!"

The football made a soft whooshing sound when it left his hand. All of us but David quit blocking and turned to watch the arc of the football as it flew. It was a beautiful tight spiral. The ball easily sailed five yards beyond Rex's reach.

McCreedy called out, "My fault. Huddle up."

In the huddle he said, "All right, we're going to try a trick play. Don't pay any attention to what I say when we get up to the line. When Rex gets close to the line of scrimmage, he's going to pitch the ball back to me so I can hit Jimmy on the fly. Any questions?" We broke huddle.

McCreedy barked, "Down. Set. Turdiwinkle Brown! Turdiwinkle Brown!" We started laughing at the ridiculous play he was calling. It was exactly what he wanted us to do. "*Hut*!"

Rex took the handoff and headed left, still laughing as he ran. Jim Coleman went deep. Suddenly Rex turned and pitched the ball back to McCreedy. In one smooth move he spun and launched it down the right sideline. Jimmy Coleman caught the bomb and legged it out for a touchdown, laughing all the way. The old Turdiwinkle Brown play had worked perfectly.

With exaggerated awe and wonder Rory McCreedy announced, "Unitas completes an impossible throw to Coleman as the opposing team is faked out of their jocks! It's unbelievable! How does he *do* it, ladies and gentlemen?"

This guy was too good to be true. We were laughing and repeating the great McCreedy quotes. Shucks, McCreedy had even cracked himself up. Meanwhile, Kenny Sprague was wheezing and trying to catch his breath.

"Time out," he called. "I need a cigarette."

He pulled out a pack of Camels and lit one up. For most of the guys I knew, cigarettes were reserved for important events or secretive clandestine meetings like our campout. Kenny was one of the few regular smokers we hung around with.

We all moaned and McCreedy said, "C'mon, Sprague. Make it fast."

Kenny said, "Give me a minute, will you. I think I pulled my groin."

Jelly muttered, "That's got to be a tiny little injury."

When Sprague had finished his smoke, he reached for another one.

"Knock it off, you boner!" Woody Coleman was ticked off. He looked at McCreedy and they both nodded.

Woody barked out, "Dog pile on Sprague!"

We knew what it meant, and we reacted with a shout of mean-spirited joy. Sprague groaned and quickly stomped out the butt. David Patterson grabbed him first and threw him roughly to the ground. David shouted, "*Dog pie!*" and flopped down on top of Sprague.

We all piled on, crisscrossing our bodies in a writhing heap of arms and legs. Finally, McCreedy called, "Okay, that's enough."

We were laughing and breathing hard as we tumbled and rolled off Kenny Sprague. David offered me his hand. Smiling, he nodded as he pulled me to a standing position and softly said, "Ay-mot, you a good guy."

I could tell he felt like he was part of the team, such as it was. I smiled back at him, and we walked over to where McCreedy was standing to wait for our next instructions. I didn't realize it then, but it would be my last impression of David Patterson.

CHAPTER 8

TRUE NORTH

Walt Sprague was Kenny's father and Dad's best friend. He was sort of a local legend. At sixteen, he'd lied his age and enlisted in the Navy to escape an abusive father. He served in Korea and was some kind of hero. Given what I have come to know, anybody who served in that war was probably a hero. He retired from the Navy after twenty years of service. His career was well documented in pictures and news clippings framed and hung on the walls of the Sprague home.

Dad and Walt were close even though they had come from very different upbringings. Walt was the well-educated academic who was born with a proverbial silver spoon in his mouth. Dad came from a blue-collar lifestyle and, as he said, an eighth-grade education derived mainly from the "school of hard knocks."

When he was discharged from the Navy, Walt got his bachelor's degree in engineering from Iowa State and his master's at the University of Minnesota. Eventually he received a PHD from the University of Wisconsin in Madison.

He also was something of a wizard when it came to boat building. Over the past twenty years, Walt had built virtually every launch employed by the Lake Pepin fishing rigs. Three were still in use. These were heavy-duty workboats, not the recreational type. They were made of fiber glassed marine plywood and coated with a heavy layer of gray epoxy paint. Walt's standard design had a partially squared-off bow and was powered by a strong V-8 motor. By most standards, they were practically indestructible.

He was pushing sixty now, but he hardly showed it. He was tall and slim and always looked tanned. Walt and Dolly Sprague lived in a cream-colored stucco house on Lakeshore Drive. Walt designed it himself. It had a flat roof and a lot of windows facing the lake. It didn't look like any other house in town.

Walt had also authored an engineering textbook for the University of Minnesota. In one of its chapters, he documented in great mathematical detail how a boat could be built from concrete, wire mesh, and only minimal use of wood as a skeleton. The unorthodox idea had been proven to work as far back as the 1860s, and yet, among the locals, the topic of Walt's writing occasionally came up as the subject of a wisecrack.

All things considered; Walt was a pretty interesting guy. He smoked a pipe and somehow, he made it look quite sophisticated, even with a cap on. He and Dolly had their hands full parenting Kenny.

A few years earlier, Walt had helped to start up a Bay City chapter of the Boy Scouts, mostly as an attempt to keep Kenny out of trouble. It hadn't worked out too well. Kenny was a classic screw-up whose main goal in life was to get some kind of attention. It was impossible to hit the standard of his dad's accomplishments, so he settled for negative attention, which was better than nothing.

Among other offenses, Kenny had been busted for shooting cats with his pellet gun and for throwing rocks through the garage windows at Brown's Seed Corn. He was a real wiseacre and not very popular, even among his buddies. He dropped out of Troop 88 a month after it was organized, but Walt stuck with it because the other Scouts were counting on him.

Among his many other interests, Walt was very knowledgeable about local Indian lore. His fascination stemmed from a deep academic respect for the people who lived on the land and then had it taken away. As a way to inspire the Scouts, Walt came up with an ambitious project.

The new Prairie View School had been built on a few acres of flat and barren land that spanned the four miles between Bay City and Hager City. Behind the school a large bluff rose out of the sand and weeds, a prime example of prehistoric glaciated topography. Most of the rocks on the bluff were sedimentary limestone and many held tiny, fossilized shells. Busloads of school kids had taken field trips there for years before the school was built.

Walt had studied many of the cultural nuances that defined the identities of the early Native American tribes. He was familiar with a theory first presented by a Minnesota archaeologist early in the twentieth century, who hypothesized a grouping of flat rocks strewn upon the bluff overlooking Prairie View was the work of early Indigenous people. He also speculated that they represented a bow and arrow, or perhaps a bird.

The theory was a bit of a stretch. The stones simply didn't look at all like the archaeologist's imagined vision. Still, the concepts made a great foundation for what Walt had in mind. The project was intended to bring an Indian legend to life for the students, and the Scouts needed all the initiative they could muster.

Walt was fairly certain the archaeological essay from over sixty years ago was unknown to virtually anyone other than himself. After pondering his options, he decided to flesh out the story a little and make a few alterations to the original rock formation for the Scouts to better understand what the primitive people *must* have meant. What was the harm?

Over a two-week period in early August, Walt carted close to a ton of the flat limestone chunks up the side of the bluff to be placed just so, with the intent to improve and enhance the shape of a bow and arrow. Several stones were added or moved. In spite of all the new rocks, it was intentionally designed to appear ancient and somewhat primitive.

When completed, it had a truly authentic look and could easily be seen from a long way off. The curved line of the bow was bisected by the improved straight line of the arrow. Clearly, the imagery was greatly enhanced.

The arc of the bow was filled in, and the straight line of arrow stones now fully intersected the curve of the bow and pointed eastward in the general direction of Bay City. Walt explained to the Scouts how the Indian tribes used such landmarks as reference points for hunting parties or as warnings to other wandering nomadic people that this ground was already taken.

Walt used a compass and a surveyor's transom to strategically place stones such that a line drawn from the lower to the upper end of the curved bow would point "true north." Of course, the Indians didn't have compasses that would have been influenced by the magnetic north pole. Instead, they used the stars and the planets that lit the night sky as their guides. He said they achieved great accuracy using this method. According to Walt, three hundred years later, the Canadian trappers and even the Lewis and Clark expedition used these giant stone markers to find their way.

This was a great legend, and Walt was an excellent storyteller. The Scouts were mesmerized and so inspired they worked their butts off clearing away copious amounts of sand burs, milkweed, and thorny wild raspberry bushes to finish in time for the fall school year. Of course, the only wrinkle was that it was a mostly fictional tale Walt had cooked up for the sole purpose of motivating the industrious Scouts. As he had hoped, the unifying message *did* inspire the Scouts to work together as a team and hopefully gain some respect for Native American traditions. There was no mistaking the bow and arrow now. However, even Walt failed to predict the extent of popularity his story would eventually generate.

Word of the Scouts' project rapidly spread. The fictitious Indian legend and the redesigned marker took on a life of its own, adding even more luster to Walt's established reputation. Within a couple of months, it was a sort of tourist attraction for locals and out-of-state visitors alike.

Walt was even interviewed by a reporter from the *Alive at Five* newscast out of Minneapolis. He posed with his pipe and answered the questions he was asked without blinking an eye.

"The Scouts moved a few of the individual stone elements of the bow and replaced some with new rocks we hauled in. It is the Scouts' intent to increase awareness of the importance of Native American influence on our modern way of life."

The *Red Wing Daily Republican Eagle* also ran a story along with a picture. The story said:

> "In the earliest days before the settlers had come to Wisconsin, the Indian tribes constructed this primitive stone marker to direct and guide their journeys across the land. This amazing bow-and-arrow marker showed the way for these early people to find their way home.
>
> "The arc of the bow measures over 180 feet, and the tip of it points straight North with accuracy rivaling the tools of modern people. It points to Lake Superior, the Checquamegon Forest, and to Canada beyond. The arrow points due east toward Lake Pepin.
>
> "It is the only known example of this kind of archaeological treasure to be found in Wisconsin. We marvel at what it has meant to our ancestors and what it still means to us today."

Even if it was made up, it was great story, and a tough one to keep entirely to himself. Walt knew Dad could keep a secret, so he shared the whole tale with him, but only after it had begun to take off.

"Cripes, Brick. I'm a little worried this is getting so much attention. I'd just as soon not get known for being a great liar."

"Don't worry, Walt. And for once, don't overthink it. Folks just need something to feel good about. It's okay to give people something they can believe in. Besides, a little fiction is sometimes the best way to do justice to a good story. Your secret is safe with me."

\+ + +

Around two o'clock Saturday afternoon, Walt showed up at the barbershop to talk. Like everyone else, he was aware that Mom was sick. He had thought about it and come up with a very practical idea to help make things a little better for her. He said he could build a toilet that would function totally without water.

"I have a specific use in mind for it. This could be a prototype for one I might want to use later on. Or, better yet, if we can figure out a way to get your holding tank built, maybe it would end up being a temporary loaner. C'mon, Brick. You'd be doing me a favor if you give it a try."

When he built our house, Dad's original plan was to just get by for a while with the outdoor privy. Afterward, I guess there never seemed to be a good time or enough money to upgrade to the holding tank. The outhouse had served its purpose, but everything was suddenly very different since Mom got sick.

"Walt, this is the strangest, and one of the greatest, ideas I've ever heard. If this can help Rachel out, I will never forget it. Can I pay you?"

"Oh, I'm pretty sure we both will never forget it. And no, this one's on me. When I get around to the project where I want to use the second one, then I might ask you for a little help. Does that sound okay?"

"Sounds great to me!"

Walt's toilet was made of welded stainless steel. The primary difference between it and a traditional toilet was that his didn't flush. It burned the refuse. Its firebox had a latching lid and was equipped with an intense propane burner that quickly reduced the solids down to a fine ash and sent the water content up an exhaust pipe as steam. Every week or so, the firebox would have to be emptied of ashes through a slide-out drawer.

Walt read all about it in *Popular Mechanics* magazine. Several brands of waterless toilets were already on the market. However, the *Popular Mechanics* plan allowed the average do-it-yourselfer to see exactly how to build it. And Walt was far from being average.

Dad had seen Walt make some pretty weird things work, including a coupling device for the fire truck's hose connections that doubled the distance water could be sprayed. Dad thought about Mom having to go outside in the coming winter. It didn't take much to convince him to try Walt's latest invention. Though it sounded a little strange, he knew it would work as designed. Walt had a way of making just about anything seem possible. It was a great opportunity and a practical way to put a toilet in our house.

Walt made it clear that he did not have a patent on the thing, and it was probably not quite street legal in one way or another. It didn't seem to matter much to Dad, nor to Walt for that matter. The finished product resembled some sort of modernistic, industrial metal sculpture.

Within two weeks it was installed in the unfinished bathroom. A copper gas line was run to a T-fitting on the big propane tank by the side of our house, and a vent pipe was run out through the roof. It was a huge improvement, and just in time.

The first time Walt hit the ignition button a flame shot up from inside the firebox and above the seat by at least a foot. The latching mechanism on the waste collection box had failed. It would have most certainly fried the bottom of anyone who might have mistakenly decided to remain seated during the "burn cycle" as Walt called it. After a few adjustments it was fine-tuned to work as planned.

Walt smiled a sheepish little smirk at Dad and said, "You should probably try not to let that happen again. Maybe you'd best stand up before activation for a while."

"Good thinking, Professor."

We called it the Burner because of the near miss during the test run. By the time it was up and running, the house was pretty livable. Rory McCreedy's mom, Doris, hung the kitchen wallpaper. She knew Mom from church, and it was her way of showing her friendship and support. It looked great. It was clean and white, and the roses were a cheerful improvement over the minty-green paint it covered up. Mom was going to love it.

The next week, Dad announced we were moving back home. We didn't have much stuff to move, and within two days the barbershop was abandoned again, with little fanfare and no hesitation.

Darla was a fixture in our household by now, and Dad really liked her. Even Jack thought she was nice. She helped hang drapes and dust off the countertops. By now I was on a first-name basis with Marty and Deedee Day. Deedee had dropped off a Spanish rice hotdish. We appeared to be getting somewhat back toward normal, if you can call a flame-powered toilet normal.

The Burner rapidly became a curiosity among my friends. Suddenly going to the bathroom became sort of a popular sport in our house. For a time, it seemed as though all of the guys who stopped by had to pee. This was never an issue with the outhouse.

Dad and Wayne Button painted the outside of the house with a fresh coat of light tan paint and chocolate-brown trim. They also built a little porch on the front of the house. There was room for two rocking chairs, which he proudly placed pointing toward each other at just the right angle. Dad couldn't wait to sit side-by-side in the rockers with his sweetheart: "One for me and one for your mom."

The little house Dad built several years ago had never looked better. Remarkably, the same flood that had caused such chaos and sorrow to enter our lives became a catalyst for the improvements made all over town. In many ways, Bay City was beginning to look like a small town with a lot of good stuff going on. The only thing left was to get Mom back again. It was still a month or so until we expected her to come home.

Dad and I were sitting in the rocking chairs just after four o'clock when the Zephyr sounded its long, moaning horn as it roared into the far end of town. Dad smiled at me and said, "Here she comes, son. Progress. Ready or not."

"Yes, Dad, progress. Ha ha, I get it."

"What? I thought you liked trains."

"Yeah, and I think you like giving me a hard time about it."

A few seconds passed as the sound of the Zephyr drew nearer. Just before the crescendo reached its peak, he whispered in an intentionally hoarse stage voice, "*Progress*."

The ground shook when the train went by, and we could feel it under the porch where we sat. The Zephyr was both beautiful and imposing in its gleaming and powerful presence. It demanded you stop what you were doing and watch as it sped past. There were only a few passenger cars, so it was gone nearly as soon as it arrived. The immediate Doppler effect was followed shortly thereafter by the softening roar, ending when the train reached the long curve in the tracks just above Deer Island. The power and speed of the Zephyr was unlike anything else I'd ever seen.

CHAPTER 9

PROGRESS

My fascination with trains began with a trip to the Minnesota State Fair when Jack and I were both pretty little. For a few bucks, Dad convinced the station manager to let us ride in the mail car. He saved a little money, and we would share an adventure we could talk about when we got older. Win-win. Not too surprisingly, our mother decided to opt out of the trip.

Shortly before seven a.m. he lifted me straight up and onto the floor of a boxcar bound for Union Depot in St. Paul. At one end, Dad and Jack sat on folding chairs along with two train men. A short wooden barrel stood among them with a checkerboard on it. Several bags of mail were carelessly piled at the other end. With those few exceptions, the car was mostly empty.

The side doors were slid open to reveal the world passing by in all its wonder. Even before we had reached cruising speed, I walked over and sat down a foot or two back from the door's opening, with my short legs crisscrossed. The only thing Dad said was, "Hold on, son. I would hate to see you fall out."

So, I held onto the side of the door, and I didn't fall out, and we rode on to St. Paul. Jack played checkers with one of the workers. I'm fairly sure he won. Dad talked about anything the men wanted to discuss. I sat there and looked and listened in amazement.

The sound of the gigantic steel wheels on the tracks was loud, hypnotic, and powerful. At every crossing and on the edge of every small town, the engineer blew the horn. We rumbled past Deer Island and Goose Lake. Herons flew away, frightened by the clamor. Geese floated in a V formation, and overhead an eagle circled. Turtles slid off their resting places on logs when they felt the thunder of the wheels.

We wound our way along the Mississippi up through Diamond Bluff and Prescott, where the tracks crossed over into Minnesota. The scent of diesel smoke occasionally wafted into the car. It wasn't unpleasant. It was the smell of work and commerce.

I thought about a textbook Jack brought home from school. Its title was *American Progress.* The cover picture portrayed a train with its headlight shining brightly and pointed straight at the reader. I turned away from the passing scenery long enough to ask, "Dad, is this progress?"

The trainmen chuckled. My father said, "Yes, son, I guess this *is* progress." He teased me about it ever since.

In truth, passenger trains were struggling with drastically declining ridership numbers. Even the mighty Zephyr had a tough time filling seats in those days. Its main competitor, the Milwaukee Railroad's Hiawatha Express, had retired from service the prior year. In our area, the Zephyr stood as a defiant example of a slowly dying breed.

When we reached Union Depot in St. Paul, we parted company with the trainmen and walked several blocks to a seedy destination called the Euclid Hotel. It smelled damp and moldy, like an old basement. Some old men sat doing nothing in the lobby. We rode a creaky old cage-style elevator to the second floor and began our afternoon and overnight stay there in the heart of the city. It was spectacular.

From the dirty window, Jack spied a bookstore across the street, so we went over to look around. The name of the place was Heaven's Gate Books. As we entered the store, I became aware of the timeless odor of the multitude of books residing on the crowded shelves. Inside the entrance door, Jack smiled as only books could make him smile. He inhaled slowly, drinking in the musty perfume.

When Jack became interested in a book, he picked it up and carefully inspected it as if it were a fragile and valuable treasure. It could have been a Fabergé egg, and he likely would not have treated it differently. Dad and I hung around near the front of the store until he was finished with his search.

Finally, we exited the dimly lit sanctity of Heaven's Gate and returned to the streets of Lowertown, St. Paul. Jack carried a beat-up copy of *Moby Dick*. He couldn't have been more delighted with the well-worn paperback than if it had been a first edition. The words were all that mattered.

Back in our room at the Euclid, he read his newfound treasure for the rest of the time he was awake. Dad eventually had to tell us both to go to bed.

"Okay, fellas, it's time to call it a night. It'll be a big day tomorrow, and I don't want anybody too tired to have fun at the State Fair."

I got ready for bed as Jack finished the chapter he was reading.

"Goodnight, guys. Get your pajamas on."

Jack slowly closed the cover of *Moby Dick*. He placed the book neatly on the nightstand next to the bed we were sharing.

I was too excited to be tired. "Good night, Jack."

He scrunched up his face and raised his eyebrows ominously. "Call me Ishmael."

I had no idea what he meant. Dad smiled at him and said, "All right, Ishmael, get your jammies on. It's time for some shuteye."

After Jack and Dad were asleep, I crawled out of bed and sat on the wide windowsill for a little while, watching the traffic go by down below. I was amazed that so many cars just drove around all night. Every time a light changed, another bunch of fast-moving engine sounds sped past with their headlights illuminating the darkness below. Such as it was, it was the first night I ever stayed in a hotel.

Next day, the fair was great fun, a sort of Disney World for the common person. Everyplace we went there were new things for Jack and me to experience. We toured the animal barns, where we saw some of the largest horses I'd ever seen. We drank all the milk we could drink for a quarter. We rode on carnival rides and ate hot dogs and onion rings. I even had a deep-fried dill pickle on a stick. And of course, we had a piece of homemade pie from the Knights of Columbus pavilion near the Midway, where all the rides were.

Dad made sure we were really tired out by the time we rode the city bus back downtown to Union Depot. As we caught the evening train back home, Jack was too spent to play checkers, and I didn't sit by the door. Instead, we both slept like cats, curled up on the bags of mail headed to Chicago and all points east.

Long after our adventurous mail car experience, I would lie in my bed at night and listen for the sound of trains. In my imagination, I played a game I called "Jim 'n Joe." Truthfully, I never liked my name very much. It was Mom's choice. I would have preferred a more common one. Either Jim or Joe would have done nicely.

They were best friends and World War II soldiers, heroically fighting the Nazis somewhere far away. Jim had black hair and Joe was blond. Except for that, they could have been twins. They both looked a lot like me. I pretended to be whichever one suited me at the time. Whether I was Jim or Joe, I was trying to save my other self from the Nazi invaders.

It was life or death, and I was personally responsible for both of us. The weight of the blankets pulled up over my head helped create an imaginary foxhole there in my little bed. I was lying in wait and plotting my next move as the Nazis marched all around me. I don't remember much shooting ever occurring, just a bunch of marching. But clearly, those marching bastards had to be stopped!

The trains passing through our town in the late evening hours were our only hope, our escape route to freedom. We needed to run and catch up before the train reached its cruising speed and was gone for good. It was our only way out of this ancient forest or that blown-up town.

We weren't sure where we were going, but we knew we had to get away from here. The train would take us to some new and wonderful place where we would be safe and happy, if only we could find a way to catch a ride.

No matter if I was Jim or Joe, I was still only me. I suppose I never really knew exactly what I was trying to save myself from, after all. But tucked in my little bed with the covers pulled over me, Jim and Joe saved the world for the cause of freedom on many cold winter nights as the trains rumbled through Bay City, just before I drifted off to sleep.

CHAPTER 10

EVERYTHING CHANGES

Just after daybreak on Saturday morning, August 19th, a knock came on our door. It was Sam Most.

"You'd better come, Brick," was all he said.

Sam hadn't walked across the street more than a few times for as long as we had lived there. This must have been important. Dad followed him as he walked back up and across the street. He veered right and headed toward the Patterson's house, his short legs churning at a surprisingly quick gait. The door was standing wide open with the frame busted where it had been kicked in.

Inside, the bodies of two men lay in pools of black coagulating blood, their hands bound behind their backs with duct tape. The tape was also wrapped several times around each of the men's ankles and around their faces to cover their mouths. It was clear Willard and David Patterson had been severely beaten.

Each had been shot once in the temple. Tiny streaks of blood and brain matter spattered the floor and the cabinet fronts. Willard's right eye bulged horribly from its socket, with the white completely replaced by dark red. There was no need to check for a pulse.

In the living room, David's uncle Art slumped on the couch. He too had been shot to death. The television was still on. Flecks of blood dotted the screen.

Being the constable of Bay City usually meant breaking up an occasional bar fight or maybe intervening on a weekend domestic squabble. Dad had no idea what to do with this. Sam had followed him inside the door.

"Are they dead?"

"Yeah, Sam. They're dead."

Sam shook his head and turned around to walk back outside. He was still shaking his head and muttering when he stepped back out into the morning air.

"Deader than shit! This is bad." Sam was right.

Dad ran home and told Jack and me to get up and get dressed. He called the Pierce County Sheriff's dispatch and explained what he had seen. Jack and I heard enough to get the picture. Then he called Dale Thorsdall and told him to come quickly. In a half hour, three county deputies and a state patrol officer were on the scene.

By ten a.m., the FBI had arrived from the Minneapolis office, and around three p.m., the news crews started showing up. Sadly, Bay City was officially on the map. In between times, mostly every man, woman, and child over the age of five who called Bay City home had taken a turn standing on the street gawking and speculating.

Crime scene barricades were put up, and the house was sealed off from all but the uniformed officers. It was a full-blown criminal investigation the likes of which had never happened in Bay City or the entire county, for that matter.

The *Alive at Five* crew got there at four o'clock and set up for the dinner-hour newscast. Rod Ramirez was the evening anchor. When Rod personally went out on assignment, it was a sign of a big story. He lined up two interviews: Dad and Sam. At five p.m. the camera operator was set up in front of the Patterson house, and Rod was ready "in five, four, three, two, one . . ."

"Hello, this is Rod Ramirez for the *Alive at Five* news team. We are on the scene in the usually quiet river town of Bay City, Wisconsin, reporting on a breaking story of mass murder. Early today, three men were shot to death in a bizarre execution-style killing. No suspects have been named at this time, and police and FBI remain on the scene. These men, Marion North and Sam Most, are neighbors of the victims, and they were the first to discover the bodies. Mr. North, what can you tell us?"

Dad said, "Very little, really. It appears they were killed sometime last night. The rest is up to the police to discover."

Ramirez spun to his left and shoved the microphone up near Sam's mouth. "How about it, Mr. Most—what did you see?"

Sam grabbed Rod Ramirez's hand and pulled the microphone close to his lips. He said, "It's bad. They're deader than shit."

Rod Ramirez was a pro. He looked back at the camera and said, "Well, that about says it all. We'll continue to follow this story and update you at ten on the late news. This has been Rod Ramirez reporting."

The light on the camera went out. Ramirez was a little miffed. "Thanks a lot, old man." Ramirez headed for the van. "Okay, I'm out of here. Somebody might want to fumigate the mayor of Hooterville, there. He's a little gamey."

Jack and I had been hanging around on the fringe of the action all day. Dad was obviously shaken up by the experience. He had been interviewed by the police several times and had patiently answered the same questions over and over. Dale Thorsdall had brought a half-pint of brandy with him. After the TV interview, he took a long pull on the bottle and offered Dad a nip as they stood behind Dale's pickup.

"No thanks, Dale. I think I'd better keep a clear head."

"Brick, I think you probably know what I'm going to say."

"Christ, Dale, I didn't sign on for this kind of duty. I don't have a clue what I'm supposed to be doing here."

"It looks like you do. Somebody just needs to be the 'go-to' guy. It seems like you've already been elected."

"Shouldn't that honor go to the mayor?"

"Shit, for a hundred bucks a month? You're asking a lot, aren't you? Besides, as you know, I'm your boss. I'm delegating it to you."

"Yeah—thanks, boss. Is this the 'easy stuff' you mentioned?"

"Brick, I get the feeling this will change our town in ways we can't even imagine yet. I'm really worried about what it will do to us. We've been pretty well insulated from all of the crap going on in the big cities. Now all of a sudden, we have our very own homegrown murder to worry about."

"Yeah, I know what you mean. Death changes everything."

Darla had come by, and we stood together in our yard, away from most of the action. She made a point of keeping Jack nearby, sometimes holding us both by the arm to make sure he didn't go off somewhere by himself. The scene across the street was suddenly strange and unfamiliar from our normally quiet neighborhood. It had become a scramble for space and for the right camera angle. There were arguments among the crews and a lot of plainclothes and uniformed police coming and going. It all seemed somehow disrespectfully casual.

After several hours, three hearses arrived, and the bodies were finally removed from the house. For the first time it began to sink in that David Patterson, a kid we played with and went to school with, was gone forever. Jack, Darla, and I spoke very little as we stared across the street in horror, disgust, and strange fascination.

When you are young, it's hard to imagine the reality of death, especially when it happens to one of your peers. In the early morning hours of August 19th while the whole town was still asleep, David Patterson, his father, and his uncle were shot to death in their home, less than a hundred yards away from ours. From that moment on, Bay City would never be the same, and neither would any of us who had known the Pattersons.

It didn't take long for the camera crews and reporters to leave once the hearses had vacated the scene. Dad said the way they scattered reminded him of crows. The police investigation would continue for several days before it began quieting down. After that an eerie, quiet fear settled in, and would remain for a long time.

After supper, Dad sat at the kitchen table, barely sipping a can of beer. I went over and sat down across from him.

"Dad, are you okay?"

"Yeah, sure, son. I'm fine. I'm just thinking about Willard. He was a good guy. I can't figure out who would want to hurt him or why."

"I know. I had the same kind of thoughts about David. I kind of feel like—maybe I should do something. You know, try to help."

His demeanor instantly shifted, and he became surprisingly angry as he began to rant.

"*Damn it, Emmet!* I need you to promise me you and your buddies won't try anything stupid. It's already a holy mess, and the last thing I need to worry about is whether you boys are rooting around like some darned private eyes. Leave it to the police and the FBI. The chances of me or you or anybody else in this town figuring out who did it are slim and none. That would take a doggone accident. Let somebody who knows what they're doing handle it. I sure don't. Hell, I didn't even hear the shots last night!"

"All right, Dad. I know, I know. I can't help but feel like there is something we *all* should be doing though. And Dad—maybe they were—you know, maybe it happened while the freight run was coming through town. It doesn't seem like *anybody* heard it."

His tone softened. "It's a good point, son. I will share it with the police. M, a lot of bad things happen in the world. Mostly, they're better left to just pass by. I'm going to tell you something I don't think I've ever shared before. And I don't want it repeated, you hear? When I was a boy—younger than you are now—my dad, your granddad, took me fishing out in the back channel west of Goose Lake in his old rowboat. Do you know where it is? Downstream from the old Edgewater Bar. It's a pretty rough place."

I nodded.

"Well, I was fishing off the side of the boat closest to shore and your grandpa was fishing off the side facing the channel. We sat there for over an hour and neither one of us had caught anything. Then, something came floating downstream in the current.

"At first, you couldn't tell what it was. When it got closer though, I could see it was a body. A dead man! It must have been in the water for quite a while. It was a *horrible* sight. I still remember how bloated and ugly the face was.

"That dead body floated within four feet of the boat on the side where I was fishing. When it got close, the current turned it over and I could see the handle of a great big knife sticking out of its back, just between the shoulder blades. I was so shocked I didn't know what to do or say. I just sat there staring."

"Geez, Dad! What happened?"

"We never found out. Your grandpa said, 'Son, why don't you come over on this side of the boat. I think the fishing is a little better over here.' And that was all. I moved over and the body just continued to float on downstream. We didn't talk any more about it."

"Gosh, Dad, somehow it just doesn't seem right."

"I know. We should have reported it to the sheriff or something. But we didn't. We just let it go on by. The body was eventually found, but we had nothing to do with it. To tell you the truth, I wish I didn't have to get involved in this whole thing either. But I guess I do. You have to promise me you'll steer clear of trouble on this, okay? Just go to the funeral and say your goodbyes like the rest of us. Find your own way to let go of your friend. Can you do that?"

"Yeah, sure. But Dad, that's not what you're going to do is it? I mean you can't just . . . Right?"

"No. I guess not. I'm not exactly sure *what* I'm going to do. Look, M . . . how about if you just stay on your side of the boat and I'll stay on mine? Deal?"

"Deal."

The next day, the Mafia all got together at my house. Before long, we ended up in the big ditch behind Pattersons' property. We just sat there looking at the house, with the crime scene warning tape still fluttering in the breeze. Between long periods of silence, we talked about David. We didn't really know him in quite the same way as we knew each other, but we agreed we would miss him a lot anyway. We decided we should do something to show our respect. But what?

We were used to making a difference in each other's lives just by being together. Today, we felt confused by the immense evil that had come upon us. We knew we couldn't fix this. It would have to be left to grown-ups and strangers who didn't know David and didn't understand our world.

In a little over a week, we would be going back to school, and then it would be hard to imagine doing much of anything. It seemed as if there should be something we could do to somehow influence this terrible thing which had suddenly become the sinister new identity of our town.

Anyone who had anything to say had already been interviewed by the police. We would soon learn that, as horrifying as they were, the Patterson murders would too quickly slip down the list of priority cases being handled by an overwhelmed police force. The reality was the Pattersons were simply poor folks living in a poor town. For the police, the consequences of *not* solving other cases outweighed the immediacy of spending more time and workforce on this one. But for now, at least, it was fresh in *our* minds, and everyone in our town seemed to have an opinion.

For the most part, I think very few actually understood the significance of the whole situation yet. It didn't stop the speculation, though. At Stella's lunch counter the theories abounded. One suggested a drifter killed them during a botched robbery attempt. Somebody had seen a blond-haired stranger lurking around town, but nobody could offer a description. Somebody else said a guy with an accent had been in Hunt's one night looking for a fight.

Sam Most even had his own take on the situation. He thought it was probably the Jehovah's Witnesses. Nobody else seemed to think so.

Another version suggested it could even be a local person who still walked among us. Wayne Button spoke out loud what others were thinking: "It could be anyone—even one of us."

This was a very chilling thought for kids and parents alike. Suddenly it was not safe to camp out at the lake, and we were told to stick together every time we left the house.

After a specialty cleaning company finished their work, the Patterson house was locked up with a big padlock. The investigation was still going on in the Minneapolis FBI office and in the Pierce County Sheriff's Department. But by all appearances, after a few days there was little local sign of any police activity. Except for the daily gossip, once everyone had been interviewed, things started quieting down.

There wasn't much our father could do to help with the investigation. He made a call every other day or so to check whether any progress had been made. Jack and I could tell he wasn't getting many answers.

Sometimes he would shake his head a little bit as he hung up the phone. He usually ended the conversation by saying something like "Now, don't forget about us down here" or "We're counting on you."

CHAPTER 11

The Funerals

Page six of Red Wing's *Daily Republican Eagle* newspaper listed the obituaries of David and his family in alphabetical order.

Patterson, Arthur. Age 50. Died unexpectedly at home on August 19.

Patterson, David. Age 16. Died unexpectedly at home on August 19.

Patterson, Willard. Age 47. Died unexpectedly at home on August 19.

The abbreviated biographies in the obituaries did not capture the essence of their lives or the gruesome way they died. However, the rest of the horrific story was posted in sensational detail above the crease on page one. The headline read, "Execution-style Murders in Bay City."

It would take several days for the morticians to finish their work. Because the Pattersons didn't attend church, decisions had to be made about which of the two ministers in town should perform the funerals. A large turnout was expected. Reverend Greeley from the Methodist church and Reverend Callin from the Lutheran church agreed to share the responsibility for the service. It made sense to hold the funeral in the Methodist church because it was larger.

A week later, on the Saturday morning following the murders, the church bells rang to signal the start of the Patterson family funerals.

The pastors were correct. Not only did the local citizenry turn out, but a lot of strangers from the surrounding area came purely out of morbid fascination. The *Alive at Five* news crew even showed up again. It had the potential of becoming a real circus, but the Reverends Greeley and Callin somehow found a way to do their jobs in the midst of the controlled chaos.

I'd been to my grandma's funeral when I was three, but I really didn't recall anything about it. David's was the first funeral service I could remember.

I grouped together with Darla, Tom, and Denny when we first arrived. Rex came soon after. We ended up standing in a line of people stretching up the church steps and into the building. Once we got inside, I realized we were moving toward the front of the church and, eventually, past the bodies. I saw McCreedy and the Coleman boys as they completed the circuitous route through the church and back out into the day.

The caskets were closed in order to supply some final degree of privacy for the three men who had been subjected to such extreme brutality. A picture was placed on a tripod in front of each one. The line slowly walked past them and, one by one, offered their respects.

Soon, Jelly started getting twitchy and uncomfortable. He thought it was pretty creepy. Darla said she would go with me if I really wanted her to, but she would rather not. Rex just said, "No way."

I told them to save me a spot in a pew at the back of the church. Somehow, I knew I should do this even though it felt a little strange.

As I reached the caskets, I silently thought of myself shouting outside his house, "Here for David!"

I looked at the smiling pictures and tried to imagine them sleeping, but it didn't seem real. They were dead. There was no pretending. An overpowering feeling of sorrow swept over me.

An older gentleman said the mortuary had "done a good job," and I wondered what he meant, given the closed caskets and all. What does a good job look like when nobody sees the work? I hoped at least David wasn't dressed in a suit. I doubt he ever wore one in his whole life. I allowed myself to wonder how the mortician handled the damage left from the bullet that killed my friend.

Just then a fly landed on David's picture and began to crawl across his face. I instantly got dizzy and felt a little queasy. A burning sensation bubbled up in the back of my throat. I choked it back and looked away.

Turning back toward the pews, I spied my dad near the back of the church. I saw my friends and our neighbors all looking toward the caskets. I read sorrow in the eyes of some and apathy in others. For a second, I imagined what it might be like if it was my own funeral. Who would come? Who would care besides my family and a few good friends? Then my eyes found Darla and I noticed how nice she looked.

I worked my way back to the pew where the Mafia was sitting. Darla quietly asked me, "Are you all right?"

"Sure." I felt like I had been punched in the stomach. "Darla?"

"Yes?"

"You're the prettiest girl at the funeral."

"Gee, thanks. I guess." She must have read the confusion on my face. She patted the back of my hand and then held onto it for the rest of the service.

After the ceremony was over, the bodies were taken to the cemetery for the burial. The five of us opted to walk down to the lakeshore together, trying to get a better grip on what we had just seen.

Tom was still a little troubled. "I can't understand how, in a modern society, we have such primitive rituals for the dead. It's like taxidermy or something. I'm glad the caskets weren't open."

Darla had a more pragmatic view of it all. "I think it's done this way to help people cope. You know? Grief is a way to say goodbye to someone who's already gone. I think it's especially important when somebody leaves as suddenly as David and his family. So c'mon, Tom—*please*—just shut up and grieve, will you?"

I had been thinking hard since we left the church. "Guys, we need to do something. Something for David. Something that fits who he was. You know, he was a little different, but he really was one of us."

Rex had an idea. "What about the Kingfish? We could carve something."

It sounded pretty good. We would carve something into the big tree and create our own tribute. David would have approved.

At some point, Denny chose to talk about his mom's death. He said, "It's not that I really mind funerals. I just wish I could remember my mom's. She's buried in Florida. Uh, I guess that was a long time ago. Sometimes it feels like we shouldn't have left her down there."

Rex put his hand on Denny's shoulder. "You told me she liked the warm weather. I think she would've wanted to be in Florida, Den."

"Yeah, I guess so."

Rex withdrew his hand. "Not to be disrespectful, but—at least you know what happened to your mom. I mean, it's horrible and all, but I don't even know where my dad is. Since he and Mom split up, he's never called me, not even once. What kind of a dad won't even call his kid? Y'know?"

There was nothing to say. He was right. We just sat mute. Then Denny fixed everything.

"Rex—ah, I hate to tell you, but—it's probably your foot."

"What? What the hell?"

"Yeah, I think your gross foot is probably why he never calls you."

"My *foot*? What does that have to do with anything? That's just stupid! Why would you say that? It's just *mean*!"

Rex was getting genuinely upset. His neck was getting all blotchy and pink. Denny only let him stew for a few seconds before he offered his reasoning.

"Well, I figure it must be why, 'cause everything else is so great. Rex, we all think you're great, man. I mean, let's face it, that foot is about the ugliest thing I've ever seen, not counting, uh—like, turkey giblets or something like that. It's got to be the only reason, because otherwise, you are such a good guy. And a really great friend. To us all."

Denny's voice changed as he got serious. "Anybody else would be proud to be your dad." A few seconds of complete silence passed. Then Denny repeated, "Has to be the foot."

They *both* understood more about loss than the rest of us.

"The foot...yeah, I guess so. Gosh, Den, for a second there I thought I might have to punch you in the face."

"Right, but did you see how I flipped it into something really good?"

"You flipped it?"

"Yeah, I flipped it." Denny made a rolling motion with his hands.

Rex shook his head. I could tell he didn't want to smile, but he just couldn't help it.

The world was right again.

After supper the five of us convened down at the Kingfish. We struggled to come up with exactly the right message. At first, we couldn't figure out what we were supposed to say using only initials carved in a tree. As far as we could tell, ours would be the first memorial message on the Kingfish. Right away we discounted R.I.P. DAVID as being too trite. After some thought Rex found a good spot on the Kingfish, and we took turns carving one letter at a time. Together we carved DAVID P—FRIEND. It was enough.

Afterward we built a fire and sat there talking about David. We tried to come up with some good stories. Mostly, we repeated things we'd said before.

When we were getting ready to leave, Tom made an unexpected comment. "Emmet, nobody offered a eulogy for them."

"What do you mean? What's a eulogy?"

"It's a speech somebody who knows you really well gives—somebody who matters. It's kind of a tribute to the dead guy. You know, about what kind of lasting mark he made in the world."

"I didn't know. I guess they didn't have anybody else."

"M, if I die, will you give my eulogy?"

"Holy crap, Tom. Knock it off!"

"C'mon, I mean it—will you?"

"Sure, Tom. Yes. I will. Now can we stop this morbid talk? You're creepin' me out."

"Promise me!" He grabbed my arm. "Don't forget! Don't ever forget. It matters."

"I promise. *Geez!*"

"Good. Good."

After we covered the campfire coals with sand, the five of us walked out of the park and split up at the intersection where Lakeshore Drive crossed Main Street. I walked Darla home and then continued on to my house and the safety of my family. It was getting late. When I got home, I found Jack curled up on his bed, reading.

"Jack, do you know what a eulogy is?"

"Yeah. Did somebody talk at the funeral today?"

"Just the ministers. They didn't seem to say anything very personal."

"Yeah, sometimes it's like that. I think funerals are mostly supposed to make you feel better about yourself somehow. The dead guys sure don't care. Their lives are like blown-out candles. The rest is just a ritual—somebody's job."

I felt my face getting warm. This time Jack had pissed me off. Like a lot of things he said, I didn't fully appreciate his imagery. But I understood enough to know I disagreed with the assumption David was just a candle to be blown out and forgotten.

"Jack, you can be a real *jerk* sometimes. This time you're wrong. Not everybody forgets. I won't. *Not ever*!"

"Yeah, I hope you're right. 'Night, M. I'm going to bed. Don't be too mad."

"'Goodnight, Jack. I'm not mad."

But I was. School was starting Monday morning, and another summer was over. And David was dead.

CHAPTER 12

THE SCHOOL YEAR BEGINS

Early autumn was quickly happening around us. The birches and soft maples were already beginning to show their fall colors. The humidity had dropped, and we were returning to class. Labor Day was next week, and it meant a long weekend off. This was fine with us. A three-day weekend at the start of the school year seemed like a bonus to the kids and the teachers alike.

Nothing much seemed to be going on with respect to actually solving the murders. There were a lot of theories and opinions, but generally the Patterson horror just sort of folded itself into the local culture and became part of Bay City's new and darker identity.

The rumors continued. One stressed how the three men had been tortured in horrible ways, like somebody was trying to get some information from them. There was speculation about all kinds of ugly stuff. Even satanic cults were mentioned.

Jack had long since finished the portrait of Mom and several other highly detailed images of people, places, and a few imaginary heroes. He signed up for Art History, Drawing and Painting, and Twentieth-Century American Writers as an elective English literature class. He'd found his niche.

I enrolled in Maritime History. This was a great class for a lot of reasons. First, it was taught by Kolby Sims, a gray-haired intellectual with a no-nonsense teaching style who was popular with students and parents alike. At six and a half feet tall, Mr. Sims commanded your attention simply by entering a room. Then he did it again when he began speaking so very eloquently in his booming baritone voice. Though we all referred to him by his first name behind his back, to his face he was, without exception, *Mr.* Sims.

His course was not taught from a single textbook. Mostly, it was a series of great stories presented orally to the class. The subject material ranged from high adventure on the open seas to the more traditional impact of exploration and commerce. The best parts were the tales of maritime disasters. Kolby Sims reveled in these, and he knew every detail of every major disaster on the oceans and inland waterways.

The second day in class, he barked at me, "Mr. North, is it true you live in Bay City, near the banks of Lake Pepin?"

"Yes, sir." I was certain he would ask me about the Patterson murders.

"Have you ever heard of the Sea Wing Disaster?"

I was somewhat pleasantly surprised. "A little. My folks have mentioned it."

"What did they say?"

"The only thing I remember is a lot of people drowned. My dad said the bodies of the victims were stacked up like cordwood on the levee wall at Red Wing."

There were a couple of groans but several of my otherwise bored classmates sat up and took notice. Mr. Sims had set the hook and was reeling them in.

"You are quite correct, Mr. North. It was a terrible sight and a horrible outcome for what started out as an afternoon pleasure cruise. The Sea Wing Disaster is one of the most infamous of all inland water accidents and is still the single worst boating disaster ever to occur on the upper Mississippi waterway."

Mr. Sims held up an old yellowish newspaper borrowed from the Historical Society.

"The following is taken from the *Pierce County Herald* of July 16, 1890. It regards the sinking of the *Sea Wing*, a steamboat captained by D. N. Wethern which encountered a storm and sank in Lake Pepin on July 13, 1890, with a great loss of life. It was reported at the time as being caused by a tornado. You will notice a disproportionate number of the victims were women, unable to tread water in their long dresses."

He cleared his throat and began reading:

> "*Pierce County Herald*, July 16, 1890. Headline: 'Perilous Lake Pepin.' Under a quiet sky Lake Pepin is a peaceful and beautiful sheet of water. It is about thirty miles in length and three miles in width, and bows to the high bluffs on either side which seem to confine the force of windstorms, and transform it into an Atlantic fury. Old river men understand this and wait for storms to exhaust themselves before venturing into its waters.
>
> "It would have been well for Captain Dave Wethern if he had obeyed the dictates of his own judgment and remained at Lake City instead of attempting to return with his 250 happy excursionists in the face of a storm that he saw approaching. But fate directed otherwise. The excursionists were anxious to get home and nearly 150 men, women, and children found their watery graves.
>
> "As nearly as we can figure, the *Sea Wing* left Diamond Bluff on a pleasure excursion early in the morning, towing a

barge fitted up for passengers. They stopped at Trenton, Red Wing and perhaps other places, taking on guests until fully 250 were on board. Shortly after leaving Lake City on the return trip, the storm broke in all its fury and almost immediately the steamer capsized.

"George Reeves, one of the excursionists on the barge, reached Ellsworth Monday night. He states that after the barge was cut loose from the boat, he saw the vessel capsize, but heard no sound nor outcry between the constant flashes of lightning that illuminated the waves, though he could distinguish the white dresses of the drowning ladies as they struggled within the dark flood."

The tall, gray-haired teacher folded his paper carefully and continued his narrative.

"There is a large granite outcropping near the confluence of the Wisconsin and Main Channels of the Mississippi, near the place where the *Sea Wing* sank. It is engraved with the name of the boat and the date she went down. There were too many victims for all of their names to be etched into the rock. The memorial is all that's left of them."

Mr. Sims kept it up for forty-five minutes. By the time class was over, the story of the Sea Wing had become a fascinating and frightening parable of the lost and drowned. There was no metaphorical resurrection here—only the cold and watery graves of those unrecovered corpses who never made it to the levee wall in Red Wing. The class was drawn to these macabre themes far more than we were interested in the historical facts and statistics of the story. Mr. Sims knew this, and he made the most of every creepy and gory detail. It is one reason why his class was always one of the first to fill every year.

"Are there any questions? Anyone?" The bell rang, ending the class and sending us on our way. "All right then, class dismissed."

Mr. Sims watched his students as they filed out of the room still talking about the ladies who drowned in their white dresses. His goal was not necessarily to sensationalize history or gross out his students. He sought to inspire conversation and make history more than just dry facts and figures.

On that day, it appeared he had succeeded. He watched as the "A" students interacted with the "C" students. At test time they would display their academic differences, but today they were similarly entwined in the story. He smiled to himself. History really *can* be exciting.

As I gathered my books, I glanced at Mr. Sims. Growing up on the lake teaches you some lessons other kids may never have to learn. I thought of the story Dad shared with me about the dead body floating past in the current.

As I left the classroom, I looked at his face and wondered to myself if he had learned some of those lessons the same way I had. He sounded like he had firsthand experience. Or maybe it was because he was such a great teacher. When he spoke, everything just seemed more real.

My thoughts went to a summer after we first moved to Bay City. I recalled seeing a boy's limp body dragged out of the lake, all bluish and apparently lifeless. His mother was frantic. A lady who happened to be walking her dog on the beach performed mouth-to-mouth resuscitation on him and seemingly brought him back to life right there in front of me. I remember the lady simply gathered up her dog and went on her way afterward, and the mother gave the boy one heck of a spanking. The whole scene was strange and scary. He was approximately my age.

I was really grateful Mr. Sims didn't ask me about David's family. For the first time in a while, Bay City's identity was not automatically connected with the murders. While it was still pretty morbid, the *Sea Wing* story was a part of river life I found more interesting than the mundane predictability of workboats, fishing, and hard-earned sweat.

I thought about the *Sea Wing* all afternoon. As I learned from my mother, it's very wrong to go out on the water if you can't swim. I could understand how the storm surprised them, though. I had heard many stories from the old river rats and had even seen a few nasty squalls blow in myself.

The eighth grade in Ellsworth Junior High was quite a different experience from the prior year. The kids who attended St. Francis Catholic School had gone as far as the curriculum allowed, and they now were mainstreamed into the public school system. This brought a whole new group of classmates into the mix—a lot of new faces and names.

Denny and Rex were adamant that Catholic girls were excessively promiscuous. I wasn't sure how they knew. I said it didn't matter anyway since I planned on staying true to Darla. Still, I was fascinated with the possibility that a conservative Catholic upbringing might lead to a backlash of wild and rebellious sexual antics to get even with their parents or their priest. At least this was Tom Freeman's theory, and I was willing to accept it as fact.

Two very pretty girls from St. Francis soon began to cause quite a stir. Faith Briggs and Jane Keener were best friends. Faith was blond and energetic. Jane was dark-haired and very outspoken. Both were smart, and both were excellent swimmers.

Almost as soon as they arrived on the scene, Jane launched a campaign to organize a swim team. She sat down with Miss Strand, the girls' physical education teacher, and Principal Fulton, and explained in great detail how this might be done. Never mind that the school didn't have its own swimming pool. Practice could be held in the pool of the motel owned by Jane's parents.

The news quickly spread that Faith and Jane were trying to put together a team. In a twist on the theme, they wanted it to be a synchronized swimming team. There was an immediate outpouring of support from the entire junior high school population. Somebody started a petition, and soon it was signed by a majority of the student body.

Rex, Denny, Jelly, and I all signed our names multiple times, including some highly transparent aliases for good measure. "Wilbur Shakespeare" and "I. P. Daily" were definitely on board. Also, among the committed was a guy named "Elvis Johnson." I guess Rex thought adding a different last name would somehow make it seem less conspicuous.

Jane and Faith were rapidly gaining in popularity. Mr. Fulton and Miss Strand gave tentative approval for the girls to start up a synchronized swimming team, which would practice after school at Keener's Motel. Miss Strand had been a competitive swimmer in college, and she highly approved of the girls' initiative. Mr. Fulton went along with it because he imagined it could be a popular decision and it didn't cost very much.

"Well, Miss Strand, I don't see any reason we shouldn't approve this plan. It seems well thought out, and these girls have done a nice job planning it—with your help, of course. Besides, the petition was signed by a couple of US presidents, and I don't think we want to look unpatriotic. Let's go for it."

Since there were no other synchronized swim teams anywhere in the district, Ellsworth's newest athletic team would not be in a competitive sport, but instead would put on a couple of exhibitions for classmates and parents in their debut season. If things went well, maybe the team would continue for next year. Mostly it was planned to be "practice, practice, practice."

Miss Strand would be the team's coach and advisor. It was clear she was excited to be part of the action. Rex and Denny asked if they could join, but Miss Strand told them the world wasn't quite ready for their unique talents.

While my buddies were trying hard to get any amount of attention from the membership of the new swim team, I was mostly content to be a spectator. Still, Faith Briggs was undeniably really something, and not just because she was so pretty. She was as nice a girl as you would ever meet. Everybody said so. Half the boys in school had a crush on her, but she was going steady with an older guy who played in a band. I guess the other half probably had a crush on Jane.

Faith and Jane were part of an elite group of girls who referred to themselves as the Gems. The Gems were a clique in every sense of the word. They were a little stuck up, a little stand-offish, and maybe a little too pleased with their own good looks. But somehow, they managed to pull it off. Rather than being resented for all they seemed to have going in their favor, they were admired as role models by both their peers and their teachers.

In many ways they exemplified a lot of the good things young women aspire to be. Academically speaking, the Gems were recognized as some of the best and brightest. They were attractive and intelligent, got good grades, and were close and true friends.

The Gems didn't name themselves. It came from a different circle of girls who were being sarcastic. ("Well, aren't *you* a bunch of gems.") It was meant to be derogatory, but they embraced it, and it stuck in a positive way.

The new team scheduled their first exhibition at a school-sponsored pizza party held poolside at Keener's Motel on the first Thursday evening after Labor Day. It didn't allow for much practice time. Miss Strand and the Lady Synchronizers were up to the challenge. Coincidentally, all five of the members were also Gems.

Besides Faith and Jane, the Gleason sisters had signed on to the team. Cari and Shari Gleason were identical twins, and they both swam like dolphins. They were raised with three brothers, and the competitive environment seemed to be working out fairly well for the fledgling team.

Zoey Hardy was the final member. She was probably the smartest girl in school, even smarter than Faith or Jane. She had a mop of curly brown hair and a large and seemingly permanent smile.

Our first week of school ended, and we were set to enjoy the three-day Labor Day weekend. There was a dance scheduled for Saturday night at Horton's, with Deedee and Marty Day as the entertainment. Dad was working security, and Darla had made certain I knew I would be her date.

"Your attendance is *not* optional!"

"Wow! You make it sound like a math test."

As usual, Jack was not planning on going. He had started a portrait of Martin Luther King Jr. It was a unique choice even for Jack. Once again, he'd managed to capture the spirit of his subject in the eyes.

He was increasingly more tuned into the implications of Dr. King's focus on freedom and humanity than most of us. When I asked him why he chose Martin Luther King as a subject for a portrait, Jack shrugged his shoulders and said, "You'll know someday. He's a true peacemaker in a time when the world really needs one. I think he'll be considered like Gandhi, in his own way."

I wasn't so sure Gandhi was very famous in Bay City, either.

At five thirty we called Mom and had our usual talk. This time we got more than we planned for. Mom said she had completed her treatments and would be coming home as soon as the doctors finished some tests to measure the results. It was nearly two weeks earlier than originally planned. We shouted and bounced around the living room.

Then she said we should all pray extra hard that all this time apart would end in a cure. They had given her the maximum number of radiation doses she could handle, and there was nothing more to do. It would have been better if they could have made the treatments last a little longer, but the cancer was far enough along to demand an aggressive approach. She said now we just had to wait and hear how well it had worked. Dad was on the kitchen phone, and Jack and I were listening to the extension phone perched between our heads, with our ears almost touching. None of us knew what to say. It was out of anyone's control.

Dad finally said, "God didn't put you through all this to see it fail, Rae. He's got something else in mind for you and for all of us. Together."

Mom asked us to pray with her, something we were not really used to doing except before meals.

She said, "Dear God, thank You for the many blessings in our life. Thank You for my family, who always believed we could beat this disease. Thank You for the many good friends who have supported us during our time of need. And thank You for the grace and goodness of this place and all the people who have helped me and so many others. Amen."

We hung up the phone and didn't say anything. Jack and I sat down on the couch together. Neither of us knew whether to feel happy or just worried. I guess it was both. Out in the kitchen, Dad looked beyond the back-door window at the sun slowly inching its way down the sky toward the horizon. Tears streamed silently down his cheeks. He hoped God was listening.

CHAPTER 13

THE DANCE

At six thirty Saturday evening, Darla showed up. A few minutes later, her folks pulled into the yard with the Riviera's radio loudly playing "Unchained Melody" by the Righteous Brothers. Marty had his hair slicked back, and he smelled heavily of Brut cologne. Deedee had on a blue sequined dress that was slit up the side, showing a significant amount of real estate.

Darla was as pretty as ever. It was a warm early fall night. She was happy and proud of her mom and dad. Even before we had the chance to properly greet each other, I blurted out "Mom is coming home!"

Deedee grabbed me and hugged me close and said, "That's just great, darlin'!" Her Memphis accent was pure southern belle.

Marty shook Dad's hand, and they both were all smiles. Darla noticed Jack standing uncomfortably off to the side of the living room. She walked right over to him and grabbed him and gave him a big smooch on the cheek.

"Jack, I'm so happy for all of you!"

Jack turned pink, then red, and then a sort of magenta color. He was speechless. Then she turned her eyes on me. Her kissing radar was pinging wildly, and she was homing in on her target. I froze. Right there in front of Marty and Deedee, Dad and Jack, and God Almighty, Darla kissed me hard on the lips. It didn't last too long, and it wasn't a passionate make-out kind of kiss, but she had clearly made a statement for all to see. I was shocked and a little embarrassed. Happily, the adults nodded and smiled in approval. Jack was still gasping for air like a goldfish out of water.

I said, "Gee, I guess good news brings out the best in all of us."

We shared a good laugh, partially out of friendship and humor, but for me it was mostly out of relief. I couldn't help admiring Darla for the way she just made a statement about our relationship without making it some kind of big deal. In my eyes, she was amazing. Maybe it was because she was a year older. Whatever it was, I was beginning to feel something strange and incredibly satisfying.

Marty finally said, "Pile in the Riv. We'll all ride together."

Jack said he needed to stay home and work. Dad and Darla and I sat in the back seat, and she held both of our hands. The radio was tuned to WGGT, Wonderful Widget, and Marty had the volume turned up high.

Darla took turns smiling at me and then at Dad. Once, she turned to me and gave an overstated wink and blew me a big, pretend Darla-kiss. I opened my eyes wide and tried to make it seem like I did not approve, but of course I did. She responded by crossing her legs and hiking up her skirt a tiny bit.

We pulled into Horton's parking lot and parked right outside the back door. Darla and I helped unload Deedee's microphone stand and a couple of old suitcases holding extension cords, microphones, and other various components for mixing sound. For their stage lighting, they used an old rotating, colored-disk light gizmo from an aluminum Christmas tree.

Deedee accompanied her vocals with an electric piano, and Marty played a drum set consisting of a small bass drum, a snare, and a high-hat cymbal.

At eight o'clock the house lights came down and the revolving, colored light was turned on. It was time to start the dance. The spinning

Christmas light reflected its colors off the mirrors lining the back and sides of the stage and from Deedee's blue sequined dress. Dad started his slow walk around the perimeter of the dance floor. He was still smiling.

Labor Day weekend brought out a lot of the local residents and nearly all of the campers from the lakeshore campground. It was the last big week of the tourist season. Wayne Button was there with Stella. Walt and Dolly Sprague were there. Even Molly and Uncle Harry were there. They hired a bartender at Hunt's for the night so they could have a little fun.

Marty and Deedee started the night with Johnny Cash's "Folsom Prison Blues." The dance floor was crowded in no time, with couples doing the jitterbug or a polka step. They played an occasional waltz for variety. Darla and I sat at a table in the back. I drank an O-So Grape, and she had a Nesbitt's Orange. I would have been content to just listen and watch. Darla put up with it for a few songs, and then:

"Hey sailor, how about a dance?" she purred in her best Mae West impersonation. I'd been afraid of this.

"Darla—I don't know how to dance. Not to this kind of music, or even to our kind."

It barely registered. "You're not getting off *that* easy. I'll show you how. We'll wait for a slow dance. You'll be fine."

Deedee chose the songs, and tonight she was mixing it up. There were pop songs and show tunes. There were several old-time country favorites like "Stand by Your Man" by Tammy Wynette and "North to Alaska" by Johnny Horton. Deedee specialized in torch songs, and she got a big response for favorites like Patsy Cline's "Crazy." When she started the intro, Darla grabbed my hand and said, "All right, you're up, fella. Don't step on my toes."

The hall was pretty dark, and nobody was paying any attention to us. Darla placed my right hand on her waist and held my left hand in her right.

She nodded and off we went. At first it was sort of awkward, but soon we were moving in time to the music, and I almost enjoyed it.

Wayne Button had his eyes closed and his cheek pressed to Stella's. When the song was finished Darla looked up at me and said, "Don't you just *love* that song?"

I smiled and said, "I do now."

"Carmen is moving to Los Angeles. Her dad works on televisions or typewriters or something. He thinks there are lots of good jobs out there. I'll really miss her."

Darla was clearly disappointed. I hadn't seen Carmen since the campout, but Darla talked about her often. Carmen was an adventurer of sorts, and she seemed to be a role model for Darla. I didn't know what to say. I just shrugged my shoulders and said, "I guess everything has a way of changing. People seem to move around more these days. How about another dance?"

It was shaping up to be a great night. The weather cooperated, and the dancers went outside whenever they needed to cool off or have a smoke. They looked up at a clear night sky and the millions of stars glittering above them.

Inside, it was too warm, but it felt kind of good, as if summer was still trying to hang around for a while. Darla held my hand between dances. She picked songs anybody could keep up with, even me. Dad checked in from time to time, and Joe and Deedee sat with us on their breaks.

Dad had told Walt and Dolly the news, and it spread quickly through the crowd. People slapped Dad on the back and told him they knew all along it would turn out well.

At about eleven thirty the Spragues came over to the little stage, and Dolly whispered something in Deedee's ear. With a nod to her friend, Deedee announced she was going to sing "a special song for a special guy."

Her voice echoed slightly from the reverb of the public address system.

"As you may know, our friend Brick North's sweetheart, Rachel, has been sick and away from home for many weeks. A little bird, who shall remain nameless (but her initials are Dolly Sprague) told me Brick and Rachel's favorite song to dance to is "There She Goes" by the great Carl Smith. Brick, I'd like to sing it for you tonight. I hope the next time we play it for you, you'll be dancin' with Rachel."

I'd heard this song many times before on the radio and on jukeboxes. Mom said it was written by a brokenhearted man whose wife walked out on him. Supposedly, he drank himself to death on the money he made from the royalties. It was a great country legend.

Marty started it off with four clicks of his drumsticks and Deedee began singing her story. Within a few seconds, Dad was turning down offers to dance with several of the local ladies. He was a good-looking guy for his age, but these ladies were just being nice. He thanked them and said he would "wait for Rachel to get home."

Deedee was in rare form. Her natural vocal twang was intentionally exaggerated as she closed her eyes to help sell the heartbroken sorrow portrayed by the lyrics.

This time, I took Darla by the hand and led her onto the dance floor. The colored lights reflecting off the windows and mirrors looked like multicolored snowflakes falling over the dancers. The couples held each other a little tighter and realized how fortunate they were to have the companionship, and maybe even a little love. We circled slowly, suspended in the moment, like dancers on a music box.

Hardly anybody stayed in their seats. I held Darla close and put both my arms around her waist. She looked straight into my eyes. Then she reached around and put her hands on mine. We smiled and I wished the song would go on for a long time.

On the outside edge of the dance floor, just beyond the reach of the colored lights, Dad walked slowly on his solitary patrol. The rest of the crowd probably thought he was alone, but in his mind, he danced every step with the love of his life. He had memorized the curve of Mom's waist from a hundred other dances, and he could almost feel her warm breath on the side of his neck as he had so many times before.

When the song ended, the crowd erupted in wild applause. That night, the dance ended late. The crowd demanded encores. Marty and Deedee had already sung every song they knew, so they repeated a couple. Nobody seemed to notice.

By the end of the night, Darla had me dancing to some of the fast songs too. I sort of bounced back and forth from one foot to the other and made random circular hand motions in front of my body. Many years later, these generally are still my signature moves.

When the crowd finally began to head home, Dad, Darla, and I pitched in and helped Marty and Deedee pack up. We hugged again in the driveway before the Day family left for home. Darla patted me on the rump and gave it a little squeeze.

"Are you still paying attention, big boy?" I most certainly was.

Jack was already asleep. Dad gave me a big hug when he said goodnight. He wasn't very prone to hugging Jack or me, though he often wrapped Mom in those big arms. As I lay in bed, I thought about all of it: the dance, Darla, Mom, and Dad walking the long looping circle over and over again.

For the first time, I wondered if Darla and I might be falling in love. It was hard to imagine what it meant at my age. The only real measuring stick I had was my parents' love for each other. Considering everything they had been through I felt a little embarrassed. But I only knew how easy everything seemed when I was with her. Like dancing, I was only beginning to learn the steps.

Homecoming was in three weeks, and half our town would make the trip to Ellsworth for the big game. As usual, our local favorite son, Rory McCreedy, would be warming the bench as backup quarterback.

Our family's homecoming would be a week earlier, when Dad and Uncle Harry went back to Madison to bring Mom home for good. It was the last thought I had before I fell asleep. Down the lake, the familiar rumble of the late train was heading our way, but I would be fast asleep by the time it rolled through town.

The dark and empty house across the street from ours served as a reminder of the murders and made certain they couldn't fade from my thoughts.

CHAPTER 14

The Pool Party

On Tuesday after Labor Day, the big buzz was about the Lady Synchronizers' upcoming demonstration at Keener's Motel. The pool area could handle a pretty large group, but by Wednesday morning Miss Strand was getting a little concerned about the potential size of the spectator crowd. Wedding receptions and Chamber of Commerce gatherings were held poolside in the past. But the notion of a large and concentrated crowd of hyperactive junior high school students promised to be a real challenge. Luckily, Mr. Fulton came up with the idea that the school would supply free pizza, but only if the crowd behaved themselves. Also: pending good behavior, we were informed the kids would be allowed to join in an open swim after the show.

The exhibition was scheduled for six o'clock Thursday evening. Darla had to babysit for some neighbors, so I had the dubious distinction of traveling solo with the Mafia for the first time in a while. By the time Thursday arrived, the synchronized swimming event was pretty big stuff. Parents came with their children, and the crowd in Keener's pool room was filled to the rafters with anticipation.

At exactly six p.m., Miss Strand strode over to a microphone placed near the edge of the pool and held her hand up.

"People, people—can I have your attention, please?"

Miss Strand was dressed in black pants and a black blazer. Her short-cropped blond hair was crisply combed and parted on the side.

Rex quietly said, "She's looking particularly dapper tonight, eh?"

The Lady Synchronizers stood behind Miss Strand. Jane Keener, Faith Briggs, the Gleason twins, and Zoey Hardy were perfectly coordinated in their black one-piece swimming suits. Still tanned from spending the summer outside and dangerously curvaceous, they turned at an angle with their right legs held straight, left legs slightly bent, and left hands on their hips.

The Mafia boys, including me, were totally knocked out. This was why we came. The moment we had been waiting for. For us, they could have skipped the entire swimming routine and just stood there all night, or at least until we passed out from oxygen deprivation.

Miss Strand thanked the parents and the students for coming, and the Keener family for hosting the event. She introduced the swim team and talked about the discipline and practice it took to put together the program. She also described the term "sculling" to the audience, explaining that it is a difficult and strenuous action of the hands and wrists that allows the swimmer to hover in place or maneuver, all without displaying the normal movements associated with swimming. Miss Strand reminded everyone about the pizza and open swimming, stressing the part about how it was still contingent upon good behavior by all.

Then she announced, "Okay, folks, let's get started."

A record player had been patched into the overhead sound system in the pool room. As the swimmers took their places at the edge of the pool, the music began to swell and fill the room. The first part of the program was set to the song "Aquarius" from the musical *Hair*. One by one, the swimmers dove into the pool. Synchronized swimming is part dance and part athleticism. Every eye was on the Lady Synchronizers, though not all for the same reasons. After all, some of us were adolescent boys.

The group circled and stretched. They arched their backs and pointed their toes to the ceiling. They moved with great ease and impressive accuracy as they formed and reformed crisp lines and circles in the middle of the pool.

When they went head-down in the pool and stretched their long and shapely legs above the surface, Rex and Denny began clapping. As they realized they were the lone clappers, they sheepishly stopped.

When the song ended the room exploded with applause. The Lady Synchronizers had done a fantastic job. However, as they climbed out of the pool, it became unmistakably obvious that the room was several degrees cooler than the water in the pool. The sensible one-piece Jantzen competition swimsuits were designed to not creep up, fall down, or let any wayward body parts escape at the wrong time. But even the Jantzen company's designers could not completely overcome the increasingly visible effects of the cold air.

Denny grabbed my arm and whispered, "I love this sport."

Jelly put an exaggerated shaking hand to his brow in a military salute. He mumbled, "I think I'm going to cry."

Rex clasped his hands and said, "It's just so—uh, stunning."

Tom and I looked at each other with a quizzical expression. Stunning?

I whispered, "It's like looking at an eclipse of the sun. I know I should turn away, but I just can't."

Miss Strand was fully aware of the rising level of testosterone in the room. She took immediate action. The last thing she needed was a controversy on their first performance night. She turned her back to the crowd and instructed her team.

"Okay, ladies, let's get some robes on. We've got a lot going on here."

It felt good to be one of the guys and act just as desperately silly and immature as the rest. I had been spending most of my free time with Darla, and I guess the boys and I were aware of it, though they didn't give me a hard time about it. They thought she was great, too.

That said, for the first time in quite a while, I wasn't Darla's date. And for a short time, I was distracted from a lot of more complicated stuff. I was just a goofy young guy, hanging out with other guys who were acting as foolishly as most guys tend to do when they get together for more than a few minutes at a time.

The second routine was performed to an instrumental by the Dave Clark Five called "Theme Without a Name." Somehow, even in spite of our intense fascination with the girls' looks, the boys and I began to see the art in this unique new sport we were viewing for the first time. It was easy to see the hours of practice that went into every move. But these young women were communicating and interacting at a level beyond the simple coordination of the individual swimming movements. These were good friends who were celebrating the joy of being together and creating something that depended on team effort as much as individual talent. As with friendship, it was clear you get back what you put into it.

This group knew they looked good, and they clearly had their routine down pat. By the time they finished the second number, we didn't feel the need to make any additional lusty comments. We clapped along with everyone else, aware we were seeing something worth serious appreciation. Still, at one point when the Gleason twins bent over to towel off their legs, Denny and Rex both sighed deeply at the same time.

The third song was the "The Pink Panther Theme," in which Jane Keener and Faith Briggs performed as a duet. They had attached pink fabric ears to their heads with bobby pins and wore some kind of black waterproof makeup on their noses. Whisker lines drawn on their cheeks completed the feline look.

The disguise was not great, but the girls were incredible. They could do nothing wrong. They vamped and played to the crowd, sometimes intentionally funny and sometimes unavoidably sexy.

These were two great-looking girls who had worked hard on their routines, and they deserved to show off. They were having fun with their act and the crowd responded accordingly. The duet was a hit. The team was on a roll.

Jane's dad loudly reminded anyone in earshot, "That's my daughter out there. Isn't she great?"

As Faith and Jane exited the pool, Zoey Hardy was standing at the microphone.

"Hello, I'm Zoey. We are happy all of you came out tonight. It wouldn't have been much of a party without you. We've worked hard on our routines, and truthfully, we weren't sure if synchronized swimming would go over very well. How do you like it?"

The crowd clapped approvingly, and whistled, and then clapped some more. Zoey continued. "The five of us have known each other for a long time. Many of you know us as members of a group called the Gems. We have been close friends for so long it's sometimes hard to imagine anything different. But in a few years, we will go off to college and eventually get married and start families. Believe me, we understand how lucky we are to be here with each other, and with you tonight."

The room grew quiet.

"We think we have saved the best for last. Faith Briggs has a solo number she worked up, and we feel it really is the artistic vision we are trying to portray with our swimming. Please stick around for the open swim and the pizza. Thanks again for coming out."

Once again, the room was filled with applause and cheers. As the crowd noise subsided, the music came up. This time though, it was very different from the other choices. Faith Briggs stood alone at the edge of the pool with her head down and her eyes closed. The Pink Panther makeup was gone. She slowly raised her head as the strains of "Ave Maria" began. This version of Schubert's masterpiece was performed on piano, accompanying the great mezzo soprano soloist, Maria Callas. Even when played on a record player, it was somber and riveting, a total departure from the earlier routines.

When she dove into the pool, Faith's body arced high and was perfectly balanced, with her hands crossed and her legs held tightly together. She barely made a splash when she entered the water.

She glided smoothly, with power and confidence. She held her hands up in silent prayer and bowed in supplication. It was a ballet, and she was the prima ballerina. The music was haunting and beautiful. All the while she moved around the pool, she was telling a story of hope, conviction, and self-sacrifice.

Her swimming was unusual and completely mesmerizing. Jane's mother held her hand up to her mouth, and Faith's mom had tears in her eyes. Out of reflex, Faith's dad found his wife's hand with his own. Everyone seemed to be aware they were seeing something special. While the other performances had been entertaining and impressively executed, this was at a different level altogether.

"Ave Maria" is a beautiful musical prayer to the Virgin Mary, but like most of the crowd, I was dumbstruck by the grace of Faith Briggs.

She was pouring her emotions into this deeply moving music. The creativity was more sophisticated and compelling than the other routines. Her teammates silently held hands at the side of the pool.

Hers was a timeless story of commitment. She offered her honest devotion in every move, and she asked only for understanding. As gifted as she was, she was able to portray both strength and humility at the same time. For me, however, the message of the dance could not transcend the beauty of the dancer. Faith continued to gather momentum until the final chord was struck.

I admit feeling a little confused at my sudden attraction to Faith. Darla had been the only girlfriend I ever had, and I cared about her deeply. After all, I was just watching a swimming exhibition. It wasn't like I was cheating on her. Still, I think I felt a little guilty because I may have forgotten about her for the four and a half minutes Faith performed her magic.

As the recorded piano sustained its final chord, we waited a bit too long in silence, not knowing whether to clap. When we finally did, even the applause was different. There were no whistles or shouting. There was only the thunderous sound of hands clapping loudly and respectfully.

Faith was obviously very tired. She had spent a tremendous amount of energy. The Gleason twins grabbed her hands and helped pull her out of the pool. Faith's cheeks were flushed. The bright pink accented the sapphire blue of her eyes. She waved, and the crowd began cheering. I stood motionless and just stared. She was in a class by herself. One of a kind.

By the end of their show, Ellsworth was a synchronized swimming town. At the completion of the school year, the administration would be talking with the County Board about building a pool. Like a lot of great ideas, it would not come to fruition due to budgetary constraints, but tonight we were a synchronized swimming town.

Afterward, we stayed around, and a lot of kids swam. Rex and Denny spent most of the time talking to the Gleason twins. With Tom in tow, I managed to find Faith and Jane as they were chatting with their parents.

"Hi Faith. Hi Jane. Gosh, you two were great tonight. You all were. Thanks for your show. It looked like a lot of work went into it."

"You're welcome, Emmet. I'm really glad you came."

Tom took the hint. "Jane, I especially liked the Pink Panther part."

"Why, Tom, I didn't realize you are such an animal lover." Jane smiled craftily as Tom's cheeks turned a little red.

Tom and I grabbed a piece of pizza and ended up out in the backyard behind the motel, sitting cross-legged in the grass. The dimming daylight was fading fast and the air just beginning to cool.

Tom Freeman was unquestionably a natural comedian. But, when he chose to, he could also reveal a more serious and thoughtful side.

"M, have you ever noticed how different girls are from guys? I mean—especially at our age."

"Are you referring to the breast-al regions, as so amply displayed this evening?"

"No, I mean it. A bunch of guys would never be able to do what they did together."

"That would be pretty creepy looking, Tom."

"You know what I mean. Girls just seem to . . . I don't know, interact better with each other. You know, communicate. I wasn't expecting all that—art. I mean, holy crap, they were great."

"Yeah, me neither. Faith's dad and mom were really proud of her. She was crying, I think. She sure is cool. Faith, I mean."

"Yeah, they all are. I think Jane Keener is the coolest one of all."

"Really? Why? I mean, she's great-looking and all, but let's face it, she's not as cool as Faith."

"I disagree, my friend. She's really smart, and I think maybe she's a little misunderstood. She's—I don't know—deep."

"Your bullshit's getting a little deep."

Tom changed the subject. "You might refuse to admit it, but I think you know that we are a little different from Denny and Rex. Most of these kids will stay here all their lives. You and I won't. But I don't know, Faith and Jane are maybe on the bubble. If they're lucky, they will escape this town and never look back. If not, they'll probably marry some football jock and breed litters of little football jocks."

"Hey, we play a little football. Do you think we stand a chance?"

We smiled at each other. He was right, of course. It was true we were a little different from Rex and Denny. We only had this kind of conversation when the two of us were alone. They likely planned to stay put in our hometown. By contrast, Tom and I often imagined elaborate adventures we would have just about anywhere in the world *except* where we grew up.

Tom looked back toward the motel. "I hope they make it out of here. They both seem like they can do just about anything they want to."

I considered what he meant and responded, "Heck, I hope *we* make it out of here."

We looked at each other and nodded. Finally, I said, "We'd better go back in. If we miss our ride, we might have to stay here all night with the swim team."

"We can't have that, can we? It could possibly screw up my commitment to lifelong celibacy."

"The leaves are starting to turn color already. I guess it's going to be an early fall."

"I guess so. Man, where'd the summer go?"

We got up and walked back to the motel and to the crowd. Jelly put his hand on my shoulder as we approached the back patio door to the pool.

"You're a good man, Mr. North."

"So are you, Mr. Freeman, so are you."

Inside, the parents and kids were happily chatting in clusters of threes and fours, unaware that a couple of young and occasionally foolish boys had somehow gotten the message tonight. It wasn't all about girls in swimsuits. While the exhibition was clearly well done, it wasn't even all about synchronized swimming.

It was about hard work, communication, and appreciation of both physical and artistic accomplishment. But most importantly, like Aretha said, it was about R-E-S-P-E-C-T.

CHAPTER 15

KEEPER OF THE KEYS

After church on Sunday and on Tuesdays after school, Faith Briggs volunteered at the hospital as a Candy Striper. She dreamed of becoming a nurse someday. She dreamed of doing many things and usually carried out the majority of what she set her sights on. Today, she looked forward to her visit with Mrs. Keyes.

Though she performed many tasks and services when she volunteered, Faith's visits with patients were always the best part of her experience. Mrs. Keyes was a long-retired interior decorator who had worked for many of the well-heeled residents of the Twin Cities. She was wealthy and well educated, a great conversationalist who always had something interesting and positive to say.

Faith's pink-and-white striped smock was perfectly clean and pressed. Her mother made sure of it. Since her family was in the dry-cleaning business, it was a public symbol of their company's quality. She walked quickly and purposefully through the front door of the hospital and past the receptionist's desk. When she reached the east wing, she checked in with the charge nurse, who gave her some assignments and an update on Mrs. Keyes's status.

Mrs. Keyes was dying of end-stage renal failure. She was very sick and weak, but nonetheless a joy to talk to. Her skin was yellowish, and her eyes were sunk deep into their sockets. In spite of her obvious illness, she wore bright red lipstick and exaggerated blue eye makeup that enhanced the brightness and intensity of her gaze. A dreadful red wig perched precariously atop her little balding head.

"Good morning, Mrs. Keyes."

"Why, hello dear. It's so nice to see you again."

"May I come in?"

"Yes! Of course, you can. Come and sit on the foot of the bed." She leaned toward Faith and whispered, "Say, do you think you could find me a martini around here somewhere? Hmm?" She raised her eyebrows and nodded affirmatively.

Faith kindly smiled and replied, "No, I suppose not, but I brought a magazine for you. I thought you might like to read awhile."

"I will do so. After you leave. I want to talk to you when I have a chance. Too bad about the martini though."

"Oh, you're sweet! What shall we talk about?"

"The *keys!* I want to tell you about my keys."

"The Keyes? You want to talk about your family?"

"No dear, *the keys*! I want to talk about *my* keys. The keys to happiness. They're over there in the drawer."

She seemed a little delusional. The nurse had said she was getting very weak and explained she was on stout doses of morphine to control her pain. Faith wasn't sure if she should humor her, but she went to the chest and opened the top drawer. Inside was an old black beaded purse, the kind carried by flappers in the 1920s. The purse was heavy, as though filled with loose coins. Inside was an assortment of keys that appeared to be from any number of different sources. There were tiny keys and rusted keys and skeleton keys, brass ones and silver ones and gold-colored ones. Mrs. Keyes nodded in approval. According to her, these were the keys to happiness.

"Well, what do we have here, Mrs. Keyes?"

"Bring them over. I'll tell you all about them."

Faith laid the keys to happiness on the bed between her and Mrs. Keyes. Slowly, the old woman picked through the collection and occasionally grasped one in her crooked fingers.

"This one came from an old grandfather's clock from the dump. And this one I got in a box at an auction. What do you think of 'em, Faith? Do you recognize any? Is your key in there?"

She cackled a thin and hoarse laugh which quickly became a cough. Faith placed her cupped hand on Mrs. Keyes's bony back, rubbing and patting until the old woman regained her breath.

"Why do you call these the 'keys to happiness'?"

"Well, to tell you the truth, I originally invented it as a marketing scheme. With a name like Keyes, I thought I could use it as an advertising gimmick. Pretty clever, eh? I decorated a lot of rooms for a lot of wealthy people. I wanted to make sure they told their friends about me so I could get more business. I hoped by giving them a key it could become my trademark. You know, a calling card. I guess maybe it did.

"During many projects, I often learned more than I really should have about the homeowners. Once I redid a whole house because the youngest son had died suddenly.

"The first time I gave someone a key, it happened to be to a lady whose husband had done something very bad. The job started out like any other. We met and talked, and I tried to make her comfortable about choosing new colors and fabrics and prints. She seemed so cold and distant at first. Gradually though, she grew more friendly, and finally she opened up a bit.

"She just seemed so sad; I knew something must be wrong. When the room was done and the two of us stood there together looking at the finished product, I just couldn't help myself. I asked her why she was so glum. She broke down and cried and told me all about how her husband had been unfaithful. Redecorating this room was his way of buying his way back into her good graces. She said she was brokenhearted, and all the redecorated rooms in the world couldn't fix that. She only wanted her husband to love her again."

"Oh my gosh! What did you say to her?"

"Well, dear, I said he was an awful man for doing it and she should have just burned the house down instead of redecorating it."

Mrs. Keyes started to laugh again and once again began to cough and sputter. Faith rubbed her back. She motioned for a Kleenex, and when Faith handed her one, she spat something terrible into it.

"What did you do then, Mrs. Keyes? How did you ever get around to giving her a key?"

"Well, we had a good laugh, and she decided against the idea of burning down the house. Then she uncorked a bottle of wine, and we drank it together. I guess you could say we bonded. Sometime after the second glass or so I got a little too bold and blurted out how I thought she had a lot more to say about the whole thing than simply to be quiet and accept the redecorated room as an even trade. I gave her a key and told her she was in charge of her personal happiness, not her husband. She, *and only she*, got to decide when and if she would forgive him. It should only happen if she was good and ready for it, and not a second before. If he was sorry, and I mean *really sorry*, then maybe she needed to forgive him and get on with their life together. God knows most every man needs forgiveness at one time or another.

"However, I told her if his idea was to get off easy by bribing her with a new living room, she should send him packing and sue him for every penny he had. Either way, with or without him, she should hold out for true love. I don't know what her final decision was, but she surely seemed grateful for the key. She held it in her fist and resolved to make the right decision. It was the last time I ever saw her."

"Mrs. Keyes, that's a great story. Are there others like it? Other people you helped?"

"Yes, I suppose so. There were lots and lots of them really—lots of redecorated rooms, at least. I guess it wasn't always quite so dramatic. I mean, not always for a bad reason. Most people just wanted a prettier house. The one thing they all had in common, though, was after the *house* was redone, they expected their *lives* would somehow be better. Every time I finished a job, I would give a key to the homeowner and tell them the redecorating was only the beginning. The key stood for her own individual happiness, and they alone could use it."

"Mrs. Keyes, this is wonderful!"

"Yes, dear, I guess it must have been. Through the years I received many letters from former customers. Some of those get-well cards on the windowsill are from people I haven't seen in many years. It's interesting how many of them mention the keys as if they somehow magically made a difference in their lives.

"I remember one lady who said she got the courage to become a nun after I gave her the key. I really didn't intend *that* to happen! I do recall at least one woman who told me she and her husband made love right on the floor for the first time in over a year. She claimed it saved their marriage. I guess maybe a little roll in the hay really *was* the key to their happiness. Oh, Faith, I am sorry. That was a little off-color."

Faith giggled. "It's okay, Mrs. Keyes; I'm old enough to handle it. Please, tell me more."

"Well, there are *so* many stories. These are the keys I collected with the intention of giving away. I never had the chance to complete the project. I just ended up with more keys than I have time. This is where you come in. I need you to take these and give them away to the right people."

"Mrs. Keyes! I can't. Besides, who *are* the right people anyway?"

"Faith, you *can,* and you *will* take them. I *need* you to do this. I am not going to be here to finish the job. You will know who the right people are. You will spot them. I did. I know you will, too. They are everywhere. They are the ones who need you to let them know the key to happiness really exists for *them*—the ones who might not see it unless you hand it to them and say exactly what it is when you do.

"It is very important you do this for me. Trust me, I have seen how this little thing can make a difference. It would be a shame if it didn't get carried on. Please, promise me you will do this. Promise?" The old lady was tired out by all the talk and the memories.

"Yes, of course. I promise, Mrs. Keyes. I'll do my best."

"Thank you, Faith. Just don't waste them. After all, they *are* the keys to happiness. Now you take one. Pick out your own key. Go on, pick one."

"Can I really? Is it all right?"

"It's more than all right, dear. You can't be the keeper of the keys to happiness without ever finding your own key. It wouldn't be proper." She smiled a mischievous little smile. Her sunken eyes twinkled.

Faith carefully examined the keys, one by one. There were fancy keys with filigree engravings. There were many old clock keys. Mrs. Keyes said they held special meaning to her because clocks were used to manage the time of our lives. There were a few old skeleton keys and even a few gold-plated keys from lockets long given away or lost. She finally found her key. It was a small solid silver one, slightly over an inch long. Its head formed a heart. It was just right!

"Oh Faith, it's your key all right! It fits your personality perfectly!"

"Yes, Mrs. Keyes, it does, doesn't it?" Faith turned it over in her hand and smiled. The silver heart key was indeed her personal key to happiness. Mrs. Keyes folded her hands and smiled a satisfied smile. She had done it again.

"Remember, Faith, the rest is up to you."

"Mrs. Keyes, I don't know exactly what to say. I am so grateful."

"Just be happy, dear. That's what life is all about."

Faith Briggs left the hospital with the keys to happiness tucked casually under her arm in the beaded purse. Mrs. Keyes died a couple of weeks later, but not until she had shared many more stories with Faith about the magic of the keys. Faith wore the silver heart key on a chain around her neck every day for several weeks after she received it.

Soon after, each of the Gems got a key. Faith told them all about Mrs. Keyes and repeated the stories as well as she could remember. She made them all promise to never, ever lose them or throw them away. I suspect they never have.

CHAPTER 16

Our Homecoming

Mom's follow-up test results were favorable. By the time Jack and I got up early Saturday morning, she was already on her way home. We put on clean clothes and tried to spiff up the house a little. Mostly we just goofed off. We were happy and excited and a little nervous about how she would feel. We wanted badly for her to like how the house looked. Dad had worked so hard.

They reached Bay City just before noon. Uncle Harry started honking the horn as soon as the Impala crossed the tracks onto Main Street. He leaned on it all the way through town, like newly married couples do after a wedding. Dad and Mom were seated together in the back seat. Neighbors working in their yards or walking on the sidewalks waved when they went by. Mom clearly did not appreciate this sort of attention, but she didn't get to decide. Dad loved it. He rolled down the window and gave a "thumbs-up" sign to everyone he saw.

When they drove in the yard, Harry finally let up on the horn. Jack and I were already out the door before the car rolled to a stop.

Our mother beamed at the sight of her two boys, and the tears started flowing at once. We stood there hugging and kissing, deeply aware we were finally reunited as a family again. Harry just smiled and leaned on the front fender of the Chevy.

This time Dad offered Harry a crisp fifty-dollar bill. He put up a little fuss, but Dad insisted. I think both men realized it was impossible to do justice to Harry's generosity. Harry and Dad shook hands and thanked each other profusely as Mom fussed over Jack and me. After a few minutes Uncle Harry wished us well and headed back down the street to check in with Molly at the tavern.

The first thing Mom noticed was the new front porch and the rocking chairs. She smiled and sat down, slowly rocking and looking at Dad.

"Nice work, mister."

Then we went into the house. She could see the wallpaper from the front door.

"Oh my! What do we have here? How in the world did you get this done? It looks like a fairy tale."

"Doris McCreedy hung it for us, but M picked it out."

"Oh! It's *wonderful*."

She cried again and we hugged her again. Mom's luggage was still on the front lawn. We forgot all about it and left it there for over an hour as she settled back in and inspected the house. All the hours Dad had spent remodeling were suddenly worth it. She was ecstatic. Dad saved the bathroom for last.

"Rachel, I've got a little surprise for you. He opened the door so she could see the curious stainless-steel device for the first time.

"Is this what I think it is?"

"Yes, my dear, it's your new washing machine!" We all laughed.

"Brick, where did you come up with this? I thought we couldn't get a permit. Are we legal?"

"Well, sort of. It's one of Walt's inventions, until we can afford the holding tank. It runs on propane, and it sort of *burns* the waste away. It seems fairly safe. And before you ask: no, it does not smell bad.

She looked at him suspiciously. "You're kidding. Does it really work?"

I piped up, "You bet it works. We've all been using it. Pretty space-age stuff, isn't it?"

Mom said, "Yes, it is. Pretty space-age stuff, all right. I always wondered how the astronauts did it."

"Rachel, I promise we will replace it as soon as possible when we can save up the thousand dollars we'll need for the holding tank."

"It's fine—much better than what we had."

Jack finally said, "Mom, I've got something for you." Dad and I had kind of forgotten about the portrait, but we knew what he meant as soon as he mentioned it. Suddenly, Jack was center stage. He went into our bedroom and returned with a cardboard tube. Inside it was the portrait he had completed several weeks ago. He unrolled it and laid it on the kitchen table.

Mom put her hand up to her mouth and whispered, "Dear Lord."

"Do you like it?"

"Jack, it's so real . . . so nice. It looks like me when I was a girl . . . except I don't think I was ever this pretty."

"Yes, Mom—yes, you were. You still are."

That did it. We all broke down again, and the waterworks started flowing. Jack's portrait was the best homecoming present Mom could have gotten. Better than the porch or the rocking chairs or the rose wallpaper. Better even than the Burner.

All the excitement had tired her out. Mom explained she would probably need quite a bit of rest for a while, and her emotions were a little fragile. She said we shouldn't worry about it. The treatments had sent her cancer into remission, but now she had to recover from the procedures themselves. She needed to take several medications, including vitamins, an iron supplement, and pain pills when she needed them. She asked us to forgive her, but she really needed to lie down after the long ride. She hugged us again and then went into the bedroom to rest.

So, there we were again. Dad and Jack and I looked at each other as if we could barely believe she was back. He patted us both on the back.

"Grab the bags, boys. She's home to stay!"

Remission seemed like the best word I'd ever heard.

Mom took a long nap, and we moved about the house with exaggerated care to be quiet. Truthfully, we just couldn't wait to see her smile and look at her face again. She finally got up around three o'clock. She moved very slowly and seemed groggy for a while. Her lack of energy was new and clearly different. But what mattered most was she was home.

I asked her if it was all right for Darla to come over. I was used to her validating mostly everything I asked for. This time she thought maybe tomorrow would be a better day for guests. I felt sort of disappointed about her answer. Darla seemed like part of our family to me. Instead, she came over Sunday morning, and Mom got along famously with her, just as I'd imagined she would.

Mom proved to be quite an attraction. In addition to Darla, our first visitors were Walt and Dolly. They stayed for over an hour, reminiscing and chatting about almost everything *except* cancer. Neighbors came and went often. They usually had a casserole or a salad, or maybe some cookies. She showed off the new wallpaper and told every visitor she could never have gone through the whole ordeal without her family and God. Many of our neighbors left with a crocheted doily or potholder.

Sam even came across the street again. He pulled some irises from in front of his house and brought them to her as a bouquet. She hugged the old bugger and sent him home with a doily and a pie someone had left.

The early days proved to be a time of readjustment. We had to learn about Mom's new sleep patterns and her nutritional needs. She ate smaller meals and sometimes needed snacks at odd times of the day and night. We were so used to fending for ourselves that it seemed a little awkward when she wanted to cook dinner or sweep the kitchen floor. Whenever she picked up the broom, one of us rushed over and asked if we could help. At first, she let us. But soon she let us know she really wanted to get back to her normal life again.

"Fellas, you are more than welcome to continue doing your share of the household chores. I appreciate it. Just know I want to do my share, too. Mind you, not *more* than my share, but—my share."

A few days after Mom got home, Dad stepped in front of her to help set the table. She put her hand on his forearm and gently took a plate from his grasp.

"Treat me like you always did. I won't break. I'm a lot stronger than you think I am. Don't worry, I know you love me. You can love me when I'm setting the table, too. Okay?"

He didn't say anything. He just pulled her close and kissed her like he did when they first met—when they first fell in love.

"Wow! Keep that up and I'll set the table ten times a day if you like it so much! The boys won't be home for a little while. Why don't we talk this over in the bedroom?"

He stood up straight and caught his breath.

"Can we—I mean, can you? Is it okay?"

"Yes, Brick, it's fine. We just need to be a little careful. But it's *really* okay. More than that. I need us to be *us* again."

The two lovers held hands and walked together into the little bedroom. They made love for the first time in months. The sorrow he felt when she first told him of the cancer was set aside. So was the misplaced shame she felt, as if getting sick was somehow her fault.

Afterward, they lay in each other's arms, smiling and counting their blessings for several minutes. Then the back door flew open and reminded them they were also the parents of two hungry boys.

"Mom, Dad? Are you home? Where are you? Are you here?"

Mom said, "We're here. We'll be right out."

Out in the kitchen Jack and I were poking around in the fridge. "What's for supper?"

Mom answered, "We're still trying to decide."

When the two finally appeared from the bedroom, they both looked a little flushed and slightly sheepish. Dad said, "So, boys, home a little early, eh?"

Jack had kind of a funny look on his face. I didn't know why. I said, "Joe and Deedee would like to know if you want to go to the Homecoming game with them tomorrow night. Darla and I are going. Want to?"

Mom said, "What about you, Jack? What are your plans?"

"I'm not really interested, Mom. I thought I'd draw a little."

Dad said, "Maybe we'd better stay home, too. Your mother might get too tired."

"I guess I feel like I would be fine, but who knows? Would you feel bad if we didn't go?"

"I guess not. It's a big game, though. We are going to put the hammer down on those River Falls creeps."

Mom asked, "Is Rory McCreedy still playing? He is such a good-looking young man."

"Well, sort of. He's the backup quarterback. He only plays if we are way ahead or way behind. I don't think he will play tomorrow night. It should be a close game."

"We will do some cheers in the living room while your dad and I watch the *Lawrence Welk Show*. Won't we, Brick?"

Jack smiled, causing him to look younger than he usually did. I guess he hadn't smiled very often while she was away.

"Pretty heavy, Mom. Are you sure you can handle all the excitement? Lawrence Welk is a real stick of dynamite."

Mom and Dad looked at each other and smiled. Dad finally said, "Don't worry about us. We should be fine. What do you say we go out for burgers at Stella's tonight?"

Mom said, "Not until I get fixed up a little bit!"

She went back into the bedroom to change clothes. Her husband came in and began tucking in his rumpled shirt. As he undid the belt, she turned and gave him a serious look.

"Uh, Brick, I don't think we have time for *that* again, do you?"

His cheeks were still a little flushed when he reentered the living room. Ten minutes later she returned in the same blue dress we had seen her wear in Madison. Her hair was still very short, but she no longer tried to cover it up.

"Let's go, boys! Time's a-wastin'! I turn into a pumpkin at midnight, so we'd better hurry up and head to the ball."

Dad said, "What do you think? Shall we take the Pontiac? It *is* kind of a special night."

Mom thought about it for a few seconds and then said, "Well, that's a good idea, . . .but, well . . . let's not press our luck. It's so nice outside, and I could use the exercise."

We walked together down the street and across the tracks to Stella's. There was a good crowd, as usual. Everyone seemed happy, and some of our neighbors made a fuss over Mom. Stella came over and ruffled my hair and gave me a hug. She didn't have to say it. I knew what she meant. She was silently letting me know how happy she was for us. I remembered the morning when she held me close and just allowed me to cry.

The burgers seemed bigger than usual, and they tasted as great as ever. Dad gave me a quarter for the jukebox. In those days it got you five choices.

He whispered "A-6" when he handed me the coin. It was "Love Me Tender."

As soon as it came on, Dad asked Mom to dance. She got all embarrassed and at first refused, giving him a poke in the side with her elbow.

He said, "I've waited a long time for this dance. I wish it could be a little more private than this, but I really need this one. C'mon Rae. Please?"

Mom and Dad got up and began dancing to the jukebox in Stella's Café as the other diners cheered and clapped. Before long Wayne Button grabbed Stella, and then everybody started pairing up. Pretty soon, the whole place was out of their booths and dancing between the tables. The room wasn't set up for dancing, so there was a fair amount of bumping into each other, but nobody seemed to care. When the song was done, Mom and Dad held onto each other while the other customers clapped and congratulated them.

A few couples lingered as the jukebox changed records. I had made the rest of the choices on my own. The next song was a high-spirited rockabilly song called "I Fought the Law" by the Bobby Fuller Four. It didn't exactly support the romantic mood. There were some good-natured chuckles as the remaining dancers meandered back to their booths.

After supper, we took our time walking home. The sun was still fairly high in the sky as lengthening traces of red began showing up near the horizon. Dad and Mom held hands. We walked past the old school and past the fish market. When we reached the Patterson house, Mom kept her eyes pointed straight ahead. She let go of Dad and took Jack's and my hands in her own, saying, "This does not concern us anymore."

Just ahead, old Sam was standing at the edge of his front yard with a hose in his hand. He appeared to be watering the cracked blacktop street.

Dad said, "Looks like you just about got it, Sam. Can I help you put your hose away?"

"Good deal, damn right you can. Rachel, you look really nice."

"Thank you, Sam. It's kind of you to say."

He smiled his crooked smile and dropped the hose right where he stood, turned around, and hiked up the broken sidewalk toward his front door. Dad nodded and gave an understanding wink to Mom. The hose lay there pulsing and still watering the street.

Mom, Jack, and I kept going toward our house while Dad shut off the water and put Sam's hose away. Tomorrow was Homecoming.

CHAPTER 17

The Other Homecoming

Friday afternoon classes ended at two o'clock, and we walked three blocks down the hill to the high school gym for a big pep rally. This was one of the rare times I got a chance to be with Darla during normal school hours. As we sat together in the bleachers, I looked around and was reminded she was a bit older than me.

The coach gave a blistering speech in which he used the term "fired up" no less than five times. He introduced the team to thundering applause. Every time one of the players came out, the cheerleaders chanted and did a cartwheel or a handstand. Mac Murphy, a senior and the first-string quarterback, made a speech too. It was not especially articulate, but it was all right, I guess. He gave a thumbs-up sign to his buddies, and he winked at his cheerleader girlfriend, Rhonda Leaf, who knelt on the edge of the gym floor. Then he guaranteed a win and ended his speech with a shrug.

"That's all I got to say."

We must have thought it was brilliant because we all cheered loudly. To punctuate the moment, Rhonda did a double cartwheel and ended it with the splits. She held her hands up above her head in a "V" with her legs straight out and flat on the floor. Now *that* was brilliant. We cheered again.

After the rally, I walked upstairs to Darla's locker with her so she could get her things before going outside to catch the bus home. While we were standing around, Billy Hooper walked over and leaned against the locker next to Darla's. He was a big, muscular farm kid who generally thought he was a little more attractive than he actually was.

"So, Darla, are you coming to the game? I plan on royally kicking some Wildcat asses tonight."

"Hi, Billy, do you know Emmet North? We're both going. You know, together." She smiled and cocked her head to one side and blinked her eyes several times.

Hooper looked me over. "*North.* Yeah, I know him. Isn't he a little young for you? What are you doing with this poor white trash? His old man is a bum and that's all he'll ever be, too. Oh, I forgot. *You* are poor white trash too. Your whole town is good for nothing. Did anybody get murdered there lately?"

Darla was rapidly getting upset. I was mad too, but I didn't bite at the chance to get punched. I calmly said, "Billy, I'll let my friend Rory McCreedy know how you feel. I'm sure he'll be interested in your opinion of Bay City. Good luck with your ass kicking."

As we turned to leave, Hooper realized his potential mistake. As tough as Billy was, McCreedy probably could take him if it came down to an actual fight.

"Hey, I didn't say nothin' about McCreedy."

Darla looked over her shoulder. "Oh, we heard you. You called him white trash. I think I heard something about his mom, too, didn't you, Emmet? I think he said Rory's mom was pretty trashy, too."

"Unfortunately, I believe I did hear something to that effect."

Hooper knew when to quit. He just waved us off and grumbled, "Ah, bullshit!"

We got home just in time to inhale a quick supper and change into some warmer Panther Booster clothing. The Riviera pulled into the yard around six, and we excitedly set off for Ellsworth.

The Friday night air was crisp, and the bleachers were packed, with all expecting a showdown. The River Falls Wildcats were in first place in the Middle Border Conference, and the Panthers were in second. With home field advantage and it being Homecoming and all, the possibility of an upset seemed very real.

The Panthers were warming up on the field. They went through their stretching exercises and their calisthenics. The Wildcats did the same, though Deedee didn't think they looked as sharp. McCreedy was throwing the ball leisurely to some second- and third-string players while the first team offense was getting down to serious pre-game business.

As Deedee got settled in, she announced with typical enthusiasm, "Man alive! That Rory is a *hunk*!"

The ref blew his whistle at seven p.m., and the game was on. Hank and Doris McCreedy snuggled together in the bleachers with a blanket over their shoulders. They waved cheerfully at Rory but did not expect him to get any playing time. It didn't matter. They were proud of their son anyway. Next year after Mac Murphy graduated, he would be the starter.

It soon became clear the matchup was everything it was billed to be. Both offenses moved the ball down the field and scored. The Panthers ran the ball nearly every down, and the Wildcats passed a lot. It was a classic confrontation between two opposing coaching philosophies and a primary reason why Rory's passing capabilities were underutilized.

Soon Panther quarterback Mac Murphy was taking charge. At any time, he was likely to dash around end and roll for a first down or a score. The "black and blue" running strategy was relentless and effective at chewing up the clock while wearing down the opposition. The season was still young, but this rivalry meant a lot to both teams.

Darla and I had decided to sit with her folks. The Mafia had checked in with us earlier. They were seated up in the back row of the bleachers making ongoing crude and disparaging remarks aimed at the Wildcats. Additionally, they made loud farting noises whenever the Wildcat players bent over to assume their down stance.

Mac Murphy's folks were sitting in front of the Mafia. Denny referred to them as Life and Death Murphy. Mrs. Murphy was a rotund woman who was extremely loud and demonstrative. She shouted at the refs and cheered unapologetically for Mac. Mr. Murphy was tall, very thin, and gray-haired. He sat almost motionless and crossed his legs in an oddly effeminate way that sort of made me cringe and imagine significant discomfort.

Life and Death Murphy sat up in the high bleacher seats with Denny, Rex, and Tom. Mrs. Murphy loved the boys and laughed at every one of their inappropriate comments, elbowing Death in the ribs with each guffaw. In the second quarter, Death even got a little excited when Mac scored a touchdown on an option play.

Both teams were successful, and by halftime the score was 21 to 14 in favor of the Wildcats. The halftime festivities included the marching band's roughshod renditions of "Louie Louie" and "Up, Up and Away." The cheerleaders gyrated just a little more than some of the parents cared to see, but the high school boys in the stands appreciated their efforts. Life Murphy yelled, "Shake it, girls!" and stood up to demonstrate what she had in mind.

After some mostly recognizable versions of popular tunes and a couple of rousing Sousa marches, the extravaganza ended with the band forming a shaky "E" on the field and playing the "Panther Fight Song." We dutifully stood up and sang our hearts out.

The third quarter opened with the Panthers on offense. Mac Murphy played like he was possessed. He ran left. He ran right. He crashed into the middle. His front line was exclusively built of big, strong farm boys who genuinely liked to push and shove and occasionally kick the opposition in the ribs. I hated to admit it, but even Billy Hooper looked good. The Panthers tied the game late in the third quarter.

The score was still tied midway through the fourth, and it was becoming clear both teams were getting tired. The Wildcat receivers were dropping passes, and Mac was getting stuffed at the line more often. Both the Wildcat and the Panther punters were getting more than their share of the action. Then, with three minutes to go in the game, disaster struck.

The Panthers were on the 20-yard line with 80 yards to go for the win. Mac Murphy took the ball and ran right. A hole in the line opened up so wide you could drive a truck through it. Mac smiled as he turned the corner and wheeled up the field. Within ten yards, he had outrun his blockers. He had done this many times before. No big deal, he knew what to do. He put his head down and shifted up a gear. Then he ran out of room.

The Wildcats had responded to Murphy's speed by leaving their fastest wide receivers in on defense. As fast as Murphy was, Kyle Thompson was even faster. The Wildcat speed demon chased Murphy down from behind and launched his body like a missile right at Mac's legs. Thompson's helmet hit him in the left knee, sending him careening out of bounds at midfield. The crowd went silent as Mac lay writhing and holding his knee.

For a moment, the only sound was Life Murphy's voice screaming like a banshee. She was standing precariously on her seat and barking like a mad dog. She looked like she could have had a heart attack at any second. The Mafia thought it was great.

"You dirty, rotten little rat-bastard! You son of a bitch! Foul! Foul! Ref! Are you blind? Disqualify those Wildcat bastards!" She was spitting white flecks of saliva with every word, and her face was as red as the Wildcat uniforms. The coach was on the field and bending over Mac.

"How bad is it? Is anything broken?"

"I don't think so. It's just a sprain. I can play. Just help me up."

"Time out, Ref! We need a time out!"

The coach was chewing his gum like crazy. By now the crowd was getting restless, and many were booing the Wildcats. As if on cue, Kyle Thompson came over to Mac and offered his hand. Mac Murphy shook his hand and the crowd clapped in recognition of the good sportsmanship.

What they didn't hear was Mac saying, "Thompson, you cheap-shot asshole. My boys are gonna break your legs off."

Thompson whispered back, "Good luck with that."

The coach walked back across the field and Murphy painfully limped back to the Panthers bench. Life and Death Murphy were both standing up now. Uncharacteristically, Death glided ghostlike down the bleacher steps to where the team was huddled up on the sidelines. He placed his large bony hand on the coach's shoulder. His sepulchral voice was deep and ominous.

"Coach Devaney, sit him down. Do not let him get hurt any worse. *Please.*" Then he turned and went back to his place in the stands.

The coach was surprised and a little ticked off because Mac's dad had chosen to come down to the field. However, the crowd interpreted this as a sign of encouragement. The excitement was building, and everyone seemed certain Death Murphy had patted the coach on the back as a sign of confidence.

In the huddle, Coach Devaney asked Murphy again, "Can you run? Your dad says he wants you to play."

"I think so."

The Panthers ran two handoffs, one to the right and one to the left. No gain. As the team broke huddle on third down, it was obvious Mac Murphy could barely walk, let alone run. Coach Devaney called him back.

"Mac, c'mon back here. You're out. *McCreedy*! Get your damned helmet on. You've got work to do."

Rory McCreedy jumped up and trotted onto the field. He looked good. There were two minutes left in the game. It was third down. Crunch time.

McCreedy said "Huddle up," and the team huddled up. "Okay men, listen up; I mean business. Let's get this done so we can go to the dance and impress some ladies. What do you say? Let's beat these Wildcat bozos."

The team agreed. McCreedy relayed the play Coach Devaney had called.

"Blue 26—right—green light—BREAK!"

"Blue 26 right" was a familiar pass play to Gene Simon, the fastest man on the team. "Green light" meant Gene should just keep running as hard as he could. McCreedy would throw the football deep and let Gene run under it for the catch.

McCreedy had no problem with the play. He had practiced it a hundred times and even made sure to call it in every playground game. He aimed to hit Simon at the 10-yard line. The crowd went silent as the Panthers came to the line of scrimmage.

"Ready—set—Hut! Hut! *Hut*!"

McCreedy slapped the ball. He backed smoothly away from his center. He looked to his left and away from Gene Simon. He pumped a fake pass. Simon was clearing the secondary and was a good three yards in front of his defender when McCreedy spun back to his right and launched a rocket. The ball sailed in a tight, perfect spiral. We all watched in taut anticipation.

Rory McCreedy overshot Gene Simon by at least five yards. The Wildcat bench and bleachers went crazy. Their defense had dodged a bullet. We couldn't believe our eyes. It was fourth down. Coach Devaney called his last timeout.

"Okay, McCreedy, settle down. This play will work. Just keep your arm under control. We have to go for it. Same play to the left." McCreedy nodded his head.

The Panthers lined up for a fourth-down miracle. It was a tie game. Even if they didn't score, time was running out, and the Wildcats would have to take over on their side of midfield. It looked like we were heading for overtime. Mac Murphy was limping back and forth on the sidelines. His knee was starting to limber up. Maybe he could get back in for the overtime.

"Down—set. Hut! Hut! *Hut*!"

McCreedy slid catlike away from center. He briefly looked left as Gene Simon cleared the line. He turned to his right to draw the defense in the wrong direction. What he saw made him catch his breath. Was that Thompson? He had let Brad Carlson run right past him and was trotting several yards behind him. He looked winded or possibly hurt.

McCreedy spun back left and looked for Gene Simon. He was streaking down the left sideline, but the Wildcat defender was right on his hip. Instinctively, McCreedy spun back to his right and rifled the ball in the direction of Brad Carlson.

As the ball cleared Rory's fingertips, Gene Simon's defender slipped and fell. Gene crossed the goal line alone and waved his hands over his head.

Brad Carlson was shocked. When McCreedy threw you a pass it was like catching a cannon ball. Instantly, he tightened up and waited for the pain. Out of the corner of his eye, Brad could see Kyle Thompson's red uniform closing in fast. He had been playing possum and now had turned on the afterburners. McCreedy's pass hit Brad Carlson perfectly in his hands in full stride at the 10-yard line. Kyle Thompson was beaten! For a millisecond the world stood still. Then the worst thing that could happen—happened. The ball caught the end of Brad's middle finger and jammed it badly. He screeched as the football bounced straight up in the air.

Kyle Thompson, the Wildcats' premier receiver who just happened to be playing defensive back, closed the final gap between him and his target, easily catching the tipped ball. He circled back to his right and ran away from the action. Ninety-four yards later, he crossed the goal line for a touchdown and the win. It was a Middle Border Conference record for a touchdown after an interception, and coincidentally, it was the worst moment of McCreedy's charmed life.

The game was suddenly over. The hometown crowd shuffled out in stunned silence as the Wildcat spectators wildly cheered and chanted. It was nearly unthinkable, but Rory McCreedy had apparently made a very bad read on the defense, and everyone had seen it. We were pretty quiet on the way home. Finally, Deedee broke the silence. "Well, no matter what else, he sure is good-lookin'."

Marty smiled. "I guess so, if you like *that* type."

"Ha! What type is *that* type? The young and handsome type? He's just the berries!"

"Dream on, Deedee. Dream on."

"Now don't worry, Sugar. Rory is just a baby. You know I like my man to be kinda old and funny lookin'. That's why I love *you* so much."

On the way home, I thought about how the Panthers lost the big game and McCreedy's unfortunate choice of receivers. Still, it was only a football game, after all. And he was still McCreedy.

CHAPTER 18

Cow Sense

Back in town at the bars and coffee shops, McCreedy was the topic of many derogatory conversations. Rory skipped the dance and drove out to a place appropriately called "The End of the Road." It earned the name when the state of Wisconsin had to abruptly suspend construction of a two-lane county road at the shore of the Isabel Creek, when the funding for a bridge was cut from the state's budget.

McCreedy sat behind the wheel of his dad's pickup, staring through the barricade at the water. He had somehow managed to blow the chance of a lifetime. He shook his head. What was he thinking? Brad Carlson couldn't catch a cold, let alone a touchdown pass.

By the time Gene Simon hit the end zone, he was so far ahead of his defender it was ridiculous. It would have been easy. Woulda – coulda - shoulda. Like the coach says, they'll get you every time. It was just the wrong call. Not because he read the defense wrong, but because he threw the ball to the wrong pair of hands. The pass was right where it needed to be. Brad Carlson just didn't have the strength to hang on to it.

But the night wasn't a total loss for everyone. Despite the game's outcome, it was almost a foregone conclusion that Homecoming included a major post-dance make-out opportunity for the players and their dates.

Rhonda Leaf was counting on it. She and Mac Murphy had been going steady for three months. They were both graduating soon, so she had begun to consider whether Mac would qualify as a potential long-term relationship or merely a temporary distraction.

While the guys tended to make crude suggestions about their lustful intentions, the girls often had discussions about deeper feelings and commitments. Rhonda envisioned her first time would be meaningful and special. It seemed questionable whether it would be with Mac. She was in charge of the decision and she was in no particular hurry. The situation had to be perfect. If not, too bad, Mac!

By the time Homecoming had come around, Rhonda's closest girlfriends and her cheerleader teammates were all included in her support team. Whatever Rhonda decided, they wanted to share vicariously in the experience.

She had borrowed her parents' camper van under the pretense that the cheerleaders would all be riding together. In fact, the cheerleaders did arrive at the game as a group, but after the dance they planned to scatter like leaves in the autumn wind. After the dance, they would reunite on top of Memorial Hill, a well-known location high above Ellsworth's ragged downtown skyline.

The Ellsworth police would predictably drive through the park at midnight when it was understood everyone would have to leave so the big gate could be locked. Neither the police nor the parkers wanted any trouble.

Rhonda was already at the dance when Mac Murphy and the other players arrived. The band was Quicksand, featuring lead guitar player Smith Morris. He was a handsome, long-haired slacker who somehow had managed to become Faith Briggs's boyfriend. Smith was sixteen, two years older than Faith. Her parents didn't exactly approve.

Because of the age difference, she was prevented from going to the dance with Smith for the same reason I didn't get to take Darla. Her dad would probably have stepped in if another reason had been necessary.

The players' hair was still wet from the showers when they came shambling into the gym. They were visibly pissed off about the way the game ended. Mac still limped badly. The loss complicated things a little, but Rhonda was dedicated as a cheerleader and a woman to help Mac get through this hard and confusing time.

Billy Hooper usually stuck close to Mac Murphy. He lacked the imagination to do anything too original. Tonight, however, Billy had managed to carry out a fine example of misplaced teenage initiative. A bottle of peppermint schnapps and a second bottle of blackberry brandy were stashed under the front seat of his Bel Air. It didn't take long for the boys to convince their dates they were too beaten up to dance without some medicinal aid.

By the time the band took their first break, Mac and Billy were sitting in Billy's car, passing the schnapps back and forth and still bitching about what a loser Rory McCreedy was. When Quicksand took their second break, the girls joined them.

After the second dose of schnapps, the boys were ready to dance. The Ellsworth football team was not synonymous with dancing excellence. These strong and athletic young men from rural America moved as stiffly and awkwardly as if Frankenstein's monster had been their dance coach. Worse yet, Coach Devaney and his wife hit the dance floor as Quicksand began a respectable version of the Doors' "Light My Fire." Despite a great song being played relatively well, the scene on the dance floor was awful. The entire Frankenstein Dance Troupe was on display.

McCreedy sat gazing at the Isabel Creek for a long time. He took a long, hard internal look at himself, too. He thought about quitting the team. He even thought about joining the Army. In the end he just drove the back roads home to Bay City.

By eleven thirty he pulled the truck into the driveway of his parents' home and turned off the engine. When he opened the front door, Rory realized his dad was watching TV with the lights off. The reflection from the old Motorola cast a jumpy greenish light onto the hallway walls.

Hank McCreedy spoke out in an exaggerated whisper, "Is it you, son?"

"Yeah, Dad, it's me."

"C'mon in here. Are you hungry?"

"No. I'm fine."

"Your mother's asleep."

Rory stood in the archway of the living room. He wanted to talk but didn't know where to start. Hank and Doris had both seen it all. He figured they might be pretty ashamed to be the parents of the guy who blew the big game. Finally, Hank said, "It was a really great pass. Right on the money."

"Yeah, I guess so. I think maybe you and I are the only ones who know it."

"Doc Steiber had to put a cast on Brad Carlson's middle finger. I think Brad knows it too."

"I'm not sure if it's enough, Pop."

"It's got to be, Rory. You know, once it's out of your hand, it's up to somebody else to make the catch. You did your part. I'm just as proud of you as I can be. You're a damned fine quarterback, but you're a better son. Believe it or not, that's a lot more important than a dropped ball."

Rory wrapped one of his long, muscular arms around his father's shoulders and rubbed his balding head with his big hand. He was nearly four inches taller than the older man. They stood there in the flickering light of the TV half-hugging each other.

"Hank, you're a true fan of the game. I love ya, Dad."

"You'd better. I'm *your biggest* fan. Hell, your mom and I might be your *only* fans right now. It'll change though, I promise. One pass and one game do not make a season." Hank smiled and Rory nodded.

"Goodnight, Dad."

"Goodnight, son. Go, Panthers!"

"Ouch."

Hank McCreedy knew Rory was in for a tough time. This was a hard lesson every quarterback had to learn. When the fans turn against you, the great athletes must find ways to play through the harsh reality of public criticism. Some just fade away. It was true in college and in the pros. Unfortunately, it was true even in high school. Hank and Doris had spoken hopefully many times about the prospect of Rory getting an athletic scholarship. Without it, it would be very hard to send him on to a good school. There was a lot at stake. Hank was pretty sure his son had the right stuff to handle it.

Back at the dance, Quicksand played "House of the Rising Sun," "Sunshine of Your Love," "I've Got a Line on You," and "It's All Right." They dedicated Eric Burden's great hit "We Gotta Get Out of This Place" to the graduating seniors. They worked hard and made sure the crowd knew it by leaning into their guitars and displaying painful expressions at just the right time during the leads. Nothing reflects beautiful teenaged angst better than a bending string on an electric guitar.

When the band took their third break at ten thirty p.m., it signaled the departure of several couples who drove straight out to Memorial Hill Park.

Rhonda had tasted the peppermint schnapps, but only enough to make her feel a bit light-headed and perhaps a little uninhibited. Mac, on the other hand, was hammered. He stumbled and groped and slurred his words.

Billy Hooper was equally loaded. He had managed to convince Traci Palace that he was in fact, a serious contender for her affection. For the time being, it appeared Traci was willing to believe it. Billy spun his tires as he left the gravel parking lot and turned toward Memorial Hill. When they reached the first stop sign, Hooper mistakenly showed his true colors.

"Hey Traci, do you know what S-T-O-P stands for?"

"No, Billy, what does S-T-O-P stand for?"

"Start—taking—off—pants! Get it?"

"Yeah, Billy, I get it. Say, wait a minute. Take me back to my car, will you? I forgot something."

"What? Yeah, okay. Crap." He made a wide U-turn and drove back to the parking lot. "What did you forget anyway?"

As the Bel Air pulled up next to Traci's VW Bug, she opened the door and jumped out. Then she leaned back in through the open passenger side window.

"Billy, for a little while, I forgot what a total jackass you are. Thanks for reminding me. Have a nice time by yourself up on Memorial Hill. Good luck, big guy."

She smiled a saccharine smile and jumped into the VW. Hooper was slack-jawed and amazed. Traci offered another exaggerated smile and gave him the finger as she drove away. Hooper was too drunk to know how to react. He was probably too drunk for a lot of things. He drove home and went to bed, still saturated, and dumbfounded at the way some girls think.

Rhonda managed to pour Mac into the front seat of the camper van, where he slumped down into a partially reclining position. She turned on the radio, nice and soft. She sighed deeply and calmly eased the van onto the street leading to her future, whatever it may be. The van smelled slightly like the pleasant scent of peppermint.

Rhonda recognized several of the cars and pickups parked up on Memorial. A couple of them blinked their lights when they saw the camper van pull in. Rhonda pulled up to the far end of the parking lot and out onto the grass framing the secluded crest of the hill. Across a fence and beyond the adjacent pasture below were the lights of Ellsworth. Rhonda said in a sultry voice, "Mac—wake uh-up. Do you want to cuddle?"

Her only answer was a loud snore. Mac Murphy was out, dead to the world. Rhonda softly put her hand on Mac's shoulder. "Ma-ac." More snoring. "Great!"

Rhonda decided to let him sleep for fifteen minutes or so. Maybe a nap would refresh him. She listened to the radio. She was starting to feel confused and a little sad. Tonight was supposed to be a turning point in their relationship.

Rhonda had even picked out the background music for the occasion. She had an eight-track recording of Percy Sledge singing his great ballad "When a Man Loves a Woman." When she got to that part in the fantasy, she snapped.

Rhonda screamed, "Mac! You muscle-bound oaf! *Wake up*!!"

She wasn't messing around anymore. This was her big night, and she aimed to have a meaningful, life-changing, Homecoming make-out experience! Nothing worked. She shoved him and pinched him and pulled his hair. Mac was down for the count. Now what?

Rhonda was getting anxious. She was certain several of her girlfriends were out there with their dates and imagined they would all find out the night of a lifetime had ended with a snore instead of fireworks. This was just embarrassing. Her mind raced. She sat back in the driver's seat and thought about what to do.

She said softly, "Stay calm. Stay calm."

Rhonda slid down into the seat. She just needed a little time to think. She closed her eyes to ponder her predicament. She repeated, "Stay calm."

As she began to doze, she heard a low-pitched female voice say, "Looo-ser. Got it?"

"Yes, I've—what—?"

The sound of her own voice startled her awake. A lone cow stood cross the fence line chewing her cud in circular bovine fashion.

"Hello, is anyone there? Are you—?" she muttered. "Oh, for Pete's sake! Now I'm talking to cows—*and they're talking back*!"

And then: "Oh crap, Mac, you really messed this up."

Rhonda shook her head and half smiled as she started the van and slowly headed down the winding road from Memorial Hill and back to town. The local police car was just entering the gates as she left.

By the time they got back to the school parking lot, the crowd had mostly left, and the band was loading out their equipment. Rhonda couldn't help noticing Smith Morris was talking to Shiela Golden. Across the street by the school, he reached out and brushed her hair over her shoulder with the back of his hand. Smooth . . . really smooth. What a womanizer he was!

Right now, Rhonda had other things to worry about than Smith Morris. She leaned over and planted a big kiss on Mac Murphy's limp and unresponsive lips. At the same time, she leaned her elbow hard into his groin. The combination had its desired effect and Murphy began to rouse from his peppermint schnapps coma.

"Where are we?"

"Oh, Mac. Wasn't it *wonderful*?"

"What? What was wonderful?"

"Don't tease me. You know what I mean. Every time I hear *our* song, I'll know that you're *that* man and I'm *that* woman."

"What the hell are you talking about? What song? What man?"

Rhonda knew it was about time to call it quits. She reached over, unlatched the door and began pushing Murphy out.

"Well, I guess it's time for me to take the van home. You'd better go. I'll call you tomorrow. Thank you for this night and these beautiful memories."

Rhonda pushed hard, and Murphy muttered in drunken confusion as he clawed his way out of the van and staggered toward his car.

Rhonda shifted the transmission into drive and asked the dashboard hula girl, "Are they all this bad or am I just unlucky?"

She pulled out of the parking lot and turned left, past Smith Morris's car. Shiela Golden was sliding across the front seat and over to the driver's side, where he sat smirking. The hula dancer didn't say a word but wiggled in agreement with every bump in the street.

By the time Monday morning classes began, the big news at Ellsworth High was what a lucky guy Mac Murphy was, and of course, what a disappointment Rory McCreedy had turned out to be.

The rumor about Shiela Golden and Smith Morris got back to Faith, and she broke up with him when he came to pick her up for lunch. It wasn't hard. She had done it before.

Rhonda's girlfriends demanded details. She thought about spinning some extravagant tale about how perfect the evening was, but somewhere inside she reminded herself about a wise cow that had spoken the truth to her in a dream.

"Sorry to disappoint you, ladies. Nothing happened. Mac passed out and I guess—well, I finally realized he is just not good enough for me. End of story, he blew it."

"We are *not* surprised."

"You deserve better."

"We all knew he was a phony."

By lunchtime Rhonda had been hearing a different version of the story, and she knew what she needed to do. She found Mac Murphy in the lunchroom with his buddies.

"Soooo, Mac—I heard you are telling everyone we had sex Friday night, and, well, I was wondering where *I* was during all that. I mean, I know where *you* were. You were passed out in the front seat of my dad's van. Maybe you forgot, so let me refresh your memory: the closest you came to having the most incredible night of your life was taking a little nap while I, in all my female glory, had to decide whether it was worth trying to wake you up or not. Guess what I decided? *RIGHT!*

"Mac, you are a failure. You lost the game Friday, and you lost the chance of a lifetime with me. So, let me just suggest this: in fifty years, when you are a tired old creep and you look back on what might have been a beautiful experience for both of us, I would like you to remember what? How you blew it!

"On the other hand, I will have the satisfaction of knowing I did *not* end up giving myself to a drunken mess like you. That's right Mac, *my* decision. This is *my* body, and *I AM IN CHARGE*!" She was building up steam.

"I do not mind everyone knowing I am still a virgin—that *WE ARE BOTH* still virgins! I still have my dignity, and you darned well can't take it away from me no matter what lies you tell. Oh, by the way, *we are finished*!"

She spun on her heel and sauntered slowly toward the door. Applause broke out in the cluster of her girlfriends. She was their queen—a goddess! Mac Murphy had been tackled for a loss. Just before she reached the door, Rhonda turned around and surveyed the carnage one last time.

Then she calmly spoke to Mac, to the crowd, and to herself, "And another thing: *that cow was right*!"

Murphy said, "What did you say? C'mon Rhonda, let's talk about it."

+ + +

Mac Murphy limped around for a couple more days to leave no doubt about how badly he had been injured.

McCreedy went about his business and kept to himself. It seemed the whole school was shunning him, all except Woody. By Wednesday, he had developed a sort of hunched-over look, almost like Denny, but different somehow. He kept his eyes pointed straight ahead and ignored the whispered comments he heard behind his back. He told himself this was part of what every athlete had to learn. Hank said so.

It was going to be a long football season. McCreedy rode the bench for the rest of the year. The Panthers went five and five playing mostly uninspired, straight-ahead running offense.

McCreedy and Woody often played catch with a football in the evenings and on the weekends, though the Saturday games seemed to evaporate. Heck, we all would have played at the drop of a hat if he had called a game. He seemed as if he had forgotten who he was, but we didn't.

CHAPTER 19

The Kingfish Legacy

After football season in the northern states, autumn quickly begins its slide into winter. There is barely enough time to pause and enjoy the short burst of incredible color before the leaves come drifting down to earth. Most families are busy getting ready for the coming snow and cold, which predictably begins quite gracefully in late November. However, by mid-December, any introductory mercy in the winter weather pattern has usually been abandoned.

Halloween is one of the last youthful outdoor holiday events before the seasons change and the sun completes its relentless march south of the equator. At our age it wasn't as much fun as it used to be, though. I guess we were getting a little too old to feel comfortable going door to door and trick-or-treating, even if it did mean loading up a pillowcase with candy.

Still, a few things seemed to make perfect sense on Halloween. We made a clear and obvious choice. We would walk through the cemetery after dark. It was the scariest and most courageous thing we could think of. If we made it out alive, we would have bragging rights for the rest of our lives. If we died at the hands of some unseen spirits, so be it. We pretended to be prepared for the worst.

I guess we didn't really believe in all the "ghosts and goblins" stuff, but I know for a fact we were scared down to our skivvies about the whole thing. It was plain creepy.

For the record, because of Denny's mom, we asked him whether he wanted to opt out. Even as crass as we sometimes could be, we didn't want to accidentally hurt his feelings. But, in typical fashion, he was up for it. Denny wasn't keen on missing out on a good caper.

We got together at Jelly's house around suppertime, and his mom made us grilled cheese sandwiches and tomato soup. We didn't talk too much during the meal. I was reconsidering the wisdom of our plan. Still, we had told too many of our classmates about it to back out.

Darla wisely stayed home with her folks, handing out candy to the trick-or-treaters. She said walking through the cemetery sounded awful and a little dumb. Her decision was fine with me. I hate to admit it, but I didn't really want to share the experience with her in case I looked as scared as I thought I might. Or worse yet, if we chickened out completely.

For dessert we had some cupcakes that Jelly's mom had made every year since he was little. Tom was sort of embarrassed his mom would serve them to us. Decorated to look like little jack o' lanterns, they clearly looked like something for younger kids. He brought them in on a plate and asked in a high and wavering voice that sounded only slightly like Julia Child's, "Who wants cake?"

We sat around for an hour or so until the sun went down and then for another hour until the moon began to rise. Finally, I decided to shame the boys into action.

"Do you still want to do this? If you guys are too scared, we can call it off. Of course, with all the people we bragged to about it, we'd be branded as sissies forever. It's your call."

"I think you're the one who's scared. I ain't no sissy." Rex was ready.

Tom reminded us of something we all had blocked out of our thoughts. "And David's grave is up there, too. I think we should find it and maybe say a few words or something."

"Geez, Tom, are you still hung up on that eulogy thing? I think we should just stay on the road and not go walking around on any graves. It would be bad luck, man." Denny was serious.

"No, I think he's right. Let's look for David's grave. I would just like to visit it. We don't have to get weird about it. I've never been there. But Den is right. We should stay off the graves." As always, I was the voice of compromise.

We looked at each other and realized we had agreed on our general plan. Now, it seemed as if there was a valid reason to do it.

"We'd better go. The vampires probably wake up pretty soon."

That comment really ticked Rex off. Though ghosts and goblins were clearly not real, maybe vampires were worth getting a little worked up about.

"Emmet, you can be a real dumbass sometimes."

"Thank you, Mr. Hillstad."

"You're welcome. Dumbass."

We left Jelly's place around eight thirty. It was already very dark. The moon was just beginning to rise. It was going to be full and bright, just right for Halloween, and just right for a walk through the cemetery.

It didn't take long to get to the front gates. Maybe we wished it would take a little longer. They were always open . . . waiting. The cemetery was isolated and intimidating. There was no false bravado now. We were all a little edgy. A breeze was beginning to blow, and the brown oak leaves still clinging to the ends of the branches made an ominous rustling noise.

Denny finally spoke. "Well, here we are. Boy, this sure is a bunch of fun so far."

The moon was still low in the sky, but it lit up the scene well enough for us to see most of the grave markers standing row on row. The road through the cemetery was a single-lane dirt driveway. It got little traffic except during the week before Memorial Day and, of course, when there was a funeral.

We stood there for about as long as we could and then we walked together through the gate and into the cemetery. I was so scared my legs were shaking. Heck, Denny was so scared he couldn't even think of a wise-crack. I could hear Rex breathing deeply. Tom was the only one of us who seemed at ease. He spoke in his normal voice.

"I think I know where David's grave is. It's over there by the big pine tree. C'mon."

He set out walking diagonally across the graves and toward the place he had pointed to. We did our best to stop him from tramping on the graves, but he just kept walking. We hissed at him in loud whispers, and I don't know why we were whispering. I suppose we were just playing it safe, in case there *were* any ghosts to wake up.

The three of us hopped over and tiptoed between the slight mounds of the graves, carefully not stepping on any we could avoid. Jelly seemed oblivious to the possibility he might be causing the spirits of the deceased to roll over and reach up to grab him by the leg. We made sure there was adequate space between him and the three of us just in case it happened.

"Here it is." Tom had found David's grave.

We could make out the names on the stones in the moonlight. There were three identical small, flat, rectangular granite markers lying side by side, one each for David, his dad, and his uncle Art. There were no mottos or statements like "Rest in Peace" or anything like that, only their names and the years of their births and deaths.

Compared to the attention they received at the time of their murders, the location of their graves was one of anonymity at the back of the cemetery and away from the larger and more ornate stones marking those of wealthier people. Jelly sat down cross-legged right on David's grave and looked straight at his stone marker.

"Uh, Tom—are you sure you want to do this?" I put my hand on his shoulder.

"It's okay, M. I don't think he would mind." Tom's voice was soft and reassuring. Denny and Rex and I looked at each other, shrugged our shoulders and sat down. I can't believe we did it, but we sat right down there in front of the Patterson family's graves like we were sitting on the beach or in our front yard.

"Man, it's hard to relate to somebody our age being gone forever."

"Yeah, Tom, it is. Do you think maybe we can go now?"

"Pretty soon, M."

Then Denny said, "Guys, this isn't as scary as I thought it would be. It's kind of a cool place in a way."

"How do you mean?" I wasn't at all convinced yet.

"Well, we talked about this once. These gravestones kind of make me think of the Kingfish. We all carve our initials on the Kingfish because we want to make some kind of—I don't know, permanent mark. I think the names on these stones are like that in a way."

We understood what he was getting at. Rex said, "Yeah, I guess so. Too bad you've got to be dead to make this kind of mark, though."

Tom finally tuned back into our talk. "Denny's right, guys. It's the same thing. We all want to leave something behind. Otherwise, you're just gone. You know what I mean? We all hope to leave some kind of—legacy. I don't think David ever had his chance."

Denny cleared his throat. "I think we did a good thing when we carved David's name on the Kingfish. We left his mark for him. I think it's a whole lot better tribute than this stone."

"Yeah, me too." Rex was running his hand across the carving on David's marker.

Tom nodded a little bit. "Yes."

I was thinking about Tom's choice of words. As usual I was intrigued by his use of the language. Legacy wasn't a common word in the conversations of guys our age. I finally understood. They were right, of course. This stuff was important. By now I was talking in my normal voice and no longer whispering.

"Guys, maybe we *are* the legacy. I mean, you know . . . of our town. Maybe all that really matters is what we do while we are here together. Maybe it's not so much about what you leave behind, but what you do when you're alive that counts. What *we* do when *we're* together.

"I know for sure I don't want a funeral like David's. Maybe I'd leave instructions for a great big cake made to look like me. Instead of a bunch of sad speeches, I'll just have Tom stand up in front of my friends and ask, 'Who wants cake?' in that goofy voice. Then you guys can remember me while you're scarfing down a big chunk of the 'me' cake. And please, spare me all the talk about how 'natural' I look. I want a big old frosting smile. *And* I want *good* music, too. Smoky Robinson and Van Morrison."

We were all smiling now.

Tom nodded at me in the moonlight. "Mr. North, you are correct as always. Your profound insight is a gift to us who merely wait and listen for your impeccable wisdom."

"I just hope you can handle your part of it, Tom. Maybe you should write down the words. Remember? 'Who—wants—cake?' Can you handle it?"

He got serious again. "I mean it, M. It's right on target. I think David spent his whole life just trying to fit in with the rest of us and trying to get through school and all. He had to work harder for everything he had, which wasn't very much. But he had us and we had him as our friend. You're right. We shared some great times with David. That's what really matters. He and his dad and uncle were part of our town. Part of our legacy."

Denny said, "Yeah, his legacy for me was when he kicked my ass playing football. Man, he could block like crazy."

"I'll always remember when we blew up his birdhouse. Do you think they will ever find the guys who killed them?"

Suddenly, I opened the wrong can of worms. The killers were still a frightening subject. I think we had pretty well decided no ghosts, or witches, or zombies were going to get us. But all at once, I think we realized how just being out at night, even with a group of friends, could prove to be dangerous.

We decided to move on out of the cemetery and head back home. We had done what we set out to do, maybe a little more than that. Now we were in a hurry. We weren't as careful as when we had come in. We walked across the graves on our way back out to the dirt road. I guess we had decided we were not doing any harm to anybody. Or maybe we were just a little scared.

The moon was climbing high in the night sky. It shone down big and bright, and we could read some of the family names of our town displayed there for the four of us as we trudged past the grave markers. We recognized a lot of them. As Rex suggested, some were the same names carved on the Kingfish many years before.

We walked down the hill and across the tracks into town. The younger kids were done with their trick-or-treating. There were some pumpkins smashed and the pieces scattered on the sidewalk along Main Street. Rex and Denny said goodnight and split off in the direction of their end of town. Jelly and I headed in the other direction, toward the safety of our houses and waiting beds.

"Tom, I thought I'd feel different after walking through the cemetery. I thought I'd feel like we won something or beat something. I don't feel it." I was walking slowly and kicking a piece of pumpkin.

"Yeah, me too. I feel good, though. I think what we did up there was—I don't know—right."

"Maybe we shouldn't talk about it. Maybe we shouldn't brag about walking through the graveyard after all."

I thought about how different the actual experience was from what we had built it up to be. We stopped and looked at each other for a second. Then we both said, "Nahhh!"

The Freeman house was a block down to Lakeshore Drive.

"This is where I get off. Are you good to walk the rest of the way alone or should we ask my mom to drive you?"

"No, I'm fine. See you, Tom."

As I watched him walk away toward the lights of his house, I felt a rush of the same irrational fear as I had experienced when we first entered the gates of the cemetery. This time I wasn't worried about some ethereal, ghostly danger. This time I was scared stiff to think I was going to walk the last six blocks all by myself with the possibility of a killer lurking somewhere close by. I was embarrassed to think I might be afraid of the dark. "Knock it off," I said out loud to myself.

I walked the first half block before instinct got the best of me. My pace began to speed up until I was moving at a trot. It only lasted a few steps before I broke into a full-throttle sprint.

I could easily see the streets and the yards in the moonlight. I kept my eyes straight ahead and tried not to look off into the darkness, where I was worried the killer could be matching my frenzied pace, stride for stride.

As I approached my block, I felt the eerie realization I had to run right past the Pattersons' house just before reaching my safe haven. There it was, dark and abandoned, an empty monument to fear and death. A haunted house if ever there was one. Since the people were gone, it was only a shell filled with mysteries unsolved and secrets no one should ever know. The light from the full moon poured in through the windowpanes, and I could see the shifting shadows of the living room furniture as I ran. At least, it's what I hoped I saw.

Fear's sharp and piercing claws grasped at my back and threatened to reach in between my shoulder blades and tear my pounding heart right out of my chest. I was overcome by real and deep fright born not from some childish imaginary goblins but from a grown-up understanding of how evil can exist even on the block where you live.

By the time I burst through the back door and into the kitchen I was gasping for breath. Dad was sitting in the living room watching the late news. How could he be so calm?

"Hi, son. Keep it down, will you? Your mom and Jack are asleep. What did you do tonight?"

I was still huffing and puffing. "Well, Dad, we . . . walked through the cemetery."

"Really?"

"Yeah."

"Hey, that's pretty good. Were you scared?"

"Not really."

"So—you just decided to go for a late-night run?"

I smiled at him. He had figured me out again like he always did. "No. It was a little weird coming home alone from Tom's place."

"I'm glad you're home M. You'd better get some sleep."

"Goodnight, Dad."

"Goodnight, pal."

"Say, Dad? Have you ever thought about what your legacy might be?"

"My . . . legacy? Well, I guess you and Jack are my legacy. You boys are about all your mom and I will ever need."

"Hmm."

"Go to bed, will you? Your questions are too hard for this late."

"I love you, Dad."

"I love you too, M."

He was probably still thinking about my odd question even after I had gone off to bed. For a little while, I lay there thinking about David smiling down at me during our last football game as he helped me up from the ground.

CHAPTER 20

CHRISTMAS 1967

There is no greater time of year than Christmas. Even part-time Christians sing along with the familiar Christmas carols and recite the proper Bible verses. Our hearts were glad, and during this very special time, we felt like better people. Certainly, this is part of what it's all about: a time for personal spiritual rebirth. At any rate, I don't know anyone who doesn't get a little extra religion during Christmas.

In our town, nativity scenes were seemingly displayed everywhere. My favorite was the one in front of the Methodist church. It was made of plaster and had been around for a lot of Christmases. At some point the baby Jesus must have gotten broken and was replaced with one which was noticeably oversized compared to Joseph, Mary, and the rest of the cast of holy characters. Denny nicknamed this version "Big J."

And of course, there are the presents. This factor varied from house to house, but even in the homes of poor people like us, there were usually a few more gifts than family members to open them.

On face value, the giving appears to be all about the person receiving the presents. But really, we all know it is about the love among family members and friends. It excites you when you are young, and it sustains you when you are no longer young. It makes the food you eat taste better and the time and space you share seem like the best place on earth. Objects can't do that, only people.

A lot of the stuff exchanged between people at Christmas eventually ends up either broken or worn out, or maybe not ever used at all. There weren't very many presents under our little tree, but there was something for everyone, and it was enough.

And, of course, there was the food. Christmas dinner is perhaps the best family gathering of the year. Food was pretty cheap in those days. Since Mom had come home, it was more plentiful, too. Cooking was a tangible reflection of her bountiful focus on family. Mom's great cooking abilities were always on display at Christmastime.

Even Dad got into the act. His strong right arm was stirring the divinity candy 'round and 'round until it got so stiff, he could barely move the wooden spoon in the big crockery bowl. Then he would solemnly proclaim, "It's time," and the sweet, white stuff was plopped into little gobs on waxed paper and allowed to cool. Well, most of it, anyway. Jack and I always managed to snitch some of the delicious goo while it was still hot. Mom pretended to object, but we knew she expected it. This same scene played out every year.

Finally, there was an important and significant part of Christmas that doesn't get a lot of consideration: two weeks off from school. True, it is a time for all people. But mostly Christmas is, as it has always been, a season for kids.

School let out at noon on December 23rd, and it wouldn't reconvene until after the New Year. In a somewhat unexpected twist, Darla's parents had decided to fly off to California and spend the holidays with Carmen's family. Darla said Carmen's dad had been talking to Marty about how great his new job was and how many opportunities there were out there.

I had sort of hoped our families could get together over Christmas, but it was not an option now. They planned to go directly to the airport in Minneapolis after her folks picked Darla up from school. We hurriedly exchanged gifts in the school lobby as she waited for them to come. She gave me a great jackknife, and I gave her a stupid little blue glass vase. She pretended it was really special.

Then suddenly Marty and Deedee were there, and she rushed outside after giving me a quick hug. "I'll see you next year! Merry Christmas, Emmet."

She waved and smiled her beautiful smile as she ran down the sidewalk and away. I looked again at the jackknife. The side panels were made of actual deer horn, and it had a little silver shield on it stamped with the brand name, Old Timer. It was a high-quality little knife meant to last a long time. I wondered if the goofy little vase would even survive the trip.

There usually seemed to be somebody invited to join us for our holiday meal. On Christmas Eve, Uncle Harry and Molly came over for supper. Old Sam was there too. At five thirty we sat down to a feast. Mom really outdid herself. She roasted a turkey *and* a ham. There were Swedish breads, Swedish date cookies, and sausages. There were white potatoes and sweet potatoes. And for good measure, Mom made Swedish meatballs. The leftovers that Mom didn't send home with our guests usually lasted several days.

As soon as I sat down, I grabbed for the bowl of mashed potatoes, only to be frozen by Mom's icy stare. I slowly pulled back my hand as she commanded: "Let us bow our heads and say grace."

I felt a little sheepish how obviously unimpressed she was with my enthusiasm for her cooking. I guess Mom had come to know that if anyone was going to say a dinner prayer, it would have to be her. Meals would be a free-for-all if it was up to Dad, Jack, and me. On the other hand, she always prayed quietly, even if it was only her.

She closed her eyes and bowed her head. We all did likewise. I kept one eye open and watched her. She was beautiful. Unlike my dream of her praying in the yard, I heard every word, and I believed.

"Dear Heavenly Father, on this, the celebration of the eve of the birth of Your Son Jesus, our personal savior, we ask Your blessing on this house and on our meal. Thank You for the love we share, and for our health. And thank You for the knowledge that You keep us safe from all evil, both seen and unseen. Dear God, we thank You for the greatest gift of all, the joy and the hope embodied in Jesus Christ and given as a gift to each and every one of us. In His name we pray. Amen."

"Amen."

She finally opened her eyes and looked at me with a stern face. Then she winked and we smiled big smiles. All was well. Immediately, we began talking and passing bowls of wonderful food and enjoying the banquet she had put before us.

I thought about how she was the source of our family's hope and inspiration. Mom getting well again was the greatest gift we could ever have.

As we ate and chatted, my mind wandered. I thought about Darla and her parents so far away out west in California. I imagined what Christmas might be like in such a place. In my mind's eye I saw a decorated palm tree in the living room of a brand-new trailer house, with Christmas lights and tinsel and a heap of brightly colored presents. I imagined Deedee and Marty singing Christmas carols in their highly stylized country/rock-and-roll/Las Vegas kind of way. I wondered if Carmen had a boyfriend and if he was eating dinner with the Day family right now instead of me. I felt a twinge when I thought of Darla, and for a minute I wondered if I should try to give her a call after supper. Regretfully, I never got around to doing it.

+ + +

While ours was a bit chaotic, the Briggs home was neat and warm and completely organized. Faith, her little sister, and her two younger brothers sat at the Duncan Phyfe dining room table and waited patiently until John and Bonnie Briggs sat down. As they had done so many times before, they joined hands and, on John's cue, began to recite the dinner prayer in unison:

"Bless us, oh Lord, and these Thy gifts, which we are about to receive from Thy bounty through Christ our Lord. Amen. In the name of the Father, and the Son, and the Holy Spirit, Amen." In perfect coordination, they let go of each other's hands and made the sign of the cross.

John Briggs nodded in approval, and Bonnie Briggs smiled lovingly at her family. Like her oldest daughter's, her smile could light up the room. She looked at them one by one and counted her blessings.

Faith was neatly dressed, as always. She was growing up so fast. Bonnie secretly hoped she had finally outgrown her on-again, off-again boyfriend, Smith, and would maybe meet someone her own age. The older boy just didn't fit with John and Bonnie's plans for Faith. She was smart and incredibly talented in so many ways. Smith just looked like trouble . . . and he played in a rock and roll band!

Her younger daughter, Lizzy, resembled a smaller version of her older sister, but her personality was all her own. A corner of the wrapping paper was picked off every one of Lizzy's presents under the tree. John Briggs had barely said "Amen" when Lizzy chirped, "Amen, and thank you, Sarge! I mean *Daddy*!"

Sarge (Daddy) offered a bit of a scowl but couldn't hold out for long. The imitation frown quickly became a smile. He had to turn his head away and chuckle.

Bonnie studied her husband's ruggedly handsome face as he carved the roast. His eyes had seen a lot of things in Korea most men would hope never to see. She looked at the faces of her two young sons and wondered how many of the little boys sitting at their Christmas Eve supper tables in 1967 would end up wading through Vietnamese rice paddies or crawling wounded in the rain forests north of Saigon. She blocked the thought from her mind and cheerfully said, "Merry Christmas, family! Let's eat!"

In the living room, the TV news was just ending. "As you know, tonight is Christmas Eve. As we report the news from around the world, it is clear not everyone is enjoying dinner with their family, and not everyone will be opening Christmas presents later this evening or tomorrow on Christmas Day. For those who are, we wish you the very best of the holiday season. And for those who may be far from home or otherwise unable to be with their loved ones, we offer you our thoughts and prayers for reunion, and the hope of the true meaning of Christmas to resonate tonight throughout this changing world we live in. I'm Walter Cronkite, and that's the way it is—tonight, December 24th, 1967. Goodnight."

CHAPTER 21

THE AMERICAN DREAM

Walt Sprague had heard all the jokes about the cement boat. Some of the locals even referred to it as "Sprague's Folly." But he had left nothing to chance when he wrote the original documents that detailed the engineering and measurements. Of course, the data was theoretical and only meant to prove the point on paper. But building the real thing had been a dream of Walt's since he first did the research. Yet somehow the quest had eluded him thus far.

Since the Patterson murders, Walt believed if ever there was a right time or a right reason to build it, this was probably it. As far as he was concerned, the hard part was not whether the boat would float. The bigger question was if it could somehow help change the image of Bay City back to what it was before the murders.

Ferro-cement boats were not a new concept. They had been built in many parts of the world and even used by the US Navy. This was where Walt first became interested in the idea. However, floating one on Lake Pepin had never been done. It was time.

First, he built an exact scale replica using the same materials called for in the prototype design. He floated the initial small one in his bathtub and then a larger one in the pond behind the house. He knew it was mathematically correct, and he was completely confident a bigger boat would float as well as the models did. To hell with the critics and jokesters! He had made a pretty penny on the textbook. Still, it always burned him a little when someone at Stella's chided him about the idea of "building a submarine for fishing on the bottom."

On the morning of Monday, January 1, 1968, Walt began building his first ever Ferro-cement boat in his pole shed, up on the higher ground at the back side of his pond. The pole shed had standard-size garage doors that hinged open on the north end of the building. Walt used the shed to change the oil on his pickup or the family car, or when he wanted to tinker with a carburetor. However, on the south end of the building, the end that faced the lake, Walt had fashioned a system of cables and pulleys attached to a large electric winch. The entire end wall of the pole shed was designed to open up like wings and swing away on each side, thus allowing Walt to build his boats inside and move them out when they were finished. Homemade heavy-duty welded hinges were attached at the corners of the building, and the entire massive contraption moved along two swinging arcs on metal wheels attached to heavy-duty axles.

Within a week he had the framework skeleton built. It could have been the backbone of a Viking longship, except for the squared-off stern. It was going to be precisely 40 feet long, a monster by Lake Pepin standards. Altogether, the boat would take around six months to build. Walt was a very disciplined and meticulous builder. He took his time and didn't cut corners. Its name would not be "Sprague's Folly." He would call her *American Dream.*

She would be powered by two gleaming V-8 Oldsmobile motors, direct from the plant in Belvedere, Illinois. The trim would be solid teak imported from Brazil and the fittings solid brass. When completed, a mast would rise ten feet above her cabin. Its only purpose would be to display the stars and stripes. The hull would be made of reinforced Ferro-cement construction. Though the mass of the boat would be considerable, she was designed to displace only two feet of water.

This one would be unlike any other boat he had ever built. His trademark workboats were fine crafts in their own right. However, they were specifically designed for utilitarian purposes. The *American Dream* would be purely a pleasure craft. The *Dream* would be Walt's finest effort. A great deal of aesthetic focus and downright luxury were needed. And of course, she had to behave just as well as the many boats he had built before her.

He aimed to take her down the Mississippi all the way to New Orleans with Dolly at his side. This boat would be the symbol of his life's work and would provide a second honeymoon for Dolly and him. Together they would take the *American Dream* all the way to the Gulf Coast shoreline and through the Keys to Miami, where the *Dream* would hopefully be sold for a respectable sum. Even before he had begun, Walt had found the broker he would use to sell the *Dream.* The broker estimated it could be worth over a hundred thousand dollars, but it had to be a proven vessel.

And then there was the other compelling reason. The town needed something to change the horrible reputation it had accidentally gained from the Patterson murders—something positive and inspiring to take the town's attention away from the ugliness of the past and onto a better image of its future.

The time Walt would spend with Dolly, cruising down the length of the greatest river in the world, would be a dream come true—*his* American dream. Now it was time to turn the vision into reality.

On January 14th, the Packers won Super Bowl II. The entire state celebrated their victory over the powerful silver-and-black-clad Raiders. Good had triumphed over evil. For the moment, things were looking right in the world.

The days stretched into weeks, and eventually, around the end of February, the thin plywood outer hull began to take shape. Dad had gotten interested early on when Walt began disappearing for extended periods without any explanation. He remembered Walt had said he had a project in mind and might need the Burner. At some point Walt had muttered something about a cement boat.

He was fascinated with his friend's remarkable imagination and wanted to be part of it in some way. Hopefully, his years and skills working with concrete could come in handy. That is, if Walt would allow anybody but himself to pick up a trowel.

Brick stayed away and let his friend work until finally he couldn't take the curiosity any longer. He showed up at Walt's garage one morning, and that was that. Walt knew why he was there, and Dad just pitched in and started helping out, and following Walt's lead. Thereafter, Dad worked side-by-side with Walt every chance he had, between plowing snow and keeping the town thawed out, shoveled, and generally running smoothly.

Walt's focus was structural perfection and engineering detail. The surface area of the thin plywood exterior hull and the interior cavity volume of the ferro concrete determined whether the total weight of the boat displaced just the right volume of water to allow it to float. This part of the design needed to be perfect.

"Uh, Walt. Can we talk?"

"Sure. What's up?"

"Well, I want to lay the cement. Not because you can't do it, but you can't do it as well as *I* can."

A quizzical look came over Walt's face. It was clear he needed additional convincing, and Dad was prepared.

"Look, I know you've done the research and I know you have the design engineering down pat. And that surely is not my thing. What I am good at—I mean *really* good at—is putting down the mud. I don't want to offend you, Walt, but I just know it will turn out better if you let me handle this part. What do you say?"

"Well, I guess you've been thinking a lot about it. Now let me ask you a couple questions. First, we need to install the screen over the plywood. Then the cement needs to be exactly two and three-quarters inches thick. Less than that, and it will not be structurally sound. If it's even three inches thick, we risk having it ride too low in the water, or worse. Okay, my friend, what do *you* say? Are *you* up for this?"

"I can handle it. You just tell me exactly what you want done and I will do it to your specs. I know how important this is to you—hell, to the whole town. I promise you won't be disappointed."

"Well, it's settled then. Do you still have your tools?"

"Thanks, Walt. Yeah, I still have what we need."

"Great. One last thing, though. I think I may need to repossess the Burner. My boat needs its toilet pretty soon. I might have come up with a different solution to your holding tank problem."

"What? Really? Now what have you got in mind?"

"Well, it's a holding tank all right, but an upgrade from most of the ones you are familiar with. When the time comes, I will let you know. Do you trust me?"

"Heck, yes, I trust you, Walt—like I would trust my own brother."

"Okay, you're officially in charge of the cement work. You realize this is the part of the plan everybody has been giving me a hard time about for years, right?"

"Don't try to talk me out of it. You can still take all the credit when it's done. Besides, an amateur like me will make a great scapegoat if anything goes wrong."

"I never thought of it that way. This is sounding better and better."

"Baaa."

"*Like hell!*"

The oversized engine compartment was designed to allow a person to stand upright, to better appreciate the motors. This was a tilt toward the novelty aspect of the boat. Because of the potential public display factor, even the engine compartment needed to look especially good. Whoever would buy this one would want to show it off.

Dad knew a guy from Red Wing named Al Kind who had perfected a painting process allowing two different colors of paint to sort of splatter together, creating a speckled look. Al called it Comet Tone. He had patented the process and there was even some talk about one of the Big Three automakers buying it to use in the trunks of their cars. So far, though, it belonged to Al.

Virtually everything he could get his hands on was Comet Toned. Even his car was Comet Toned. Al had managed to convince his friend Shorty Black to Comet Tone all the booths at Shorty's Tavern in Red Wing. He used a combination of red and blue splatter. The result had a somewhat disturbing effect on one's vision. When you entered Shorty's, your eyes took a moment to adjust to the clash of colors, and customers occasionally reported slight dizziness. Al delighted in this, but Shorty wasn't thrilled. Still, Al had given him a big price break, and he couldn't afford a do-over. So far, Comet Tone hadn't crossed the river to Bay City.

Dad suggested Al's Comet Tone system would really set off the design of an otherwise common part of the boat. Walt thought this was great. The engine room would be Comet Toned, though Walt said he wanted to pick out the color combination. Now they only needed to convince Al.

Walt also planned to install one of his fire-powered toilets in the boat's head. The *American Dream* was shaping up to be a veritable World's Fair of inventions and forward thinking. Walt's genius was driving the project, but Dad supplied a lot of the muscle, and there was no question both men were passionate about the eventual outcome.

Walt thought he could finish the project sometime in late June. Dad suggested, "Why don't we talk to Dale about having a parade on the Fourth of July? It could end in Lakeshore Park, and you could launch the *Dream* on Independence Day."

Walt smiled and lit up his pipe. He smiled and shook Dad's hand. With a big wink he said, "Outstanding!"

Dad nodded his head and repeated "Outstanding! We'd better try to get Dale down here. You talk to Dale, and I'll call Al Kind."

Walt left the whole Comet Tone matter up to Brick. Since he wasn't very much of a salesman, Dad figured the best way to convince Al Kind to be part of the *American Dream* project would involve beer, lots and lots of beer. Mom would clearly not approve. Dad called Al while she was resting. He kept his voice low.

"Hello Al—Brick. Yeah! How are you? Long time, no see. How about getting together for a few beers? Well, how about Friday night? All right. Why don't you come over and we'll hit Hunt's for a couple cold ones? I've got something I want to show you. Okay, I'll see you then."

Mom appeared at the bedroom door.

"I heard every word you said, Marion. What are you cooking up? Who is Al? You had better not come in late expecting any attention from me, mister! If you stay out late, I will not be awake when you get home."

"Rae, this is important. I need to introduce Al Kind to Walt. It's something about the boat he's building. Don't ask me too many questions, okay?"

"Try to be quiet when you get home, and do not do anything illegal or dangerous."

"Dang. It sort of takes all the fun out of it, doesn't it?"

They smiled at each other, and Mom shook her head. The trap was set, and Al Kind was about to be captured.

Friday night arrived, and Dad went to meet Al at Hunt's Tavern around seven. Walt was planning on coincidentally being there, too. After a few drinks, they would all go down to the shed to see the boat. There was no way Al could turn them down if he had the chance to see the *Dream* in person.

Al Kind was a man of diverse interests. The Comet Tone gig was only part of his story. Besides Al's painting business, he was a professional clown. He worked at the local carnivals and parades in summer, and he hired on to the circuses when they passed through the Twin Cities. In the fall, Al worked at the Minnesota State Fair. As he said, he was always "clowning around." He was in his forties but tried to act and talk younger. He wasn't really a hippie but more like an alum of the Beatnik period.

Late Friday afternoon, Al had made a visit to St. John's Hospital in his clown makeup to cheer up a little girl with leukemia. Al joked that St. John's Hospital had a hotline with his number on it. As he also said: "Clowning isn't all fun and games."

He always managed to keep his clown persona intact while he visited the sick kids, but he occasionally broke down in his car afterward. This was one of those days.

He would have had time to change out of his clown gear, but Al figured Brick would get a kick out him showing up at Hunt's as "Bobo." Also, it was a great way to meet women.

At seven o'clock, Dad and Walt were stationed at the bar. It was a pretty good night, with a crowd of the usual natives mingling with campers and a few stray visitors from out of town. At 7:10 the door flew open, and there was Bobo the Clown in all his glory.

Bobo was patterned after a "sad clown" persona with the ragged suit, crumpled top hat, and painted-on frown. Al's shtick in a bar was very different from the sensitive role he had played earlier on in the day. This was his chance to cut loose. It seems a clown disguise allows you to get by with saying just about anything to anybody without getting punched out for it. Bobo made the most of it.

"Yo, tar-bender, I mean bartender, fix me up with a cold one. You there with the fat ass, how about letting me sit down? I've been on my feet all day."

With that, he held up one of his giant flat shoes. Immediately the crowd was on his side and laughter was breaking out all over the room.

Bobo's pockets were filled with magic tricks and pranks of every kind. He had a buzzer on his middle finger to tickle the palm of an unsuspecting sucker who shook hands with him. There was a plastic mustard container with a piece of yellow string crafted to look like a stream of mustard shooting out at his victim. And of course, Bobo had a bouquet of plastic flowers tucked up his sleeve and ready to present to some lucky young lady. Over the course of the night, each of these would make an appearance when the time was right.

Molly Hunt bought him his first beer, and Uncle Harry set it up. And so, it began. Dad knew Al well, but he wasn't exactly sure what to do about the whole clown thing. He hadn't planned for this. Walt frowned and quipped, "So, this *clown* is the guy you told me about?"

"Very funny, Walt. Trust me, the Comet Tone idea will work. We just need to get him down to your shed to see the *Dream*."

Just then Bobo spotted Dad. "Brick the Bear! Ist dat you, Mein Herr? Ha! I'm a poet and I didn't know it!"

"Hi, Al., C'mon over."

The clown skipped across the barroom floor and hopped up onto Dad's lap. "Kiss me, you big lug!" Bobo planted one right on Dad's lips.

So far, this was definitely not going according to plan. Hunt's Bar was in a state of utter chaos. Though Dad was popular, he was possibly the least likely character to take part in Bobo's personal vaudeville routine. Several of the customers were in tears, and others were laughing so hard they were having trouble catching their breath.

"Oh man, Al, knock it off, will you? I've got something important to talk to you about. This is Walt Sprague. Walt is building a boat, and, well, we need Comet Tone."

Immediately Bobo the Clown began to melt away and Al Kind, the entrepreneur, quickly emerged. The kooky vocal inflections were gone, and a serious look came over his painted face. Now they were talking about Al's true passion, his greatest achievement. Al Kind, still dressed as Bobo the Clown, shifted into his best marketing pitch.

"Gentlemen, Comet Tone *is* the future, and the future is now. If we are talking about Comet Tone, I can only imagine we are talking about something so new, so different, only Comet Tone will do. Did you say something about a boat? Comet Tone has natural waterproofing qualities unsurpassed for strength and durability."

Walt stared in disbelief at the unstoppable selling machine that was Al, alias Bobo. This was just a little too strange. He muttered under his breath, "Am I hallucinating?"

Dad put his hand on Al's forearm. "Al, I think we all need to drink a lot more. We need this done for free, at least for a while."

For a second Al's facial expression mimicked Bobo's frown. "Brick, are you telling me that you brought me over here to hustle me for free paint? That's just not cool, man. I thought we were friends. Just not cool, man."

"Hold on now, Al. You need to hear me out on this. This is a very good thing." Al was starting to get a little steamed. The Comet Tone deal was quickly disintegrating. Walt intervened.

"Al, Brick says this Comet Tone of yours is the real thing. I would like very much for your paint system to be part of the *American Dream*, which I am building in my backyard. I am willing to pay for it if I have to, but I really can't afford much. My wife and I have wiped out most of our savings to build this boat because our town needs something to be proud of, and this is something I can do.

"Are you familiar with the story of the Patterson murders? Besides being a heck of a piece of engineering, I want this boat to help change everybody's feeling of what Bay City is like. It's a good town, Al, with a lot of good people here. I hate that our hometown is famous for something as horrible as those murders. What do you say?"

Al shut up and listened for the first time. "Maybe we'd better order a pitcher."

For the next hour or so, the three men huddled together and discussed the Patterson murders and the numbing effect they had on Bay City. Walt shared his vision of the boat with Al, and he also assured him that when it sold, he would likely be paid well and would settle up for the paint job then. Since it was not conventional construction, it would somewhat limit the number of people who might be interested in it. However, those who were would probably recognize the value. This was the nature of the *Dream.*

By the time he finished telling the story, all three of the conspirators were fairly loaded, and Al Kind was generally on board with the plan.

"Gentlemen, I think we need to have a look at this *American Dream* of yours. Tar-bender! A fifth of tequila to go, fine sir! Brick, please pay the man. Let's vamonos!"

The three of them left, with Bobo taking a bow as he made his grand departure. They walked together down the steep Main Street hill and around the corner to Walt's pole shed. Walt and Al passed the bottle of tequila as they went. Bobo's clown feet caused soft slapping sounds as the men made their way in the cold, clear, late February night. By the time they reached the shed, each had tasted the tequila more than a few times and were serenely intoxicated. Walt flipped the light switch, and Al saw the *American Dream* for the first time.

"Holy macaroni! This sure is a big boat. Did you say this thing is made of concrete?"

"No, not just concrete. It's Ferro-cement. So, there's a composite of chicken wire, and plywood, and glue, and a lot of other stuff."

"And you really think this thing will float?"

"Yup. I know it will."

"I think you're dreaming!"

"Well, yes, I guess I am, Al. I figure you can only do big things if you dream big dreams, don't you think? The paint needs to be heavy. It acts as the inside skin over the cement. There will be tiny wire ends that will be close to the surface of the concrete because that's how we know how to get the right thickness, and—"

Al Kind held up his white-gloved hand to interrupt Walt.

"Oh man! This is too good to be true. And you guys think *I'm* crazy! I have *got* to be in on this. I gotta say I don't understand the smarty-pants science lingo, man. But I know a little about paint. As far as I can tell, Comet Tone was *made* for a job like this. It'll be almost like a rubber membrane. Now why don't you show me those jacked-up motors you told me about? I think I will understand the *vroom-vroom* part."

They continued to crawl around on the partly finished boat for over an hour, laughing and talking, with Al and Walt passing the tequila bottle between them.

Finally, Al leaned over to Dad and said, "Am I drunk enough yet? I really could use some sleep. Okay, I'll paint this thing for you. No charge. I think I'd better head home now before you decide I need to pay *you* for the privilege."

"Not in this condition, you're not. You can stay at our house tonight. Rachel just loves clowns."

"Too easy, Brick. You're makin' it too easy."

"What do mean? I don't get it."

"All right, I guess you're gonna make me say it: *she must—she married you, didn't she?*"

"Oh, good one."

Dad and Al headed slowly back up the hill to Hunt's where Al's car was parked. Walt walked across the backyard, stopping only briefly to pee. Dale Thorsdall was coming over in the morning for a look at the *Dream.*

Al shut off the lights and turned off the ignition as they rolled silently into our front yard. They agreed to do their best not to wake up Mom. The medication she was taking would help out some. She slept deeply because of the effects of the pain pills.

They managed to sneak in undiscovered, and Dad showed Al where he would sleep. Then Dad led Al to the bathroom and mimed a demonstration of how the burner on the toilet worked. It was totally lost on Al, who thought the toilet was just a funny-looking conventional water version.

Al closed the door. His head was spinning, and he almost tipped forward into the big stainless-steel toilet. He decided he'd better sit down. When he did, the nearly empty tequila bottle fell out of his oversized pocket and made a clanging noise on the metal stool. He quickly grabbed the bottle mid-bounce and smiled proudly to himself, considering the terrific catch he had just made.

Al had seen enough of the tequila for one night. He stood up and dumped the last remnants of the bottle into the toilet. Still bending over, he pushed the ignition button as his friend had showed him. Instantly, the tequila caught fire and a blue flame shot straight up out of the toilet.

As he tried to slide unnoticed into bed next to Mom, Dad heard Al make a startled sound and he quietly slid back out again, whispering, "Oh no."

Mom groggily asked, "Brick, is that you? Who is out there in our bathroom?"

"Hi, honey, it's nothing. Al Kind is sleeping on the couch tonight. Go back to sleep. I'll check it out."

A slightly singed Al appeared at the door of the bathroom as Dad came around the corner in the short hall separating the bedrooms. Both men were startled and let out a short "AHH!"

Fortunately, Al did not appear to have sustained any burns, though the air smelled acrid from the combination of burnt clown hair and real hair.

Al croaked, "Brick, is there anything you want to tell me?"

Dad sheepishly whispered, "Walt is putting one of these in the boat, too. Pretty nifty, eh?"

The two men giggled like little boys. They held their index fingers up to their mouths and said, "SHHHH!" Then Al hugged his old friend, and they laughed some more.

So, there they were: co-conspirators in a great caper, laughing at a crazy exploding toilet in the middle of the night. Al was definitely the right man to paint the *American Dream.*

Next morning, Al sneaked out before anyone else was up at our house. He must have made quite a sight driving back to Red Wing that Saturday morning, still a little scorched from his adventures of the night before. He left a big brown cigar on the kitchen table for Dad.

Walt, the stoic academic, awoke with an epic hangover. Even the stout coffee brewing in the kitchen sounded too loud. He had invited Dale Thorsdall over to see the *Dream* and possibly talk about a parade. When he arrived, Dale posed the familiar question usually asked about a Ferro-cement boat.

"Will she float, Walt?"

"Without a doubt. It's all in the weight-versus-displacement conversions."

"Yeah, yeah, Walt, sure, I believe you. Uh, I don't want to sound negative here or anything, but is this thing insured?"

"You know Dale, I think maybe you are on to something. I didn't think about insuring it when it was just a pile of plywood and chicken wire, but by God, she's a real boat now, isn't she? What do you think of her?"

"By Jesus, Walt, this is one *beautiful* boat. What in the holy land of Canaan ever inspired you to build this thing? It looks like something the president should be riding around in on the Potomac River—or me, maybe."

"Well, I'll admit it's pretty big, but I don't think it's quite up to presidential standards. Besides, that old goat is a Democrat."

"Hey, watch it! *I'm* a Democrat! Do you want to get this thing insured or not?"

"Sorry, old boy. What do you say? Can you get me some coverage?"

"Well, not every company will insure boats, especially high end or specialty craft like this one. This is a Limited Market Placement if there ever was one. Farmers and Mechanics might do it. I'll have to check. What did it cost to build her, anyway?"

"I guess I have about seventy-five thousand or so into the materials. Oh hell, Dale, I've got just about everything we own into it. If something happens to her, I'm sunk. No pun intended."

"Yeah, interesting choice of words, Walt. *Whoo-ee!* It's a lot of bucks. I think maybe we'd better go for some excess coverage on this one. Y'know? The market value is likely over and above the actual cost. It's not like you could just go out and buy another one if something happens to her. I'll see what I can do. If I understand it, you only need it insured until it sells in Florida, right?"

"Yep, that's right. Dolly and I plan to leave on the trip downriver around November 1st, just before the snow starts flying and the ice moves in. The trip should take a couple weeks maybe, and hopefully we can unload her in Miami and come home. I guess I need the policy for around five months."

"How much do you think you can sell her for?"

"I don't know, I thought I'd ask one-ten and go from there. If she sells for a little less, I just need to cover my costs and hope we have enough left over for bus fare home."

"I'll ask F and M for two hundred fifty thousand. All they can do is say no. They'll want to take a look at it. Heck Walt, once they see this *American Dream* of yours, you'll get your policy. I'm pretty sure they'll set it up for six months. It seems like a pretty low risk. It will still be expensive, but what the hell, it's only money, right?"

"Yeah, right. *My* money. Just about every last cent of it."

"What about this Fourth of July launch? As mayor of our fair village, I proclaim this a hell of a good idea! I'm all for it! What can I do to help set it up?"

"Well, we'll need to use the village tractor to tow it down to the landing ramp, and we need a parade. And I think it would be great if we had some kind of picnic or dance or something afterward. Shoot, one of the reasons I started this crazy project was so Bay City could get known for something besides the Patterson murders. I want to celebrate a little. What do you think?"

"I think I can handle it. Shit-fire Walt, I'll go you one better. We'll have a firework display like this town has never seen before! We'll light up the sky over the harbor, and your *American Dream* will be christened with a bottle of champagne the way they do the big ocean liners. As far as I can tell, it's about the same size as one of 'em! Sound good?"

"Outstanding."

CHAPTER 22

THE WOLF

Fritz Michaels was not a good-looking man. He might have been, if not for the ugly scar on his upper lip. Heavy and purplish, it carved his mouth into a permanent sneer. It was a gift from his father at a very early age. It wasn't the only scar he carried courtesy of his father, just the only visible one. It all combined into a constant, festering hatred, which, above all else, is what made him the truly repulsive human being he turned out to be.

After his mother died, Fritz was raised by his grandmother. She moved them away from the bad memories in Iowa, up north to Minneapolis. She legally changed his last name to hers in an attempt to erase all evidence of the evil the little boy had endured. It didn't quite do the job.

In his early teens he quit going to school. When he wanted a car, he took the keys from his grandmother. He used as much force as necessary. It never really took very much. Usually, he just had to shove her around a little. Once in a while, a little more. Eventually, she called the police, and they helped him move out. At sixteen, he was on his own.

Michaels worked many odd jobs but never really settled into anything for more than a few months. He had been a cook at a local diner for a while, and after that he was an orderly in a psychiatric hospital. He lost the job when he was caught stealing medications from the patients. It got him a year's probation and his first brush with the court system. It wasn't his last.

Even before he was legally old enough to drink, he found ways to get booze, and he started getting high on Benzedrine whenever he could buy a few tablets from one of the drivers at the Starlight truck stop. One night in a drunken, speed-induced rage, he started a woman's car on fire because she refused to give him her phone number. She was twice his age. That decision got him a year at the Stillwater prison.

Fritz Michaels was bound to be bad. All the signs were there: traumatized and abused as a child, a violent temper, drug and alcohol abuse. He did his time with only a few altercations with the other prisoners and turned twenty-one behind bars. When he finally walked out a free man, he managed to stay out of trouble for only three weeks. Then he killed his first man.

On a beautiful night in August, he was staggering home from McGrath's Tavern and stopped to pee in an alley just off Selby Street. A guy who happened to walk into the same alley from the other end of the block merely made an unfortunate choice. He paid for it with his life. There was no quarrel, no fight. The guy just startled him when he walked too close, and Michaels happened to have a gun.

The police arrested him the next morning while he was still in bed. He was in the back seat of the squad car before he could remember what he had done.

Michaels went back to Stillwater, this time in the maximum-security section. The rules were a lot tougher than in medium security. So were the inmates. The things he experienced in prison at first broke him down but then slowly built him up into something different and even more frightening. He was hardened by the fights and by obsessively lifting weights. He had borne witness to virtually every sort of dehumanizing treatment imaginable, whether by the guards or by the other inmates. He inflicted as much pain and degradation as he experienced. Eventually, there was little left of human emotion.

Fritz had a lot of time to think about what it would take to make things right again. After what seemed a lifetime, he completed his sentence in Stillwater. By the time he got out, he was nearly thirty. He was cold and soulless—an angry, dangerous, and completely feral human animal.

The first thing he did on the outside was get a large tattoo of a snarling wolf in the middle of his chest. Among all the others, it was his first done by a professional. The next thing he did was try to enlist in the Army. When the recruiters discovered he had just gotten out of prison, the conversation ended abruptly. Even to Michaels, this seemed crazy. All he wanted to do was kill people, and he was not going to be able to do it because he had already done it. This seemed genuinely illogical. It didn't take him long to adjust his original plans. Since he couldn't kill the Viet Cong or the North Vietnamese commie regulars, he decided to focus on a different target. Somebody had to pay. He knew exactly what he needed to do.

Michaels found his father fairly easily. He was living in a ramshackle farmhouse just outside Iowa City. He followed him around town for the better part of the afternoon. Mostly, it was from bar to bar. After the old bum was sufficiently loaded, it was time for him to go home.

He followed the old man to the farmhouse, and when he unlocked his door, Michaels made his move. He shoved him inside through the open door and knocked him down hard onto the floor, breaking his hip. With his knee in the old man's back, Michaels took out a roll of duct tape and began his terrifying work.

Michaels sneered, "Don't worry, I won't hurt you."

As he said the words, he remembered the last time he had heard them over twenty-five years before. Michaels growled again, "Don't worry, I won't hurt you."

But he did. Over and over in ways hard to imagine. Finally, he bent over and put his lips next to the place where the man's ear had been.

"Do you know who I am? Who am I? *Who am I?*" The old man could only make mewing sounds under the layers of tape covering his shattered mouth.

By the time he ended it, Michaels had killed his second victim. The first one was a reflex action. This one was out of revenge and pure enjoyment. Rejection from military service no longer seemed to be a problem. He was waging his own war.

CHAPTER 23

ALMOST

Jobs had always been scarce in Bay City. In winter, when work was even harder to find, some of the local men harvested ice from the lake and sold it for a few dollars to Mick and Hap Swenson. Generally, this happened between Christmas and the end of February when the ice was safe to drive on and thick enough for its designated use.

The large blocks were stacked in the big icehouse next to the fish market. Each row was packed in heavy sawdust for insulation. Even with the expected melting, the ice blocks lasted all summer long.

In summer, the blocks would be fed into the hopper of a giant crusher to use for packing the fish into slatted wooden boxes. Most of the fish caught during the summer season were shipped alive to market in tank trucks, but a lot of the catfish were cleaned and packed, ready for the retail grocery stores. Some of the best carp also were iced for later use at the Bay City market, eventually becoming delicious chunks of the Swenson Brothers' signature smoked fish.

The ice on the lake was often two feet thick or more. Conventional chain saws had to be modified to cut it. They were fitted with four-foot-long bars and the chains equipped with longer, more vicious-looking teeth. Two-by-three-foot blocks were cut, which then were slid up a wooden ramp onto the waiting flatbed truck. The truck and equipment belonged to Swenson's Market, and anybody who was brave enough and tough enough to cut ice was free to borrow them.

Uncle Harry and Wayne Button had been cutting ice all day. It was brutal work, but they had managed four truckloads. Each made forty dollars from the sale. Harry asked Wayne to stop at the supermarket so he could get a loaf of bread and a few other groceries. After the grocery run, Wayne suggested they stop for a beer before heading home. Ice cutting is widely recognized as being very thirsty work.

Besides Molly Hunt's Bar and Horton's Ballroom, Ron and Rosie's Tavern was a little joint on the far end of town. The bar was formerly called Ron and Sal's, but Sal divorced him and moved to Milwaukee. Ron Nelson painted over the sign and renamed the place when he married Rosie. You could still see a faint outline of Sal's name bleeding through the paint under Rosie's, but nobody seemed to care, not even Rosie. She was a good-looking woman who worked hard to make a go of the shabby tavern. Everybody agreed Ron had married up.

Wayne pulled the truck into Ron and Rosie's, and the two tired men went inside to slake their thirst.

"Hello, gentlemen. You look like you've been icing. How about a beer?"

Harry said, "Hi, Ronny. Two Schmidts, please."

Wayne added, "And a couple shots of brandy, for the cold."

Harry drank a fair amount of beer, but he mostly steered clear of hard liquor. Still, it was very bad style to turn down another man's offer of a drink.

"Uh, Wayne, maybe just one, okay? I'm not too big on shots. Hard liquor has sort of a Jekyll and Hyde effect on me."

"No kidding. I'd like to see that."

The two men sat at one end of the bar, and the bartender sat at the other end, talking to a rather trail-worn woman neither of them recognized as a local. She likely owned the Cadillac parked outside. Until Harry and Wayne arrived, Ron and the Cadillac lady had had the place to themselves.

She chain-smoked as Ron pushed rum and cokes at her and alternated between telling her bad jokes and flagrant lies. Rose was out of town, and Ron's reputation was a little sketchy even when he was sober. The lady appeared to be pretty loaded. She laughed at all of Ron's jokes and confirmed the lies by repeating variations of "oh my" or "do tell."

Harry and Wayne did not appreciate what they were seeing, but they initially intended to overlook Ron's apparent intent.

The first shot went down before Ron had returned to his stool at the other end of the bar. Wayne ordered another and Ron waived his hand. "I'll be right there."

"No, really, Wayne. I'd better stick to beer. Bad things happen when I drink booze."

"Like what? What could possibly go wrong by drinking shots?"

"Right. Well, I almost did an awfully bad thing. *That's* what can happen."

"Oh no, DWI?"

"Worse."

"C'mon, Harry. Now you *have* to tell me. What happened?"

"Well, I almost ran over a little boy."

"Oh, crap! You said 'almost,' right? Right? Please tell me the kid was okay."

"Yeah. I stopped in time, but it was a really close call. The police showed up, and I paid a fine and lost my license for about a year."

"Cripes, Harry, the world is full of 'almosts,' good ones *and* bad ones. Think of it this way: when something bad *almost* happens—well, that's a *good* thing, because it didn't actually happen. When something good *almost* happens but doesn't, it's a disappointment. Get it?"

"All right, I get your point. What about you? What kind of 'almost' have you seen or done?"

"Huh, c'mon, Harry. You know what people say about me. No goals, no future, drinks too much. Hell, I guess that part is true. There's a heck of a lot of 'almost' in me. But here's a good one for you: I'm *almost* ready to propose to Stella."

"No kidding! Great! Are you thinkin' you'll do it anytime soon? Like tonight?"

"Maybe."

"No maybes! There's no time like the present."

"I guess so. But I need another brandy. Are you with me?"

"What the heck can I say? I don't want to be your excuse for not proposing."

Ron Nelson sat talking for a few more minutes and finally got up and delivered the next round. Harry held the shot glass up, pretending to propose a toast.

"Here's to you, Dr. Jekyll."

"And to you, Mr. Hyde."

Harry ordered the next round, and Ron took even longer. The two men were dehydrated from working and sweating in their coveralls all day. The alcohol was assimilating into their bloodstreams quickly.

This went on for quite a while. Soon Wayne and Uncle Harry were trading one-liners about how bad the service was.

"Maybe we'd get better service if Rosie was here."

Ron wasn't paying any attention to their comments. After the fifth or sixth shot and beer, Harry and Wayne were plastered. The booze had gifted the men with a rare sense of humor. Each thought the other was the funniest man on the planet. Harry would laugh at Wayne's bad-service jokes and Wayne at Harry's. They were two very, very funny men.

Uncle Harry leaned over toward Wayne and asked, "Hey Wayne, have you got change for a Hern?" He guffawed at his cleverness. "Get it? A Hern!" He slapped Wayne on the back.

"Uh, I don't get it. What's a Hern?"

"Ah, never mind."

Finally, the bad-service jokes settled onto a theme: "Hey Ronny, maybe this bar is too long."

"Yeah, it's a pretty long walk from your end all the way down to this end."

"Maybe we should join you two lovebirds. What do say? Should we come down to your end?"

"Comin' right up, boys."

Ron continued to talk, ignoring the loopy icers. In their hazy, drunken state, this seemed like a challenge that simply could not be overlooked. Harry and Wayne silently agreed something needed to be done, if for no other reason than to teach Ron Nelson a lesson about infidelity.

Years later, when Harry finally decided I was old enough to hear this story, he would portray the critical moment as if he were somehow the victim of bad luck or fate. Harry's version of what happened next went something like, "Emmet, it never would have happened, but the saw started on the first pull."

Harry stood up from the barstool and went out to the truck. The ice-saw indeed started on the first pull. Ron's eyes nearly popped out of his head when he saw the seemingly deranged man coming through the door with a four-foot-long chain saw growling loudly.

"Let's see, Wayne, how much of this bar do I need to cut off in order to get better service around here? I guess maybe about half of it."

"Sound's just about right, Harry. Ron, does that sound right to you?"

"No! No! Stop now!"

"Don't worry, this will just take a minute. Then you won't have as far to walk to deliver our drinks. Trust me, Ronald. It's a *good* thing."

Ron was beginning to hyperventilate. His face was bright red, and he began making unintelligible moaning noises between gasps for air.

Harry held the saw just above the top of the bar. Slowly he began to lower the roaring machine toward the shining mahogany surface. Finally, Ron just covered his ears and began half-shouting and half-crying, "*Oh god! Oh god! Oh god!*"

Just before the jagged saw teeth hit their target, Harry hit the kill switch. As the chainsaw fell silent, he calmly said "There you go, Ronny Boy. Do we have your attention? Maybe the service will get a little better now."

Wayne ordered one final round and Ron brought it right away. He was a beaten man. Wayne insisted he join them in a shot. The Cadillac woman thought the whole scene was hilarious. *She* thought the shot was a great idea. Harry and Wayne raised up their shot glasses and said, "*Hoy-hoy!*"

Ron just drank his shot and said, "Guys, please go home now. Okay?"

Harry agreed.

"Yes! You are correct! We should go home now! We have done enough work for one day. Mr. Nelson, thank you for your excellent service. Good evening, ma'am. He's married, you know."

She rasped, "I really don't care."

The two men laughed their way out the door and into the truck. They slapped each other on the back. They knew they just *had* to be the funniest guys in the world.

"You know, Harry, I'd say you *almost* cut that bar in half."

"Wayne, I believe you're right. I *almost* did."

By the time Wayne dropped Harry off at Hunt's, it was dark out and long past suppertime. Molly could hear him even before he reached the back door. He was singing "When Irish Eyes Are Smiling." Molly met him at the door with her hands on her hips. His cap was turned sideways so the bill stuck out at an angle over his left ear. Under his arm he carried a badly crushed loaf of bread.

"*Hell-oh*, my dear." He bowed deeply and almost tipped over.

"Harry! You look like the devil!"

He stood up straight with an exaggerated sinister look on his face. "Maybe I *AM* the devil!" He laughed a sinister laugh and wiggled his two index fingers in front of his forehead like devil horns.

She was still mad, but even in this state, he had somehow managed to charm her . . . a little bit. She just steered him toward the couch.

Across the tracks an extremely inebriated Wayne Button made his way slowly and carefully up the back steps of Stella's Café. When he got to the landing he stopped and caught his breath. From the inside pocket of his herringbone wool vest, he pulled out a small box holding a diamond ring.

He softly said to himself, "Hello, Stella. I hope you will allow me the privilege of becoming your husband. Will you please marry me?"

Just to make sure he got it right he started in again. "Hello Stella. I hope..." Then he remembered he should get down on one knee to propose. As he knelt down, he bumped into the back door. When the light came on inside, he stood up too quickly and began to lose his balance.

As Stella opened the door, all she saw was Wayne Button waving his arms wildly as he tipped over and began somersaulting backward down the steps. It wasn't a long trip down, but it could easily have been a fatal one. Fortunately, Wayne was as loose as multiple shots of brandy could make him. His gangly frame had turned to rubber. It may have saved his life. Wayne turned over once and then again, landing in a heap at the bottom of the steps.

Stella screamed, "*Ahhh!*"

At the bottom of the steps Wayne shook his head to clear the cobwebs and looked up in shock at her standing there in her nightgown and slippers. He still held the ring between his thumb and index finger. He cleared his throat and began delivering the speech as he had practiced.

"Hello, Stella. I hope you will allow me the privilege of becoming your husband. Will you please marry me?"

"Wayne?"

"Yes, Stella, who did you think it was?"

"Are you proposing?"

"I sure am."

"Are you sober?"

"Uh, almost."

"*Almost?*"

There was a long silence. "Well, not quite, honey, but one more trip down these steps and I should be."

There was another long silence. "Wayne! *Oh, get up here!*"

"So, what do you say? Will you marry me?"

"Ask me again when you sober up. You won't forget, will you?"

Before he bedded down, Stella put Wayne on formal notice: either he quit drinking or there would be no wedding. The line was drawn. It was his moment of truth. Wayne swore off booze the very next morning. His hangover made the decision a little easier. Stella was wearing the engagement ring by the time she opened the café.

CHAPTER 24

MARCH WINDS OF CHANGE

On March 1, 1968, President Johnson appointed the Kerner Commission to explore the underlying causes of 1967's widespread race riots in American cities. The commission's findings would later declare the nation was "moving toward two societies, one black, one white, separate and unequal."

March 6: President Johnson signed Executive Order 11399, establishing the National Council on Indian Opportunity (NCIO). President Johnson said, "The time has come to focus our efforts on the plight of the American Indian," and he added that NCIO's formation would "launch an undivided, Government-wide effort in this area." The president tried to connect the nation's responsibilities to the tribes and nations with contemporary issues for African American civil rights, an area with which he was much more familiar.

March 16: Senator Robert F. Kennedy of New York entered the race for the Democratic presidential nomination, saying Eugene McCarthy's showing in New Hampshire "has proven how deep are the present divisions within our party and country. It is now unmistakably clear that we can change these disastrous, divisive policies only by changing the men who make them."

On March 31, 1968, President Johnson shocked the nation when he announced on live television that he would not run again for the presidency. By then, right-wing political opinion had become disenchanted with LBJ's social programs, including Medicaid and Medicare. To make matters worse, the liberal voters were angry and worn out by the bloody marathon that was the Vietnam War.

"With America's sons in the fields far away; with America's future under challenge right here at home; with our hopes and the world's hopes for peace in the balance every day," Johnson said, "I do not believe that I should devote an hour or a day of my time to any personal partisan causes or to any duties other than the awesome duties of this office, the Presidency of your country."

The more likely reason was that LBJ was running third in the polls, and it would be disastrous for a sitting president to lose badly in the primaries of his own party. President Johnson was a savvy politician who knew when to retreat for the greater good of the Democratic Party.

The very next day in New Hampshire, Richard Nixon announced his candidacy for the Republican presidential nomination.

The buzz at Stella's seemed to ping-pong between those who thought LBJ was too much of a puppet for the military and those who couldn't quite identify what it was about Nixon they didn't trust. His "beady little eyes" were mentioned, and the word "shifty" seemed to be a frequent definition. Once again, the winds of change were swirling.

Hap Swenson grumbled how he hadn't voted for a Democrat in thirty years, but Nixon just might end his streak.

Consensus opinion seemed to show that another Kennedy in the White House might be a welcome change from Lyndon Johnson's bulldozing style.

CHAPTER 25

The Killing of Martin Luther King Jr.

The evening of Monday, April 4, 1968, began like a lot of others at our house. We had eaten supper, and Jack and I were busy doing our homework. Mom and Dad were washing dishes in the kitchen with the TV news in the background.

As usual, the headlines were presented first, then the weather and the sports. The meteorologist had finished his optimistic appraisal of the week ahead, and the sports announcer had completed his assessment of the winners and losers. The news anchor signed off, and the channel went to some commercials.

Gunsmoke was just beginning when the show abruptly was interrupted by a national news alert from New York.

"Good evening, ladies and gentlemen. This story is still unfolding as we bring it to you. It is with great regret that we must report on this day, April 4, 1968, while standing on the balcony of the Lorraine Motel in Memphis, Tennessee, Martin Luther King Jr., Nobel Peace Prize winner and civil rights leader, was assassinated. Dr. King was in Memphis to lead a protest march in sympathy with striking garbage workers of that city. His famous 'I Have a Dream' speech has been cited as one of the greatest inspirational speeches of our century.

"He is survived by his wife, Coretta Scott King, their two sons, and two daughters. Dr. Martin Luther King Jr., dead at age thirty-nine from an assassin's bullet. We will have a more complete report on the evening news at nine. Once again, Martin Luther King Jr. has been assassinated in Memphis, Tennessee, while standing on the balcony of his hotel."

The horror was still sinking in when the network reporter ended his report.

"We will provide the full report as soon as we receive more details. This has been Leonard Reasons with this special report."

Mom and Dad stopped what they were doing and went quickly into the living room as soon as the initial announcement was made.

Jack stood up from the chair and was staring at the TV screen in disbelief. Both his hands were clenched in fists, and his eyes were filling up with tears.

He rarely showed his emotions by crying. Mostly, he internalized his anger. Now he was doing both. Jack stood there with his eyes brimming as his fists opened and closed again in disbelief and rage. He was visibly shaking. I was aware of who Martin Luther King was and how important he seemed to Jack, but at the moment, I was more focused on Jack's visible anger and frustration.

Mom saw it too. "Jack, are you all right? I think we need to talk about this."

"No, Mom." He spoke in a low tone. "I'm not all right. Do you know what this means?"

"Well yes, honey, I think I do. Your father and I both realize this is a very serious matter." Dad was surveying the scene and waiting for his role to be revealed.

"Son, I know you admired Dr. King and what he stood for. But you can't take this personally. There are some things we just can't change, and this is one of them."

Jack just stared at Dad with a surprised look on his face. "Dad, how can you say that? It *is* personal—*very* personal. A hundred years from now this will still be important. Whether a white person or a black person killed him, this will set back the peace movement and the equal rights movement more than any of us can realize. Don't you know that when he said, 'I have a dream,' he was talking about us too? If I don't take it personally—if *we* don't take it personally—*what the hell do we stand for, anyway*?"

He hadn't raised his voice, and it was clear that Jack was not upset with Mom or Dad. I don't think they had ever heard him swear before. He was deeply troubled and drifting toward a black hole of emotions. He looked like he was about to explode.

"I—I need to just think." He slowly turned and went into our bedroom and closed the door.

Mom and Dad looked at each other and then at me. Dad cleared his throat and spoke to me. "Son, I think we'd better give Jack some space. Maybe we should keep the TV on and try to get some more information about this whole mess."

We watched the regular programming until seven thirty, when the network interrupted again with another special report. They were broadcasting live from New York.

"Good evening. This is Leonard Reasons reporting. As we reported earlier, Dr. Martin Luther King was gunned down tonight in Memphis, Tennessee."

The report essentially repeated what had been said before, except the network had polished it up and added some clips of Dr. King and his family. However, they added something new at the end.

"This evening we also had a news team in Indianapolis, Indiana. That team was traveling with Senator Robert Kennedy on the campaign trail for the Democratic presidential nomination. Senator Kennedy was preparing to address a crowd with a campaign speech. The assassination caused him to change his plans, and he used the time to speak about the events in Memphis and to express his own feelings. Tonight, we close this report with Senator Kennedy's very eloquent speech to his supporters."

The camera cut to the scene in Indianapolis. Some local politician introduced Bobby Kennedy as he approached the podium and began to speak. At the same time, Jack appeared in the bedroom doorway.

"Ladies and gentlemen: I'm only going to talk to you just for a minute or so this evening because I have some very sad news for all of you. Could you lower those signs, please? I have some very sad news for all of you, and, I think, sad news for all of our fellow citizens, and people who love peace all over the world; and that is that Martin Luther King was shot and was killed tonight in Memphis, Tennessee. Martin Luther King dedicated his life to love and to justice between fellow human beings. He died in the cause of that effort. In this difficult day, in this difficult time for the United States, it's perhaps well to ask what kind of a nation we are and what direction we want to move in. For those of you who are black—considering the evidence evidently is that there were white people who were responsible—you can be filled with bitterness, and with hatred, and a desire for revenge.

"We can move in that direction as a country, in greater polarization—black people amongst blacks, and white amongst whites, filled with hatred toward one another. Or we can make an effort, as Martin Luther

King did, to understand, and to comprehend, and replace that violence, that stain of bloodshed that has spread across our land, with an effort to understand, compassion, and love. For those of you who are black and are tempted to be filled with hatred and mistrust of the injustice of such an act, against all white people, I would only say that I can also feel in my own heart the same kind of feeling. I had a member of my family killed, but he was killed by a white man. We have to make an effort in the United States, we have to make an effort to understand, to get beyond, or go beyond these rather difficult times. My favorite poet was Aeschylus. And he once wrote:

> 'Even in our sleep, pain which cannot forget
> falls drop by drop upon the heart,
> until, in our own despair,
> against our will,
> comes wisdom
> through the awful grace of God.'

"What we need in the United States is not division; what we need in the United States is not hatred; what we need in the United States is not violence and lawlessness, but is love and wisdom, and compassion toward one another, and a feeling of justice toward those who still suffer within our country, whether they be white or whether they be black.

"So, I ask you tonight to return home, to say a prayer for the family of Martin Luther King—yeah, it's true—but more importantly to say a prayer for our own country, which all of us love—a prayer for understanding and that compassion of which I spoke. We can do well in this country. We will have difficult times. We've had difficult times in the past. And we will have difficult times in the future. It is not the end of violence; it is not the end of lawlessness; and it's not the end of disorder.

"But the vast majority of white people and the vast majority of black people in this country want to live together, want to improve the quality of our life, and want justice for all human beings that abide in our land. Let us dedicate ourselves to what the Greeks wrote so many years ago: to tame the savageness of man and make gentle the life of this world. Let us dedicate ourselves to that and say a prayer for our country and for our people. Thank you very much."

Jack's tears spilled over and streamed down his cheeks. He said nothing. When the speech was finished, he nodded silently, slowly turned around, and went back into his sanctuary.

I went outside and sat in one of rocking chairs on the front porch. I looked down our street and rocked slowly. The streetlights were beginning to come on, and I could see the lights in the windows of our neighbors' houses. I wondered if anybody else was having the same sort of conversation as the one in our house. I suspected most people in our town might not get quite as emotional as Jack did about Dr. King's death. I wondered how I should react to it all. Where did I fit into this? Once again, I considered about how personally threatened I felt when David and his family were killed, so close our home.

A vague sense of doubt and dread began clouding my thoughts. Whether or not it affected the rest of the world more than ours, Jack was right in feeling outraged and profoundly frustrated. He wanted to do something, but there was nothing he could do. At that moment, Jack's was the voice of my conscience. I began to feel *his* rage welling up inside me. The realization poured into me and suddenly I understood we *all* should feel as angry and afraid of what had already happened, and more ominously, what was likely yet to come.

Dad came out and sat down in the other rocker. "Are you okay?"

"Sure. I was just thinking about what Jack said, and what Mr. Kennedy said. What do you think?"

"I think Bobby Kennedy is a great man like Dr. King was. I hope he can help keep things from getting out of control."

"What do you think about what Jack said? Shouldn't it be . . . *personal?* You know, shouldn't we try to do something?"

"I suppose so. I just don't think we can do very much. I think it's one of those things we should let somebody else handle. It's too big for us. We already have our hands full with our own issues."

"I don't know, Dad. I think Jack's right. Somehow, this is about us too. It's like with David's family. We can't look away. No matter what else is going on, I think we need to—*I* need to pay attention. Dad, the world is changing, isn't it?"

"Maybe so, M. Maybe so. Hey, aren't *I* supposed to be giving *you* the advice here?"

"Don't worry, Dad, who do you think I learned this stuff from?"

As much as I wish I could say the Martin Luther King tragedy remained at the forefront of our attention, this seemed to be true only for a few weeks. Even at school, we touched on the subject from time to time, but the topic gradually faded away. For most, the sadness, fear, and anger soon began to dissipate like a cold, hard spring rain sinking into the earth. An exception was Jack, of course.

CHAPTER 26

COMMERCIAL FISHING

By the time Wayne Button announced to the Swenson Brothers he was quitting the fishing crew to help Stella run the café, the news had been well-circulated about how he had sworn off drinking for good. After that, a lot of things seemed possible and not quite as surprising.

"Mick, Hap—you've been good to me, but it's time for me to move on. You probably heard I quit drinking. I want to try to make it work with Stella, and she won't put up with anything but the straight and narrow. She wants me to help her run the restaurant, and I even asked her to marry me. What do you think of that?"

Mick said, "You mean you are going to be waiting tables? *Our* table? Pouring *my* coffee? And calling *my* breakfast 'Shit on a Shingle.' Yeah, there's something to look forward to, all right."

Mick and Hap looked at each other and shrugged their shoulders. Finally, Hap delivered the official company opinion: "I guess if you want to get all goofy about it, we can't stop you. You're not the first fisherman who gave up the lake because a woman asked him to get off the boat. Shoot, love screws up a whole lot of good fishing. We need to find a new guy, though. Do you think Stella can wait until we get it figured out, or should we just sell the business right now? If we do that, maybe we'll all be waiting on tables. Look, just make sure you wash your hands really good. You've been working with the fish so long I'd hate for everything I eat to taste like carp."

Hap and Mick had already been notified that their other crew member from last summer had decided to stay in Madison and play bass in a rock band called the Restless Souls. The money wouldn't be as good, but there would be a lot more girls. This was too bad; he was a hard worker and a darned good fisherman.

Mick's two boys, Pat and Rick, were going to take his place. Even with the two-to-one replacement ratio, the loss more than outweighed the gain. With Wayne hanging up his waders, it was tough to imagine starting over with a whole new crew. The summer of 1968 was shaping up to be a real corker.

Wayne was smiling. He knew Hap wouldn't waste his breath giving him such a hard time if he didn't approve.

"I think she'll wait. Do you have anybody in mind for my job?"

Mick looked serious. "I don't know. I thought we'd see if we could maybe get hold of a chimpanzee somewhere."

"Very funny, very funny. That chimp better have a good sense of humor to put up with you jokers. Seriously though, what about it? Any ideas? What about Brick's boy, Emmet?"

Hap wrinkled up his brow and took his cap off, a sure sign of a big decision coming.

"The North kid? He's a pretty good-sized boy, and he isn't old enough to go running off and getting married anytime in the near future. It would be good to have somebody for a few years. Shoot, Wayne, you might have finally got something right and now you're leaving. Anyway, where the hell are we going to get a chimp?"

Mick agreed. Chimps were hard to come by.

"Yeah, Emmet North—Brick's boy. Hard work usually runs in a family. Do you think he can swim? He's gotta know how to swim. I'll give Brick a call."

Before I was approached, Mick Swenson called my dad, and together they decided it would be a good thing. The job was mine. Decision made. While most of my friends were still on an allowance or maybe mowing an occasional lawn for a couple bucks, I was about to begin a real job.

I didn't have to apply for it. I never really even had much of a say in whether I wanted it. This was the first summer in quite a while when a job on the fishing rig had opened up, and now the whole crew had turned over.

A fishing-crew job was recognized as a good option for a young guy. It paid pretty well, and we needed every penny we could get coming into our house. In spite of that, it was deliriously hard work and did not appeal to everybody.

Nobody bothered to ask what I thought about it. Dad came home one afternoon in the last week of school and awarded it to me. Slightly confused, I accepted the job and the obligatory handshake. My hand nearly disappeared inside his huge fist. He was so proud. I guess I was a little too surprised to respond, one way or another.

I wasn't sure I wanted to work a job yet. Dad just assumed I would. Shucks, at sixteen he was already running his grandfather's farm. I'd heard that story many times. At any rate, the deal was set, and I was going to be a commercial fisherman.

Dad said, "You start Saturday morning. Be at the fish market at seven."

School got out at noon on Friday. This year there would be no summer vacation. I really could have used at least a day or two before I started my new job, but at seven o'clock on Saturday morning, June first, I was standing in front of the fish market door. At the same time, Wayne Button was happily pouring coffee and serving hot, greasy breakfasts at Stella's Café.

I knocked on the door of the fish market. Nothing happened. I knocked again. Still nothing. Finally, the door flew open, and Hap Swenson was standing there. I immediately noticed the nasty stump of a cigar he held clasped in his teeth. It was foul-looking and soaking wet, obviously unlit and looking like it just *had* to taste very bad. For all appearances, it could have been lodged there in the corner of his mouth for a long time.

"Good morning, Mr. Swenson. I'm ready to work."

For a moment, he looked over the top of his glasses at me. Then:

"*Jesus Christ on a bicycle, North! Would you please get your greenhorn ass in here? I don't have time to host a goddamned tea party. We need to jump to it! There are fish to be caught. By God, you're a fisherman now. Get in here and let's get started, boy!*"

I sheepishly crossed the doorstep to my new job. The market was wet and busy and fishy- smelling. I felt like I'd just landed in one of the greatest places on earth. I had been in the market before with Dad, but this morning the crew was getting set to start the main season, and everything seemed to be happening at once. And I was part of the crew.

I imagined it looked a little like a firehouse just after the siren rang. The quick motions and deliberate activities made the crew look like they were preparing for some sudden adventure or crisis. I would soon learn fishing was a little of both.

An older man with a hose was washing down the stainless-steel counters, and a long-haired woman with a very bad overbite was lining up raincoats and waders on a modified coat rack on the end of the building by the back door. I recognized them from Horton's fish fry.

"Emmet, this is Boris and Shirley Rose."

They barely acknowledged the introduction and went right back to work. I later learned that Shirley almost drowned after falling through early ice on the lake when she was a young girl. Boris was fishing nearby, and he pulled her out, but only after she slid under and away from the place where she had gone in. Boris managed to find her distorted outline through the thin ice, and he used an ice chisel to chop her free.

Years later Shirley married Boris out of gratitude or love or some other mysterious reasoning. In the market as with the Friday night fish fry, they worked so smoothly and coordinated as to appear they could read each other's mind. By all evidence, she may have been his perfect match.

"I think you've met Mick."

Mick Swenson was going in and out the back door, loading boxes of gear and piles of ropes and other things into the back of the truck parked out back. Mick shouted down to me, "Hi Emmet, glad to have you working with us." Then he disappeared outside again.

"Emmet, you know Mick's boys, don't you? Pat and Rick?"

"Hi Pat. Hi Rick. So, you're going fishing too, eh?"

Pat said, "Yeah, Dad's making us."

Hap called us together. Boris and Shirley stopped what they were doing and wiped their hands on their aprons. Even Mick came over and listened as the older man got ready to speak to his new crew. Mick had heard this speech many times before, but he always enjoyed it. It was a rite of summer and the closest thing to a formal welcome we would experience.

"Boys, you are fishermen now. You've got a lot to learn in a damned short time. I don't mind showing you how to do things, but I don't like to have to show you twice. Pay attention, and you'll learn fast. We pay twenty dollars a haul and a dollar per thousand pounds. Every time we go out, there is a chance to make some good money if you're smart and if you work hard. There's also a chance you'll drown if you're not. But by God, it's not going to happen on my watch! We've never lost a man yet, and we're not going to start this summer!

"Drowning is just about the stupidest thing an angler can do. It is not an option! If it happens to any one of you, I promise you I will not feel the least bit sorry for you. No sir! I will leave you for the turtles and dance a jig on your grave. And then I'll go out and hire a man who knows how to look out for himself.

"Know this: we need to honor the lake because it's how we make our living. And the best way to do that is to *stay safe*! Every time before we make a haul, I want you to think about it. When I say, 'Fishermen's Luck,' I mean nobody's going to drown today. I also mean we are going to catch a bunch of fish. And by God, I mean we are going to make some serious money! I want you all to repeat 'Fishermen's Luck,' and you'd better convince me you mean it! Any questions so far?"

There were no questions.

"All right, the only other thing you need to know is this: no matter what the lake brings us, we'll have no regrets. If we have a bad day or a weak haul, we'll not whine about it. No sir! Every day is a new day and a chance to better our lot in life. Everything is an experience and a lesson to be learned. Get it? If I say, 'No Regrets,' I want you to say it right back to me, and you'd darned well better mean that, too."

I was in awe. Hap was utterly inspiring. I felt like if he wanted to, he could probably just part the waters like Moses if it meant a better haul.

"Let's get started then. We're all in this together. I am counting on you guys, and I want you to know you can count on me and Mick, too. There are fish to be caught, and there's money to be made!"

The hell-bent-for-leather speech amounted to the entire new employee educational program for the three of us. The rest would be on-the-job training out on the water. When Hap finished bringing the heat, we trudged over and got our waders and raincoats and headed out the back door.

Mick said, "You skipped the part about staying sober on the job."

"Yeah, I figured they were too young. Maybe I should have mentioned it."

The brothers smiled, and we piled onto the back of an old yellow Chevy stake-bed truck and drove off for the lake.

By eight o'clock we were inside the big workboat they referred to as the launch and slowly heading out of the harbor with the seine boat and three live boats in tow. Mick drove the launch. Hap went ahead in an aluminum jon boat with a forty-horsepower Johnson outboard motor. He was a wizard at "bumping" fish. Hap would go to one of the many shallow areas of the lake and float the boat slowly through the cattails using an oar to softly touch the sides of the huge carp all herded up like cattle in the water weeds. On a quiet morning you could actually hear them feeding. This technique allowed an experienced fisherman like Hap to accurately estimate the potential catch.

With Mick at wheel, we made our way to a neutral place on the lake and waited for Hap to report back about which haul location we would fish.

Pat, Rick, and I sat together quietly taking it all in. None of the three of us had a clue about what we were going to do exactly. The Swenson boys had been along on a few hauls just to watch and goof off, so they might have seen some of the techniques we would need to learn. But more likely, they were about as green as I was. Rick Swenson turned to his brother and asked the question that had been bothering him since we left the market.

"Gosh, Hap's our uncle. Do you really think he would dance a jig on our graves?"

"Nah. He was just trying to psych you out. He wants to make sure we know he doesn't want us to drown. Shucks, Hap can't dance worth crap anyway."

In a half hour or so Hap appeared on the far side of the lake, speeding toward us from out across the Flats. As he pulled the jon boat alongside the launch, he smiled up at his waiting crew.

"All right boys, it's time to get to work. Mick, let's head for Lily Pond."

"Got it. Fellas, Hap is the boss when it comes to where and when we fish. Let's get moving."

We entered the mouth of the Catherine (pronounced 'Cath-reen'), a deep cut with fast-moving water found right at the head of the lake. The big launch motor was unfazed by the current working against us. Birds seemed to be everywhere, sitting in the trees lining the shore and circling overhead. Turtles sunned themselves on fallen trees and rocks, and the occasional muskrat or beaver could be seen busily working on some industrious project only they could understand.

At the end of the Catherine, we turned southeast into the Wisconsin channel of the Mississippi. Today we had to go pretty far downstream. The added force of the current helped us make good time. We passed several places whose names would become familiar to me later on as seining hauls. This morning they included Fishermen's Landing, Point No Point, Duck Pond, and Towhead.

No matter where we were, the smell of the lake was the same. As I drew the heavy, humid air into my lungs, it made me feel like a part of something infinitely larger. I felt I was getting to know a part of myself for the first time—that something was awakening.

We had been on the water for half an hour or so when we approached the big granite outcropping known as Steamboat Rock. It had been deposited in this spot a million or more years ago when the glaciers cut the river valley and dumped countless tons of moraine material like a child moves sand in a sandbox. It was a tangible reminder of the incredible force of nature. On the side facing the river's main channel, stonecutter William Krause had carefully carved the words "Rest with God, ye souls of the Sea Wing, July 13, 1890."

"Do you see that stone marker?" Mick knew we were all looking at it.

"Sure."

"It's Steamboat Rock—a good reminder of why we need to be careful out here." I vividly remembered Mr. Sims's lecture.

We sat quietly as we glided past the granite monolith and crossed into the deepest part of the lake. The main channel ran along the far side where the shoreline marked the eastern edge of Minnesota. A mile or so above Lake City, Minnesota, we pulled into the shallow water of Lily Pond, where we would make our first haul as a working seining crew. Hap was sitting there in his jon boat and smiling at us in the morning sun.

As we arrived at Lily Pond, Hap nodded his head and said, "Okay, boys, Fishermen's Luck."

We all responded loudly, "Fishermen's Luck!"

"And No Regrets!"

"No Regrets!" I loved it.

We started the first real work I had ever done around mid-morning. There was no hourly wage. We worked on "shares." There would be no paid time off or holiday pay, no sick time or workers' compensation. No employment benefits of any sort, only the work and payment for our sweat. It seemed fair.

Lily Pond turned out to be a relatively light haul. Hap spent most of the time on the deck of the seine boat teaching us our roles. He had us switch off when we had learned one job and then he would teach us another role. One guy handled the cork line and another guy the lead line. The third man worked the pulling gear, a mechanical device that hauled in the nets and set the relentless pace for our work.

The first lesson we learned was that the pulleys of the gear were fully exposed and therefore could be very dangerous. Hap explained that if we lost a finger, we'd damned well better not come crying to him, by God!

Mick and Hap both finished the haul in jon boats, mainly making sure the nets didn't get hung up on underwater stumps or other debris.

When all went well, the seine, or net, was laid out in an expansive circle that grew smaller and tighter as the pulling gear did its work. The large lead sinkers slid along the lake bottom, and the cork line floated on the surface. Eventually, the fish would be crowded into the big net bag, and the lead line would be lifted up and draped on the side of a live boat. When one was filled to capacity, it was moved out, and another took its place.

The mouth of the bag created a wide, open pool where we would stand nearly chest deep in water and flopping fish, hand-sorting each one into the live boats according to size. There were "jumbos" and "number ones" and "number twos." Anything smaller had to be turned back into the lake.

Game fish were strictly off limits. Many trophy walleyes and northern pike were turned loose with barely an acknowledgment. Mick and Hap made sure we never broke the rules.

The live boats were an interesting and very important part of the fishing rig. They were generally shaped like a regular boat, with a pointed bow and a slightly squared-off stern, but the sides were made of thin wooden slats with horizontal openings to let the water flow through the boat when it was submerged. Bulkheads were strategically located in the bow and stern. It floated high and dry when the bulkheads were empty and filled only with air. When it was pumped full of water, the deck of the live boat floated level with the surface of the lake. If a live boat was anchored in the current, the fish could be kept alive for several days. It was an essential part of selling the catch and getting it off to the markets.

After a good haul, the live boats would be brimming. Then, back on shore, the catch would be loaded into a big cart that ran up a ramp on steel railroad tracks to a weighing platform. This structure was built for the big tank trucks to drive under. The slippery cargo spilled down a short slide and into a tank of water hooked up to an air compressor, which aerated the water and kept the fish alive until they reached the markets in Chicago or New York. The load-out was tantamount to counting the dollars adding up as the fish slid flipping and flopping down the chute and into the live trucks. If one managed to flip out onto the ground, Hap or Mick quickly retrieved it.

Mostly, we were after the carp, which were extremely plentiful in Lake Pepin. But we also took other rough fish, the most notable being catfish. One of the great perks of working at the fish market was that we could help ourselves to one fish every day we made a haul. This was a big deal to me. A couple channel cats made a good meal. I had a chance to put food on the table for my entire family. It was a new and gratifying feeling for me.

The first haul went well. We weren't very sharp, but the three of us rookies learned a lot the first day. Pat and Rick liked to argue about how things should be done. I mostly ran the pulling gear and stayed out of the discussion. I could tell from the beginning I was going to like this life. Nature was all around us, and the work was remarkable, both in its simplicity and yet in its massive scope. Except for the motorized pulling gear, we were probably doing what fishermen had done for thousands of years.

At the end of the day, we had caught a total of twelve thousand pounds of carp. It seemed like a gigantic load to me. Hap and Mick said it was a short haul, but a good way to learn. An average one would be twice as big. No regrets.

We headed home across the Main Channel and past Steamboat Rock, upstream past Towhead and Duck Pond. Pat and Rick and I flopped across the bunks in the back of the launch. It was late afternoon. I couldn't imagine how we could possibly handle a bigger load than the one we just made. I was wet and tired, and my muscles ached like crazy, but I had put in my first real workday.

I was beginning to see why Dad seemed so proud I had been offered this job. His values centered squarely on hard work. It was the measure of a man. He had done it his whole life. I know he thought I should follow his example. That was good enough for me.

Darla came over after supper expecting to hear how my first day at work went. I was already out cold on top of my bed. She stuck around for an hour or so, and Mom showed her some crochet stitches. I slept through the night from sheer exhaustion.

Monday, we loaded out the haul. After all the fish were weighed and dumped into the waiting live truck, I had made thirty-two dollars. It was the first payday I ever had. I offered the money to Mom and Dad, but they turned me down. There would be a lot of paychecks in my future for which I would never remember the exact amounts. But I will probably always remember that first one.

Tuesday morning, we began the cycle of our work again. We planned to haul Fishermen's Landing. As I began to be more comfortable with new work duties, I was able to look around more, and appreciate the panoramic beauty of the lake. The sights and sounds combined to create the most remarkable workplace a kid could ever imagine. The hot sun overhead helped to remind me it was summer after all, even though we were working our butts off. We caught nearly twenty thousand pounds.

I started picking up on some of the knots we used in our work. Mostly we used half-hitches, which could easily and quickly be undone for tying up the boats at dockside, and we used a slip-hitch on the big pulley wheel of the pulling gear.

The bowline knot was the hardest for me to learn. It creates a solid and permanent loop, which is good for hooking onto a boat in a hurry. Hap could tie one in only a few seconds. I took a lot longer and couldn't seem to keep my tongue out of the corner of my mouth when I was making it. When I completed my first one Hap nodded his approval, which was a pretty big deal all by itself.

Mick said within a few hauls we would begin to predict what to do even before we had to do it. He was right. By the end of the second haul, I could just about tell when Mick was going to signal me to speed it up or slow it down. Hap usually ranged around the outside of the seine in an aluminum jon boat and looked for problems. Once in a while he would drag a chunk of wood out and ease it over the cork line. Occasionally a turtle was freed and paddled away into the lake. Above all else, the nets were to be protected from damage if at all possible. We knew they were our livelihood, and we all looked after them with great care. We were gradually becoming fishermen.

CHAPTER 27

June 5th, 1968: Robert Kennedy Is Killed

I woke up early Wednesday morning planning for another routine workday. From the bedroom I could hear our TV. I opened the door to see Mom and Dad standing together in the living room. Every channel was reporting the shooting of Senator Robert Kennedy in Los Angeles. At 12:15 a.m., just after making an acceptance speech for winning the California presidential primary, Bobby Kennedy was gunned down by a Palestinian national named Sirhan Sirhan. He was mortally injured and pronounced dead at 1:44 a.m. The gunman was already in custody.

Mom and Dad watched the TV set in disbelief. It was as though they were seeing something they couldn't quite understand. My father muttered, "Not again."

I came out of the bedroom rubbing my eyes. "What's up? Why are you watching TV?"

Jack was still asleep. Mom shushed me and I knew something big was happening. I went over to where they stood and listened as the announcer repeated the story for maximum dramatic effect. Another famous person had been killed.

Even the brother of President Kennedy, a guy who was running for president himself, wasn't safe anymore. All of a sudden, the reality of how much killing was going on seemed close and personal again.

Once again, I was anxious and afraid. If men like John and Bobby Kennedy and Martin Luther King could be assassinated in cold blood, then average people like *my family and me* were surely not exempt. Whatever was going on in our country's collective psyche was becoming increasingly violent, and it seemed there was nothing anyone could do about it. There were just too many images of death on TV to sort out—constant reminders that no one and no place were ever really completely safe. And David and his family had been murdered *right across the street from our house.*

By the time I got to work, I was feeling downright paranoid. The Swenson crew was talking about it when I arrived at the market. As always, there wasn't much time for conversation, but I listened while I worked. Boris Rose thought he had it all figured out.

"Dat asshole, Herbert Hoo-fer, kilt bote of dose Kennedy bois and dat preacher King, too. He and LBJ are in cahoots! I'm tellin' you, Hoo-fer is behind it all! He figgered day vas socialites or communists but day vernt. Day vas just Cat-licks! Everybody knows dat!"

As always, Boris's opinions were somewhat stronger than the facts to back them up. I didn't know what to think. This killing seemed so senseless, so random—like Dr. King, or David and his family. For all I knew, David Patterson's killer was still in town, and—who knew? —maybe I could be next, or my dad, or my mom, or Jack. If anybody my age was going to be accused of being a communist sympathizer, it would probably be Jack. Heck, maybe he *was* a communist. I wasn't sure what communists believed. I only knew they were different from the rest of us, and Jack definitely fell into such a category.

Hap wasn't amused. "Boris, don't go spreading that foolishness around. I don't want J. Edgar Hoover or the FBI sniffing around here. We might get slapped with some health code violation. And they would probably shut us down for a while *and* none of us would earn a dime, and *that* would seriously piss me off! And another thing: they were social-*ists*, not social-*ites*. Except Jackie Kennedy. She really is a socialite, I guess."

Hap turned his attention to his crew with his usual crotchety demeanor. "Never mind all that crap, fellas. C'mon boys, there's fish to catch! We've got a job to do, and the job is fishing, not solving murders!"

As Boris ranted, I watched Shirley gutting a big carp and cutting it into pieces to be prepared for the smoke house. Her skilled hands worked with precision as she slit the large round belly from between the fish's gills and in a perfectly straight line ending near its tail. She opened the body of the carp, reached in with her bare hand and aggressively scooped out the guts. In one smooth motion, she yanked the tangled gut-ball free and slid the pile down the length of the stainless-steel table and into the waiting barrel. It was a gross form of perfection, and she obviously was a master of gut-ology.

The head was then removed and also slid into the barrel. Finally, the body was cut into large chunks and pierced with sharpened S hooks to be hung on the smokehouse racks. Shirley noticed I was watching. When she had the opportunity to say something she nodded to me and spoke in a matter-of-fact way.

"Beautiful, ain't it? Nothin' ever goes to waste."

I nodded back and pondered the implications of her statement. "What does the guy do with the guts when he picks up the barrel?"

"Feeds 'em to his pigs."

Shirley had already begun butchering another big carp. I wished I hadn't asked. For a few seconds I thought about how much I used to like bacon.

Around town, tongues were busily wagging about the latest tragedy disfiguring our national identity and clawing at the pride of our fathers. It wasn't so different from what our town was experiencing after the Patterson murders. People seemed to be getting shot all over.

Out on the water, though, we kept our minds on the job, enjoyed the good weather and the work. Hap chose Duck Pond, a relatively easy haul. The challenges of fishing beat the heck out of a lot of life's other realities.

The June morning air felt especially good. The water outside my waders felt warm around my legs. My muscles strained under the weight of the fish in the nets. Rick and Pat sniped at each other, as always. In spite of being a new crew, we were catching on pretty well. It turned out to be a good haul.

When I got home for supper, Mom was frying catfish. Dad and Jack were sitting in the living room with the news on. Not surprisingly, it was all about Bobby Kennedy. I took a wash basin full of water and a change of clothes out into the backyard to get cleaned up. When I came back inside, Sam Most was at the front door. He had a newspaper clutched under his arm. He didn't knock. He just stood there. Dad saw him through the screen door and walked across the linoleum floor to greet him.

"I'm scared, Brick. They're killing the president again. Can I come in?"

Sam's version of the story was a little off center. But we knew what he meant.

"C'mon in, Sam. We're all a little scared. Can you stay for supper? Rachel's frying fish."

"I like fish. It's easy to chew."

We sat together at our kitchen table and ate supper. As always, the food was good. But nobody said much. I guess we were just keeping our thoughts to ourselves.

After supper Jack and I went into our bedroom. Dad and Mom sat in the living room with Sam. Eventually, he drifted off to sleep sitting straight up on the couch. Jack and I talked about Bobby Kennedy.

"Jack, do you think there will be riots because of this?"

"What do you mean, white people rioting because of Bobby Kennedy's death? I don't really know. I'm just sick about it though. I hope not. I'm not sure it's the same thing as when Dr. King was killed. There could be demonstrations, I guess."

"What do you mean, 'it's not the same'? It's the same to me. Weren't they alike? Weren't Dr. King and Mr. Kennedy both men of peace? It didn't seem to stop anybody from raising hell when Dr. King was killed. I'm scared. I don't get how violence is supposed to cure violence."

"Yes, I guess so. In a lot of ways, they were probably alike. I can't really explain it."

"I see students on TV rioting, both blacks and whites. I know it's mostly about the war, but won't white people riot because Bobby Kennedy was killed? I mean, maybe even here in our town." It might have been the first time I ever saw Jack at a loss for words.

"Stop asking me questions, will you? Do you *want* a riot to break out here? Geez! It's the same thing, all right? People are frustrated and scared. *I am frustrated and I'm scared, too!*"

Mom tucked her head in through the bedroom door and put her finger over her mouth, signaling us to keep quiet because Sam was still asleep. Just then he began to stir.

"Mary!" He called out his dead wife's name as he awoke.

Dad said, "It's all right, Sam. We're here."

"Oh! I thought she . . ."

"I know. It's all right." Dad went over to the couch and sat down next to the old man.

"Can I walk you back home? I'd feel better if I knew you were inside, and the door was locked behind me."

Sam smiled a sad, tired old smile. "I'd like that."

I followed them out the screen door and sat down on the front stoop. Dad and Sam walked across the street to his home. He made sure Sam was all right, and he told him to lock the door behind him when he left.

As he walked out Sam said, "Thanks, Brick. Do ya think it was the Jehovah's Witnesses again?"

"No, Sam, I don't think so. Those guys are okay. Don't worry. They already caught the guy who did it."

Staring down the street, I could only wonder at what was going on inside the houses of our neighbors and friends. Were they outraged at Bobby Kennedy's death? Was it any different from Martin Luther King's assassination because Kennedy was white? Did anybody even think about David Patterson and his family much anymore? I couldn't tell. Our town still looked about the same as it did the day before.

The air smelled slightly of the fried catfish combined with fresh-cut grass from a nearby lawn. This time of day, everybody was inside finishing up with supper. I stood up and stretched. I was tired, and my muscles were sore. In a way, I was beginning to like the physical feeling of work. Besides the paycheck and the occasional bonus of fresh catfish, it helped me to think about something besides Darla.

Dad was looking pretty tired, too, as he crossed the street and slowly walked back toward our house.

"He's a good old guy."

"You're a good old guy, too, Dad."

"We're all getting a little older, son." He winked and smiled a little as he opened the door. I followed him into the house, and for the first time I could remember, he locked the door behind us.

CHAPTER 28

STELLA AND WAYNE

Whatever else happens in the world, one thing never stops: no matter how crazy things get, people keep falling in love.

Considering looks alone, Wayne Button and Stella Person were a seriously mismatched couple. He was tall and skinny and bowlegged, and she was short and wide, and in general, Stella had some noteworthy horizontal surfaces while Wayne's profile was mostly vertical.

But in all the ways that mattered, they were great together. He told her jokes, and she laughed at every one, even if she'd heard it before. They took turns cooking special dinners in the café after closing time and danced to the jukebox when they were all alone together. It was true love.

Nobody was too surprised when they announced their intention to marry. What *was* a sort of surprise, though, was their open invitation for the whole town to join them in the café for a free meal as a kind of combination open house and wedding reception. The ceremony itself would be held in the Methodist church, and when it was over, everyone in attendance could walk across the railroad tracks and Highway 35 and over to Stella's café for supper.

Handmade signs were posted all over town, and the wedding of Stella and Wayne quickly became one of the most talked-about social events of the summer. It is a well-known fact that people will turn out for free food, and Stella was widely recognized as a great cook.

Wayne and Stella's personalities were also distinctive, each very popular in their own way. In simple terms, they were characters, part of the local color. Between the two of them, they seemed somehow connected to just about everybody. Their wedding would surely be a big day in Bay City.

"Hey, what's another hundred or so guests? We'll find a way to get everybody fed. We always do." Wayne shrugged his bony shoulders and smiled.

"Easy for you to say! I do most of the cooking!"

Stella pretended to complain, but she was proud everyone was so excited about the wedding dinner. It also gave her something to keep her mind off the wedding itself. She was a pro at the restaurant business, but when it came to the wedding, she was as nervous as any bride-to-be. She confided her concerns to Mom and Deedee.

"I just want to look pretty. I know I'm a big gal, and I don't want to embarrass myself. Wayne deserves a pretty bride. It's not likely I'm going to get skinny before the wedding, so I guess I better just make the most of what I got.

"Girls, among other things, I need a fancy new bra—one to provide support—one to shape and lift—a lot. If there's some sort of top-secret new technology the government is trying out, I might be a good choice for a test project. Only . . . it has to be really pretty."

Stella asked Deedee and Mom to go with her and shop for her wedding dress and "a few special things only a husband should see."

Mom and Deedee were up for the task. They were flattered and happy to help. Mom didn't get to shop for clothes too often, and I think she figured it would be fun helping spend someone else's money. Deedee just flat-out liked to shop.

"Shop till you drop! That's my motto. Then, after you drop, crawl over to the next sale rack."

Thursday nights the stores were open late in Red Wing. It was the night when a lot of farm families came to town to buy groceries and other supplies. Joy's Bridal Emporium was the logical choice. The shop was owned and run by Linda Joy. She was a fifty-year-old, slightly graying former accounting executive with thinning hair who had followed her dream and opened the store despite her family's criticism. She loved helping people, and weddings were her passion. The business had been kind to her, financially speaking.

Deedee called her and set up an appointment. Confidentially, she told Linda to plan on some extra time for the fitting. When she asked approximately what size Stella was, Deedee just said, "She's a big gal."

A little bell jangled above the door as the three friends entered the shop.

"Hi, Joy, how's the rag business?" Deedee asked with her usual brassiness. "This is my friend Rachel North, and *this* is Stella Person. She's the lucky lady."

"Greetings, Deedee, thanks for calling me. I am really excited to help you find the right dress. Hello, Mrs. North, it's nice to meet you. Stella, I'm Linda Joy, but everybody just calls me Joy."

"Hello, Miss Joy. I hope you can help. I need to look beautiful. Are you a miracle worker?"

"Stella, you *are* beautiful. Trust me, girl, you don't need any help in that department. I just need to come up with the right dress to show off your face. It's all about the bride's face. Well, in your case it might have something to do with the chest, too. Don't worry, sweetie, I have some really nice things to show you."

Stella, Deedee, and Mom spent the next two hours looking at catalogs and dresses on the racks and talking and measuring and dreaming out loud about the wedding. Little by little, Joy helped Stella feel as if she were one of the most important brides she'd ever worked with. She said the results would, in fact, be striking. When the process was done, Stella had been fitted for an ankle-length, ivory-colored gown with a beaded bodice, a thin ribbon at the waist, and a bow on the back.

"It's the bow your husband gets to pull when he unwraps his present. That's *you*, darlin'!" Stella giggled like a girl. Mom and Deedee chuckled too.

"Joy, now we need to get down to some serious business." Deedee took charge. "Stella needs some underwear, and I mean the stuff you can't put out in the front window. Just between me and you, she has already given Wayne a preview of the movie and a matinee or two, if you know what I mean. We need to show him something like he's never seen before."

Mom snorted a little through her nose. "Deedee, you're just awful," she said with wicked amusement.

Stella blushed and said, "I think I should plead the fifth on that one."

"Anyway, Joy, she needs to make sure Wayne gets a really good feeling about the whole marriage thing. What have you got for mature audiences only?"

"Now you're talking. I'm going to lock the front door and turn off the sign, so we don't get interrupted by any of those sweet young things and their faint-hearted mommas. Let's get naughty, girls!"

Joy turned the sign in the window and closed up shop.

"Okay, girls, get ready for the main event!" Joy brought out an array of silky and lacy things imported from Paris, Milan, and Las Vegas. Mom and Stella covered their eyes and laughed, saying "Oh my God!" after every new piece was laid out.

"Oh, for Christ's sake, girls, get over it! Haven't you ever worn nice underwear before? I'm sorry, Joy. I didn't realize I was bringing a couple of virgins into your store."

"I understand, Deedee. If *they* like it, think how the groom will feel. Stella, your guy Wayne is in for a real treat."

Stella picked out some pretty steamy stuff. The bra didn't turn out to be as big a challenge as originally thought. The French designers had long ago figured out how to conquer the force of gravity.

"What about this little number for the wedding night? You're going to need a nice nightie for your trousseau." Joy held up a pink lace teddy, slit at the hips and scooped deeply at the bust. Tiny straps over the shoulders offered only an ornamental function.

Stella wondered out loud, "Can I *do* this? I mean, can I really pull this off?"

"Honey, you definitely have the groceries to fill this order! What do you think? Sexy, eh?"

In her usual sassy fashion, Deedee quipped, "Besides, if things go according to plan, it'll be Wayne who pulls it off."

"Oh, my Lord, I think it's very wishful thinking. What about—support? I can't wear a fancy French brassiere to bed. Wayne is used to seeing me in a T-shirt or an old sweatshirt in cold weather. We'll probably have the lights out anyway. I wouldn't want to give him a heart attack on his wedding night."

Joy became incensed at the thought. "Oh *puh-lease*! There will be no T-shirts! Look under here . . . there is a built-in underwire bra, and believe me, it's got the right stuff. You could balance a table on your boobs, and they would still stand out like a flag in a stiff breeze. It's the latest thing, and it's designed for a *real* woman like you, Stella. Let me get your size and you can try it on."

Joy handed Stella a fancy box and offered an encouraging nod as she went into the dressing room. There was quiet expectation among the troops as Stella took her time wiggling into the teddy. Finally, after several minutes, Stella broke the silence. "Ohhh, baby! Joy, you're a genius!"

The Mom-and-Deedee team hugged and laughed and felt like together, they had helped create greatness. Stella came out of the dressing room a few minutes later. Right away Deedee started giving her a hard time.

"I thought you would show us how you looked. What's up with this? C'mon, get back in there and give *us* a peek! Inquiring minds need to know!"

"Not on your life. That surprise is reserved for Wayne and Wayne alone. But trust me, girls. I look *fabulous*! I have never been so *out there* before!" She held her hands in front of chest.

"You're 'out there,' all right. We'd all like to be out there like you are! Or maybe about half of what you've got. Oh crap, you know what I mean." Deedee stumbled over her own choice of words. "Stella, hurry up and pay the nice lady before I make a fool out of myself again."

"Don't worry, Deedee. I hope you ladies just think of me as a friend. It's been my pleasure to help out. You are all just delightful!"

Deedee went over and gave Linda Joy a big hug and planted one on her cheek. "Thank you, baby. You are a really sweet gal. We couldn't have done this without you."

"You are welcome, and congratulations to you, Stella. The dress should be here soonish, and we can do any alterations then. You are going to be a beautiful bride, and your teddy is *so* nice! Thanks for coming in. I will call you when the dress gets here. Bye for now!"

Stella was all set. Mom and Deedee felt a little smug about the entire event. It could have taken a lot longer, but Joy really came through for them. The wedding was still a month away.

On the way to the car Stella said, "Maybe I should ask Wayne to start taking vitamins. He's going to need them!"

Mom hooked her arm in Stella's as they walked. "You might be surprised. When he sees that teddy, it might be *you* that needs the extra energy!"

"Don't worry about me. I can keep my motor running as long as it takes. I might even leave a light on! Heck, I might leave *all* the lights on!"

"Stella you are *such* a slut!" Deedee nearly spit because she was laughing so hard.

Back in the store, Linda Joy smiled and poured herself a glass of red wine. She had done it again. Stella would be breathtaking. She smiled to herself and sighed deeply. "Here's to you, honey. You're beautiful."

The next few weeks flew by. It seemed like everyone who came into the café was planning on attending the wedding, or at least the wedding dinner. The dress came in and Joy made a few alterations, but nothing too serious. Stella hid the teddy and the French undergarments in a box on the top shelf of her closet. She even talked Wayne into buying a new suit.

When the day was finally at hand, everyone sped home after work to change clothes and get ready for the wedding. The organ music started pouring out the front doors of the Methodist church at 5:45 p.m., and the townsfolk all headed toward the church.

By six o'clock, the church was completely filled, and the crowd was spilling out onto the front steps. Several of the husbands and most of the kids were happy to volunteer to be out in the yard. It was the first big church event since the Patterson funerals.

Reverend Greeley was always pleased to perform a ceremony for a couple who were already living together. He began in the usual way:

"Dearly Beloved, we are gathered today to celebrate the marriage of Stella and Wayne. The holy state of matrimony is sacred indeed, but it is also a condition that should not be entered into without forethought."

He smiled at the couple standing in front of him.

"If I may be so bold, the two of you appear to be a major attraction. As pastor of this church, I sure wish it was customary to pass the collection plate at a wedding! Have you ever seen anything like this in your life?"

The crowd inside the church clapped and cheered. Though they weren't exactly sure why, the crowd outside on the steps and the lawn did too.

There they were: an unlikely looking pair of people whose perfect feelings for each other far outweighed anything else. Facing each other, they stood in virtually the same place where David's casket had been. The ceremony was brief, and the crowd appreciated it. As always, the highlight was when Reverend Greeley told the groom: "You may kiss the bride."

Right on cue, Wayne enthusiastically obeyed, and Stella pretended to swoon. So much for the nuptials. The crowd was hungry, and across the tracks two of Stella's servers were heating up enormous pots of spaghetti, sauce, and meatballs.

After the "I do's," Stella and Wayne walked hand-in-hand across the backyard of the church and over the railroad tracks, then across Highway 35 and up to the front door of the café with a small sea of people trailing right behind them. When they reached the landing in front of the door, Stella turned and hollered at the crowd, "Just give us a second to change and we'll get started! I don't want to wreck this dress! Right?"

As they turned to head into the café, Wayne stopped her and spun her sideways. He gave her a long and passionate kiss. The crowd responded with a roar. Then, amazingly, the skinny and bowlegged Wayne swept Stella up in his arms and carried her across the threshold into the café. This unexpected display of virility drew a serious round of respectful applause, especially from the men. Wayne was a heck of a man!

Stella and Wayne hurried through the café, out the back door onto the landing, and upstairs to change their clothes. Stella laid out her dress neatly on the bed. Wayne draped his suit coat over a chair and rolled up the sleeves of his white shirt. He was ready. Stella put on a new pink uniform and Wayne pinned her wedding corsage on it. Before they headed downstairs to feed the hungry masses, Stella took Wayne by the hand and softly kissed him on the lips. "I'm really glad," she said.

"For what, honey?"

"For you turning out to be the man I hoped you were." She had little tears in the corners of her eyes.

"Stella, do you think maybe we could get by with just staying up here?"

"I don't think so. How about you?"

"No, I suppose not."

"All I ask is that you don't work too hard down there. You're in for the night of your life!"

Wayne winked and said, "Darlin', so are you!"

She threw her hands up and rolled her eyes. "*Hallelujah! I'm a married woman!*"

The newlyweds went back downstairs and opened the front door to the café. The crowd filed in. Many had gifts which they placed on the counter. Wayne and Stella greeted them one by one, and everyone congratulated the couple, as happens in the receiving line after virtually every wedding. Immediately after, each guest was rewarded with a heaping mound of spaghetti and meatballs on double-stacked paper plates.

The spaghetti dinner team rivaled the best efforts of any busy factory assembly line. The guests came through by the dozens; in the front door and out the back, and then down the steps to one of many picnic tables set up in the backyard. When the tables were full, people spilled over to the front parking lot, with some even dining off the hoods of their cars.

When Dad and Mom arrived, Stella loudly proclaimed how Mom had helped pick out the wedding dress and a few other things. Wayne thanked her for helping and shook Dad's hand briskly. Stella elbowed Wayne in the ribs and said, "You ain't seen nothin' yet! I have a little surprise for later. You'll thank Rachel, all right. And Deedee, and the good Lord above!"

When Uncle Harry and Molly came through the line, Wayne blurted out, "Harry, leave the saw outside. Okay?"

"Ix-nay, Wayne." They smiled broadly. The two had shared a great caper that would be part of the local lore for many years. Though they were grown men, it really wasn't too different from the infamous burning-bird-house incident David Patterson, and I had shared a few years earlier.

Together with their serving staff, Stella and Wayne managed to put out over a hundred and fifty plates of spaghetti, equal to nearly half the entire population of Bay City. It took the better part of two hours to get everyone fed. Many of the big eaters had seconds and some even thirds. There were plenty of leftovers and take-home boxes.

As the guests finished, most headed home or toward Horton's. The Ramblers were playing, and Wayne and Stella planned to join everyone at the dance. It was a pretty good deal to have a wedding dance just down the street and not have to hire the band. And Horton's had the added advantage of the wedding crowd entourage.

Wayne and Stella changed back into their wedding finery before walking down to the dance hall. Wayne drank orange pop and Stella strawberry sodas. They danced nearly every dance until they suddenly disappeared just before the last set.

When they arrived on the landing at the top of the stairs leading to the apartment above the restaurant, Wayne paused after unlocking the door. Bending over, he reached out and under his bride.

"Wayne! What the heck are you trying to do?"

"Relax, Stella, I'm going to carry you over the threshold. Now hold still and let me get a grip on you."

"*I don't think so.* I could hardly believe it the first time! How about if we just hold hands and cross it together? I would hate to see you wear yourself out or get a rupture or something. I've got better things in mind for you."

"Baby, I love you."

"I love you too, Wayne."

Later, after the dance ended and Mom and Dad were walking home along the railroad tracks leading past the café, they couldn't help noticing the lights were on in the upstairs apartment. *All* the lights. Mom smiled and murmured softly to herself, "*Oooh, baby!*"

CHAPTER 29

A New Job

Martin Day had been with 3M for over ten years. They paid well and had good benefits. The only trouble was, they tended to occasionally move people around like chess pieces, crisscrossing the entire country. Despite the financial benefits, he and his family had bounced around nearly the whole time.

Marty's job in logistics was to set up systems to make sure supplies and parts were shipped to and from the right places to create a broad spectrum of 3M products. Most assignments lasted a couple of years. Once the systems were in place and the job was completed, he was reassigned.

When he was called into the plant manager's office late on a Wednesday afternoon, Marty wasn't really prepared to hear that 3M needed him back in California ASAP. It must have been something pretty important to move him so soon.

The boss's name was Fred Colletti, but the guys on the line called him Dago Fred or Freddy Spaghetti. He said the company could give him about thirty days, but not much more. By the middle of July, Marty needed to be in Anaheim. It would mean a nice raise, and 3M would rent a place for the family until they could find permanent housing.

"Sure. Fine, Fred. You can count on me. I, well, I guess I'll get going. I'll need to talk to Deedee and Darla. They loved California. I'm sure this will be okay with them. I'll see you tomorrow."

When he was driving home, Marty thought about how many times he'd had the same conversation with his wife and daughter. The last time was when they had moved to Wisconsin from California, just about a year before. Deedee hadn't been too keen on the idea. Darla threw a fit. She made it seem as if they were moving to the middle of Siberia.

A year later, it seemed like they both had settled in and actually enjoyed the place. Marty liked a lot about Bay City, too. He fit in. He had friends here. When he and Deedee played at Horton's, their neighbors treated them like they were Hollywood stars. In California they could barely get a gig. This was not going to be easy.

"Are you for real? I mean, are you for flippin' real, Marty? I barely got all the boxes unpacked from the last move and now you want to move me back to Anaheim. For cryin' out loud! I guess our little trip at Christmas wasn't enough, huh? Y'know, someday an earthquake is going to rip the whole darned state off from the lower forty-eight and sink it in the Pacific Ocean. I was kinda' thinkin' maybe we wouldn't want to be anywhere close by when it happened!"

"Now Deedee, you know I really don't have much of a choice on this. When the big boys say jump, I jump. At least I'll be getting a nice raise out of it."

"*Really*, a raise? Are you kiddin' me, or are you just *tryin'* to piss me off? Or maybe just convince yourself? California was about the hardest place we ever lived. This place is our home. I like it here! I like my friends. Rachel and Stella are about as nice a couple of girls as I've ever known. *Please*, Sugar, let's not do this! Not this time. Let's stay right here and put down some roots!"

"Deedee, I'm sorry. We need to be there around the middle of July."

"Well, just flippin' great. You're going to tell Darla this time. I'm not gonna do it!"

"I will."

"Darned tootin' you will! You know they shot . . . oh *crap*, never mind!"

"What Deedee? What were you going to say?"

"Well Marty, I was going to say they shot Bobby Kennedy out there, but hell, they shoot people here too, I guess. *Dammit*!"

The back door opened as Deedee finished her sentence.

"What's going on?"

Deedee's tone softened up as she said to her daughter, "Honey, I think you'd better sit down. Your father has something he needs to tell you."

Darla knew what was coming before he cleared his throat to talk. Even though Deedee insisted Marty was on his own, she helped Darla understand how the whole thing worked and how the company got to decide where they needed her father the most.

"Honey, your Daddy is a smart and talented man, and 3M probably wouldn't get a single truck on the road without him. I know this ain't fair, and I don't like it either. But we both love your dad, and we go where he goes. We're a family, after all."

"I know, I know. I guess I've known all along we would move again sometime. I just didn't think it would be this soon." Her voice started to quiver. "I have really nice friends here. I have . . . *Emmet*! Oh, Mama!"

Darla buried her face in her mother's shoulder and cried as hard as she had ever cried before. Marty put his arms around both of them.

"Baby, I know this one's different. You're old enough to know what's goin' on. I won't try to talk you into believing this is something it ain't. He's a really nice boy."

After supper, Darla called me and told me what happened. I asked if I could come over and talk about it, but for the first time I could recall, she shut me out.

"No, I can't see you tonight, Emmet. Let's deal with this tomorrow. I have moved so many times I can hardly remember. It's best if we just try to enjoy the time we have left together and act like nothing is going to change. If we don't, it'll wreck what's left for us. I'll see you tomorrow. Okay?"

"But Darla, I . . . okay, sure." As she hung up the phone, I whispered, "*Oh no.*"

CHAPTER 30

The Dream Becomes Reality

By the third week in June, the *American Dream* was just about done. Dad's concrete work was impeccable. The Comet Tone skin was perfect. The smooth, creamy walls gave no clue about the unique composition beneath. Walt installed nearly all of the finishing touches himself, the last of which was to hang the American flag on the mast. Dolly handled the decorating touches in the main sleeping cabin. In keeping with the red, white, and blue color scheme, she included some nautical motifs along with some patriotic ones.

After he had stared at it alone for nearly an hour to make sure it was really finished, Walt called Dad, Al, and Dale to come over. He invited the men to come inside the dark pole shed before turning on the lights.

"Gentlemen, I present to you the *American Dream*."

She was big and clean and shiny and, above all, massively impressive. Al Kind had convinced Walt that Comet Tone should be used on part of the outside hull as well as the inside walls and the engine room. Walt agreed, with the stipulation that most of the color would be below the waterline. The majority of the hull was bright white, with the bottom and keel painted royal blue. It looked tremendous.

As a nod to Al, the engine room was a speckled gray-and-white combination. The brass fittings gleamed, and the teak trim was regal-looking. Even the seats were spectacular. Walt had hired an upholsterer from Lake City to do them up in fake white leather.

Down in the engine room, smack dab in the middle of all the gray and white Comet Tone were two of the sweetest V-8 Oldsmobile motors ever to come out of Belvedere, Illinois. They were customized with a whole lot of unnecessary chrome, and every inch of the blocks was painted red, white, or blue.

"Wow! She's beautiful." Dale was mesmerized.

"She sure is. Are you sure she will float?" Al still needed some assurance.

"Well, I guess it's time to find out. I think she'll be fine as long as there aren't any cracks. The whole concept depends on the integrity of the hull. If it takes on any water, the weight of the cement will take her down like a ton of bricks. Sorry, Brick—no pun intended."

It was the first time Walt had answered such a question any other way than with a resounding affirmative.

"We need to move her first. Honestly, it could be the tricky part. Once she's in the water she'll be fine. It's all in the mathematics."

Dale changed the subject. "Guys, we probably need this parade more than we ever thought we would. Our whole goddamned country is just about ready to split down the middle and break out in a civil war. Since Dr. King got shot, I'm scared to even drive through some of the neighborhoods in Minneapolis. And now, after Bobby Kennedy was killed too, I'm not even a hundred percent sure if we can trust our own government. Christ! Two Kennedys! Do you think *that's* a coincidence?"

"C'mon Dale, you don't subscribe to all the conspiracy stuff, do you?" Walt began filling his pipe. This sounded like it was going to become one of Dale's speeches.

"I don't know. I hope not. But I do know this: we need this Fourth of July celebration to turn out right, and I am convinced that includes making damned sure this boat is floating in the harbor by the time the fireworks go off. Walt, you'd better be right about this. F and M will have my ass if it sinks before it even gets launched."

Dad put his arm around Dale Thorsdall's shoulder and said, "Mr. Mayor, with due respect, you worry too much. It's a good boat—the best. Walt did his part, and now I'll make sure it gets into the harbor. Don't you worry."

Dale pulled the last pieces of the parade together and personally helped pick out the fireworks. Not surprisingly, the volunteer firemen were some of the biggest fans of controlled explosions and large showers of sparks and flames. (Operative word: controlled.)

Everything was set for the big Fourth of July launch of the *American Dream*. It wasn't going to be a very long parade, but as Dale said, "What the hell, Bay City is a small town!"

The village's lone fire truck would lead off with its siren sounding. Then the Humane Society would have a bunch of dogs for which they were trying to find homes by letting the pups show what good pets they would make.

The Ellsworth Panther marching band planned to show off their best and flashiest songs. Bobo the Clown would be waving and throwing candy to the kids. Then, just after dark, the crew from the fire department would supervise the fireworks display.

Deedee and Marty Day agreed to perform at Horton's on the night before they left town for good. The dance would cap off the celebration nicely, and (thanks to the Days) it didn't cost Dale or the village a dime.

July Fourth was on a Thursday, and this meant the holiday weekend would last four days. The park would be packed with campers. The tourist dollars were very important to the local businesses.

It was going to be a big day and a big night. But the main attraction would be the *Dream*. The overall success of it depended on an uneventful launch. It was a great story for certain—one that nearly writes itself. The paper would cover it, and maybe even the TV news. Bay City was going to get its much-needed positive press. It all sounded great. The only thing left to think about was how the story would end.

Dale was still a little worried about whether the *American Dream* would float. If she did, this would go down in history as the greatest celebration our town had ever seen. It could potentially change the public's opinion about Bay City and rehabilitate our image for good. If it sunk, we would all look like a bunch of fools and even bigger losers than we already appeared. It was too late to turn back now.

He thought to himself, *Jesus H. Christ! It's made out of* cement! *It's going to take a goddamned miracle for it not to sink. Maybe he is just crazy. Oh hell, if he is, it's a pretty good kind of crazy.*

On the morning of the Fourth, the weather looked great, and all systems were "go." Walt slowly opened the front wall of the pole shed, and Dad backed the blue Village of Bay City tractor in, hooking it up to the front of the big trailer cradling the *American Dream*. The tractor strained as it pulled the huge boat across the yard and up to the edge of Lakeshore Drive. By eight thirty, she had rolled out of her place of birth and stood gleaming in the morning sunshine.

The parade was to begin in Horton's parking lot and wind its way across the tracks, past the old barbershop and Hunt's Tavern and then down the hill, finally reaching the place where the *Dream* would assume its position for the rest of the way down Lakeshore and through the park to the boat ramp. Walt had measured the width of the ramp and even made some borings to test the thickness of the blacktop to make certain there would be no surprises. Everything looked good.

Dad and Walt were stationed down on Lakeshore Drive with the *Dream*. Dale was up at Horton's, organizing the order of the parade participants. Since he helped plan the event, he figured it was only right that he named himself Grand Marshal. Uncle Harry offered the Impala to be Dale's wheels. With Molly beside him in the front seat, Harry (and Dale) would be at the head of the whole shebang.

By doing so Dale realized he would be the face of Bay City's relative success or the potential failure of everything. Basically, it all boiled down to whether the *American Dream* could float. Win, lose, or sink like a stone, Dale was all in.

After a couple of calming pulls on his flask, he was ready. He thought, *Ah, to hell with it. Let's have some fun.*

The lawn chairs were already beginning to appear by eight o'clock, and by nine, the sidewalks were filling up with local citizens and even some visitors from surrounding towns who were not having a celebration of their own. Lakeshore Drive was pretty packed. A lot of people were interested in the *Dream*, and a crowd had formed around her with some folks taking snap shots even before she took her parade position. There were kids, and grandmas and grandpas, and moms and dads. All were expecting something special.

Many carried American flags or some other red, white, and blue Independence Day symbols. There wasn't a cloud in the sky, and by all indications it was going to be a fine event. Bay City could have been any small town in America: proud and excited about the celebration and everybody wanting to be part of it in their own small way. And yet, no other place in the entire country likely had a giant concrete boat in their parade.

+ + +

Everything was packed up, and Darla and her parents were leaving the next day, the day after our big Fourth of July happening. The moving crew would finish the job and meet them in California. It would take three days to drive to the West Coast. Six weeks later, she would be starting school in California. Until now, Darla and I hadn't talked that much about her leaving. Denial seemed to me like the only realistic way to handle it. Now, I had to admit the end had finally arrived. As we walked along the street in front of the old schoolhouse, she reached for my hand and spoke in a quiet voice.

"Let's take the old station wagon out for a drive tonight. We can do it right after the fireworks when everybody goes to the dance. What do you say? One for the road?"

I smiled as I remembered our first and only adventure in that car. "Sure, one for the ditch. I mean, for the road."

We walked down to Main Street and sat down on the curb in front of the barbershop. It was the place where I'd first met Darla. From where we sat, we could see across the tracks to Horton's. The parade was beginning to get lined up.

I said, "I think we'd better get down to the boat pretty soon."

"Yeah, I just wanted to feel this place one more time. You know, this is where we . . ."

"I know."

We stayed a little longer and then started toward the lake. It was a busy scene. People were walking back and forth across the street, and some kids were laughing and playing catch while others were riding their bikes. I tried to shut the rest of the world out of our little bubble. Saying goodbye was going to be awful.

Dale Thorsdall was just about ready to signal the start of the parade. Harry and his cheerful copilot, Molly, had the red Impala idling and ready to go. Dale was getting set to climb into the back seat when he saw Sam Most come barreling over the railroad crossing on an old riding lawn mower. One front wheel teetered noticeably from side to side as he made his way. He didn't look when he crossed the tracks, or again when he crossed Highway 35 and entered Horton's parking lot. By the time Sam drove up to where he was standing, Dale had recited two heartfelt prayers that the crazy old coot wouldn't get hit by a car, or maybe a train. It would have screwed up the whole parade.

Sam pulled up and shifted the mower into neutral. He was wearing an Army private's hat. The smell of mothballs was pungent. Dale squinted and looked closely at it. It was from World War I. A small flag on a little wooden stick was taped to the front support of the mower's cracked steering wheel.

"I wanna be a parade."

"Uh, hi, Sam. Do you mean you want to be *in* the parade?"

"That's what I said. Where do you want me?"

Dale sized up the situation. Sam was the oldest guy in town and a World War I veteran. He rarely left his own yard. Riding in the parade must have meant a lot to him. How he managed to maneuver his dilapidated lawn mower this far was a wonder all by itself. To hope it would make it all the way to the end of Lakeshore Park was not a good bet.

"Sam, I'll tell you what. I'm happy you want to be in the parade today. Would you do me the great honor of being co-Grand Marshal? I'd appreciate it if you'd ride with me in Harry's convertible at the head of the parade. All you gotta do is wave once in a while."

Then Dale put his hand up to his mouth and whispered loudly so Sam could hear it: "It's an election year, Sam. It would sure be good for my campaign if a World War I vet would help me out."

Sam smiled proudly. "You bet, Dale."

"Climb in, Sam. Harry, hold her steady, a World War I vet is coming on board."

"Absolutely. Hi, Sam. It's good to see you."

Dale climbed in next to Sam and raised his hand to start the parade. Without hesitation, Sam started waving at nobody. He wouldn't stop until they reached the end of the line. Sam was so short he could barely see over the top of the door, but the sun was warm and felt good on his aching knees. And suddenly, he was co-Grand Marshal of the greatest parade he had ever seen. This was one of the best days of his life.

Darla and I had found our way down to where Dad and Walt were stationed with the *Dream*. They both looked a little nervous.

"Your Mom and Dolly are down by the park entrance. I think Jack is there, too. Why don't you and Darla head over there and see if you can find 'em?"

"How about you, Dad? Are you feeling all right?"

"Sure . . . I guess. To be honest with you, I guess I'll feel a lot better when this boat is in the harbor. I'm not a hundred percent sure the tractor is up to pulling this big thing. It's really heavy."

"Dad don't worry. Everything will be fine. Uh, Mom is feeling really good these days."

At first, he wasn't sure why I had said it. Then he understood and his expression changed.

"Yes, she is, isn't she?" He was smiling. It was what really mattered. I smiled back at him. "Still," he continued, "it will really be great when this boat is floating."

"I'll see you down at the boat ramp. Good luck, Dad. Good luck, Walt!"

Down at the end of Lakeshore Drive where the road curved sharply and headed up the steep hill onto Main Street, Harry's car was just coming into sight. People were cheering and clapping. I didn't know Dale was so popular. Then I saw Sam Most waving and smiling at the crowd. There was something perfect, even beautiful about it.

"We'd better get going, Darla."

"I know, just a minute."

Darla waved at Walt. Then she ran over to the big blue tractor and scrambled up onto the running board where she could get her arms around Dad. She gave him a big hug and kissed him on the cheek.

"We're really proud of you two. I'll miss you and Jack and Rachel, Brick. So badly." Then we both ran off toward the park.

We found Mom, Dolly, and Jack where Dad said they would be. They made some room for us so Darla and I could wiggle in between them, and we sat down cross-legged on the side of the road.

The Mafia came winding through the crowd at about the same time. They didn't seem to notice how much they were ticking people off as they wormed their way through the crowd and to the front row. Denny smiled an exaggerated smile and waved at Darla and me.

"Hi, sis! Hi, bro! Thanks for saving your family a little place to watch the parade."

Tom was busy saying "Excuse me—excuse him—excuse us" to everyone Rex and Denny were pushing past. Rex wasn't talking. He was acting as a sort of human battering ram in front of Denny. I think he liked the contact. When they saw Mom and Dolly they settled down and got almost respectable.

"Hi, Mrs. North, Mrs. Sprague."

"Hello, boys. Now sit down and let's watch this wonderful parade."

When Harry's Impala came by, we all cheered. Sam Most was waving and saluting the crowd. He was smiling like there was no tomorrow. I couldn't help but notice he had his dentures in. I waved at Harry and Molly, and they waved back. Harry gave me a wink and a "thumbs up."

Dale Thorsdall sat back with his arms stretched across the back of the seat and smiled. He was smoking a big cigar and just soaking in the scenery. He didn't even have to wave. Sam was handling his official duties nicely. Occasionally he looked back at the parade stretching out behind him. Everything looked perfect so far. The boat ramp and all it stood for was five hundred yards ahead at the end of the park.

After Harry's lead car, a group of volunteers from the Humane Society came walking some of the most adoptable dogs in the county.

Next came the fire truck. It was overpopulated with zealous volunteer firefighters who shouted at people they knew. Frequently, they surprised the crowd with a burst from the loud, train-like horn.

Right behind the fire truck, Al Kind as Bobo the Clown bumbled along with a large, red-striped satchel filled with candy. He ran from one side of the road to the other and dished out handfuls of sweets to the kids and the pretty girls. He made sure Darla and I got more than our share. There was a recipe card tucked into the band of his crushed and worn-out top hat. "Comet Tone" was neatly printed on it in magic marker.

Dale had made it known that almost anyone was welcome to take part in the event. Several old cars and some people riding horses paraded past the crowd with great appreciation. If you had a new pickup truck, it was reason enough.

We sat there watching our neighbors and friends pass us by, waving and smiling. Jerry Wold surprised everyone when he drove past in a shiny new, bright-yellow sewage pumper truck. A large sign with a bee painted on the side of the tank proclaimed, "Honey Wagon." Inside the cab, Jerry was wearing a rented tuxedo.

The new rig was much larger than his old one. The tank was stainless steel, and the truck's bumpers, running boards, and several pieces of trim were sparkling chrome. Considering its use, the Honey Wagon was downright deluxe.

The newly wedded couple, Stella and Wayne Button, rode a bicycle built for two. They were having a great time. A hand-written sign was attached to the fender of the rear wheel. It simply said, "Eat at Stella and Wayne's place." As soon as the parade ended, they would hurriedly ride it back to the restaurant for an expected post-parade rush.

Then the Ellsworth High School marching band came strutting down the street. We could hear them from a block away as they mercilessly pounded out the melody of Credence Clearwater Revival's "Proud Mary."

When they reached the entrance to the park, they stopped right in front of us and began to massacre "Brown Eyed Girl." First a group of brash trumpets took a turn, and then a quintet of clarinets tried to replicate Van Morrison's unmistakable vocal parts.

When they got to the familiar chorus, Denny and Rex pretended to hold microphones in front of their mouths and started singing "*Sha-la-la-la*" at the top of their lungs. Tom shrugged his shoulders and joined them. Even Mom and Dolly started singing along. When the moms broke into song, Darla and I joined in, and pretty soon everybody around us was singing loudly and gloriously out of tune.

Finally, the band decided it was time to put Van the Man's big hit out of its misery, so they did it the only way that possibly could have been worse than the stiff military version itself: the drum major raised his baton and, at just the right moment, spiked it toward the earth, as the band punctuated the summer air with a wretched "cha-cha-cha" ending. We clapped as though the curtain had just fallen at Carnegie Hall.

The first time I remember hearing the song was when Darla and I heisted the old station wagon. I'm pretty sure the sentiment was what kept me from upchucking in response to the marching band's frightful rendition. Still, the song choice couldn't have been timelier.

As the band continued its program while marching on into the park, we became aware of the main attraction of the day arriving. Behind the last row of percussionists loomed the upper half of the *American Dream*, all shiny and impressive. Dad was setting a very slow pace and managed to keep a suitable distance between the blue tractor and the drum line at the rear of the band. Up in the steering cabin and behind the big teak wheel, Walt Sprague was smoking his pipe and waving down at us. He pointed straight at Dolly when he saw her and blew her a kiss. She pretended to catch it on her lips and blew one back at him.

Mom was gazing proudly at Dad. He looked a little nervous, but he managed a quick wave as they approached, with the Village of Bay City tractor laboring to pull the *American Dream* and looking like the *Little Engine That Could.* Underpowered as it was for this job, the tractor had all it could do to keep the big boat's weight moving along the path toward its watery destination.

Jack leaned over to me and said, "Man, do you see the irony in all this?" I didn't have a clue what he meant.

The toiling blue tractor moved slowly past us with Dad at the wheel towing the *Dream* and Walt looking down at his neighbors from his place of honor. Dad was praying he had the skill to back the boat down the ramp and into the water.

He had done it a hundred times before for himself and for countless campers too inexperienced to maneuver their own boats into the harbor. But this was different. Walt's *American Dream* was easily the biggest thing Dad had ever handled. There was no rehearsing for it. He had to get it right the first time. He had imagined it in his mind over and over for many months. Though it seemed like a big responsibility, he was pretty sure he could handle it. Still, the tractor was beginning to run hot, and it had quite a distance yet to travel.

As he passed us there at the side of the road, he thought about how nice his wife looked and how quickly his boys seemed to be growing up.

Then he looked ahead into the park where the parade participants were beginning to pull off to the side near the end of the lot. Whatever the outcome, the end was in sight.

The Village of Bay City tractor eased the *American Dream* through the gates of Lakeshore Park and down the length of the parking lot with the rows of campers neatly arranged for maximum occupancy. The Fourth of July campers clapped in appreciation for the parade ending at their doorsteps. Men pointed, and women waved. Beer bottles were tilted as the *Dream* was toasted with Old Milwaukee or Miller High Life.

As the marching band ended its last song and the band members dispersed, Dad brought the *Dream* to a stop on the blacktop loop near the end of the parking lot, just at the top of the ramp. The boat would need to be maneuvered around the loop in a wide semi-circle and then backed down the ramp into the harbor. He left the tractor idling and walked back to the boat trailer as Walt climbed down the chrome ladder at the stern.

"Well, Brick, here we are."

"It's not too late, you know. We can quit while we're still ahead."

"Hmmm, fine with me."

"What? Are you nuts?"

"I'm just joshing. Besides, I kind of want to see if this thing floats, don't you?"

"Trust me, Walt, nobody is more interested in that subject than I am right now. Well, nobody but you, I guess."

"Don't worry, my friend, this boat will float. A lot of things worth doing seem impossible until you try them. Don't you agree? It's what makes a dream worth dreaming."

"If you say so. Let's put 'er in, then. What do you say, Walt?"

"I say, let's put 'er in." He bit down on the stem of his pipe in such a way that it pointed up at a forty-five-degree angle and made a face intended to look a little crazy.

Dad got back on the tractor and throttled it up. The diesel motor snorted loudly as he shifted into a low forward gear. Walt walked alongside the *Dream*, and Dad continued around the loop, cautiously lining up the big boat with the top of the ramp.

When he shifted the tractor into reverse, Dad breathed out an audible sigh before letting out the clutch. The crowd gathered closer around. All eyes were on my father and on the *American Dream*. Walt looked squarely into Dad's eyes and motioned with the fingers of his right hand to bring her backward and onto the ramp. Dad nodded his head and started the backward push.

At first, the *Dream* moved slowly and deliberately in a straight line, back toward the waiting harbor. When the trailer reached the top of the ramp, it seemed to pause and teeter for just a second before beginning the descent. Dad was sweating profusely. The big boat blocked his view of the water. Though Walt was directing him, he couldn't see where he was going. It was a blind approach.

"Looks good, Brick, keep her coming."

Dad eased the boat over the peak to begin the intended slow-motion trip down the ramp. The weight of the boat pulled hard on the tractor, and it began to speed up. He quickly realized he wasn't going to be able to stop the process even if he wanted to. I think everyone probably saw it at about the same time. The muscles of his arms were bulging, and his forearms were aching from the sheer effort of trying to keep the Dream on its course. Walt wasn't looking at Dad anymore. He was concentrating on the water.

He said, "Keep her coming, it looks good."

Dad couldn't have stopped even if he had wanted to. In one smooth motion, the *American Dream* powered down the boat ramp and into the harbor, causing a little more splash than planned. The blue tractor's rear wheels were touching the water before enough of the weight was buoyed up to allow Dad to regain some control of the situation. It all happened in a matter of a few seconds. Unbelievably, it appeared as though Dad had done it so many times before he could make it happen in his sleep. When Walt stepped around the front of the tractor Dad's eyes were open wide and his hands were shaking.

Now, everybody was cheering and clapping.

"Wow, Brick! You sure made it look easy-peasy. Nice job!"

"Walt—I had my foot on the brakes all the way down the ramp. It stopped when it was ready. I had nothing to do with it."

"Very funny, Brick, very funny. I'll untie the guy lines and then I need you to back her out another five or six feet. Sound good?"

"Sure. Then I think I'll go home and change my boxers."

Walt waded out into the water and untethered the *Dream*. Dad backed her a little further out into the harbor. Finally, Walt motioned for Dad to stop.

"Perfect, Brick. Right there. Leave her right there!"

The *American Dream* floated high and gracefully on the sparkling surface of the harbor. As Walt suggested, she drew almost exactly two feet of water.

Dale Thorsdall came bounding down the ramp with Dolly Sprague and Mom on his arms and a bottle of cheap champagne in one hand.

"Gentlemen! It's a great day for a boat launch! What do you think? Shall we send this one off with a pop?"

Walt looked at Dale and said in a very dry and serious tone, "Dale, I was always pretty sure this boat was going to float. But I never tested her hull to see if she could withstand a blast of Cold Duck. If she sinks, it's all on you."

"What? No! Are you kidding? He's kidding, right? You're kidding, Walt . . . aren't you?"

"Yes, Dale. I'm kidding. Dolly, I think you should do the honor. C'mon out here, sweetheart."

"Out in the water? Well, okay!" Dolly Sprague kicked off her sandals and splashed out to where her husband stood. She bunched up her cotton dress and held it in her left hand. In her right was a $1.99 bottle of Cold Duck that Dale had bought the day before. It could have been Dom Perignon.

Mom came over to where Dad was standing and hooked her arm in his. He looked relieved. Walt looked over at Dad and gave him a big wink.

"Here we go, boys! Dolly, let 'er fly!" The band had reassembled at the top of the boat ramp. As Walt gave Dolly her cue, the director pointed his baton at a single drummer who crisply delivered a tight roll on the snare.

Dolly leaned back and made a roundhouse motion with the Cold Duck. With a cymbal crash from the band, the bottle burst on the rounded point of the bow in a pinkish, purplish explosion of cheap wine and glass. Walt put his shoulder against the boat and pushed hard.

The *American Dream* floated easily backward into the harbor while our entire town and all our visitors cheered wildly. Not only did she float; she was magnificent. The band broke into the national anthem. We reflexively put our hands over our hearts and began to sing. It was quite a scene. There we were: a whole town of newly converted believers.

"Did you see *that*? I always knew it would float!"

"You liar! You told me it would sink like a stone. I'm the one who said it would float."

"Oh, it floats all right. *The American Dream. Wow!*"

CHAPTER 31

GOODBYE

The sun was warm overhead, and the sky was blue and free of any clouds in every direction. Walt eased the *American Dream* over to the main dock, and he and Dad secured the bow and stern lines to the big brass turnbuckles.

After the national anthem ended, Walt started the Belvedere engines up. The crowd cheered again as the engines first rumbled loudly and then settled into a throaty purr down below in the engine room.

Then Walt looked at Dad and said, "Well, does anybody want to go for a boat ride? All I ask is for everybody to use the park's bathroom before we go out. I don't have the toilet installed just yet."

Dad, Mom, Jack, Darla, and I piled onto the *Dream*. Deedee and Marty came along too. Al Kind and his alter ego, Bobo the Clown, both came along on the maiden voyage. Dale Thorsdall climbed aboard too, but not before locating Sam Most.

Surprisingly, Kenny Sprague appeared just as we were going aboard.

"Hi Dad. Permission to board? Is it all right if I join you?"

Walt smiled and glanced at Dolly. "Heck yes, Kenny. Your mom and I are really glad you made it. C'mon aboard!"

The Mafia boys were the last to board. Dad untied the lines, and Walt easily maneuvered the *Dream* away from the dock and out of the harbor.

We cruised around on the lake for over two hours. Walt was the epitome of a relaxed and happy man. Lake Pepin sparkled like a billion diamonds. The sky reflected off the dark water of the lake and gave the illusion of pristine, ocean-blue purity. Dale passed out cigars and made sure all the men had one. Deedee theatrically tapped him on the shoulder and demanded one of her own, which Dale was happy to provide.

Mom had one arm around Dad as she tossed her hair in the breeze and smiled. It had grown out, but not nearly enough to braid yet. To me, she looked like Jack's portrait of her at a much younger age. I got a lump in my throat but managed to smile anyway. Even Jack was grinning at the scene.

My three best friends were laughing and mugging for the camera as Dolly snapped shot after shot. Darla was her usual wonderful self. She sat next to Sam and engaged everyone in conversation, making each of us feel special. Walt even asked Kenny to drive the boat. Geez, Kenny was sort of behaving like a regular, good guy for a change.

My period of denial was finally over. I was intensely aware she would be gone by this time tomorrow. I tried not to let it ruin the moment. Darla was right. We needed this carefree and easy time, each of us for our own reasons. For the time being we were miles away from any problems in our lives and especially those of our troubled nation.

Sam just smiled and looked at the water. Once in a while he'd say, "Look at that!" I'm not sure we were looking at the same things Sam was seeing, but it didn't matter.

Near the end of our ride, Mom went over and sat down next to Darla. Without saying a word, they held hands and smiled at each other. It was just so beautiful. I couldn't help noticing they both had tears in their eyes. I had to look away.

Finally, Walt took us back to the dock. The launch and maiden voyage had gone perfectly. It was after four o'clock by the time we left the dock and headed home. Everyone was to meet back in the park after supper for the fireworks display. Dale thought they would start at about nine. Then everyone would probably move uptown for Marty and Deedee's farewell appearance at Horton's.

All day long, I had been thinking about being with Darla for our last night together and taking her parents' car for a farewell spin. "One for the road," as she had said. I replayed the first incident in my mind and vowed to myself it wouldn't happen again. What if my crappy driving was the last thing Darla remembered about me? By the end of the day, I was fixated on doing a better job than I had managed the first time. I couldn't seem to think past it.

I told Mom and Dad we were planning on skipping the dance and getting together on the lakeshore for a bonfire after the fireworks. Dad shrugged and Mom gave the final approval.

"It's fine, Emmet. Don't stay out too late."

"We won't. Is midnight too late?"

"Not this time. We'll be at the dance. We should be home a little after midnight, too."

As mom turned away, Dad placed his hand on my wrist. "Emmet, we trust you to do what's right. Understand?"

There it was again: *the right thing*. When it came to my last night with Darla, I was so unsure of what the right thing was that all I could say was, "Uh huh."

I walked over to Darla's house a little before seven. We sat around for a while talking with Marty and Deedee. They were happy to be playing Horton's one last time before leaving town for good—musical troupers till the end. It was sort of a going-away party, and they were getting paid to attend. When the parade and fireworks hoopla came along, it just made it all the more special.

"Now, sugar, you can come and visit us anytime you like. We would be really glad to see you. You're a real sweet boy, and we know Darla will miss you."

Marty echoed Deedee's sentiment. "If you learn how to play guitar, you can come out and join the band, as long as it's not one of those souped-up electric guitars."

"No problem, Marty. I think you're safe for a while. I can barely whistle."

Sometime around seven thirty, Darla and I went for a walk. The fireworks wouldn't start for over an hour. We held hands and just walked without saying anything. We crisscrossed most of our town before heading down Lakeshore Drive, back toward the park. Once in a while we looked at each other and smiled. We didn't need to say too much. The memories we had made together spoke to both of us.

"It was a good day, wasn't it?"

"Sure, Darla, it was really good. Did you see how proud my dad was about backing the big boat down the ramp?"

"I sure did. And your mom, too."

"You seemed to like the boat ride."

"I'll remember it forever." She smiled sweetly and a little sadly. "I think it's what a miracle feels like."

+ + +

After the parade, when most folks in town were enjoying their holiday leisure time, Walt Sprague returned to his shed and tidied up. It had been over six months since he began construction on the *American Dream*. Now it was time to start a different project. Around five thirty, Jerry Wold pulled up in front of the open gull-wing doors of Walt's shed.

“Pull ’er right in, Jerry.”

Jerry parked the old pumper truck inside. The two men had been talking about this since before Jerry bought his new truck. Walt took out his billfold and counted out five crisp hundred-dollar bills.

“What do you have in mind for the old boy, Walt? There are still a few miles left on the engine, and the tank isn’t very old at all. I just needed more volume.”

“Do you think it’ll make a good holding tank for Brick and his family?”

“Well, yeah. Sure. This tank will probably last a hundred years.”

“I guess that’ll have to do then.” Walt smiled at Jerry.

Jerry asked, “What about the old truck? What’s your plan?”

“Well, believe it or not, I don’t really have a plan for the truck. Can you use it for anything?”

Jerry grinned. “Well, heck yes, I can. Since the tank is going to the North family, I think it’s proper for me to buy the old truck back from you for the generous price of, shall we say, five hundred dollars?”

The two men smiled, and the money changed hands for the second time.

“Thanks, Jerry. I’ll bring the truck to you after I take the tank off.”

“It’s a pleasure doing business with you, Walt. You drive a hard bargain.”

“Say, Jerry, I don’t mean to pry, but—are you all right? Except for the parade I haven’t seen you around much.”

“I’m fine, Walt. Just a few things on my mind, I guess. Nothing you need to worry about.”

The park was full of people getting excited about the upcoming fireworks display. It was pretty close to nine o’clock and beginning to get dark. I knew where to look for the Mafia.

We found them down by the Kingfish drinking Mountain Dews and smarting off at each other. They knew all about Darla leaving the next day, and I think they wanted to be on their best behavior during her last night in town.

Denny spotted us first. "Hello there, you two. It's nice you could come."

"Hi, guys."

Darla pretended shyness and made it seem flirtatious. "Hi, Tommy. Hi, Rex. Hello, Denny. I wouldn't want to miss a chance to say goodbye to my favorite men."

Denny began his usual schtick. "Darla, it's really too bad you're leaving. You know, you could have had any of us. I can't believe you settled for Emmet. He's so, so—ah, who am I kidding, he's the coolest one of us and we know it. You can't blame me for trying, though, can you? I don't suppose there's any chance Carmen is going to make an appearance for your sendoff, is there?"

"Sorry, Den, no such luck."

"Crap. I wore swimming trunks under my cutoffs, just in case she wanted to take a little dip again. *Kidding! I'm kidding!*"

Rex seldom tried to express his thoughts on anything too deep, and nobody would ever mistake him as being sentimental. He surprised us when he pulled a little wrapped package out of his shirt and handed it to Darla.

"Uh, Darla, I want you to have this. It's kind of from all of us in a way."

"Rex, thank you. You didn't have to do this!"

"It's not so much really, I just . . ." He ran out of words right about then. Darla opened the wrapping paper and the little cardboard box beneath it. Inside was a little piece of broken brown pottery. The guys all knew exactly what it was, but Darla didn't understand.

"Rex, I think I have to ask you to explain this. I don't know what it is exactly."

"It's Indian pottery I found here on the beach. We used to hunt for it when we were a little younger. This is one of the best pieces I have. I—*we* want you to have it, you know—to remember Bay City."

"It's wonderful. Really wonderful. Thank you—thank you all."

Most of the ancient pottery shards are gone now. Decades of tourists have picked the beach pretty clean. The only thing rarer is finding a decent arrowhead. Our parents had luck finding both on the beach or in the fields high above the lake where the Indigenous people lived and hunted. Walt Sprague had an entire collection of arrowheads and pottery harvested over decades of intentional searching. But my friends and I generally had to settle for an occasional small shard. Even those were getting scarce. It was quite a statement for Rex to give away one from his prized collection.

I felt ashamed. I didn't have a going-away gift for Darla, and I was pretty sure I wouldn't be able to come up with anything before tomorrow. Still, the Indian pottery shard was about as good a reminder of our town as there was.

Technically, the town owned the beach. But no one does, really. Others before us and others after will leave their footprints on the same sand. If only for the time being, it was ours to walk on, and for a while it had been Darla's.

We had grown up on this lake, and the pottery shards we sometimes found while walking barefoot along the shore were a unique part of the life we shared. We understood enough to realize a great people with a strong and beautiful culture had lived where we now live and that their remarkable life had been stolen away. What was left behind is legendary. Rex had somehow come up with the perfect gift for Darla.

Just then the first barrage of fireworks rocketed skyward over the harbor and exploded with a rain of silver fire and light. Instinctively, we said "Oooo, ahhh" in unison with the rest of the crowd.

The fireworks continued for a half hour or so. The red, blue, silver, and multicolored bursts of sparks lit up the sky over the park and illuminated the scene below. The *American Dream* floated serenely in the harbor as the strobe-like bursts of fireworks played on the illustrated skin of the Kingfish, causing the storied tree to intermittently cast its shadow over its children below.

When the display was finally over, the boys asked us to stick around and build a fire. I made only the flimsiest attempt to explain why we couldn't.

"Sorry, guys, we can't. We've got some—stuff to do."

Tom understood. "Oh sure. Stuff. That's important, too. You kids run along. We won't wait up for you."

Darla hugged each of them once more and we walked out of the park heading toward her house.

By the time we got back to the pink trailer, Marty and Deedee had already left for the dance. Because of the equipment loading, they wouldn't get home until around one in the morning. The gray Ford wagon was parked there, just waiting for us to take it for one last spin. Darla got the keys and a rolled up sleeping bag.

"You drive. Try to stay on the road, will you?"

"Hey! Do you think you're dealing with an amateur?"

"No, not an amateur, just a guy who drives like he's blindfolded."

I slid in behind the wheel. "Where to, miss?"

"Oh, I don't know. How about Johnson's Woods?"

"It's dark and scary out there. I might need someone to hold my hand."

"You're catching on."

This was the moment when I first realized I was not prepared for all the possibilities. Specifically, I was not in possession of a condom. Some of the guys I knew bragged about keeping rubbers in their wallet "just in case," but for me it had never been an issue. Until now, maybe.

We drove slowly down the street away from Darla's house and straight through the center of town like we owned it. We were just another couple out on a date. As we crossed the tracks and turned left on Highway 35 in front of Horton's, we could hear Deedee belting out "Stand by Your Man." Anyone who spotted us might have recognized what was going on, but we slowly drove by, completely unnoticed.

A short way past the edge of town we turned onto the dirt road just inside the back entrance to Johnson's Woods. This one was used mostly by hunters. I had walked it many times before but, of course, had never driven on it. We crept along trying to avoid the branches sticking out and threatening to scratch the wagon's already scratched-up paint. Near the end of the road was a turnaround. We parked the car in the big dirt circle and shut off the lights. The bright moon cast long shadows off the tree branches over the clearing where we parked.

It had become so easy to talk with her. I had gotten used to simply saying whatever was on my mind and knowing she would allow me my thoughts without any criticism. I hope she felt the same way. For a while, we exchanged our feelings about little things we would miss about spending time together. I still didn't want to talk about her actually leaving, but eventually, we did.

"You know, you could just break up with me like other girls do. You don't have to move clear across the country."

"Sorry, Emmet, it's what we do."

"I just wish there was some way you could stay and finish out the next school year."

"Me too. I'm always scared about starting in a new school. My gosh, it's just a month and a half away!"

We sat there in silence for a few seconds pondering the whole idea of a new school and everything it meant. Then I blurted out the question I had been considering for several months.

"Darla, are we in love?"

I didn't imagine she would start to cry. Her beautiful eyes welled up and she turned away as the tears spilled down her cheeks. I put my arm around her, and she cried harder. She buried her face in my chest and sobbed. I cried too, and finally knew the answer to my question. Then I did the only thing I could think of to try to fix this sad situation, and I kissed her.

We kissed for a while, and the kisses ranged from little sweet ones to deep passionate ones that made me feel like I could blow up at any second. We folded down the back seat and spread the sleeping bag out in the back of the wagon. Then we scrambled back, took off our shoes, and snuggled into the warmth of the bag.

"I guess we maybe *are* in love, Emmet. I used to think we were kind of a different couple. I mean, me being older than you and all. I never thought of myself as a cradle robber, though, did you?"

"Geez, Darla, I'm not a child!"

She laughed. "I know. You're a big, strong, macho fisher-*man*."

Then she got serious. "Don't you think it's really hard being our age and having strong feelings for someone? We're too young to make a real commitment. I mean, like marriage. But I guess we're old enough to have our hearts broken. I'm pretty sure I know *that* feeling."

She started to cry again, and I held her close.

"Emmet, I'm sorry. I wanted us to . . . have a special last night together tonight. I'm ruining everything!"

"Darla, I'm probably really going to regret this, but, uh, do you think we can just hang onto each other here tonight? I mean *just* hold each other. I know you brought the sleeping bag out here and all, but to tell you the truth, I don't know if I'm ready for it. Sex, I mean."

She mimicked indignation and slapped my cheek lightly. "You have a dirty mind, young man! Just what kind of girl do you think I am anyway?"

I thought about it before I answered. "I think you are the sweetest, and the funniest, and the greatest girlfriend any guy ever had. I just don't want to mess it up somehow on our last night together. I think it might change everything. Maybe it would change what we shared so far; I don't know. Besides, I . . ."

"What Emmet? What is it?"

"Aren't we supposed to have some, you know—protection? I don't . . ."

"Well! I brought the sleeping bag. Did you forget something?

"I guess so. I—well I guess I wasn't thinking about—oh man, Darla. I really messed up. I just don't want this to end up like . . ."

"Like what, Emmet?"

"Nothing. Nothing, I guess."

"What? Nothing is *always* something. What is it? Please don't tell me there was someone before me."

"No, Darla. No! There's nobody like you. I just don't want our last night to be like the first time I drove the car."

For a couple seconds Darla got the strangest look on her face. Then suddenly, she threw back her head and began laughing uncontrollably.

"Oh my god, Emmet! *Oh my god, that's hilarious!* Did you just compare me to this broken-down old Ford?"

She howled with laughter again and I started laughing, too.

"Emmet, you are so special. This is what I mean! How could I not fall in love with you? For the record, I am not prepared either. I'll tell you what: let's make a pact. The next time we get together in person, we will make crazy, mad, passionate love, even if it means we will hate each other afterward. Deal?"

"Deal."

We were quiet then for a time, just lying there wrapped in each other's arms. I was relieved. Maybe Darla was too. Finally, she broke the silence.

"I always thought you would be the one, my first. I guess I imagined we would have a lot more time together. The truth is, I know I am not ready yet, either. I don't mean 'prepared,' I mean *ready*. It's better this way."

I couldn't answer right away. I thought about it, carefully considering her words. Then I said what I had been thinking for a long time.

"I think—I *know* that you're *my* first, Darla, the first girl I ever loved. I hope you know it's true, because I feel it and it's real. I'll never get over you."

She squeezed my hand in hers and whispered, "I know. I love you too. I always will."

Altogether, we must have stayed there for well over an hour, just talking and occasionally kissing, but that was all. Finally, we put our shoes back on and climbed back into the front seat. We had the station wagon back in the yard just after eleven thirty. A little before midnight, I kissed her one last time as she stood on her steps and turned to walk toward home.

"Good night, Sweet Boy. I'll see you in the morning."

I turned back to see her face one more time, but she was already halfway through the door. I whispered, "Goodbye, Sweet Girl."

I took the long way, hiking alone down the back route to the park and across the catwalk over the spillway from Northwestern Pond. I thought about the day I introduced Darla and Carmen to the boys and tried to recall every detail of the night when we went swimming together and the conversations around the fire.

I wasn't worried about walking alone in the moonlit night. Maybe I should have been. But knowing Darla felt the same way I did, knowing we really did love each other, kept me from thinking about anything else. For a little while there was no fear.

I walked through the park where the campers were enjoying their bonfires and beer. Turning east, I walked the shoreline past Tom's house and the Spragues', and then all along the lake until I reached the road leading home.

I thought about the difference between love and sex and whether you could have one without the other. I guess we'll find out.

I kept walking on up the hill past Hunt's Tavern and finally onto the railroad tracks running parallel to Highway 35 through the middle of town. I was right about where we'd started the night, in front of Horton's. Inside, I imagined my folks having fun. I could hear Marty and Deedee's music clearly in the night air. Deedee was wailing the last few lines of "There She Goes." I hoped Dad and Mom were dancing. It was nearly midnight.

Ever since then, the song has never been the same for me. I followed the tracks along the entire length of town and past the back of the Patterson property. Though I looked at the house as I walked by, I was no longer afraid. Soon I was home and in my bed. I heard Mom and Dad come in a short time later. As I waited for sleep, I wished Friday would never come, but of course it did.

It felt like Darla, and I had spent every free minute together since her dad announced they were moving. Now I knew we might never get another chance to be together the way we had been last night. I was an idiot! What was I thinking? If the Mafia ever got wind of it, I would have to join the French Foreign Legion out of pure shame.

Mom and Dad were already up.

"How was your night? We didn't see you at the fireworks."

"Sorry, Mom, we were over by the Kingfish."

"Oh. Say, I got you a little something for Darla. You know, a little going-away present. I hope she likes it."

"Mom, it's great! Whatever it is, it's great! I really didn't think about . . ."

"I know. It's what moms are for. I'll help you wrap it if you like." She handed me a little frame with a picture of Darla and me in it. I remembered her taking it in our front yard shortly after she got home from Madison. It was just right.

"I have one of these for you too."

"Thanks, Mom. It's wonderful."

Dad said, "We'd better get over to the trailer or we might miss them."

Rubbing his eyes, Jack came out of our bedroom dressed in the same clothes he'd worn the day before.

"Wait for me, will you? I think I'm still asleep."

Marty planned on getting an early start. The sendoff committee met at the Day house around seven thirty a.m. Mom had made ham sandwiches to send along for the trip. Dad helped Marty tighten up some ropes tying down the stuff on the roof of the Ford. Deedee would drive the Riviera, and Marty would lead in the wagon.

The Mafia even showed up. This was generally much earlier than the natural waking hour for any of the boys. Their eyes and hair looked as though they had just climbed out of bed, but it meant a lot to Darla to have them there. She hugged the boys one by one and gave Tom a smooch on the cheek.

"I'll never wash my face again."

Our moms hugged and our dads shook hands and promised to write and call once in a while. Darla and I stood together at the back of the Riv trying to find a little privacy in the midst of our families and friends. I tried to say something meaningful, but my voice was beginning to crack, and I didn't want to cry in front of everybody.

"Darla, I—*you* taught me a lot about who I always want to be. This is for you."

I gave her the picture and she slowly unwrapped it without tearing the paper. Once again, her eyes began to tear up as she looked at it.

"Thank you, Emmet. I promise I will never forget you for as long as I live."

We had tried to be brave, but we just couldn't hold it in any longer. We clung to each other and cried without shame, right there in front of everyone.

Marty waited until we were done hugging and then he said, "I, uh—guess it's time."

Darla kissed me one last beautiful time and got into the back seat of the Riviera. Afterward, I held my tongue between my lips for a few seconds and tasted the salty combination of our tears and our sorrow. Marty and Deedee started the engines, and we waved goodbye.

The two cars rolled down the street, away from the pink trailer and toward a new life. Darla stood on her knees with her arms up on the window ledge behind the back seat and her right hand held up with the palm facing toward me. I raised my right arm and held it motionless with the elbow slightly bent and the palm of my hand turned toward hers. By the time the cars were two blocks away I could no longer make out the features of her pretty face. She was gone from my life almost as quickly as she had appeared.

The next week, Stella and Wayne Button moved into the pink trailer and made it their home, though I would always think of it as Darla's house. The two-seater bike was parked out front and received some occasional use.

I essentially worked and moped the rest of the summer away. I lost weight and started building up muscles. I was tanned from working outside all summer long with my shirt off. Each time I thought of her, the deep sadness returned.

The boys never pressed me about what Darla, and I did or didn't do on our last night together. In the end I guess I didn't really regret it too long. Somehow, I think we both understood we were just too young to handle either the responsibility or any more frustrations that may have come from a hurried attempt to prove something when we already knew it was ending.

In my heart, I knew we had done as my father had advised, but it didn't make it feel any better. All I know is that doing the right thing sometimes is pretty complicated. But as Dad also said, "It means doing it even when nobody is looking."

Two weeks later the tank from Jerry Wold's old pumper truck became the holding tank in our backyard, and the Burner assumed its rightful place in the *American Dream*. This milestone also marked the removal of the infamous slop hole.

CHAPTER 32

A New Beginning

A day didn't pass without me thinking of Darla and wondering what it was like for her starting in a new school so far away in California. We had talked on the phone a few times, but it was changing a little with every call.

I began the year at Ellsworth High without any intention of trying to find a new girlfriend. I hadn't seen a lot of my classmates over the summer, but when I finally ran into Faith and Jane, it was instantly apparent how quickly we were growing up.

"Hi, Emmet. How are you doing? How was your summer? You look good."

"Oh, hi, Faith. It was pretty good. I worked. How about you? Did you have a nice summer?"

Jane interrupted. "She had a great summer without her creepy ex-boyfriend."

"Shush! It was fine. I spent a lot of time volunteering at the hospital. I heard Darla and her family moved to California."

"Yeah."

"Well, does that mean you are available if I ask you to go to the Sadie Hawkins Dance next week?"

The Sadie Hawkins Dance was patterned after Sadie Hawkins Day, an event imagined by Al Capp in his serial newspaper cartoon *Li'l Abner*. As in Al Capp's comic, the logic was if boys were left the responsibility of asking a girl to an organized dance, there would never *be* one. So, for this event, the girls asked the boys. The dance was set up to bring us all together for some fun dancing to records and maybe even help teach us some boy-girl etiquette.

"Huh? Dance? Uh . . ."

"Is that a 'yes'? You'd better not say 'no' or I will be very embarrassed, and my feelings will be hurt. You wouldn't want that to happen, would you?"

"No, I . . ."

"Is this 'no' you won't go to the dance with me or 'no' you don't want to hurt my feelings?" She stuck her lower lip out and pretended to pout.

Girls have a distinct advantage over boys at this age. They are maturing both physically and intellectually at a much faster rate. She was toying with me like a cat plays with a mouse just before eating it for dinner.

"Yes! No! I mean—I would really *like* to go to the dance with you."

"Terrific! Now where is that friend of yours, Tom Freeman? Jane needs a date, and we thought it would be fun if we all went together.

"Tom? Uh, he's around, I guess. I can tell him you want to talk to him."

Jane held up her hand with her palm out. "Hold it right there, buddy. I forbid you to try to set me up with your friend. That would be pathetic. I am capable of handling this without any assistance from you, Emmet. Thanks anyway. C'mon, Faith, let's hunt him down."

"Bye, Emmet. See you in class."

Jane was dragging her away by the arm. I hardly knew what had hit me. Tom didn't stand a chance either. Jane found him in the cafeteria and pounced on him before he could think of a way to appropriately express his deep appreciation. She didn't so much ask him to the dance as tell him he was going to go with her. He just stood there in suspended animation while she gave him her list of expectations: meeting her at the school, what to wear, and so on. Then Tom found me.

"M, Jane just asked me to the Sadie Hawkins Dance, and she said you were going with Faith! Am I in some deep and dreamlike hypnotic state? If so, don't wake me up."

"I know! Can you believe it? Did you see how great they looked? Geez! They're even better-looking than they were last year. They seem—older."

Just then, Rex and Denny came sidling up.

"Greetings fellow students, and welcome to Ellsworth High School, home of the Purple Panthers and the famous boy genius, Dennis Berg."

"Hi guys. You'll never guess what just happened to us! Tom and I got asked to the Sadie Hawkins Dance by Faith Briggs and Jane Keener! Can you believe it?"

Rex and Denny were only mildly impressed. Rex said, "Well that's pretty cool, all right, but Denny and I are going with the Gleason twins! Double your pleasure, double your fun!"

Jelly just smiled that all-knowing smile of his and said, "Gentlemen, we are living in very interesting times."

The Sadie Hawkins Dance was held on a Thursday night. Rex's mom gave us a ride. The gym was decorated with crepe paper streamers and balloons. Though the posters for the dance assured us of having a groovy time and encouraged us to enjoy the far-out music, I had to believe the conservative school administration didn't really want us to get *too* groovy or far-out.

The Baytown Mafia sauntered in like they owned the place. The Gleason twins waved at Rex and Denny as the two began to strut across the hardwood floor toward their dates. The Gleason girls looked very good. They wore similar short skirts that showed off their legs and clingy sweaters that enhanced their slightly top-heavy figures.

Denny turned back toward us and away from the Gleason girls. Flashing a two-thumbs-up sign in front of his chest, he squinted and mouthed, "Wow."

When he turned back, he grinned and insipidly called out, "Hi, girls."

Tom and I stood around trying to look nonchalant for a while and hoping Jane and Faith would show up soon. Heck, I just hoped Faith would show up at all. Then they magically appeared in the doorway.

Jelly mumbled, "Holy Hannah!"

He was right. Jane's miniskirt was impossible to not notice. Faith wore a blue sweater and a short paisley print dress. Her eyes were even bluer than her sweater. She waved at me as they entered the gym. I couldn't believe she was my date.

"Hi, fellas! Have you been here long?"

"No. Gosh, Faith, you look—really excellent."

"Thanks for noticing. Emmet, I think there's hope for you yet!"

"Jane, you look pretty good, too." The second the words were out of his mouth, Tom realized he had made a grave mistake.

"*Pretty good?* No kidding, Tom, maybe I should go home and change into something a little more flattering."

"No! No! I mean excellent! Really excellent! Uh—*stunning*!"

"I know, Tom, cut the crap. I *know* I look good. C'mon, let's see if you dance any better than you give a compliment."

We danced to nearly every record. Faith was tireless. Sometimes she closed her eyes when she moved to the music. Sometimes she threw her arms up over her head and shook her hair from side to side. Her knees and hips swayed in time to the music. She was . . . incredible. And I was still just me.

She preened and glided. Her dancing was pretty, and hip, and sexy all at the same time. Her moves reminded me a little of that day in the swimming pool at Keener's. In my mind she was the center of attention with every song. I was in way over my head. The only real dancing I had ever done was with Darla, and it was mostly to our parents' slow songs. Still, I was genuinely grateful to Darla for those early lessons. Faith was as good as any dancer on Dick Clark's *American Bandstand* TV show.

When a slow song came along, I sometimes looked around to see Jane or the Gleason girls. It was easy to tell that the boys were doing the same thing. I only wished I could get a better look at Faith. At this moment in time, life could not have been scripted any better.

When "Baby, I Need Your Loving" by Johnny Rivers came on, we all got up and moved out onto the gym floor. Faith maneuvered us over closer to Tom and Jane. They seemed like they were enjoying themselves. Then it happened.

I could see Tom was really getting into the music. His eyes were closed, and his lips were silently moving to the words.

Jane's short dress got even shorter with her arms around Tom's shoulders. The tiniest hint of snow-white lace showed just below the hemline.

Tom nestled into Jane's shoulder as she squirmed a bit and attempted to fend off his advances. She tried to keep a little air between the two of them, but Tom was taller, and he gradually managed to pull her closer. I stared, transfixed in horror as his hands began to migrate slowly down her back. It was like watching a car sliding on ice in slow motion, just before a wreck.

This could only end badly. Jane was capable of dismantling the average guy using only words as her weapon. Dumbfounded and paralyzed,

I watched and waited for the ugly conflict I was sure was now only seconds away. Slowly, ever so slowly, Tom's hand inched toward the target of his desire.

Faith gracefully swayed back and forth. She tried to turn me around so she would be facing Tom and Jane, but I didn't budge. Tom's hand was nearing the danger zone. My eyes were getting bigger, and my mouth was dry. I was pretty sure he was about to lose a couple of fingers, if not the entire hand. When his fingertips reached Jane's bottom, I just closed my eyes, waited, and listened. What I heard was completely unexpected. Jane's voice was calm and matter of fact.

"Tom, is that your hand on my ass?"

Several seconds went by. Then Jelly said in a wavering and strangely high-pitched voice, "Yes. It would seem so."

Faith spun around to see what was going on. Jane's right hand clenched the front of Tom's pants in a vice-like grip. She was still swaying slowly to the music.

"Tom, do you think maybe you could take your paws off me and never touch me again? If you do, I promise I'll do the same."

His eyes watered as she squeezed even harder on the front of his pants. His hands slid quickly and respectfully up to her shoulders. In response, her right hand returned to its position on his waist.

"Thank you, Tom. You made a good decision."

"You're welcome, Jane. I'm *really* sorry."

"Uh huh."

She never quit dancing.

Faith laughed a delightfully evil laugh and swept me away to the far end of the gym floor, where Rex and Denny were putting on quite an exhibition. It's an understatement to say the boys were not good dancers, but they didn't seem to realize it. Or if they did, they didn't care. They were with two very attractive girls who seemed to enjoy their unorthodox style.

On the other hand, the Gleason twins were *very* good. They had obviously learned by dancing together, as their moves looked almost exactly alike. The four of them commanded the entire end of the gym floor under the basketball hoop.

When the Johnny Rivers tune ended, James Brown's "I Feel Good" came on. Denny and Rex did their best to mimic the Godfather of Soul's famous footwork. The girls were greatly amused.

On breaks from the music, we helped ourselves to glasses of pink liquid stuff made from a mixture of Seven Up, Hawaiian Punch, and orange sherbet. The high sugar content only helped to fuel our energetic gyrations. We talked and laughed and generally had a great time.

After the Unfortunate Incident, Tom's attempts at conversation with Jane amounted to extremely polite small talk. Faith was very kind and happy to chat. She made me feel like a much better date than I actually was. Like a lot of the other couples, we eventually drifted out the back door to stroll around the sidewalks encircling the school building.

"Let's get some fresh air. I need a break."

"Sure."

"Strange Brew" by Cream had just finished. Eric Clapton's amazing electric guitar leads were still reverberating in the gym like a lightning strike when Faith took me by the hand.

We strolled and talked easily. Faith made sure of it. She asked me questions, making certain I had to give more than a one-word answer. She wanted to know about my job on the fishing boat. She asked me about my mom. She seemed genuinely interested in what I said.

I asked her about swimming and the Gems. We were getting along well. Then a car rolled up and pulled over next to the curb right where we were walking. It was Smith Morris. I thought to myself, *geez, he drives a Camaro!*

"Hi Faith. How's it going?"

"Hi Smith. What do *you* want?"

"Oh, I don't know. I was sitting here outside the old school, listening to the music, and I thought maybe I'd ask you to take a ride. I'd like to talk to you. That is, unless you're too busy."

He looked ominously at me. My pulse began to speed up. I thought to myself, *here we go.*

I imagined Faith hopping in the front seat and cruelly laughing and waving at me as the Camaro sped away. It was over. I lost. The older guy with the nice car wins. It's an age-old plot that nearly always ends the same way. But surprisingly, Faith was about to rewrite history and add a new twist.

"Fat chance, Smith! What's wrong? Did you run out of bimbos to impress with your rock-star image? Can't you see I'm on a date here? Get lost."

"Okay, Faith. *Fine.* If you want to go out slumming with Charlie Brown there, he's all yours. By the way, I was listening to the band you hired. They really stink! Quicksand does a ten-times-better job on 'Strange Brew' than those phonies."

He squealed his tires as he pulled away.

"I'm really sorry, Emmet."

I smiled at her and said, "Uh, don't you mean Charlie?" We both laughed. "Charlie Brown! Do I really look like Charlie Brown?"

"Well maybe just the haircut a little bit! Smith is such a jerk." She giggled.

"I sort of hate to point this out, but he drives a pretty nice car, and he plays in a rock band. And his name even *sounds* like rock and roll. I feel like I didn't even dress well enough to be seen with you tonight. Why didn't you go with him?"

"What? Are you kidding me? Emmet, I didn't ask you to the Sadie Hawkins Dance because I thought you were a snappy dresser. I asked you because I think you are a nice guy—smart and funny—somebody I could have a good time with. He treated me like dirt! But please don't be too disappointed if I tell you that I'm not looking for a new boyfriend tonight. I know Darla just moved away. I thought we might have something in common. I need a friend, and I thought maybe you could use one too."

"Hmm—so you just want to be friends, huh? Only a date with a friend? I guess it's a good thing I'm such a terrific dancer then."

She giggled. "I wouldn't go quite so far, but you do have some potential."

Faith was so great! I had been feeling so confused about Darla leaving that I'd nearly forgotten to appreciate my extremely good fortune at having one of the prettiest girls in school as my date.

"Thanks, Faith."

"For what?"

"I think you know."

"Emmet, I'm not letting you off the hook completely. It's still three years until we graduate. Who knows? Every couple starts somewhere. What if this is our moment? Do you ever just ask yourself, 'What if?'"

"Now I'm a little confused. Are we going to just be friends . . . for now?"

"Absolutely! Now let's go back in and show off some of those fancy moves of yours."

As we turned back toward the school, she took my hand again and turned me around, so I faced her. She smiled sweetly and said, "I have something for you."

My face started to flush, and I was sure she was about to kiss me. All the "just friends" talk was clearly a ploy. I may have even begun to slightly pucker up.

Instead, she reached in her purse and handed me an old and tarnished brass key.

"Uh, what's this?"

"It's the key to happiness. I want you to keep it and know it's *your* special key. Will you keep it?"

I was a little confused, but I played along. The metal key felt cool in the palm of my hand. I looked at it and turned it over. It was a neat old key.

"Sure, I will. I'll keep it. I think you are going to be a very good friend to have, Faith."

"So are you, Emmet. By the way, you never know, I might ask you whether you still have the key sometime later on."

"Ask me anytime. I'll still have it."

When the music was finished, the parents came to pick up their kids. Faith's dad pulled up while we waited together in front of the school. John Briggs was a Korean War hero who owned his own dry-cleaning business. His nickname was Sarge. In the war, he had survived an enemy ambush and managed to get his platoon out without losing a single man. He did well in his business because he worked hard at it. The whole family did. Faith's mom, Bonnie, ran the family business's books besides working part-time at the credit union. When she wasn't volunteering at the hospital, Faith worked in the store after school and on weekends.

Her dad parked at the curb and came around to the front of the car to meet me. I could tell he was sizing me up as he did. The creases in his pants and shirt were so crisp and sharp he could have split wood with them. The part in his hair was straight, and not a single one was out of place.

I thought he must have seen a hundred guys like us before. Faith introduced me to him and then the boys. He already knew the girls.

"So, did you have a nice time?"

"Yes, Daddy."

"Are you ready to go home?"

"Yes. Can you give Shari and Cari a ride home? And Jane?"

"I sure can. Hop in, girls. It was nice to meet you, boys."

John Briggs walked back around the front of his car. He opened the door and began to get in. Then he stopped and stood back up, leaning one elbow on the roof. He looked us over.

I was a little intimidated by his stare. He had led a seriously out-manned tank crew through an enemy attack at night in one of the most godforsaken places on earth. The story made all the papers. I wondered what he was thinking about us. We were ants. If he had sneezed, I think we would have fainted.

"Emmet North—are you Brick and Rachel's boy?"

"Yes sir, I am."

"Are you in Faith's grade?"

"Yes sir."

"I've met your folks. Good people. Stop by the house sometime."

The Gleason twins waved at Rex and Denny from the back seat. Jane crossed her legs and smiled, knowing when she did, she owned the world. Faith waved at me from the front seat, and they drove away.

Denny mimicked a deep and Sarge Briggs-ish voice. "'Stop by the house sometime.' I think he likes you."

It wasn't long before Rex's mom picked us up and drove us home. "How was the dance, boys?"

"Okay."

"Yeah, it was all right."

"Not bad."

I thought to myself how unbelievably wonderful it had been, how perfect Faith had been. Reaching into my front pocket, I ran my fingers over the key to happiness. For a second, I allowed myself to wonder "What if?" Nah, I don't think so. No way.

Friday morning while we waited for the school bus, we talked about our dates like most guys our age do. Jelly said Jane was about the scariest girl he had ever met. She was great-looking and all, but he couldn't seem to get anywhere with her. Because he was my best friend, I gently reminded him of his indiscretion.

"Tom, you are such a dumbass moron! You put your stupid hand on her behind! A lot of girls would have slapped you silly and gone home. I think she was a pretty good sport."

"I guess so. She didn't have to squeeze my nuts so hard though. I just got a little carried away."

I imitated Tom's style of quasi-intellectual humor: "I believe the correct term is 'groin-itals.'"

We laughed. Tom corrected me just to make sure we had taken the joke as far as we could go with it. "Actually, M, the correct anatomical term is 'groin-italia.'"

"How about you? Did you and Faith have fun?"

I said I had a really good time. I told the boys Faith, and I were just friends, and we had a really good time. I must have said "really good time" once too often. Jelly mocked me, "But did you have a *good* time? I mean—was it a *really good* time—or just a *good* time?"

"You're just jealous. Next time you can have the sweet, wonderful girl and I'll take the friend who won't let anybody touch her butt."

Near the end of the dance, Rex and Denny had disappeared with the Gleason girls for nearly an hour. I decided to explore.

"So, boys, let's have it. Where did you and the Gleason twins go? Give us the scoop. What happened?"

They both said "Nothing" at the same time, which of course meant something must have happened. Jelly egged them on.

"C'mon, let me live vicariously through your experiences. I need to know what I missed. Did Rex at least show the girls his foot?"

"I think you might say we had a good time. And when I say a good time, I mean a *great* time." Rex was grinning from ear to ear.

Denny looked at us with his usual sad-eyed basset hound expression and said, "Fellows, you might as well know it. We had sex. Lots and lots of s-e-x. Hot, crazy sex! *Life-changing* sex! I'm surprised I can even walk."

Jelly and I were amazed! "Are you kidding? *With the Gleason twins?* Holy crap, alert the media! Is this for real?"

Denny continued with his deadpan delivery. "Yes, boys, we did it on the street and on the boulevard. We did it in the backyard of St. Francis parish. It made me feel very dirty and I *really* liked it. *No, you idiots!* We went for a walk around the block and just talked with them! You guys are so gullible it's pathetic."

Jelly was disappointed. "No s-e-x?"

Rex shook his head. "No sex, just dancing. Of course, the way I do it it's pretty close to the same thing." He gave a short reprise of his James Brown shuffle. "You can't do this with all ten toes."

Denny brought us back down to earth.

"You guys—geez, get real. We're in the ninth grade! Besides, look at me. I'm only a teenager and I already look like somebody's grandpa. I'll probably never get laid, let alone with a Gleason twin."

There was an awkward truth to what he said. Denny was kind of different looking. The Gleason girls had been sort of a package deal. When Shari asked Rex to the Sadie Hawkins Dance, Cari asked Denny because he was Rex's friend. She probably wasn't really too attracted to him. It's just the way things worked. He was right. He probably would never get laid.

At first, we didn't say anything. Then Tom tried to make sure Denny knew how much we cared.

"Uh, don't take this wrong, but—like, if I was a girl, I'd probably do it with you, Den."

It was our big chance to get even for him taking us for a ride with his "hot sex" story.

I joined in, "Yeah, Denny, I would too. Definitely."

"Me too. Hubba-hubba." Rex batted his eyes at Denny.

"Yeah, not exactly what I had in mind. You freakin' weirdos! Is this supposed to make me feel good?"

Mercifully, the bus pulled up and spared Denny any further concerns.

When we got to school there was a newspaper cartoon strip taped to the door of my locker. It was *Peanuts* by Charles Schulz. There were four little cartoon boxes. The Lucy character was talking to Schroeder while Charlie Brown stood nearby.

Lucy asked, "Are you smarter than Charlie Brown?"

Schroeder said, "Yes!"

Lucy asked, "Are you faster than Charlie Brown?"

"Yes! Of course!" All the while Charlie Brown was getting increasingly dejected.

"Are you better-looking than Charlie Brown?"

"Yes, definitely!"

In the last box Lucy asked Schroeder, "Then why don't I like you as much as I like Charlie Brown?"

Charlie Brown's broad moon face was wearing a wide, upwardly curving single line of a smile. I folded it up and put it in the back of one of my notebooks. Right about then, I must have been smiling the same way.

CHAPTER 33

Jerry Comes Clean

Jerry Wold hadn't exactly been himself lately. He had been a loner all his life, and though his work didn't exactly inspire popularity, something was different in recent months. His septic tank pumping business was as steady as ever. Heck, he had even bought a new truck. Most mornings he still showed up at Stella's. But he had begun sitting by himself and leaving right after eating his breakfast, as if he was in a hurry and worried about being late. Dad wasn't the only one who noticed it.

After the Patterson murders, the FBI and the Sheriff's Department told Dad to keep his eyes and ears open and let them know if he noticed anything suspicious. Jerry was a nice guy who did his job and never had a bad word to say about anybody. Perhaps he drank a little too much sometimes, but it hardly qualified as conspicuous behavior in Bay City. Still, Dad took his constable role seriously.

Just before nine o'clock on Saturday morning, September 21, he followed Jerry out of the café. The day had started out unseasonably warm and humid, but now the rain was beginning to come down hard, and the temperature was dropping fast.

"Jerry, how about a lift home? I need to talk to you about pumping out our new tank."

"Sure, Brick. Hop in."

They climbed up into the cab of the Honey Wagon. The 'new truck smell' had already been replaced by a slight stench of raw sewage. It was a short ride, only ten or twelve blocks. Dad didn't waste any time: "Jerry, I get the feeling something might be bothering you."

"No. Not really."

"C'mon, Jerry, we've known each other a long time. What's going on?"

"Brick, you're a good guy, and I know you and Rachel have been through a lot. Just leave me be, Brick."

"I can't Jerry. I need to know what you know. It's sort of my job. Now you need to tell me what's up so I can help you."

Jerry pulled into the alley behind Brown's Seed Corn and turned off the motor. The rain was pouring down, and the noise all but drowned out the sound of Jerry's voice as he spoke in faltering sentences.

"I think—I might know something. I mean, I'm not sure. Maybe I should have said something sooner. I was drunk. I didn't mean it!"

"Jerry, what have you done?" Dad was getting worried. "Is this about the Pattersons?"

"It's not what you think, Brick. Sometimes I just can't seem to keep my big mouth shut."

After Jerry calmed down, he poured out a story about being in Hunt's Tavern on the night of the murders. He was three sheets to the wind by the time Willard Patterson stopped in for a beer after work. It was sometime before midnight, maybe eleven o'clock. Willard sat down next to Jerry.

"Hey there, Willard, how's the old shoe factory? Did you save any soles tonight?"

Willard was a good guy and he smiled at Jerry's familiar pun, "Two at a time, Jerry. The left one goes with the right one and they both go in the box."

It was payday, and Willard cashed his check at Hunt's every other Friday night. Uncle Harry knew this and made sure there was enough cash tucked under the coin drawer in the register. It was a ritual, and the men didn't need any discussion. Both Willard and Harry knew the drill. When Willard sat down, Harry slid a pen across the bar. Willard signed his paycheck and slid it back. The money was counted out on the bar in front of Willard, and both men nodded at the end. Willard always bought Harry a beer, and tonight he bought one for Jerry, too.

Jerry raised his glass and spoke in a loud voice that carried across the room, "Whoa, big spender! Mr. Millionaire! Thank you for opening your big safe and sharing some of your loot with us little people."

Jerry was pretty loaded, and Willard had seen this act before. He joined in.

"That's right, Jer. Every now and then I need to sweep out the safe and get rid of the small bills."

Over at the pool table two strangers paused in their game and looked at each other. Both were very intoxicated. One was a blond man with long hair pulled back behind his ears. The other appeared to be Hispanic. They had kept to themselves since they came in and were drinking shots of whiskey and beers. Between the tourist anglers and the occasional barge workers, it was not unusual for strangers to be drinking at Hunt's on Friday nights. Now they seemed to be discussing something in loud drunken whispers. Suddenly, they were scuffling.

Harry yelled from the bar, "Hey! Break it up you two. Take it outside."

The dark-haired guy said to the blond stranger, "You're on your own, man." He turned and left the bar.

The blond-haired man gulped the last of his beer and followed the other guy outside. It was almost closing time.

At midnight Harry announced, "last call" and began shutting down the bar. Willard got in his Mercury and drove away. Jerry nearly tipped off his stool when he spun sideways while attempting to aim his feet toward the door. He was hammered. When he got outside, he took a look at the Honey Wagon parked across the street and then at the county squad car down the block by the railroad crossing, with only its parking lights on. It seemed like a good night to walk home.

Jerry lived up on top of the hill by the cemetery. Even if he was sober, the climb would have taken his breath away. When he got to the top of the hill, he turned onto Cemetery Road. To further hamper his progress, Jerry sprained his ankle as he stumbled down into the ditch to pee. He was more than halfway home when a van pulled over and a raspy voice said, "Need a ride?"

He didn't recognize the guy, but the sore ankle made the decision an easy one. Jerry opened the door and half fell onto the front seat. The van smelled like stale whiskey and smoke. The driver asked, "Where ya wanna go, man?"

"Last house on the right. The one with the pole shed."

Jerry was very tired from the booze and the long walk. He slumped down and began to doze off. The blond man reached over and shook his shoulder.

"Hey Jughead, don't fall asleep on me. I don't know where you live."

Jerry raised his head and pointed with a limp wrist. "Onward, my man."

The surly driver started talking. "I saw you at the bar tonight. You were sitting next to the guy with all the money."

Jerry was in and out. "Yeah—money."

He kept talking. "What about the safe? Is the guy really rich?"

Jerry chuckled in his drunken half-sleep, "Yeah, rich. Goddamned millionaire."

"What about the safe, man? Tell me where he keeps it. Now!"

There was no safe. It was just a dumb joke Jerry had made. This was much too hard to explain to the guy. Better to just tell him something to make him quit asking questions. "I don't know. It's there somewhere."

The van pulled into driveway. The blond guy punched Jerry hard on the shoulder.

"Where's his house, Jughead?"

The punch woke Jerry up and made him amply aware this guy was nobody to mess with. Even in a drunken stupor, Jerry knew he meant business. He just mumbled, "West end—Main Street—white house with green trim."

Jerry was relieved when the van stopped in his driveway. "Beat it, man."

He got out and staggered to his house, where he fell asleep with his clothes still on.

+ + +

Willard Patterson's Mercury was parked in his driveway and the hood was still warm when Fritz Michaels pulled in behind Swenson's Fish Market and killed the engine. A small box inside the double back doors of the van contained the tools of his trade. He took out a pistol, a box cutter, a hammer, and a full roll of duct tape. Within a few minutes he was ready to begin his grim night's work.

Out beyond the city limits, the late-run freight sounded its horn. Even in his current state of stoned drunkenness, Michaels understood the value of a long and noisy train passing close to the house he was about to invade. There was no sense in waking the neighbors.

"Brick, I swear I didn't mean anything. I don't know for sure, but I think maybe he was the guy. The one who killed 'em."

Jerry's eyes were bleary and bloodshot from too many nights of troubled sleep.

Dad said, "It's not too bad, Jerry. Maybe he was the guy and maybe he wasn't. You'd better talk to the police, though, what do you think?"

"Yeah, I guess maybe I'd better. Will you be there when I do?"

"Sure. Absolutely. Jerry, Walt told me about the deal you gave us on the holding tank. I will do my best to honor our friendship and still try to steer us through this mess."

Jerry and Dad called the sheriff from our house. They talked for several minutes, and Jerry repeated what he had told Dad. After Jerry told his story, Dad took the phone and talked for a while. As usual, he ended by saying, "Now don't forget about us; we're counting on you."

After Jerry left, Dad turned his attention to his family. "Did the crew go out today?"

Mom said, "Yes. M said they were fishing Towhead today."

A few seconds passed as they looked deeply into each other's eyes. Then Dad said, "Don't worry. Mick and Hap have seen bad weather before. They know what they're doing."

CHAPTER 34

THE STORM

As usual, Swenson's seine crew left the harbor around seven thirty a.m. on Saturday, September 21st. Except for the Sadie Hawkins Dance, I had immersed myself in my job ever since Darla left to make up for the relationship I did not have, a strategy I would later perfect in my middle years.

Now the fishing season was coming to an end too. After school started, only an occasional large haul was made on the weekend. Otherwise, Mick and Hap worked at the market smoking fish, or they made a short haul with the light rig or the gill nets.

This was to be the last big lake haul before Mick and Hap went upriver for some deep fishing near Prescott. The deep fishing was smaller scale and could be handled by the two older men after the Swenson brothers and I were back in the classroom.

Our crew had been amply coached about how hard and dangerous commercial fishing is. A lot of things happen that nobody can begin to predict. Sometimes it can be a beautiful day, but there are no fish to be found anywhere. Other times, like today, the weather can be pretty lousy, and you might run into a school so big you just have to take a chance on the weather holding up long enough to finish the haul. The barometer had a lot to do with the behavior of the fish, and a large pressure drop would sometimes really bring them in.

Hap had gone out ahead of the launch in his jon boat as always. Today, he came back early and obviously excited.

"It's a big one! Towhead is loaded! There could be a hundred and twenty thousand, maybe more. We'd better hurry! C'mon, boys. Get it moving!"

I loved this part of the haul. There was a lot of activity and hurried preparations to get done before the seine could clear the deck and slide into the water. If Hap said there was a hundred and twenty, there was a hundred and twenty. This could be the biggest load of the season by twenty tons. It could pay off big for all of us. We jumped to it, and Mick aimed the launch toward Towhead.

The southwestern sky was taking on a sort of green, purple, and black tint all at the same time. Low, rolling thunder was sounding in the distance. Mick caught Hap's eye and nodded at the horizon. They both saw it.

As lifelong river rats, they knew a storm was brewing, and it was probably going to be a doozy. But the catch of the season was waiting. If the barometric pressure changed or the storm hit too soon, the fish might scatter into the deeper water. Right now, everything was right for a huge haul and an equally lucrative payday. Everything but the weather.

Hap acknowledged Mick's nod with one of his own. The men silently agreed we would try to make the haul. When it was history and the money was in the bank, we would talk about how smart we were to push on when lesser fishermen might have played it safe and stayed in the harbor. But that would come later. Right now, there's a lot of work to be done.

Mick turned the launch, and we worked our way back up the lake against the swift current of the Catherine. Once through its channel, we turned and went downstream with the current again, through the Flats, and then eventually around the large sand point known as Towhead.

Towhead was a treacherous haul even in the best of conditions. The wide, flat sandbar was usually good and clean in many ways, but it sat right on the edge of the main channel's deep and fast-moving current. You had to be extremely careful when you laid out the nets. They had to follow closely to the edge of the sandbar and yet precariously near to the drop-off.

One false step, and a man could be over his head with his waders full of water in a few seconds. It's one of the worst fears of any commercial fisherman. No matter how powerful a swimmer you are, nobody can do it with his boots on.

Mick and Hap were quick to point out they had never lost a man to drowning. They had amply shamed us into thinking it was just so stupid we would be branded as bad fishermen if we drowned. Somehow, your death was not really the point of it but whether you were a decent river man.

The launch reached Towhead at eight twenty a.m. Immediately we began the methodical ritual of laying out the net, staking the bag, and quietly surrounding the fish. All this was done within a half hour. A steady rain began just as we finished.

We had worked in bad weather before, and this was nothing new. We put on our raincoats and jumped to it. As always, I was on the seine boat with the Swenson boys. Pat ran the cork line, and Rick handled the lead line. I ran the pulling gear. Business as usual. So far, the weather was a non-issue.

Hap supplied his usual encouragement. "All right fellas, there's a lot of carp out there. Let's get moving. Fishermen's Luck, no regrets. Sound good?"

"Fishermen's Luck, no regrets!" We meant it.

The rain stayed fairly moderate for the better part of an hour. We wiped the water from our eyes and strained to see Hap and Mick's hand-signals telling us to speed it up or slow it down based on how the fish crowded together. As always, Hap clenched a mummified cigar stub between his teeth. As always, it was drenched far beyond being able to be lit.

By ten thirty, we were about halfway to having the fish crowded into the bag. It was clear we had hit it big. The fish always became agitated when they began crowding up. Occasionally, a few would jump and flip in the air. Today, the jumping was constant for as far as we could see, like popcorn popping.

Off to the south and west, the purple and black cloud bank loomed like a mountain, and the wind was picking up even more. Flashes of orange and green lightning continuously lit the clouds now. Whitecaps were starting to show all across the lake as the seine boat bobbed like a cork. We were having a hard time keeping our footing on the slippery deck. Still, we worked like madmen.

Across the water, at the far side of the nets, Hap pulled his way along the cork line and over to where Mick was hanging on. Both men were fighting against the ever-increasing pounding of the waves. With every passing minute, the wind blew harder. It was beginning to make a low howling sound. The thunder and lightning were almost constant now, and the rain began pelting us horizontally. It was getting very cold. The sky was nearly pitch black. This was a bad sign.

Hap cupped his hand to his mouth and looked squarely at his younger brother. He shouted, "We can't finish! We have to get to shore! I think there's a twister coming!"

"We're all right. I think we're good. Let's give it a shot. It's too late in the year for a tornado."

"Mick, we gotta get off the water. It's all over for today."

"*No*, goddamn it! This is the biggest haul all year. Maybe the biggest one for the last five! I'm not giving up! The price was up fifteen cents this morning! *We need this!*"

"Mick. *Mick!* Look at your boys. They'll do whatever you say."

On the seine boat we were slipping and sliding and trying to work the pulling gear against the waves and the wind. We were scared stiff, but still we kept focused. Pat and Rick were not sniping at each other now. We were silently and feverishly working as the lake grew angrier and angrier.

"C'mon Mick, what do you say? We'll catch these slippery bastards again someday. It's time to quit. I'm gonna cut the nets loose. Okay with you? C'mon now, no regrets."

"I guess so. I guess so, *goddamn it*!"

Mick held up his hand and made a fist, the sign to stop the pulling-gear. I disengaged the clutch and let out ten feet or so of the net to create a little slack. The change in tension only served to make the seine boat bob more randomly in the wild waves. By now, it was almost impossible to see the shoreline of Towhead's sandbar.

Somehow Mick managed to pull-start his motor and slowly made his way toward the launch. At times he was in full sight, riding the crest of a huge wave. At other times he was completely out of sight, down behind another mountainous swell. Instinctively, we knew what this meant.

Hap was trying to angle his jon boat around the back side of the bag where the big spud pole anchored the netting into the sandy bottom. A short piece of very heavy webbing was woven to the bag and sewn to the post in four places. A strong leader rope was threaded through the four knots. If you cut the main leader line from the post and untied it from the seine boat, the bag and the seine would float free of the spud pole and drift with the current. This was a desperate move meant to save the nets in the absolute worst-case scenario. It was a measure reserved for a time exactly like this.

Mick made it to the launch, and after securing the jon boat, he started the big V-8 engine. It leaped to life with a comforting and powerful rumble. This boat was the safest craft you could hope for in a bad storm. Walt Sprague built it that way. It was heavy and stable. Mick pointed her into the wind and throttled back until the big boat began to drift slowly downstream. He skillfully pulled her alongside the seine boat and shouted to us as we struggled to maintain our balance.

"Jump on! We're gonna take the rest of the day off. Are you with me?"

Pat and Rick dove for the safety of the launch as the hail started rattling on the deck surface. I shouted back, "I'll untie the gear!" and turned to undo the last of the ropes connecting the other end of the nets to the machinery of the boat.

This knot was the first bowline I ever tied, and it had been wet and dried a hundred times. Try as I might, it still remained too tight for my cold fingers, and I didn't have a knife. If Hap succeeded in cutting the leader-line, the seine would be free to float as soon as I untied the rope on the gear. But the knot had to be freed up or the maneuver would fail.

I could no longer see the place where Hap had been working only a few minutes ago. The rain and hail were dark metallic gray and coming down in sheets. The hail was big enough to hurt, and the seine boat's deck was quickly getting iced up and incredibly slippery. We had stayed on the lake too long, and we were paying the price.

My fingers were red and stiff, and they hurt badly by the time I shakily finished untying the last of the gear's ropes and cast them off. Just as I did, the seine boat pitched high on top of a big whitecap.

My feet left the deck, and I flew through the air. When I landed, I was flat on my back. My wet waders and raincoat began to slide on the slippery surface. Suddenly, I was spinning toward the edge of the seine boat and the churning black water beyond . . .completely disoriented and out of control. I didn't even have time to panic. As I went over the edge of the boat all I could think of was, "*Great!*"

I kicked my feet as my desperate fingers clawed at the side of the boat, but I was sinking fast as my waders began to fill. The pressure of the water compressed the legs of the rubber waders tight against my thighs even as the lake poured over the top of the bib and spilled in around my chest and waist. I sucked in a large gasp of air as my head went under. My feet hit bottom almost immediately, and I realized it was the hard sand of Towhead. The surface was only a few inches over my head—just enough to drown. I pushed hard with both legs but barely moved.

There was no visible sunlight to penetrate the storm clouds or the darkness of the water. Above my head the surface of the lake churned crazily. The motion of the waves swept me back and forth in rhythm with the stormy chop. Air bubbles escaped from my waders, adding to the confusion. In the slow-motion underwater delirium, I began unhooking the suspenders of my waders and managed to peel them down to my waist. Below the knees the boots were made of stiffer rubber, and they didn't want to budge. Another big wave hit me, and I began to topple sideways underwater. Somehow, it helped to free my left foot.

The ghosts of all the fisher men and women, and all the barge workers who had ever drowned began whispering softly in my ears. I thought to myself, *NOT TODAY! NOT NOW! OH GOD!*

"C'mon boy—come and join us. It's not so bad. You'll like it down here."

The drowned *Sea Wing* ladies whose bodies had never been recovered sat patiently nearby in the main channel, waiting for another lost soul to join them. Their skeletal arms were folded, and their tattered dresses streamed in the current. Or maybe it was a section of the seine netting. It was impossible to tell.

My lungs were burning fiercely, and I was getting lightheaded as I pried the top of my right boot open a little further, allowing the water to fill it the rest of the way and help loosen its grip on my foot. I was almost out of air. I felt my eyelids begin to flutter open.

My brain screamed, *NO REGRETS! NO REGRETS! OH NO!*

As the whispered voices of the dead grew louder, I was sure I heard David Patterson's voice above the rest.

"Hee-foh Ay-mot!"

My lungs were on fire. I mustered the strength I had left and gave a final heave. Incredibly, my right foot popped out. With my brain spinning downward into darkness, I planted both feet solidly against the bottom and pushed as hard as I could. Thirty feet further into the lake and the riverbed would have been pure Mississippi mud. I would have just sunk up to my knees. But the sandy bottom of Towhead held firm.

It seemed like hours since I had slipped off the deck, but in reality, it was a very short time. When my head burst out above the waves, I violently inhaled a combination of air and water in a rasping, gurgling aspiration which quickly became an uncontrollable cough.

I had drifted downstream a fair distance from the launch, where Mick was having a hard time keeping the bow pointing into the wind. Still, he spotted me right away. In less than a minute, he pulled within a few feet of where I surfaced. I was still violently coughing and choking, treading water in the black and frightening mess that was Lake Pepin.

Mick shouted to Pat, "Hold her right here!"

Pat took the wheel and held it steady. Mick took down a long, slim pole we used to push the launch through the shallow waters where the motor had to be shut down. He shoved the pole at me, hitting me hard in the shoulder. It hurt like hell, but I gratefully grabbed it and held on tight. Hand-over-hand, Mick towed me over to the boat, where he and Rick awkwardly hoisted me back onto the launch and away from the whispers of the dead.

I flopped onto the floor, wheezing and retching but happy just to be alive. There was no time to think about it. We had to get right to it! Still coughing and puking, I pulled myself up.

Mick took the wheel back from Pat, and he headed the launch upstream in the general direction of where he thought the solid ground could be.

The wind was wailing so loudly we could barely hear our own shouting voices. The hail was piercing and getting larger in diameter.

"Hang on! I'm gonna beach her!"

We slid and bounced across the water with the rain and sleet hammering the bow deck and windshield. Big, chunky hailstones cracked the windshield and threatened to shatter it in on us. We couldn't see anything. At the last second, Mick caught a glimpse of some trees, and he throttled back as we hit the beach, much too hard. We fell forward and landed in a heap in front of the steering wheel. The motor still idled smoothly even after we grounded her.

As we lay there, I managed to grunt out, "Where's Hap?"

"I don't know, still on the lake, I guess." Mick's voice sounded very worried.

As we struggled to get up, we looked at each other, and I knew we were all thinking the same thing. There was no way Hap could ride out a tornado on the lake. We feared the worst had already happened. All we could do was wait.

Then, as we huddled together in the front of the launch with the storm raging around us, we seemed to hear it at the same time: the faint sound of an outboard motor. We couldn't see him, and he couldn't see us, but Hap was trying to find land. We scrambled to the back of the launch and started hollering with all our might.

"Hap, over here! Hap, we're over here!"

The hum of the motor got a little louder. And then, louder yet. We kept shouting.

"Over here! Over here! *Haaap!*"

It faded out a bit and we shouted even louder. Suddenly Hap's jon boat appeared from the darkness as if it had been shot out of a cannon. He hit the beach at full throttle and catapulted headfirst out across the entire length of the boat and forward over the bow, into the tall grass of the shoreline. The motor flipped up when the prop hit the sand and nearly tore out the transom. The sight of Hap's body somersaulting through the air made us freeze. For several seconds we heard only the moaning sounds of the wind and the storm. Then Hap's unmistakable voice came from out of the darkness:

"Shit!"

We laughed with nervous relief and somehow, beyond all reason, Hap came stumbling and slogging out of the storm, limping and cussing all the way to the meager but welcome safety of the launch. He still clenched the tiny stump of his saturated cigar between his front teeth. When he reached us, he took it from his mouth and looked at it one last time before tossing it into the raging lake. Mick pulled him on board.

"I thought you drowned."

"Not yet," was all he said.

There was a big notch of flesh gouged out of the top of his left ear where a hailstone had hit him. One lens of his glasses was missing, and the other was badly cracked. His pants legs were shredded from the knees down, and there were ugly, peeled-back flaps of skin where he scraped his shins on the edge of the front bench seat when he went airborne. He was a bloody mess and soaked to the gills, still shivering from the cold and fatigue, but Hap was alive.

"I guess I got turned around out there. I couldn't tell east from west. Then I heard you calling my name. I figured you had made land, so I just goosed the motor and hoped I wouldn't rear-end you."

Mick pointed at me. "The kid there took a swim, too. He went in the drink with his boots on. I don't know how the hell he got 'em off. He was under for at least twenty minutes."

Hap seemed amazed. "Is it true? You pulled 'em off underwater? That's got to be a first. It's never been done, I tell you! It's good luck, by God!

Fishermen's Luck, I say! We're going to be okay. *Nobody ever did it before.* Do you hear me? It's Fishermen's Luck!"

His hands clenched my shoulders as he ranted. The pain reminded me where Mick had poked me with the pole. It also reminded me how fortunate I was to be alive. I gritted my teeth and relished the discomfort the old man was inflicting.

"Grab the devil by his tail and give it a good yank, boys! This storm isn't sinking us today, no sir! We're *fishermen*, all right, and damned good ones for sure! Grab that bastard by his tail and by his horns! We're not going down!"

He sounded half crazy. Puddles of bloody water were forming around his feet from the nasty gashes on his legs. A smeary streak ran down his face from the ugly wound in his ear and dripped off the point of his chin.

My god, he looked horrifying standing there in the flashes of lightning. Still, his raving somehow made me feel a little better. I was a good-luck charm. We were going to be all right. Hap said so. I was still a river man, and a good one at that.

The wind shrieked and moaned, and the launch rocked on its keel even though we were halfway onto the beach. Hap turned toward the lake, shook his fist, and shouted at the storm.

"Aaahhh!" Almost instinctually, we began imitating his primal cry. "Aaahhh!" Maybe we were all a little crazy.

Though we couldn't see it, a giant twister was cutting its way across the islands and sloughs, headed straight for Bay City and leaving apocalyptic destruction in its path. If it missed us at all, it would surely be coming close to where the launch was beached.

Either way, it was very bad. Debris was swirling in the air and falling all around us. Trees made loud whining sounds as though in great pain from being stretched and twisted by the unrelenting slate-black wind. I looked out the back of the shaking launch at the wild scene and whispered to myself, "No regrets."

Out at the end of Fisherman's Point, the locomotive-force wind was bending even the mighty Kingfish. The giant old tree had withstood bad weather before, but it was younger then. Its old roots were not as deep as they once were and its branches a bit more brittle. Across the slough the frightening specter of the hungry tornado appeared, winding toward the Point. Toward the Kingfish. Two miles away at Towhead, we sat low and close to each other in the launch, waiting for whatever was coming next.

The twister barely missed landfall at the Point. The powerful wind tore up the shoreline and scuttled several boats in the normally protected harbor. A tremendous lightning bolt struck the Kingfish, partially uprooting and breaking off the largest and oldest cottonwood tree any of us had ever known. The wind and the current did the rest.

The huge, blackened stump was cocked over at an angle toward the lake. Its trunk fell into the raging water, and the howling wind from the funnel cloud caught hold of its crown like a sail. Within a few minutes, the big tree and its hundreds of carved names were swept out into the pull of the current and on down the lake as the Kingfish disappeared into the tempest.

Nobody would realize the loss until several hours later when the storm was over, and we began sorting out the damage and assessing the cost.

Some of it would be easy to see and count. Other damage would be less evident to the eye but far more costly in the realm of human emotions and other fragile things we value most. The charred stump still showed remnants of the scrawled names, but little else remained.

The Kingfish was far from being the only casualty of the storm. At the height of the maelstrom, when the wind churned the waves on the harbor into black walls of water, the *American Dream* broke loose from its moorings and washed out into the lake, dragging a chunk of her dock still tied to the end of her stern line. She hammered into a couple of smaller boats as she extricated herself from harbor, turned in the wind, and aimed her bow toward open water.

At first, she performed beautifully, just as she was designed to. Her bow nosed straight and true, plowing through the waves with relative ease. The wind caught her squarely on the transom, and she sailed as freely as she had in the best weather. The storm was driving the boat. The wind screamed on the big mast and whistled around the brass fittings and railings. The flag above the pilot house flapped deliriously and nearly stuck straight out from the mast. It began to shred at the edges and soon was only a tattered remnant.

When the *Dream* reached the current's outbound pull, the combination of wind and water made her pick up speed. Soon she was moving much too fast. Because she wasn't being pushed along by the predictable thrust of the engines, there was no control.

The *American Dream* careened over the rolling waves and slid across the lake in a sort of sidelong drunken reel, bounding through the huge whitecaps and bulldozing over debris swept from the islands by the storm. Ahead lay Steamboat Rock. The *Dream* relentlessly shambled on without a competent hand on the wheel to change its fateful course toward disaster.

When the *Dream* hit Steamboat Rock, the starboard side of the hull caved in and allowed the lake to stream into the engine room. Within seconds the cabin was filling. Still, she crashed on ahead, stubbornly dragging her injured side along the Rock and increasing the damage as she went. Onward she plowed into the deep river channel, slowly sinking and filling up with muddy Mississippi water. First it overcame the main deck, and then it swallowed the upper pilot's cabin. The mast was the last evidence of the great boat, with its ripped and rain-soaked American flag still waving desperately in the wind. Soon, it also dipped below the surface.

The *American Dream* went down in one of the deepest parts of Lake Pepin, just where the Mississippi's main channel joins the Wisconsin branch and just west of where the *Sea Wing* sank so many years before. Unlike the *Sea Wing*, there were no lives lost in this disaster, only the *Dream*.

CHAPTER 35

AFTER THE STORM

By four o'clock, the storm had passed, and we managed to muscle the launch off the beach and back into the waters of Lake Pepin. The lake remained roily and muddy from the action of the wind and waves. Above us, long moments of bright sun were interspersed with leftover fast-moving black clouds trying their best to catch up to the storm.

We didn't say much as we rounded up the seine boat and the live boats. The seine itself was probably far down the lake or tangled in the rushes someplace near shore. At any rate, it would have to wait until tomorrow. We were done for the day and just lucky to be alive.

We rounded the Point at about a quarter after five. We had made it back to the safety of the harbor, but it was a mess. Tree limbs and all sorts of debris floated randomly up and down the harbor and deep into the slough. A couple of small fishing boats were scuttled, and a couple more were washed up on the shore. The *American Dream* was conspicuously absent.

Onshore our families were lined up and waiting. Dad, Mom, and Jack stood close together down at the waterline. I couldn't help but notice the Pontiac was parked at the top of the bank.

A small crowd of our neighbors and a few campers were there, too. They cheered when we came into sight as if we were heroes. I don't know, maybe we were. We'd managed to save our own lives. At the moment, it seemed like enough to me.

As Mick maneuvered the launch up to the dock I jumped out and wrapped the big bow rope around a post in a double half hitch. Pat Swenson did the same with the stern line. Hap guided the seine boat into its place beside the launch, and Rick Swenson anchored the line of live boats in the harbor channel. We had performed this routine many times before. It took less than twenty minutes.

As soon as I stepped on shore, Mom grabbed me and planted a kiss right on my lips. I must have been a mess, but she didn't seem to notice. I was wet and muddy and proud all at the same time.

I said, "It's fine. We're fine. It wasn't too bad."

"M, you are the worst liar in the world!" She had tears in her eyes.

"Maybe so, but I'm a pretty good fisherman." I managed a weak smile.

Char Swenson was hugging and kissing Mick and the boys. Hap stood off on the side of the dock. As a widower, he was fairly used to being the odd one out. Jack moved slowly over to where he stood.

In an uncharacteristic gesture he held out his hand to the older man and said, "Thanks, Hap. Thanks for getting him back home."

Hap smiled and nodded his head. They were both a little awkward. Then Mick walked up and said to Hap, "I think we'd better drive to over to St. John's and have the docs take a look at you. You might need some stitches. Does that sound right?"

"Maybe so, but let's stop at the market first."

Then Mom marched right up and kissed Hap and Mick on the cheek several times.

Dad asked me, "Are you *really* all right?"

"Sure. It's not as bad as it looks. Was our house damaged?"

"We lost a few shingles, but it's not bad. What do you say? Feel like going home?"

Mom left Mick and Hap and came quickly to where we were standing.

"Um, would it be all right with you if I rode back up to the market with the crew?"

Dad and Mom looked at each other. Then Dad broke the silence. "Sure, M. We'll see you at home."

"Thanks, Dad. Uh, Mom and Jack: I'm glad you were here today."

I crawled up on the back of the old flatbed truck with the Swenson boys. Mick and Hap climbed into the cab. Dad handed him a dry cigar through the driver's side window. Hap said "Thanks, Brick. Here's to the ones that got away."

Dad smiled. "Yeah, and a few guys who didn't."

Hap started the engine and drove the truck slowly down Lakeshore Drive. Mom and Dad waved. Mom raised her hand and held it suspended and motionless with her elbow slightly bent. I did the same as we drove away. I watched her image grow smaller and smaller, and then we were out of sight.

Maybe it was a mistake to ride back with the crew. For a second, I got a familiar bad feeling I might never see her again, like I felt when Darla was waving goodbye from the back seat of wagon as it pulled away. My God! What if I had drowned?

The three of us sat quietly bumping along on the flatbed and thinking about what we had just been through. I pushed the strange and frightening thoughts out of my mind and said a silent prayer of thanks to the God of my mother.

When we got back to the market, Boris and Shirley Rose were all over us. Hap and Mick bragged about how I ended up in the lake and how I was going to be a good-luck charm from now on.

"Vat vas it like? Did you black out? Did you get the *varm feeling*?"

Shirley grabbed my sore arm and looked deep into my eyes. "Did'ja hear anything? Did'ja hear the voices? *Did'ja?*"

She had a crazy and intense look on her face. Her lips formed a tight, straight line. Her grip on my arm was strong and masculine. She was trying to see inside me and examine something only she knew what to look for. I turned my eyes downward toward the floor and said, "No, nothing like that. I was just—lucky, I guess."

Boris wrapped up two freshly cleaned catfish for me to take home, and as I left, Mick and Hap both rubbed my head for luck. I was very tired. Though riding together from the lake seemed somehow important, all I wanted now was to get away from the market and go home. Beyond being physically exhausted, I felt weary.

After I got far enough away for anyone to see, all the anger and fear came pouring out. I'd nearly drowned! And I heard those voices—even David's! I lost all control and couldn't help it. I felt foolish and naked standing there, yelling out what sounded like gibberish while clutching my package of fish. Shivering from the wet cold and from all the emotions associated with nearly dying, I felt like I was about to shed my skin. I shouted unintelligible noises, cursing and ranting at the top of my still-burning lungs. In a frustrated fit, I threw the package of fish as far down the street as I could.

When I finally regained my composure, I walked back and retrieved it. It was food for the family. Then I trudged home.

Down at Lakeshore Park, Walt Sprague stood on the shore surveying the damage. The *American Dream* was nowhere in sight. He stood virtually motionless, staring out at the water for several minutes and trying to imagine what must have happened. He knew the boat well and knew what she was capable of, even if no one was at the helm. If she had sunk in the harbor, some part of the *Dream* would still be visible above the surface. For a long way down the lake, the water probably wasn't deep enough to fully submerge the entire boat. He tried to look beyond the Flats and out past Towhead where the water was deeper.

Walt also examined the giant jagged stump of the Kingfish. The great tree that had provided shade for over a hundred years had vanished. If the Kingfish could disappear, it shouldn't be too hard to believe the *American Dream* met a similar fate.

Finally, Walt sat down on the wet sandy beach. How could one storm do so much damage? The *Dream* might have helped rehabilitate Bay City's reputation, but now . . . He lit his pipe and sat there until the Saturday evening sun was nearly set. Then he went home and called Dale Thorsdall.

"Dale, I hope my insurance policy covers tornadoes. I'm pretty sure you know the *Dream* went down. I don't know where yet. I only know she's gone. How is my coverage?"

"Well, Walt, I think maybe you are going to come out all right, but I don't think the insurance company is going to be so happy. At least, they sure as hell are not going to be happy with *me*. If you remember, we insured it as a one-of-a-kind item, sort of like a work of art or like Marilyn Monroe's legs. I don't remember how much you said it cost to build, but I think you should get the full two hundred and fifty thousand for her."

The phone was silent. "Hello? Did you hear me?"

Walt asked calmly, "Are you sure?"

"Well, hell yes, *shit* yes, Walt! I went all the way out on a limb for that boat. Yes, you're goddamned right, I'm sure. I'm going to have some royal bitch-ass explaining to do, but I'm sure. I'll get started with the claim in the morning. Right now, I need a drink. Hell, I need lots of drinks."

"Thanks, Dale. I appreciate what you did for us on this."

"Don't thank me yet. I might just decide to climb up on my roof and jump off later on tonight. When those boys at Farmers and Mechanics start asking me questions, I'm going to need some pretty good answers. You're going to have to teach me enough about that crazy Ferro-cement boat of yours so I can sound like I know what the hell I'm talking about."

"I will. Thanks again, Dale. You're a good guy to know."

"Goodbye, Walt. Do me a favor and don't ever build another one, okay?"

"I couldn't do it if I wanted to. She really was one of a kind. Good night, Dale."

The next morning Mick and Hap set off down the lake to collect what was left of the nets and assess the damage. It was Sunday morning. The Swenson boys and I didn't have to go.

It would have been a great day to sleep in, but Mom didn't see it that way. She roused Jack and me at eight o'clock. Dad was already up and dressed. We ate an epic breakfast and went to the nine o'clock service at the Methodist church. It was kind of a rare occasion for Dad. Since Mom had gotten home, she attended church almost every Sunday. Jack and I sometimes joined her out of respect. She never really insisted on it, but today I guess our family just needed to be together and give thanks.

I stood looking up at the stained-glass window near the front of the church. It depicted Jesus with his palms turned upward and smiling. Under the scene was the phrase, "I am with you always."

Dad sang the hymns loudly and acknowledged the pastor's words with a nod of his head. Except for Mom, I suppose we had been a family of part-time Christians for the majority of our lives. As we left the church, Reverend Greeley said how nice it was to see us all together. When Dad shook his hand, the pastor didn't let go of his grip until he looked Dad straight in the eyes and said, "It's very gratifying to see you here this morning, Marion. Come back again soon, will you?"

"Yes, Reverend, I will. You can count on it." Dad's cheeks were flushed a little when he finally retrieved his hand.

By the time we got home, Mick and Hap had just about finished the thankless chore of untangling and pulling the nets onto the seine boat by hand. It was slow and messy work. Every stick and every clump of weeds had to be cleaned from the mesh. Every hole needing to be patched was tied in a knot and pulled off to the side of the boat for mending later.

They found the seine on the far shore near a place called Lyle's Haul. An old angler named Lyle Tolliver named it after himself, and then he drowned there in 1958. It was a heck of a way to make sure the name stuck. Besides reclaiming the nets, the men discovered something else. The huge trunk and crown of the Kingfish had gotten lodged in the shallows of Lyle's Haul, rocking and partially submerged in the waves. As the two men worked, they began reminiscing.

"I carved Char's name in the bark of that old tree when we were in high school," Mick said.

Hap shook his head. "Yep, me too. I carved Lorna's name on it when there were not more than a couple hundred others. I kinda think we ought to try to do something about this, don't you?"

By the time they finished loading the seine they had hatched a plan. Late Sunday afternoon, after Mick and Hap had retrieved the seine, they returned to Lyle's Haul with chain saws. They cut the crown of the old Kingfish off and trimmed the shattered end of the trunk to a clean, square end. What remained was a giant log, close to thirty feet long and over four feet across.

The majority of the names were there. They were crowded tight together on the stump end but thinned out as they neared what used to be the top. The men slowly towed the big log behind the launch like some giant mythical fish. They reached the harbor right around sunset.

Monday morning Mick and Hap enlisted several local guys to laboriously pull what remained of the Kingfish back onshore and close to where it had spent its life. With the help of a small platoon of men and two tractors, the log was rolled and dragged up to its final resting place on the crest of Fisherman's Point. Four short pieces of railroad ties were placed under the log, so the body of the Kingfish could clear the ground. It would help preserve it from rotting and allow most of the names to be read all the way around the trunk.

The part that had previously been too far off the ground to reach now offered room for many future lovers to testify. Nearly eight feet of the trunk remained relatively untouched for new names to be carved.

The enormous, bleached carcass of the Kingfish lay in its wooden cradle like the giant white whale of Melville's imagination, its skin tattooed with the scars of too many pocketknives to count. But if the Kingfish embodied Moby Dick, then Hap surely must have been Ahab. Unlike in Melville's tale, this time Ahab survived. Thanks to Hap and Mick, so had the recorded legacy of the Kingfish. In the coming years, many visitors would have their pictures taken while pointing at their own initials. And many more would yet be engraved.

It only took Jack a week to complete Hap's portrait. As always, the eyes were remarkable. In his likeness, Jack had captured the wisdom and experience of sixty years spent half on the water and half on land. In addition, there was the slight but unmistakable sadness that was also present in Hap's actual gaze.

When he was done with it, he rolled it up, put it in a cardboard tube, and walked all the way to Hap's house to hand it to him across the doorstep. Neither of them said a word. Jack just smiled at the old man and handed him the tube.

Hap unrolled it on the kitchen table after Jack left. He thought to himself, *God, do I really look this old? I guess so. The older North kid—Jack—he sure has a gift.*

He rolled it back up and put it into the cardboard tube it came in. Then he placed it in the drawer of the big highboy where Lorna's picture and their wedding pictures were kept. I doubt it ever mattered to Jack whether or not Hap put the portrait on display. Both of them knew it was a private act of great respect shared between two guys who had spent their lives slightly out of the mainstream.

Dad ran into Walt Monday morning at Stella's. He was pretty down.

"Mornin' Walt."

"Mornin'."

There was a long and awkward silence. Finally, Dad said, "Would you like me to take you out back and put you out of your misery or something?"

Walt's eyes were drooping, but he smiled a little bit and swiveled his head sideways just enough to look at his best friend.

"Yeah, I think that would be about right."

The two men sat together drinking their coffee and sharing the painful loss. For Walt, it was the best boat-building effort of his life, and now it was gone. For Dad, it was the frustration of knowing his friend was hurting and would never get to take Dolly on the second honeymoon they had planned.

"Is there anything I can do?"

Another long silence. "Well, I guess I'd like to go fishing. Will you go with me?"

"Sure. Of course."

After lunch, when Dad should have been busy cleaning up our town after the storm, he went fishing instead. It was unlike him to walk away from any job that needed to be done. I guess maybe he felt that tending to a broken heart was more important than picking up branches and broken glass.

They fished the Flats and caught a couple of nice walleyes. They fished the channel, and Dad caught a catfish. Afterward, Walt started the outboard motor on the old Alumacraft and headed downstream toward Towhead and beyond. He was aimed toward the deepest part of the lake, and Dad must have realized he was searching for a glimpse of the *Dream.*

As they passed by Steamboat Rock, Walt pointed to a large scrape and a foot-wide smudge of Comet Tone paint that had undoubtedly gotten scrubbed off and left behind as the only evidence of where the *American Dream* ended its voyage.

"Jesus, Walt, it made it all the way down here with nobody behind the wheel. I don't think I've ever seen anything like it—not ever. If we find it, how in blazes do we get it out of the water? It's deep out here."

"I guess the insurance company will handle the recovery work. I kind of think they will need to see it in order to decide what they want to pay for it. I just needed to know where she ended up."

Walt lit up his pipe. He nosed the fishing boat upstream into the current and idled the motor. He imagined the *Dream* surging through the waves without any engine power or steering capabilities before crashing into the Rock and sinking in the deep water. Ironically, the monument to souls lost long ago on the *Sea Wing* had killed the *Dream.*

"She was a dandy, wasn't she?"

"The best I ever saw. I'm really sorry, Walt. I was hoping I'd get to see some pictures of you and Dolly in New Orleans or Florida. I know this is really hard for you, but you can't let it get you down. You said it yourself: you can only make big things happen if you dream big dreams. Maybe we could build another one, an *American Dream Two.*"

Walt smiled his downtrodden smile again and said, "I don't think so. Shoot, Brick, it was just a boat after all. Let's go home. I think Dolly's making a pot roast tonight."

"Funny, I think Rachel is too."

The two men returned to the harbor and then to their houses. When the day was ended, each man went to bed with the woman he loved and, before drifting off to sleep, thought about what was most important in his life.

Somehow, it was true. The *American Dream* was just a boat after all—a damned fine one, but just a boat. And yet, it stood for something important that was lost forever.

CHAPTER 36

A Meeting with the Feds

The cleanup work was grueling and tedious, but, as in most catastrophes, it brought the best out in a lot of people. Neighbors helped neighbors, and even groups of volunteers from other communities streamed into Bay City, all willing to clean up and help repair our town as much as possible.

By Tuesday evening the storm was still a pretty big story on local TV and in the newspapers. The *Red Wing Republican Eagle* ran a substantial human-interest pictorial about the damage it caused and the ongoing community cleanup effort.

They even took a picture of the Kingfish in its new location on the crest of the beach. The reporter interviewed a few people who had sworn their true love by carving the initials of their girlfriend or boyfriend into the old tree.

All in all, it was a good journalistic feature. The story effectively chronicled uprooted trees, overturned lumber piles, and a couple of wrecked garages the twister had left in its fearsome path. Most importantly, it captured the genuine hope inspired by people helping people. The article made Bay City sound like a good place to live.

Thankfully, the *American Dream* wasn't mentioned. Neither did the fishing crew get any press from our narrow escape. We wouldn't have wanted any. Mick and Hap were not proud of the way we got caught in the storm. We all just wanted to get on with repairing the nets and maybe catching one last decent haul if the weather held up into October.

Mom read parts of the story aloud to Jack and me. Then she handed the paper over to Dad. He had a quirky habit of reading grocery ads out loud. After he settled into his big, dented spot on the couch, there was a period of silence before the familiar recitation began.

"Pork chops: ninety-nine cents a pound. Green beans: four cans for a dollar. One free head of lettuce with a ten-dollar order. Rachel, there's free lettuce!"

Jack and I occasionally mimicked him. It usually ended the reading with an accompanying frown, but we knew he kind of liked it, anyway.

Jack chided him. "Dad, how much is succotash? We really need to know."

"Succotash: two dollars. We can't afford it." He never missed a beat, but he read on silently after Jack's poke.

Somewhere in the middle of the paper Dad came upon a report about an old lady who had been killed in her home on Summit Avenue in St. Paul. The mansions on Summit symbolized the wealth from a bygone era, the kind derived from lumber and railroads. It was a brutal murder, according to the story. She was a former resident of Red Wing. Had the murder happened there, the story would have assuredly made the front page.

Miss Blossom French was a spinster lady whose father had willed her the house on Summit after he passed away. Shortly after, she moved from Red Wing to the home of her childhood. She lived alone in the big old house and managed quite well on the estate her lumber baron father had left her. Apparently, she had never worked a day in her life.

By all accounts she was an eccentric and lonely old woman. Even her nearest neighbors knew little about her and didn't have much to say about her death except as it pertained to their feelings about a lack of community safety. She had been bound hand and foot with duct tape and her mouth had been taped over. A single bullet to her temple caused her death. The article said the police believed robbery was the motive.

As he read, the hair stood up on the back of his neck. It sounded exactly like the Patterson murders. Once again, as had happened so many times, his mind returned to the horror of an early fall morning from the previous year. In his mind's eye he saw the sprawling bodies in their awkward, unnatural positions. He saw the streaks of the blood trails and tiny specks of brain matter. And once again he smelled the rank and damp stench of death.

His hands began to shake badly until the newspaper made a soft rustling sound, startling him back into the present. He was breathing hard and had broken a sweat. He wondered if anyone else realized this was the exact *modus operandi* as in the Patterson case. Had a sharp-eyed FBI agent caught it in a morning briefing in Minneapolis? Had the Pierce County deputies already been consulted about the Bay City murders?

It seemed unlikely. There hadn't been much interaction with any of them for a few months now. Maybe it was time to give somebody a call. He folded up the newspaper and set it on the end table.

"Don't throw this paper out, okay? I want to keep the story about the storm."

Mom asked him, "Are you sure it's not the grocery store ads you're saving? I bet you have a bunch of 'em stashed somewhere."

He forced a smile, as if it hurt a little to do it. Then he got up and went for a walk. By the time he returned he had come up with a plan. He would call and make an appointment with the Minneapolis FBI and try to get an update on the Patterson case. He would show them the story about Miss Blossom French and explain again exactly what he had seen in the Patterson house. If the Patterson case had grown cold, perhaps Miss French's untimely death would spur some renewed interest.

Monday morning, he would call the FBI office and set up an appointment. Then he would call Uncle Harry and hope to arrange for his usual driver. Brick was certain Harry would be more than willing to help out as always. He was once again resolved to at least try to make a difference on this. The news story was a punch in the gut. He couldn't just let this one float by. Not this time.

The earliest he could get an appointment with the FBI was on Friday morning. Harry arrived at six fifteen a.m. Dad was wearing a light blue long-sleeved shirt and navy-blue pants with a crease. Mom made sure he looked professional. His constable badge was pinned to the shirt pocket, and his hair was slicked back with Tiger Balm and neatly combed. His black shoes shined like a wet street.

By seven thirty, they were sitting at the counter of Mickey's Diner in downtown St. Paul with coffee and steaming plates of potatoes O'Brien. Summit Avenue was less than a mile away, overlooking the city.

The posh neighborhood could have been light years away from the daily comings and goings of Mickey's. A true local icon, the old, converted streetcar had been in the same location for decades. It had a way of bringing millionaires and street people together in the same place largely because the food was so great.

On any morning, a hooker could be sitting next to a cop, or a wealthy businessperson beside some guy fresh out of prison on parole, and no one would know the difference.

The two men sat at one end of the breakfast counter. At the other end was a disheveled-looking man with long, stringy blond hair. He looked the two over as they entered the diner. His eyes were nearly crimson, as if he hadn't slept in a long time, or maybe he had been very drunk the night before. He wore an Army jacket. He thought he recognized one of the men from somewhere. Though he couldn't exactly remember where, he did not associate it with a good memory. He decided it was best to leave.

The blond-haired man turned away and finished his coffee, leaving two dollars on the counter before walking slowly out the door. He continued to avert his face as he passed Dad and Harry. Harry noticed his jacket and said, "Hey soldier, thanks for your service."

The guy said nothing in return but raised his right hand up near his forehead in an approximation of a salute. Neither of the two other men saw his face or paid too much attention to him. A week earlier, Miss Blossom French had been in Mickey's for breakfast on the day she died.

By eight thirty, they were back in the Impala and crossing the river to Minneapolis. At five minutes to nine, Dad was walking up the steps of the courthouse with Harry in tow.

The FBI offices are in the Federal Court House building on Tenth and Nicollet in downtown Minneapolis. The three-story limestone building with granite pillars out front presented an imposing old building with a storied past. Lucky Lindy once received a key to the city here after his famous flight across the Atlantic. Harry took one last drag on his cigarette and snuffed the butt out under his foot as they reached the top of the steps.

Inside the courthouse, people were hurriedly moving about trying to get to meetings and to the courtrooms on the second floor. A guard stood near a small desk at the side of the huge rotunda that served as a lobby. Dad asked directions to the FBI offices.

"They're on the second floor. At the end of the hall, past courtroom three."

"Thanks."

"Don't mention it. Where are you from?" The guard had noticed Dad's constable badge.

"Bay City, Wisconsin."

"Never heard of it."

"I suppose not. Thanks again."

Dad and Harry climbed another set of steps up to the second floor. By the time they reached the top, Harry was winded. Dad waited a moment for him to catch his breath. When Harry nodded, they continued down the hall.

The FBI offices were in a long and narrow room. There were many rows of government-issued gray metal desks, all stacked with manila files and strewn with the odds and ends of unsolved cases. The men and women of the FBI were gradually finding their ways to their places and their endless work. Some smoked, and most had a cup of coffee.

An older woman with hair dyed jet black asked in a rather disinterested tone, "What can I do for you?"

"We're here to see Agent Craft. We have a ten-thirty appointment."

"Ten thirty, huh? Do you know what time it is? It's nine o'clock. Maybe you guys would like to take in a movie or go bowling or something. Agent Craft isn't even in the building until ten a.m." She paused and added, "I'll tell you what, there's nice murder case just down the hall in courtroom three this morning. Why don't you boys sit in and enjoy the show? It's not Perry Mason, but it ain't bad. I'll come and get you when Craft gets in. Now scoot. I gotta do my nails."

Dad and Harry went back out into the hallway. They looked at each other and shrugged. Then they quietly opened the door to courtroom three and slipped unnoticed into a long maple bench in the last row, near the back of the room. There weren't many people in the courtroom. Not surprisingly, those who were appeared to be present not by their own choice but because they had to be. Except for Dad and Harry, the sparse crowd was made up exclusively of attorneys and their clients, waiting for their turn before the judge.

It didn't take long to figure out what was going on. This was a hearing on charges having something to do with a woman who had shot her estranged husband for sleeping with her sister.

The defendant's name was Norma Zack, and she was seated at a table in the front of the room with a modestly dressed public defender. Just beyond them and facing the gallery sat Judge William Ross Bennett behind an elevated desk. His impeccable gray hair was perfectly combed, and his piercing eyes were steely blue. At the moment, he was trying to figure out just how the hell Norma Zack had thought she could get away with a crime of such monumental stupidity.

"Miss Zack, help me recreate this story, please. How did you end up with a shotgun in your estranged husband's home?"

"Well, judge, Jimmy and I were separated. I left him before I had my accident."

"Accident? Please explain."

"Well, judge, after I left Jimmy for messing around with other women, I moved in with my girlfriend, Jessica Price. That's J-e-s-s—"

"I get the picture. Please continue."

"Well, me and Jessica decided since that bastard Jimmy was cheatin', maybe I should have some fun, too. So, Jessica had these fake leather pants she let me wear, and we went out to the Parrot Cage for some dancin' and, you know, man huntin.' I looked pretty darned good in those pants, Judge."

The public defender put his face in his hands and shook his head noticeably. Judge Bennett confirmed the point. "I'm sure you did. Please continue, Miss Zack."

"Okay. So, we had a few drinks and we danced with some pretty nice guys from Fridley, but they were married so we didn't want to go out with them or anything. Anyway, it got kinda late so we decided to pro-ceed to an establishment where we could get some food. When we left the Parrot Cage, I got hit by a pickup truck in the parking lot."

"Really? Were you injured?"

"Damned right, I was! I was in a goddamned coma for three days and two nights. When I finally came to, guess who was sitting there at my bedside? Jimmy! Well, I thought maybe he wasn't such a bastard after all, so in a couple days when I got out of the hospital, I got my stuff from Jessica's house and decided to surprise him by coming home. So, I borrowed Jessica's pants again. Ha! Some great idea that turned out to be."

"So, you got out of the hospital, and you went to Jimmy's house?"

"*Our* house, Judge! Well, not right away. I had to pick up some deodorant and a toothbrush, but I suppose it was within a couple hours of getting out."

The public defender looked at the tabletop in front of him and muttered, "Sure, why not?"

The judge said, "Mr. Anderson, do you wish to make a comment?"

"No sir, Your Honor."

"Well then, what happened, Miss Zack?"

"Well, I think you can pretty much figure out for yourself how this part ends. When I got to Jimmy's and my place, the door was open, and I walked in. I said 'Honey, I'm home!' and I walked down the hall to the back bedroom. Surprise! There they were! My whore of a sister and that son of a bitch Jimmy in our bed! *Naked!* Judge, I was real pissed off, but I kept my cool."

"You did?"

"I did. I just said Jimmy, Marlene—you are two of a kind and you deserve each other. Then I turned around and headed back to Jessica's. I guess on the way to Jessica's I got more and more upset, and I started crying and all. Judge, it was my sister! He could have been with anybody else, and

I probably would have just gave up on him. I guess that's when my head started achin."

Suddenly, the public defender was interested. "Judge, may I ask a question?"

"Not just yet, Mr. Anderson, but in a minute. So, Miss Zack, you got a headache?"

"Yes, Judge, I did. And not just a little one. This was a humdinger of a migraine. Did I mention that I bumped my head really hard on the fender of that pickup? I still have a case pending on that accident, but it's in a different court. Do you know Judge Michael Chase?"

"Only by name. What happened after you got your headache?"

"Well, I guess it's about the time I bought the gun. I can't remember too clearly 'cause it's all a blur." She squinted and made a waving motion in front of her face. "But I guess I went to the Kmart, and I walked back to the sporting goods department and bought a cheap, double-barreled Mossberg and a box of shells. It was on sale, so I put 'em on my Mastercard."

"And did you then go back to the house?"

"Hell yes, I did! The only trouble is, for some stupid reason I stopped at Jessica's to load the gun, and I ended up leaving the rest of the shells on her kitchen table."

"You did? *Then* did you go back to Jimmy's?"

"Yes sir, I did. I drove over there thinking I'd give them both the scare of their lives. That was all I planned on doing. I was only gonna scare 'em. When I got there, wouldn't you know it, they were still in the bedroom and they were *doin'* it again, Judge! Even after I drove way back across town and bought a gun and all, they were still goin' at it! Jimmy *never* did it like that with me! I guess it's when I lost my temper. I can't really remember everything. Y'know? I kinda blacked out, I guess."

"Miss Zack, now I want you to slow down and tell me exactly what happened next."

Norma Zack did as she was told. She deliberately slowed her speech down and looked straight at the Judge. "Well, Judge—I shot that son of a bitch."

"Miss Zack, I need to ask you to elaborate a bit on your statement, please."

"Okay, Judge. I shot that son of a bitch when he tried to jump out the window. I meant to miss him, but, well, my finger twitched and there you go. I figured I was already in a world of trouble, so I put the gun up to Marlene's head and I pulled the trigger on the other barrel."

"What happened then, Miss Zack?"

"Nothing happened, Judge. The trigger just clicked. I guess the gun jammed. I unloaded the shells and then I realized I had left the box back at Jessica's, so I went out to the car. I left her there cryin' and throwin' up. Well, the cops caught up to me at Jessica's house and—fast forward—I ended up here today. If the gun wouldn't have jammed there's no telling where I'd be. Can you believe it? I just bought that gun!"

Attorney Anderson spoke up. "Your Honor, based on the prior medical condition obviously causing her to black out, which in turn drove Miss Zack to her unfortunate actions, would you consider a reduced charge in exchange for a plea? It seems clear this crime was not premeditated. Fortunately, we are not talking about the sister, correct?"

"Correct. I am willing to let that marinate for a minute and see what we can come up with. Are you suggesting manslaughter? You may be catching me at a good time, Mr. Anderson. Would you like to confer with your client?"

"Yes, Your Honor, thank you."

Norma Zack said, "I don't need to confer with Mr. Anderson there. If you are willing to go with manslaughter, I figure it's a pretty good deal. I killed him and—"

"Miss Zack! As your attorney, I strongly advise you not to say anymore!"

The judge agreed. "Good advice, Mr. Anderson."

"Wait a minute, Judge. I just need to tell you something." Norma Zack got serious, and her voice got a little softer. "I am awful glad I didn't kill her. Marlene's the only sister I got."

"So am I, Miss Zack, so am I. As I am called to do, I recognize Mr. Anderson's request of reducing the charge to manslaughter, which I will duly consider. Let's meet again next Monday, at nine a.m. I will see you both then."

"See you Monday, Judge."

"Thank you, Your Honor."

"As always, Mr. Anderson, it's been interesting."

As the deputy led Norma Zack out of the courtroom, Judge Bennett pounded his gavel and said, "Next case, please."

The black-haired secretary had been waiting just outside the door. At the sound of the gavel, she walked into the courtroom and tapped Dad on the shoulder.

"Okay, big boy, you're up. Agent Craft is here now, and he will fit you in a little early. He's the second to the last desk down by the water cooler."

Then she turned and shambled back across the hall with Dad and Harry following close behind. Her brilliant red fingernails were flawless.

Harry said, "If it's all right with you, Brick, I'll sit out here and wait. Maybe I can get forty winks."

"It's fine with me, Harry. Just don't let your pocket get picked."

Harry sat down, and Dad went into the FBI offices, continuing past the rows of desks to the one by the water cooler where Agent Craft spent the majority of his waking hours.

Agent Don Craft was a Bureau lifer. As he stepped out from behind his desk, it was evident he had a prosthetic leg. The steel hinge was visible, and he limped noticeably. The flesh-toned fiberglass ankle and the top of the foot showed through his thin, white sock. A stack of cardboard banker's boxes sat next to his desk. They were labeled Robberies, Homicides, and Drugs. His desk was neat, with the manila files separated and arranged in three piles. At a glance, Agent Craft's desk appeared to be better organized than many of his colleagues'.

"Good morning, Mr. North. I'm Don Craft." He held out his hand, and Dad did the same.

"Call me Brick."

"Okay, Brick, what brings you to Minneapolis?"

"I wanted to talk to somebody about a story I read in the *Red Wing Eagle* last week. It's about the lady who was killed over on Summit Avenue, Miss French. Are you familiar with the case?"

"Yes, as a matter of fact I am. The St. Paul Metro Squad is handling it. We really are not actively involved at this point. What about it caught your eye?"

"The way the killer used duct tape was exactly the same as in a murder last year in my town. I think it's the same guy."

Brick unfolded the newspaper and showed the article to Agent Craft, who got out a pad of paper and a pen and started taking notes. The agent asked several questions about the Patterson murders, sometimes interrupting in order to get the details straight in his mind. His interview lasted about twenty minutes.

"It sounds like you may be onto something. The Bureau got involved in the Patterson cases because we suspected the killer was from Minnesota and might have done something bad in Iowa. When he crossed the state line, it became ours. As the crime scenes suggest, this guy seems to enjoy his work.

"The Summit Avenue crime sounds a lot like the one we connected to the Patterson murders. Two years ago, an old man in Iowa died almost the same way, maybe even more brutally, though. So far, we're not exactly sure if that one fits. Robbery didn't seem to be a motive. I'll get a report on the Summit Avenue case. I doubt we'll get a clear tie-in, but Ballistics suggests he used the same weapon in the two other crimes. If we can match the gun, we have a case."

"Jesus, Don, I wasn't expecting all this. I figured the Pattersons to be a random killing by some drifter. Has anything been going on specifically with the Patterson case? Do you have any other leads? Any other suspects?"

"Uh, well Brick, I think it's fair to say we're not too much closer to solving the case today than we were a year ago. To be honest with you, the bad guys have a much bigger club than we do. And quite frankly, Bay City is a long way from here when it comes to high-profile crimes. No offense."

"None taken. I figured that out pretty early on, Don. Is *anybody* still working on it? What about the similarities to the Summit Avenue case? What do you say, can you keep it open somehow? A lot of people are counting on me, and I don't exactly know what the hell I'm doing here. I'm not a cop. Just a guy who gives a damn about our town."

"I can't make any promises, but I will make some calls over to St. Paul Metro, and I will get them a copy of the Red Wing newspaper article. Miss French was Jewish and pretty well off. Her real name was Beatrice Steinberg. The Jewish community is up in arms about an anti-Semitic killer. You're not Jewish, are you?"

"No, I'm, uh, Methodist."

"Yeah, well, the Jewish community has a fair amount of political clout, and I think the Metro guys are scrambling. If Metro agrees with your assessment, maybe between the two departments we can get a little something going again. But probably only if we connect it to the Summit Avenue crime. It's about the best I can offer."

"I guess it'll have to do, then. Thanks, Don. I appreciate it a lot."

The two men shook hands again, and Dad walked past the black-haired lady's desk and back out into the hall where Harry was slumped in a chair.

"Harry, time to go."

Uncle Harry awoke and stood up quickly.

"How was your nap? This isn't much of a hotel, is it?"

"No, not really. It wasn't easy getting any rest with all these innocent people talking about the crimes they didn't commit." Harry smiled. "How did you do?"

"Well, I think maybe I heard that dead rich people get a little more attention than dead poor folks."

"Maybe so, but I reckon they're all still dead, aren't they? At least the Pattersons had each other. From what you said, the other old lady died all alone."

"Yeah, these days it seems like death is easier to come by than either love or money. The agent I talked to is a good man. He said there may be a little hope for a renewed effort on the Patterson case, but I guess I won't hold my breath. Let's go home, Harry. I think we've done about all we can do."

"Good idea."

It was almost noon. They drove back east on University Avenue, across the river and past the Minnesota State Capitol building. They turned down the Jackson Street hill and onto Kellogg Street, past Union Railroad Station where the trains came and went as usual, hauling people and freight and mail.

Five hours earlier, the Zephyr had sat at the station with its big diesel engine idling and its sleek stainless-steel body gleaming in the sun as it awaited its morning run to Chicago. In a few more hours it would be back again on the afternoon run. In between, the big silver train would streak down the gleaming parallel tracks at seventy miles an hour, like a bullet cutting through the relative calm of the Wisconsin and Minnesota countryside.

Harry turned right onto Highway 61. The Impala purred as always, and the two men sat together in the front seat without talking. Brick wondered if they would ever find the guys who killed the Pattersons. So many things seemed to happen for no reason at all, like there was no real pattern to life or, in this case, death. Reverend Greeley talked about how everything was part of some master plan only God knew. It sure was hard to see the connections sometimes.

Across town, Fritz Michaels went to bed for the first time in a couple of days. He was burned out and shaking, coming down hard from last night's amphetamines and whiskey. Something had to give. The old woman on Summit had a lot of expensive jewelry, enough to pay for a different kind of deal. A bigger deal. Something to last more than just a couple of weeks.

The Colombian worked on the barges, but he made his real living as a smuggler. He would be back in town soon, and it meant the possibility of a fresh load of cocaine brought up from the Gulf on the barge line. An ounce or two was all he needed.

For now, it would have to wait. He was tired. So very tired. For the rest of the day, he would endure the sleep of the damned.

CHAPTER 37

UNITAS FADES BACK

Saturday, October 19th. Though I didn't yet know it, my time of reckoning was at hand. All day I had been feeling conflicted. The fishing season had ended for the year. The storm took care of that. The lake was a mess, and I was still a little shaken up from the whole ordeal.

I still missed Darla terribly, but I really enjoyed the time I had spent with Faith, too. I felt guilty. After all Darla and I had shared, I couldn't quite bring myself to believe it could be over for good. And Faith made it pretty clear she just wanted to be friends.

This was the sort of stuff I couldn't talk about, even with Tom. I wanted to be alone and sort things out. By mid-afternoon I'd moped around the house long enough for Mom to suggest maybe I should take a walk or something.

Darla had been gone long enough for me to finally understand it was permanent. There would be no cross-country treks to keep our relationship alive. There would be no reunion and no future between us. I wrestled with whether she might end up being the one true love of my life, even at such an early age.

I was only beginning to understand how much it meant. It seemed unfair anyone my age should need to know this feeling, but the awful emptiness was similar to what I had known before, when Mom went off to Madison for her cancer treatment.

Around three o'clock I headed up to the end of our street and continued onto the train tracks. I walked a long time, pacing my steps to skip every other railroad tie. I kept trudging along, past the viaduct and Johnson's Woods, all the way to Deer Island. Just walking and thinking.

+ + +

Rory McCreedy was not having a great day either. He wanted to be alone, too. He had gone hunting in Johnson's Woods after lunch and managed to lose a box of .22 rifle shells from out of his jacket pocket. Afterward, he technically wasn't hunting anymore, only carrying a rifle. Still, the woods were peaceful, and it was good to be by himself.

For the most part, he was slowly getting over the Homecoming loss. At least, it's what he told himself. The new season had started, and McCreedy couldn't imagine a repeat of last year. Mac Murphy had graduated, and Rory's opportunity was at hand. He needed to regain his confidence.

It wasn't optional. So far, he had been splitting playing time with a young upstart quarterback whose running style was a copy version of Mac Murphy's. He simply couldn't end up spending this season riding the bench. Absent a scholarship, college was a remote possibility at best.

McCreedy walked a long way. Eventually he found himself standing atop a steep embankment at the far edge of Johnson's Woods and directly above Deer Island.

+ + +

A week earlier, Fritz Michaels had gotten a call from the Colombian. When he answered the phone, a familiar voice asked, "Do you want to go *fishing*, amigo?"

"I was just thinking of you. Yeah, fishing sounds really good. When would you like to go?"

"Saturday. Same spot; same time."

The trouble was he only had half of the money he needed to make the purchase. Even so, if he could just get this deal done, he could quit the other stuff altogether and maybe move to Mexico and start fresh. He was beginning to think he needed to be more careful. Sooner or later, he would get caught. Still, he recognized the high he felt from killing. He didn't always have to do it, but it made him feel powerful.

Late Friday afternoon, Fritz Michaels parked his old white Chevy van at Pike Heaven Resort, paid the two-dollar overnight camping fee, and walked unnoticed three miles up the tracks to his rendezvous location. It was best to put some time between his arrival and the deal.

Michaels camped on Deer Island and woke up Saturday morning with a pounding headache, a bad case of the shakes, and a nasty disposition. A railroad trestle bridged Deer Island on either end. Between them, Fritz Michaels planned his next big move. Once he was on shore, there would be no place for Colombian to go. Michaels would convince him to agree to the new deal one way or another.

They had done many transactions before, but Michaels needed this one badly. He could only hope the Colombian would understand. If not, maybe he'd need some convincing. Regardless of what the Colombian thought, he couldn't allow it to fail.

He hunkered down and waited. It was important to keep out of sight. At four o'clock he would meet a small boat at the far west end of the island and get two ounces of cocaine, which he would consume and sell in whatever amounts suited him.

The Colombian moved unnoticed up and down river on the barge lines and brought the stuff up from New Orleans hidden in grain bins destined for the flour mills in the Twin Cities. From there it was a simple matter to borrow one of the many aluminum workboats and make a delivery under the guise of going fishing. The drop location was moved around to one of a half dozen remote places between Bay City and South St. Paul. He arrived shortly after four as planned.

Michaels held up his hand. "*Amigo!*"

The Colombian waved back. He beached the aluminum boat and jumped nimbly onto the shore.

"What did you bring me this time, my friend?"

The Colombian started his sales pitch. "I bring what I always bring: the very best. This shipment came straight from Bogota—very high quality. You'll see." Under his breath he whispered, "Asshole."

Unaware, I rounded a bend in the path leading to the shore just as the two men began sampling the drug. Even to my inexperienced eyes it was pretty obvious what was happening. I instantly felt the dull ache of adrenaline as I became petrified with fear. Seeking some minimal protection, I hid behind a bush and consciously tried to control my breathing.

They sniffed several generous amounts up their noses and rubbed it on their gums. Their comments indicated the drug was pure and strong. Michaels said he was sure he could cut it by half and still pass it off as uncut. Then he added, "*Mi amigo*. There is only a small problem. I need to pay you half today and the rest after I make a sale."

The Colombian frowned. "This is not our deal, Fritz. Tomorrow, I'll go back downriver. I need the money now. I won't be back for a month, and if the river ices in early, I might not be back until spring. You pay for half, you get half."

Michaels's emotional fuse was short. He could feel the rage beginning to build. It was becoming hard not to blow up. He tried to fake a crooked smile.

"C'mon, man, we've done a lot of business together. I really need a break. You know I'm good for it."

"Fritz, you are a burned-out addict who cannot be trusted with a dime bag, let alone two ounces. If I front you this deal, it'll just go up your nose. Don't waste my time, man. I can sell this in New Orleans as easily as I can on this end of the river." The Colombian began packing up his product.

"I've never shorted you yet. C'mon, you know I'm good for it."

"What are you gonna do? Kill another poor family for their life savings? What did you get that time, a couple hundred bucks? Man, you are an idiot. I can't believe you try to talk me into this kind of crap."

"Shut up, man. There was a safe there somewhere. If the kid hadn't panicked and started yelling at me, it never would have happened."

From my hiding place, I suddenly understood. These were the guys who killed David Patterson and his family. I started breathing harder and my face became hot. I was scared and mad at the same time—overcome with anger, fear, and a hellish realization of the predicament I suddenly found myself in.

Fritz Michaels felt his deal slipping away. His head was pounding, and the powerful cocaine had him completely wired. His hands were shaking, and his mind raced, trying to think of what to do. He needed the whole two ounces. Half wouldn't do.

Instinct took over. When the Colombian turned away for a split second, Michaels grabbed a piece of firewood and hit him squarely in the head. He went down, bleeding from the blow. The raging man was on him like a wild animal, and suddenly they were rolling around near the shoreline.

The fight lasted less than a minute. The blond man pulled out a small handgun as they wrestled for control. A shot went off as the Colombian rolled over, pulling them both into the slough and causing the gun to pitch into the dirty water. Michaels ended up on top. He held the other man down with his face shoved into the soft mud. The Colombian was drowning.

I had no idea what to do but I knew I couldn't wait any longer. I jumped out from behind my bush and started shouting.

"Stop it! I see you! Stop it, you bastard! I know what you did! You killed David, you son of a bitch!"

The man didn't stop. He looked straight at me as he finished drowning his partner. For an instant too long, I froze.

He made certain his immediate job was completed. Then he stood up, grabbed the small brown package of drugs, and came for me. The wolf tattoo on his chest mirrored the snarling look on his face. When I realized I was in serious and immediate danger, I spun around and ran as hard as I could.

Up the steep embankment and across the tracks, Rory McCreedy heard a shot. The wind was blowing steadily, and it was hard to tell, but he thought he heard someone shouting. Maybe there had been a hunting accident. He began moving quickly and purposefully down the hill to take a look. His path angled toward the west trestle bridge.

Stumbling, I ran up the winding ribbon of the dirt path leading to higher ground and back to the railroad tracks. The blond man followed with his head hunched down as he lunged forward. The frenzy of his kill was still upon him, and yet, he hungered for more. He was a predator on the hunt, and I was his prey. On the other side of the tracks, McCreedy was making his way toward the noise.

For a split second, I lost my footing. That was all he needed. The killer overtook me in the ditch just below the tracks. His first blow broke my jaw. His second one knocked me unconscious. The last sound I heard as I began to pass out was the distant sound of a train. Subconsciously, I knew it was the Zephyr announcing its imminent arrival as it always did.

In about three minutes it would blow through Bay City at over sixty miles an hour. Less than a minute later it would be passing the spot where I was about to be killed.

Half conscious, I was aware of the horrendous pain and the sensation of being dragged up the hill. I was helpless to do anything. The killer dumped me on the tracks and went down into the ditch to find a suitable club to finish the job.

Rory McCreedy came up onto the tracks from the other side just as Michaels returned to the place where I was lying. McCreedy understood what was going on. This was not a fight; it was something much worse. His mind began rapidly clicking off options as he tried to find his next, best move. Out of reflex, he pointed his useless gun at the killer.

"I think maybe you'd better back away."

Michaels dropped the chunk of wood. He turned and began to walk slowly toward McCreedy, half smiling and cajoling as he walked.

"This isn't your problem, dude. It's just a little disagreement. Nothing for you to worry about. Why don't you just turn around and head back to your squirrel hunting."

This guy was older and looked a hell of a lot tougher than Rory, and he knew it. It was easy to see I was in bad shape. If he had a bullet in the .22, Rory might have already shot at him. But he did not. McCreedy felt a warm rush, but he held steady. The killer had closed to within ten feet. His scarred lip turned his face into a mask of hatred and evil.

McCreedy shouted, "Stop! Don't come another step closer! I'll shoot, goddamn it!" His voice was shaking. The Zephyr sounded its horn again. It was louder now. The train would soon be hitting the outskirts of Bay City.

The killer stopped and held his hands out with palms up. He was looking closely at McCreedy and trying to figure out if he really meant it. His fingers slowly clenched into fists. His red-rimmed eyes narrowed, and he hissed out the words, "You better run back into the woods, farm boy, before I shove that rifle down your throat."

A drop of blood formed in the corner of his left eye and spilled over the bottom lid. The killer's cocaine-stoked temper was about to boil over.

A calm came over McCreedy as he settled into his dangerous role. He knew his gun was empty and this man could probably kill him if he chose. Emmet too. He needed to make exactly the right call. He aimed his rifle at the killer's forehead and spoke in a low and unwavering tone.

"Mister, if you come any closer, I *will* send you straight to hell."

Michaels's eyes narrowed and a guttural growl rolled over in the back of his throat. His scarred lip curled back and showed his clenched teeth. Blood trickled from one of his nostrils and ran down over the stubble above his broken lip and into his mouth. For a moment he paused. Then, abruptly, he turned and began running down the tracks back toward town.

Shaking badly, Rory quickly came over and bent down beside me. "M, are you all right? Jesus, what happened? I'm here. I'm with you." Out of the corner of his eye McCreedy saw the killer trip and sprawl headfirst onto the tracks.

I was barely conscious. Blood was in my eyes and all over my face. My jaw was so swollen I could hardly mumble. Pieces of shattered teeth mixed with bloody saliva were beginning to choke off my airway. For a split second I imagined hearing Jesus on the Methodist stained-glass window saying, "*I am with you.*" Then I realized it was McCreedy. I grabbed him loosely by the shirt sleeve.

"Don't let him get away, Rory! He killed David Patterson and now he's killed me. Shoot him, Rory! Shoot him!"

McCreedy half pulled, and half carried my limp body off the tracks and over the embankment. Down the tracks, the Burlington Zephyr's headlight shone like a star. The diesel horn blared a long blast. It was almost upon us. The killer was slowly getting away, now limping badly alongside the tracks and heading toward the approaching train.

McCreedy was dazed, and the adrenaline pumping through his body made his muscles ache. His anger and fear combined with the terrifying realization that this was the guy who killed David Patterson's family. Unlike the insanely angry Michaels, McCreedy went deep inside himself and made his decision. He simply could not allow the killer to escape.

McCreedy's eyes darted left and right as he surveyed the ground around him. He exhaled as he bent down and picked up a smooth, oblong rock about the size of his fist. Standing between the rails he inhaled deeply and mumbled to himself, "Unitas fades back . . ."

Then he took a couple steps backward, squarely set his feet, and launched the stone.

Fritz Michaels had almost gotten away. Even as he was awkwardly running down the tracks, he was planning to circle back around through the woods and take the Colombian's boat upriver to Pike Heaven Resort. If he was lucky, the train would kill both of the local punks who nearly screwed up his deal. If not, he was sure the older one would be busy trying to be a hero, and he could get lost in the backwaters. If he had to abandon the van, it was the drugs that mattered now. He could buy ten vans with the money he would make. He was almost in the clear.

Michaels could not have realized why he suddenly pitched forward and landed on the railroad ties in a twisted heap. Likewise, he never felt the impact of the Zephyr when it rolled over him with its unimaginable force. There, between the tracks and only a few yards away from the headlight of the speeding Zephyr, he had run out of time.

When the Zephyr hit the killer's body, all hell broke loose. It was a horrible scene. The collision of steel and flesh caused a ghastly explosion on the front of the engine. It took nearly a quarter mile of track to finally stop the Zephyr. When it passed McCreedy, all he could see was blood and hair and some shreds of the killer's shirt all splattered and smeared together on the shiny stainless-steel front of the engine and swooshed upward onto the glass of its windshield. A disgusting lump of human remains bumped and dragged along under the engine.

Even before the Zephyr had completely stopped, trainmen were jumping down from the engine and from the passenger cars. McCreedy hoisted me up in his arms and carried me down the tracks to where the Zephyr was parked with its huge diesel engines idling. The engineer was shaking noticeably and muttering softly as he walked.

"I never even saw him! What was he doing anyway? *Oh my God! Oh my God!* It looked like he tripped and fell right in front of us!"

It didn't take long to figure out I needed immediate attention, or that the guy who had been hit was far beyond any help. Rory hurriedly told the group of trainmen and passengers the dead man was a killer. He had attacked me, and I needed to get to a doctor right away. His natural leadership ability placed him in position of control, whether he wanted it or not. McCreedy put his hand on the engineer's shoulder.

"C'mon, guys, we better get going. Okay?"

I was lifted up into one of the passenger cars, and the Zephyr reversed its engines and backed into town and away from the horrifying accident. Somewhere during the trip, I lost consciousness again.

I woke up in a bed in Saint John's Hospital in Red Wing. I had been out for two days and nights. Jack was sitting in a chair by the bed, looking at me. My mouth was as dry as dirt, and my jaw ached badly.

"Gee, Jack, you look like crap." I could hardly recognize my own voice.

Jack leaned forward. "Are you awake?"

"Sort of."

"You really worried us, kid."

"What do mean us? Have you got a mouse in your pocket? Where are Mom and Dad?" I realized my jaw was immobilized and I had to speak between clenched teeth.

"They just left to get a cup of coffee. I'll go get 'em."

"No. Wait. I need to wake up first. Just talk to me for a while. I could use a drink of water. Okay?"

"Sure."

As he poured a glass, Jack told me the whole town thought Rory McCreedy and I were heroes. He told me all about the Colombian and the blond-haired man. The police had learned a great deal about them upon investigating their deaths. They both had extensive criminal histories.

The paper ran a story about Fritz Michaels and how he had killed the Colombian and then, in a drug-induced frenzy, beat me up and managed to run headlong into the Zephyr. The police report said he had stumbled and fallen in front of the train. Although the engineer tried everything to stop the mighty Zephyr, the killer had been run over in a grisly fashion. There wasn't even enough of him left to do an autopsy.

"He was a real scary guy, Emmet. The paper told his whole crummy life story. They found his gun down where—well, down by the water. He killed other people, including his own father. It's lucky you are alive. He was a real psycho. McCreedy has been in the news every night. I guess he saved your life, huh?"

"Yeah, Jack. He sure did."

"I don't want to think about what might have happened if Rory hadn't come along."

"Yup, I know."

"All of a sudden, Bay City is on the map again. Instead of being just a crime scene, Bay City is now officially the home of 'two heroic teens.' Somehow, you managed to redeem our sorry-ass reputation as a poor fishing village. Now we've been elevated to a 'blue-collar working-class river town.' I feel better about that, don't you?"

"For sure. I feel terrific."

Then Jack did something I don't ever remember him doing ever before or since. He bent over me and kissed me on the cheek for a long time. It hurt like hell. He hugged me really hard and began sobbing.

"I'm sorry, M. I'm sorry. I should have been there for you! I wasn't around—like so many other times."

I stroked his hair and for the first time noticed I had an IV line in the large vein on the top of my hand. "It's all right. Don't worry. I know, I know."

Jack had a lot of pent-up emotions he'd kept hidden away for a long time. I guess my second near-death experience triggered their release. I couldn't be certain of everything he was sorry for, but I was pretty sure it was more than my current state of injury.

I was sorry, too—about a lot of things. Sorry I almost got killed. Sorry Jack and I weren't closer. Sorry we didn't have very much in common. Sorry we were so different from each other. But one thing was certain, I was glad he was my brother, and I wouldn't change a single thing about him even if I could.

Mom and Dad walked in. Mom dropped her vending-machine coffee cup right on the floor, ran over, and started hugging me. Dad stood back and watched. His lower lip stuck out and was trembling. He looked me in the eyes and nodded his head slowly as if to say, "I knew you'd make it."

I managed to mumble, "Mom, I'm sort of hungry. Can I eat?"

"Anything you want, son."

"Uh, soup, I guess. And ice cream. Okay?"

"Anything."

The word stuck in my mind. "Anything" surely covered a long list right about then. My mind was a jumbled movie of random thoughts. I wished I had never seen the crazy killer who nearly ended my life. I wished the pain would lighten up a bit. And I wished I was really over Darla. I thought again about how important the short time we had together was, and I vividly recalled my arm around her waist as we stood chest-deep in the moonlit lake. I was trying to remember as many of our conversations as I could, but I knew I was beginning to forget some of them. My confused thoughts were swirling, and my vision was blurry. I hoped it was the pain medication.

Mom, Dad, and Jack stuck around for quite a while. I managed to eat some chicken noodle soup and a little ice cream. By the time I finished my meal, my jaw was really throbbing. My nurse came in and fiddled with my IV line to increase my medication.

In the dimming twilight of the hospital room and enveloped in the warm sensation of the morphine, I began getting drowsy. In spite of the pain, I managed to fall asleep again somewhere in the middle of considering all the things I still missed about Darla.

CHAPTER 38

THE AFTERMATH

I stayed in St. John's for three more days. I got plants and flowers and baskets of fruit enough to feed a small army. Some of it was from people I'd never met. The Mafia showed up and nearly managed to get kicked out barely after they got there. They had randomly found a linen closet before getting to my room and came in wearing lab coats and white rubber gloves.

Needless to say, my nurse was not amused. She let them stay only after I convincingly pleaded the insanity defense for them. By then, I think the nurses were really rooting for me.

Rory McCreedy dropped by the hospital, and we talked for quite a while. He told me he had gotten a call from Rhonda Leaf to congratulate him. He said he thanked her and found a way to politely turn her down when she suggested they should go out sometime. She told him, "It figures. The good ones are never available."

He didn't stay long, and we didn't talk about the accident—mostly just small talk.

Faith and Jane came by and brought me some flowers. Smith Morris drove them in his stupid Camaro. He stayed outside in his car while they came in. I could tell they were a little shocked by the way my face looked. They both said a lot of nice things to me, and Faith squeezed my hand hard when she said goodbye. Still no kisses, though. Who could blame her? The bathroom mirror told me all I needed to know.

Darla called too. She did most of the talking after I mumbled an explanation about my broken jaw. She knew all about the accident and was pretty worried. I found a way to say a few things to downplay the madness of it all.

Eventually she got around to talking about her new life. She told me about her school and about a lot of new friends. She didn't come right out and say it, but I think one of the guys she talked about was probably a new boyfriend. She seemed to have a different tone in her voice. Just before she hung up, she said, "I love you, Emmet. Always will."

I managed to hold back the tears long enough to say only, "'Goodbye, Darla."

It felt awful. The pain in my stomach was nearly as bad as the one in my broken jaw. In spite of how badly it hurt, it was great to hear her voice.

Al Kind came to visit. Not as Bobo the Clown, but as himself. Uncle Harry and Molly stopped by twice. The second time they brought me a copy of the new Smokey Robinson and the Miracles album.

Walt and Dolly Sprague came, too. They stayed a long time and talked quietly with Mom and Dad as I dozed. I know they were talking about more than the accident. I thought I heard Dad say something about signing some papers. I guess it had something to do with our house and the bill we owed to the hospital.

The newspaper sent a guy over to interview me, but Mom told the reporter I couldn't talk and shooed him away. Thankfully, I wasn't newsworthy for very long. I was discharged from the hospital on Friday afternoon and went home to try to pick up on my old life again.

Mom's health was good, and Dad felt relieved about the Patterson murders finally being solved, even though he hated the way it happened. Jack never seemed to run out of creative energy and subject matter.

So, he worked on his art, and Dad and Mom went about their usual lives while I mostly sat around the house and mended. Altogether, I guess I missed over two weeks of school. When I finally went back, I still looked pretty rough. A lot of my classmates left me alone. I still had stitches and bruising and a few lumps and bumps where there shouldn't be any. The Mafia stuck with me though. So did the headaches and nightmares.

On the field, McCreedy was tearing apart opposing defenses and on pace to set records in the Middle Border Conference.

The first week in November, Hubert Humphrey lost the presidential election to Richard Nixon. Independent segregationist George Wallace received thirteen percent of the vote and carried five southern states. Wallace ran on the American Independent Party with a slogan of "Stand Up for America."

Newly elected President Nixon promised a fresh start. He said it was time for our country to come together again as a *United* States of America, *one* nation under God, indivisible, with liberty and justice for *all*!

My parents were surely hoping he meant it. But they seemed worried about Wallace for some reason, even though he lost badly. His strident and angry resistance to racial equality appeared to resonate with a growing percentage of northern voters, even though his base remained geographically far south. Unfortunately, a voice of hatred and bigotry disguised as patriotism can inspire a form of bravery among some people. As the saying goes, it's "the last refuge of a scoundrel."

I had to have some more surgery on the jaw and some restorative dental work done just before Thanksgiving. By December, I hadn't fully recovered. Though still emotionally shaken by the incident, I at least looked a lot better after the operations.

Shortly after the initial attention began to die down, the bills started pouring in. Though I never heard them talk about it out loud, Mom and Dad whispered sometimes, and I knew they were discussing how to handle the cost of my medical care. There was no insurance. Over the previous two months, I became aware that the envelopes had changed color on the bills from St. John's Hospital. This was the extent of my knowledge about how close we were to losing everything.

The people of our town raised some money through a variety of creative fundraising events, including a huge spaghetti dinner at Stella and Wayne's place. This time it wasn't free, and many people donated extra to help out with my bills. It was a great gesture, but it amounted to a drop in the bucket as far as the debts were concerned.

Even after my jaw was mostly fixed, I had a tough time sleeping. The nightmares continued long afterward. Mostly I saw the face of the guy who nearly killed me. Or his snarling wolf tattoo alive and writhing on his skin. Sometimes he would step suddenly out of the shadows and grab me, and sometimes I was running to get away from him but never quite able to escape the inevitable beating I had memorized and replayed over and over in my mind. Gradually, they became less frequent.

Occasionally, I dreamed about Darla too. Usually, she was smiling and waving to me from across the street or from a couple of blocks away. Sometimes I saw her in the back seat of the Riv as it drove away. Eventually those dreams stopped too, and I didn't think as much about her as I used to. But I still felt angry sometimes and couldn't figure out why.

Late one Saturday afternoon in early December and long after the park was vacated by the summer campers and duck hunters, I found myself standing there on the Point, all alone with the Kingfish.

I found a good spot near the end of what used to be the base of the tree and carved my initials and Darla's inside a heart, using the knife she gave me for Christmas the year before. I hurried as if I didn't want to be discovered. I felt like I was stealing something I didn't really deserve anymore. Still, I was satisfied after I had finally done it. It had been unfinished business.

The first snow of winter, 1968, started falling as I walked out of the park. I turned up my collar against the wind blowing in off the lake. Looking up, I tasted the snowflakes with my tongue as I hiked along the shore. Soon it would ice up, and the endless cycle would begin again. The men would cut ice through the winter, and in spring the boats would go out again, chasing an honest day's work and a decent payday. I hoped I would be strong enough to go fishing by the time next summer rolled around.

For now, I just gazed out across the steely gray water and thought about how beautiful it looked with the snow coming down. I felt like I'd grown up a lot over the past year and wondered if I was ready for the next new season of my life. I surely was ready to be done with the last one.

Down the lake, the Zephyr sounded its horn. I looked straight ahead and tried not to think about what that sound had come to represent. The wind was getting colder. I put my bare hands in my pockets and walked a little faster. It was time to go home.

Sometime just before Christmas, Walt and Dolly called and asked if they could come over. This was kind of rare. Mostly Walt just showed up whenever he pleased, but Dolly seldom came with him. Mom made coffee, and the four sat around in our living room and talked as old friends do. It was a school day, and Jack and I had just gotten home. We eavesdropped from inside our bedroom.

At some point after the small talk, Walt turned to Mom and said, "Rachel, it's quite a pair of boys you have there." He smiled broadly like he had a secret.

Mom said, "Walt, you look like the cat who ate the canary! What's on your mind, anyway?"

Dolly turned to Dad and smiled and said, "Two really nice boys, Brick."

Now Dad and Mom were a little confused. Dad said, "We like them all right, Dolly. They keep things interesting. Why, do you want one of 'em?"

Now Jack and I were listening as hard as we could.

Walt cleared his throat and his voice lowered. "Brick, Rachel—we got the settlement last week from Farmers and Mechanics. I stopped at St. John's yesterday and wrote 'em a check from the *American Dream*'s insurance money."

Dad blurted out, "*WHAT?* No, Walt! You can't! We can't let you!"

"I knew you'd say that. We just knew you would try to find a way to stop us, but you know what? The hospital was extremely happy about it! They took the check, and they shook my hand and everything! They smiled a heck of a lot more than either of you are right now. And anyway, Brick, it's like I said, it was just a boat after all."

Mom sat back and folded her hands while Dad tried to find new ways to tell Walt how he and Dolly shouldn't have done it. The Spragues patiently explained he had no choice in the matter, and he might as well just deal with it.

"We put aside enough to cover Kenny's education. Hopefully he will use it someday. This was what we wanted to do, and it's the best thing we could *possibly* do with the money."

Finally, Mom quietly said in her calm and wise way, "My dear friends, we are indebted to you forever. We have no words to thank you. We had no way to pay those bills. I guess all we can say is it's the most generous thing anyone has ever done for us. Thank you."

Dad's big old chin started quivering and he covered his eyes with his hand as if he was ashamed, and maybe he was. But pride was lost in the midst of the surprising gesture of this kind and unassuming couple we had known most of our lives. Walt came around the chair and put his arm around his good friend's shoulders. Dolly hugged Mom.

"Brick, it really makes us happy to be able to do this. I never planned to get rich from the *Dream*. All I ever wanted was to get back what I had into building her, and maybe come out a little ahead in the end. Dale had her pretty well-insured, and we can afford to do it. Heck, I'm even going to send a check to Al Kind for the paint job. Besides, it's what friends are for. You know darned well if the shoe was on the other foot, you and Rachel would be doing the same for us."

"Walt, if the shoe was on the other foot, it would probably have a hole in it! I don't know how to thank you—really."

Jack kept motioning for me to go out and say something. I felt awkward and unsure just how to enter the conversation. Finally, I stepped out from the bedroom and stood there by the little bookcase outside our room. Jack stood behind me framed in the doorway.

I cleared my throat and said, "Mr. and Mrs. Sprague, I heard what you did. I thought I should thank you both myself. If I ever can, I'll pay you back. I promise."

Nobody laughed. I was dead serious, and they knew it. Dolly said, "Emmet, if you ever strike it rich, just do something nice for someone else. There are a lot of good people in the world who have bad things happen to them and it's not their fault."

It was the first time anyone had said out loud that the whole crazy attack was not my fault. I don't know if I believed it or not. My face felt hot as Jack put his hand on my shoulder. He whispered from behind me, "Hey, remember me? I could use a few bucks, big shot." I smiled at him, and he smiled back. We both had tears in our eyes.

After they left, the four of us stayed together in our living room for a while. I think Dad and Mom were still in a mild state of shock. Jack and

I only vaguely understood the power of what they had done. Mom finally put the whole thing into focus.

"I think we all know we have been greatly blessed today. We needed help, and by the grace of God and some true friends, we got it. Walt and Dolly are special people, and we shall never, ever forget this act of kindness. Right?"

"Mom, Dad—how poor are we?" It was a silly question. They looked at each other and then at us. Dad's eyes looked tired and old, like he had just laid down the weight of the world and needed a long rest.

Mom smiled her calm and knowing smile. She said, "Emmet, we're not so poor, not really. Do you remember the story of Rumpelstiltskin? I read it to both you boys when you were a little."

"Yeah, I guess."

"Rumpelstiltskin was not a particularly nice fellow. But I always admired him for his one unique talent. Remember? He could spin straw into gold on his magic spinning wheel. I think this is what life is all about. It's not how much money you have, but how well you are able to turn an ordinary life into something extraordinary. That's what we do . . . we spin straw into gold every day. In our case, it's about *love*.

"When you got hurt, I prayed harder than I ever had before for you to be all right. While you were sleeping—I mean, you know—asleep, I begged God to spare your life. I couldn't imagine He would give me back my health only to take you from us now. And He did. He brought you back to us. It's the greatest gift we could hope for—even more than what Walt and Dolly did. Because we love each other, and because we have friends like the Spragues, we are very, very rich indeed. Don't you agree?"

"Yes, Mom, if you say so, I know it's true."

In that moment I didn't really get it, but now, I am as sure of it as anything. And yet, I felt there was a lot more to the story. Not everything was a good memory, after all.

Walt and Dolly received a portrait from Jack for Christmas. I think he finished it in less than a week. It was a large watercolor painting of the two of them posed on a sofa that didn't exist and wearing clothes they never owned. But, as always, it was a perfect likeness.

Stella and Wayne also got one, though it was delivered after the holiday. It was a nice pen-and-ink rendering. On New Year's Day, they hung it on the wall over the couch in Darla's old house.

I hope they *all* still hang on somebody's wall—somebody who cares about Walt and Dolly, or Wayne and Stella, or Mick and Hap. Especially Hap. They all deserve to be remembered as the truly fine people they were.

CHAPTER 39

WHERE LIFE LEADS US

In the summer before my sophomore year in the fall of 1969, the first African American family moved to Bay City from east St. Paul. While I am certain it was not easy to be the only black family in town, the Wilsons and their children seemed well liked. Mr. Wilson taught math at Ellsworth High School. It was our first real-life introduction to race relations, though it's doubtful anyone thought of it in those terms, except maybe Jack. Like many other things, I do not recall anyone making a very big deal of it.

The Wilsons seemed to be nice people, though I admit Mr. Wilson wasn't my favorite teacher. He gave me a C. By the end of the school year, a second African American family had purchased a farm just outside of Bay City.

For Jack's senior year art project, he painted a mural on one of the high school's hallway walls. By then, he was good enough for school administration to realize a bargain when they saw it. It depicted President John F. Kennedy, his brother Robert Kennedy, and Martin Luther King Jr., side-by-side. The portraits were as tall as the wall. Along the bottom Jack wrote, "Lest we forget," from a poem by Rudyard Kipling. The mural is still there today.

In the fall of 1969, McCreedy started as first team quarterback and captain of the Ellsworth Panther football team. He broke single season records for pass completions, touchdown passes, and total yards and became known for his accuracy as well as his arm strength. Hank and Doris attended every game. In spite of his undeniable gift for calling ridiculous audibles, the old Turdiwinkle Brown play was never summoned again.

Life and Death Murphy were just as enthusiastic as ever—at least, Mrs. Murphy was. It was harder to tell with Mr. Murphy.

Mac Murphy and Billy Hooper even attended a couple of the home games. When it became obvious the team was better than when he was playing, Mac stopped coming.

Eventually Billy got drafted into the Army and, within three months, was killed by a sniper's bullet while on patrol in a rainforest somewhere in Vietnam. He was given a hero's burial, and all the newspapers wrote about him like he had been a great guy.

It's strange how getting killed could turn a jerk like Billy into a hero. He surely didn't deserve to die, but I found it hard to consider him as more than just an average young guy from a small town who ended up in the wrong place at the wrong time. A little like me, I guess. And then again, I'm still around and he's gone.

The Panthers won the conference and took second at state. It was their best showing in nearly twenty years. It earned McCreedy a football scholarship to the University of Wisconsin in Madison, where he started three of his four years. After graduation, he opted to intern in Washington as a page for Senator Gaylord Nelson, Wisconsin's great conservationist.

I saw him a few times through the years. We never discussed the specific details of how he saved my life that day or the incredible "Hail Mary" throw that redeemed the reputation of our town at the same time.

I stress that nobody, including McCreedy, was completely certain if the rock hit its mark and caused the killer to fall down for a second time before the train ran over him. As a matter of due diligence, the police checked McCreedy's rifle and found it had not been fired. The official cause of death was listed as accidental.

I have contemplated the differences between wrong and right many times. Sometimes I think there is an infinitely thin line where one becomes the other. In our case and in one exact moment, they were the same.

We have likely all heard this sort of thing referred to as a gray area, where black and white become an equal shade of both, but I don't believe it is really the case in this instance. For a short time, black was white, and white was black, and good and bad were the same thing. Not a blended value, but an undeniable example of each.

Whether the rock hit the killer or not, McCreedy clearly *intended* for it to happen. He didn't have to throw it. He had already chased off my attacker. Adrenaline and instinct took over, and in an instant something profound occurred. Exactly what it was will forever be a mystery.

At any rate, I am glad he did it. For David. In my heart I know it is wrong to wish death on anyone, even someone as bad as his killer. And yet, I know I wished for revenge without any reservations. Still, the throw was nearly impossible, and the odds were stacked heavily against it actually hitting its mark. Regardless of the differing possibilities, this is the reality McCreedy, and I will share for the rest of our lives.

Eventually, Rory McCreedy bought a Chevy dealership in Madison and settled into a happy and profitable life. He married his college sweetheart, and together they raised three children. He was elected and served several terms on the Madison school board. Funding for athletics reached an all-time high during those years, and everybody seemed to think it was all right. In my estimation, he deserves every bit of his success. Heck, I owe him my life.

After high school, Tom Freeman and I went off to college as roommates at the University of Wisconsin in Eau Claire. That arrangement didn't last very long. Fortunately, the friendship didn't suffer too badly from the experience. After college, he moved to California and settled in Palm Springs. He played golf and worked as a social worker, dealing primarily with Latino boys and girls.

Over the next few years, Tom and I saw each other infrequently. When we did, it seemed time had hardly passed since our last visit. We just dusted off the friendship and picked up right where we left off. We never seemed to run out of things to talk about.

Tom moved from Palm Springs to San Diego, and from San Diego to Los Angeles, and then from L.A. to Oakland. He married and divorced.

His health started to fail. Every move and every version of Tom's life seemed a little more difficult than the last. He began to look tired and a little washed out, like the paint slowly peeling off the clapboard siding on his old house in our hometown. During the same period, Tom became significantly depressed. I lost track of him somewhere during those years.

Then, out of the blue, he called me up one night. We talked awhile, and it was good to reminisce. Eventually, his voice began to quiver as he once again asked me if I would deliver the eulogy at his funeral when he died. He reminded me I'd made that promise a long time ago. I told him I would do it, but it was going to be a long way off. Even as I said it, I wasn't so sure.

Afterward, I didn't hear from him for over a year, and I didn't try to call him. When he finally phoned again, it was obvious he was stronger and feeling better. He was living just north of Mendocino in a little coastal town called Fort Bragg. We talked about his kids, and I figure they must have been the main reasons for his renewed strength. He described the exhilaration of swimming in the ocean and the serenity of walking among the Redwood trees in the ancient forests.

He said he hadn't made a lot of friends, but those he had were good and true. He thought maybe he'd finally found his place. At last Tom sounded at peace with himself. Compared to my life at the time, I admit I was a little jealous of him.

I said maybe the older we got, the less important it was to have a lot of friends, and the more important it was to have a few we could count on.

Though we didn't say it, his call offered a chance for both of us to apologize. We promised to do a better job of staying in touch, and I am pretty sure we will. I miss him in a way unlike anyone else. It's as though there are two different people: the man he grew up to be, and the friend he was when we were young boys—when he was still happy. I wonder if I will ever see that version again.

Whenever I mention Tom to any of our mutual friends, most speak fondly about him, though some shake their head and wonder out loud exactly what it was about him we liked so much. For me, it was essentially everything.

After he moved to California, he started talking about the earthquakes. They reminded him how insignificant he was compared with the power of nature. Maybe Tom didn't feel too different from the way I've felt many times, just searching for some solid ground to land on and catch my breath for a while. I really hope he has found his.

The world can be uncaring when it comes to childhood friendships. Time and distance can erode even the strongest ones. But if we are lucky, a few of the finest memories will be kept like souvenir pictures from the greatest years of our lives.

The love shared between childhood best friends is surely as strong as any between blood relatives. It's just different. When best friends grow up and grow apart, there will always be a place in the heart reserved for those special feelings, and a sadness reserved for the lost youth and innocence.

As adults, we can never seem to recapture the hilarity, the wonder, or the intimacy of it all.

Jack got his degree in art. He married a model when he was in his thirties, and she divorced him after only a year. I think he is just too hard for most people to handle full time. No matter what else, he is married to his paints and pencils. They are the defining features of his passion and his torment, his sin and salvation. I am convinced the arts represent the conscience of any culture. For me, Jack was that conscience.

I wish I thought we were always good sons and brothers. We were not. But I can honestly say we tried the best we could. At times I have been terrifically frustrated with trying to figure him out, and he with me. Still, we love each other as only brothers can.

Rex and Denny never left Bay City. They settled in and settled down into the only life they really had ever known. They both work at the Red Wing Shoe Company and ride to work together every day. Somehow, beyond all odds, they managed to marry the Gleason twins.

Their families get together on weekends to have a beer and reminisce about high school. They drive nice pickup trucks and make a pretty good living. Their kids swim in Northwestern Pond and play along the lake, though they are never allowed to camp out alone overnight on the shore. After the Patterson murders, I imagine very few kids ever will again.

Except for their annual pilgrimage to see the Green Bay Packers play in Lambeau Field, neither one of them has ever traveled too far from Bay City. All things considered, the roots they had put down were something that for a lot of years I thought I might never have.

For quite a while I made a point of visiting Rex and Denny. I went to their weddings and sometimes stopped by to drink a beer with them on weekends. Eventually I started visiting less as my career caused me to travel. They seemed okay with it. I guess we just ran out of stories about high school. Their shared histories and focus have shifted to the shoe factory, their work experiences, and their families, as it should.

Woody Coleman stayed, too. He ended up as mayor of Bay City for nearly twenty years. Though he seemed an unlikely heir to Dale Thorsdall, I guess those pop-bottle glasses might have helped him keep an eye on the town.

Mom and Dad lived out the rest of their lives in our little house in Bay City. Thankfully, they had each other for many years, even when Jack and I were absent. After Mom died, I didn't seem to get together with Dad or Jack very often. I was traveling a lot, and it was easy for me to convince myself it was my job that was keeping me away.

Dad passed away four years after Mom. Since then, I have tried to tell him many times about how sorry I am, while visiting his grave and Mom's. I hope he knows that whatever reasons I had for not coming home were not for a lack of love.

If it sounds a little cynical or even a little tragic, it is not meant to be. I think we all simply live our lives and make our own choices. We grow up and scatter to all points of the compass. We go in different directions and become different people from the ones we were when we were children. It is just the way life unfolds.

A few weeks become a few years, and eventually, we are middle-aged caricatures of the young men and women we once were. Jobs become lifestyles, and we follow the money trail, wherever it takes us. It took me all over the world, to many places I couldn't wait to leave and to some I could have stayed in forever. In a way, I guess I got what I had wished for when I was a little boy.

I married too young and spent the majority of the relationship hoping for a miracle. Though the marriage was destined to end, the miracle came in the form of a daughter, who remains the greatest example of her mother's best qualities and hopefully my own, yet different and better than each of us.

Sometime just after she was born, Darla called unexpectedly one evening after supper. I hadn't heard her voice in nearly fifteen years. She was doing well and seemed very happy, married with a son and living in Oregon.

Marty and Deedee still played and sang together, but mostly just for funerals. It was a lot easier than the four-hour gigs at Horton's Ballroom. They only had to perform a couple of songs, and usually lunch was served in the church basement after the service. Darla said they jokingly referred to their act as the Dead Beats. We both laughed at that one. She was delighted to hear I was a father and said I must be a good one.

It was a wonderful conversation. When we were done talking, we promised to call each other again sometime. So far, we haven't made good on the promise, but I wouldn't count either of us out completely. One thing is certain, though: the pact we made so long ago is out of the question now. It's for the best, I suppose. Just getting *past* the time we shared was hard enough. Getting *over* her—well, that's a completely different story.

If we are fortunate, what we feel when love has ended is not remorse but nostalgia. That is what fuels our curiosity about the past and creates a hopeless optimism about a future as gentle and wondrous as our childhood—one that we cannot possibly recreate.

After the divorce, I took a job in River Falls. Just when I thought I could go about the business of becoming a stodgy, middle-aged curmudgeon, I ran into Faith Briggs at a fundraiser for the new hospital, where she worked as a registered nurse.

Of all the people I have ever known, she was the least changed by time, still as vibrant, pretty, and completely alive as I remembered her. She too was recently divorced.

Only the tiny wrinkles in the corners of her incredible blue eyes gave her true age away. I chose not to notice them. As it turned out, she overlooked a great deal more of my flaws and shortcomings. We married two years after our chance encounter. The wedding took place on a big boat in middle of the St. Croix River, somewhere between Minnesota and Wisconsin. She still loves the water.

I now understand that Faith is the ultimate destination I was looking for, after all the twists and turns of my life's journey. Not Darla, nor even the mother of my beautiful daughter, or any of the ones in between. So many times, I turned away, as if I were not deserving. Or perhaps I just didn't want to work as hard as it might take to be truly happy. Faith made me want to try again.

I guess when you finally stumble upon the love you've been searching for over the course of your lifetime, you tell yourself just one day of it is really all you'll ever need. "If only to be completely alive for just one day." But once you've had that one most perfect day, you want another, and then another.

Together, the three remarkable kids we brought into our combined family represent our life's treasure. And thanks to Faith, each of the kids has a key of their own, their personal keys to happiness.

Jane Keener became an art teacher in Chicago. She and Faith have remained lifelong best friends. Jane and her husband George come to visit a couple of times a year. We often end up in the pool looking at the stars and recounting our stories of times long past. Usually, if Faith and Jane have had even one margarita, it takes very little prompting for them to offer up a mini demonstration of the famous synchronized swimming routine. With their legs stretching above the surface and their toes pointed skyward, George and I shamelessly show our appreciation with applause or cat calls.

Remarkably, the Gems still get together. This extraordinary group of women continues to impress and amaze me, just as they did when they were young girls. Together, they have experienced successes and failures, raised families, have been married and divorced, laughed and cried, and always remained true to each other.

Unlike the Baytown Mafia, the Gems have defied the notion that childhood chums will inevitably grow apart. They have grown up and grown older together as a close-knit group without ever losing their individual identities. They have remained kind and powerful, strong, vulnerable, and compassionate—the truest of friends.

Last year the Gems lost their first member. Zoey Hardy died after a courageous battle with cancer. After so many years, that damned disease continues to be one of the worst scourges of humanity. And yet there is a measure of satisfaction knowing how much the treatment strategies have improved and how many more people survive today. In my eyes, my mother will always be a hero.

CHAPTER 40

HOME

A month before I wrote these words, I went home again. It had been two years since I was last there. Since Dad and Mom passed away, I have far less incentive to go. Many of the people I knew have moved out, moved on, or passed away. This time I had to work up the courage to face down some personal ghosts.

**These are not the spirits of my parents, or the Pattersons or even the frightful vision of the *Sea Wing* ladies who may still be patiently waiting in the dark waters of the Mississippi. What haunts me are the friendships I once held so closely but no longer keep.

Now, only the apparitions remain, shadows cast by relationships mostly long gone for me. They are the promises of "always" and "never" that were quietly broken and left in pieces along the way, like shards of pottery from a different time.

Old friends, ex-lovers, former anyones or anythings—I am uncomfortable that I might run into one of the men or women I knew so well when I was a kid and not know what to say. And yet, no matter how long I have stayed away from home, many of the reasons to go back will remain the same as they have always been.

Driving the familiar route down Highway 63, I made the turn east onto Highway 35 just outside Hager City. From this intersection, it was four miles to Bay City. On my left and across a cornfield stood Prairie View School. In the distance I could see the faint outline of Walt Sprague's stone bow and arrow. Up ahead I noticed something that caused me to pull off the road.

I spoke aloud: "I'll be darned."

A small sign posted by the side of the highway points toward a parking lot, and simply says, "Historical Marker." I turned onto the blacktop lot and drove up to a larger, rustic-looking sign. The message told of an Indian legend. The title at the top of the sign said, "BOW AND ARROW."

A quarter mile away on the side hill of the bluff, the stones were painted white, so there was no missing the subject of the story.

The sign reads:

The rock outline you see on the distant bluff is an archaeological curiosity. Jacob V. Brower, a Minnesota archaeologist, observed this formation in 1902 and interpreted it as a bow and arrow. In 1903 he wrote, "Some of the stones representing the bowstring are displaced. The intention seems to have been to portray a bow and arrow drawn to shoot toward Lake Pepin."

Modern archaeologists think the boulders may form a bird effigy, but no one has reached a definite conclusion. Although it is an old, well-known landmark, perhaps even ancient, its origin and age are unknown, and it is not part of the Indian lore of this region. Boulder alignments made by Indians exist in other states, but this is the only one known in Wisconsin. Was it made by Indians? Is it a bow and arrow or a bird? It is still a mystery.

As I pulled out of the parking lot and turned toward Bay City, I couldn't help but smile. Walt's Boy Scout project, which he created from his imagination, had become reality. For many years I have kept in confidence the story once shared between Walt and my father. Though I kept this secret while they were both still alive, I guess I'm sharing it now.

Driving the rest of the way to my hometown, I reflected on the universal need to return to the place of one's childhood. We say it's somehow connected to matters of the heart. Part clock and part compass, its cadence marks the minutes, hours, and seasons of our lives. And always, it causes us to retrace the footsteps we left along the path of our personal life's journey, always compelling us to seek our own True North and the way back home.

It commands us to reclaim our history and examine how past experiences still relate, no matter what age we were at the time. Sometimes this means reflecting on what we lost along the way, or maybe what we never really had to begin with.

The Kingfish was beginning to decay. As with every dead and living thing, the passage of time leads to an eventual return to the earth from which it came. Many new initials have been carved since I left town—a whole new generation. I located the memorial message we left for David Patterson. I also found my initials beside Darla's. At the time, I wanted so intensely for those feelings to last, or at least for the carved tribute to be something more permanent than the relationship itself ever could have been.

My knees made a muffled crunching sound as I knelt next to the Kingfish. I took an old jackknife out the front pocket of my blue jeans, the one Darla had given me a long time ago. The "Old Timer" brand name on the side panel finally fits.

Carefully, I carved Faith's name in a spot that is a respectful distance from my original work. I made sure the new letters were a little bigger than the ones I'd carved so many years before.

When I finished, I admit to being very pleased with myself. Though it may sound foolish, I will surely ask her to come to the lake sometime so I can show it to her.

I could say, "See what I've done," as if it measures up to all she has done for me.

I am likely approaching the final chapters of my journey. Whatever amount of time is left, it can never be enough now that I have Faith. We are among the lucky ones. We found our redemption. As a reminder, I have a small brass key on my ring, alongside my car key and the one to the front door of our home. Mostly, I am happy.

The sign on the edge of town now reflects a population of 441. It also proclaims Bay City to be "The Gateway to Lake Pepin." It's a good image for our town.

Horton's dance hall burned down long ago, and the hardware store is now a thrift shop. The old bank building is gone, and the Methodist church is a VFW hall.

These examples aside, my hometown shows some unmistakable evidence of (dare I suggest?) *progress*. A delightful new coffee shop has replaced Stella's Café. And best of all, Bay City is now home to Pierce County's Historical Society Museum. Located in the former Lutheran church at the east end of town, the museum offers our town the opportunity to tell its worthy story . . . to explain Bay City's legacy to all who wish to know. Regardless of the town's relative standing in the world, all of this seems incredibly important to me.

The carvings etched on the body of the Kingfish are hieroglyphics left behind in what seems at first glance to be a small and insignificant society. But it is one that I will forever be connected to. It is my birthright. Among all the rest, my name is recorded there as part of our town's history. And though they cannot be seen, the names of my loved ones and friends are equally etched into my soul.

And so, I have come to recount these diverse and precious remembrances of my childhood and once again explore the origins of what I have come to believe in. In this place, and in this time, I can recall parts of my life now long past, memories flowing like the water in an ever-moving river.

For me, this means spending a half hour or so at the cemetery, driving past the old barbershop and the lot where our house used to stand, and then heading down Lakeshore Drive to the Point.

I roll down the window so I can inhale the musky scent of the lake through my nostrils and deep into my lungs. I usually walk along the shore to the place where we camped as kids. Carved initials are beginning to show up on a fairly large cottonwood standing at the end of the Point, where it juts out into the bay. It's nowhere near the size of the Kingfish yet, but it could be someday if it manages to survive the summer storms and spring floods.

Here the great Mississippi River spreads out to become Lake Pepin, and then downstream, the lake becomes the river again as it continues on its timeless path to the sea. As always, the current of the Great Mississippi offers new water to replace that which has passed, just as life offers new life.

If I am there at just the right time, I will sometimes hear a train coming from over on the far shore and along the bluffs. That sound will never again be what it was when I was a young boy lying in my bed and dreaming of far-off places.

I have never walked back up the tracks to the place where I almost was killed. Why would I intentionally seek it out again? Instead, I will choose to experience the singular texture of Lake Pepin's primeval mud. In spite of all the other changes, the Mississippi mud squishing between my toes will always feel the same. I wonder if it might appear a bit odd to a passerby who spots a lone man with graying hair wading in the shallows with his pants rolled up to his knees. But in these moments, I am young again.

Except that the lake is so large, and I am small, we are made of essentially the same stuff and will forever be connected in the endless flow of time. For as much as any town I have ever lived in or house I ever shared with people I love, this is my home.

Once again in the waning light of a late September afternoon, I found myself on the shoreline. Seated on a rock not far from the Kingfish, I was brushing the sand from my bare feet when I caught a glimpse of something. Even before I picked it up, I knew what it was. Holding the arrowhead in my palm, I turned it over a couple of times and realized it was as perfect as any I had ever seen. Then I returned it to the place where I found it.

As for Lake Pepin, the waves continue to find their way to the shore, as they have always done. They advance and subside in a never-ending pattern older than even life itself. Depending on the day, they can be a calming influence or a fearsome one. Like the young people who are the legacy of this place, each wave washing onto the beach is completely unique unto itself.

EPILOGUE

More than anything else, our lives will be measured by the ways we treat others. To this end, let us share our most cherished memories with our dearest friends, our children, and our children's children, so we can be certain love will endure.

Likewise, let us remember and share the parts of our history we hope never to repeat, because they are aspects of a greater truth and cannot be denied.

Many things can cause a bygone memory to transcend time or distance and become new again. It might be the faintest smell of a campfire's smoke, the fragment of a song heard through the open window of a passing car, or maybe the feel of the first snowflakes of another winter as they land softly on your face.

For me, it is the sound of a train in the distance.

A MESSAGE FROM THE AUTHOR

Writing *Sounds of a Distant Train* allowed me to express my admiration and respect for small town life, and especially for Bay City, Wisconsin, where I grew up. In my heart, I will always be a small-town guy.

I am fortunate beyond words to share my life with my incredible wife, Susie, our three kids, and our four grandchildren. Susie and I spend our time between our home in Hudson, Wisconsin and our home on Long Lake, just north of St. Croix Falls, Wisconsin. Lake life is still very much a part of my DNA.

I hope you enjoyed the book. If you ever wonder what growing up along the great Mississippi River is like, I urge you to find a place where you can safely wade out from the shore far enough to feel the mud between your toes. That feeling never changes, though, in some small way, I suggest you will be changed forever.

I know I was.